The Sound You Made

DERRYAN DERROUGH

ISBN: 0-9973915-0-2
ISBN-13: 978-0-9973915-0-3

DEDICATION

This is my gift to the dream chasers of the world. When you catch them, hold on tight, and enjoy the ride.

ACKNOWLEDGMENTS

First and foremost, I'd like to thank Elaine, for being a great support system for me. Jordan, for keeping me young. My mom and dad, for teaching me valuable lessons. Janekka and Karryn, for setting an awesome example. Kenny, for keeping me laughing. Batch, for his leadership. Jenny, for letting me bounce ideas off her. And finally, Felicity, for the awesome book cover.

Chapter 1

Vanessa Vaughn, a golden brown haired 19-year old, hopped onto one of the two hotel room beds. Her feet barely touched the floor as the rest of her body lay prone on the smooth comforter. Her day was finally over. She grabbed one of the plush hotel room pillows and settled it behind her head.

"The perks of a five star hotel in Texas are endless," she said. Her English accent was light. "Everything is bigger here, even the hotels."

She rubbed her stomach. "It's easily been four, maybe five hours. When are we eating?" The young lady asked her parents. She popped up from her prone position and sighed. "I'm growing. I need sustenance. I want food in my belly, a warm shower and a mint book. Kill me now," she smiled, outstretching her arms and plopping back on the bed again.

"Vanessa, we only just got home," her mother told her, her English accent more prominent. "When we all get clean, we all eat, as always. Sounds easy enough, right?"

Vanessa's mother and father slid their watches off and placed them on the small table by the bed.

"Moreover…if you're going to serve your country well, the last thing on your mind should be eating."

Vanessa's parents strode about the room as if they were in a rush. The manner in which they got themselves ready to shower was on another level.

"I'm first," her father announced. He walked into the bathroom and shut the door.

"It's only proper for your father go first," her mom said, stifling a laugh.

Vanessa's mother had more the stomach for this line of work. They were agents for their government, off the grid and laying low for weeks. They took Vanessa with them this time. They hoped she would hate it, and quickly revert back to her aforementioned, "food, shower and a book" self.

She was around 12 when she found out what her parents did, old enough to know Santa Claus and the Easter Bunny weren't real, and her parents were government agents.

"So…"

"It's not bad. It's too quiet. I don't know if I can handle all the quiet. It's just not right," Vanessa told her mother. Her eyes fixed on the contours of the ceiling.

"Well, it's not exactly the answer I was searching for, but it's good you thought it was quite boring. I'm sure you'll find your passion. It just so happens, your father and I found ours early."

The two looked at each other.

"He's going to be in there a while, isn't he?" Vanessa asked.

Her mother nodded her head yes. "I'm afraid so."

"I know. I don't know what takes him so long."

"Maybe we can find something to watch in the meantime? What do you say?"

"The book suits me right now. I don't want to rot my brain right yet."

Vanessa smiled and rolled over to her side. She grabbed the book off the nightstand and opened it up to the page she dog-eared earlier. The plot was formed and the story was getting good. Vanessa couldn't pass up a good book, or some reality TV.

There was a knock at the door.

Vanessa took a moment to look at the door, and then placed her eyes back in the book. "Oh, do tell me that's room service with food," Vanessa sighed. "I'm going to die, seriously."

"I didn't order a thing. I haven't rung anyone in weeks. I don't think your father has, either. Just for dramatic purposes, would you be a lamb and fall under the bed?"

Vanessa's eyebrows dipped low, her face, quizzical. She started to speak, then didn't. She lay on her stomach and army crawled backward until her body was hidden completely.

Once her daughter was safely under the bed, Vanessa's mother turned her attention to the door. "Coming!" Her voice was upbeat. She lightly rapped on the bathroom door before she arrived at the hotel room door.

The knocking at the hotel room door persisted.

"All right…hold your horses," Vanessa's mother muttered, looking into the peephole while placing her hand on the doorknob, barely turning it to pull the door ajar.

"I don't think we ord–"

A single muffled gunshot, quick as the snapping of fingers. Her mother's body hit the carpet. Her body twitched. Blood slowly ran from her head. A single gunshot hadn't killed her, but rendered her nearly motionless.

Vanessa saw two pairs of feet. Her eyes were wide with horror.

Two more muffled gunshots. Vanessa's mother's body jumped twice, as if she'd been electrocuted. Her eyes remained open, her body, still.

Vanessa was frozen underneath the bed. Her breathing muted. She was sure her mother was dead. She heard the bathroom door open. Steam by her father's feet rose.

"No," Vanessa whispered. She closed her eyes.

Three muffled gunshots, a bevy of loud sounds, and another body hit the floor. To Vanessa, it sounded like someone slipped. Blood ran from the bathroom, onto the carpet. Everything was so abrupt, she couldn't cry.

In the blink of an eye, Vanessa's life was ripped apart. She placed one of her trembling hands over her mouth as tears streamed down her face. She looked in her mother's dull, lifeless eyes. She remembered how vibrant they were, just moments ago.

"Had it coming," she heard one of them say.

Vanessa ran her hand over her mouth and chin. She'd stopped crying, and now, her fists were clenched. She had two things that helped to motivate her: the fury of her parent's murder and a newly-found sense of desperation. She didn't care if she died tonight; she was already dead, in her mind.

As she plotted her next move, she saw another pair of feet.

Tap…Tap-Tap-Tap-Tap-Tap…Tap-Tap

There stood a stranger, dressed head-to-toe in a tight, black spandex suit. His lean and defined build easily showed through. A blue upside-down triangle surrounded each eye, along with two small cutouts for each.

The room filled with anxiety. He surveyed the scene. Two dead, two remained. One of the men was a scraggly, husky fellow. The other was a bit smaller, but also husky. The stranger looked back and forth between the two.

They laughed at him.

"This has to be some kind of uh…joke, right? Sure we're not in some kind of fantasy land?" One said.

"Nope, this ain't no fantasy land," the other said, pushing his words through his amusement. "I wish it was. He'd fit right in! I mean–"

The masked one pulled out a rod the size of a small flashlight, interrupting the man's speech. After a quick shake, the rod extended to the size of a police baton, clicking and locking into place. He cocked his head to the side.

"What're you going to do with that? You might as well bring a stick to a gun fight!" One of the men said to him. "You've been watching too many movies, my man. That kind of stuff? It don't end too well…this ain't the movies."

The stranger mockingly pointed his index finger and rolled his wrist. He wanted the guy to stop talking and make his move. He wanted to tap into his enemy's emotional side by provoking him. Hopefully, he wouldn't be able to think straight, because of it.

"What, you want me to get on with it?! Am I boring you?!" He asked. His lips barely parted. The scraggly assailant grabbed his gun from his waistband and pointed it at the stranger's face.

The baton flung without hesitation and cracked the gunman in the face, exploding his nose on impact.

As the other reached into his waistband, the stranger unleashed two consecutive roundhouse kicks, snatching up his baton between kicks. The force slammed his enemy against the wall, and onto the ground.

The stranger picked up the first gunman's weapon and disassembled it, rendering it useless. He tossed it to the ground and gazed intensely at his target.

"What…what are you going to do, k-kill me?" The conscious one asked. He backtracked on his hands and knees, inching toward one of the spacious windows in the room that overlooked the city. His nose was a mess: knocked crooked, swollen, and still bleeding.

The stranger brought his index finger to his mouth, indicating that this man should invest in some quiet time.

"Whoever you are, you're going to pay for this," the gunman said. "I promise, you're going to p–"

One quick and hard swipe of the baton to a nearby wood desk broke up the thug's incessant speech. This guy didn't know when to shut his mouth.

A voice yelped from under the bed.

A second later, Vanessa scurried out from underneath with a gun in hand. Her hands shook. Her index finger was steady on the trigger, ready to pull. Her face was flushed; she intended to kill these men.

Both men placed their hands in the air. With tears streaming down her face, Vanessa pointed the gun at one of her parents' murderers.

The masked one turned and faced Vanessa, still in surrender. His eyes remained on hers. "Don't do this. You'll regret it," he said to her. His voice was rugged. The baton returned to its normal state with the push of a button. After he quickly holstered it, he carefully inched towards her, keeping himself between her and the lone coherent assailant.

"I won't hurt you."

He grasped the barrel of Vanessa's pointed gun. His other hand remained up. She could pull the trigger and leave him in a compromising position. She didn't think he was part of the problem. With a quick movement, he disassembled the gun and tossed it to the side.

"This won't work in anyone's favor," the masked man said to her. "No one else is dying tonight."

Vanessa was still shaking. Her eyes were fixed on the one that rested by the broken desk. When the incapacitated perpetrator came to, the stranger smashed his jaw again and knocked him out a second time. He turned his attention to the only conscious threat.

"I-I…I won't follow you, I promise," the gunman said.

"I know," the stranger replied.

Vanessa would never forget the faces of her parents' murderers. Every mannerism, their voices, every tidbit of information was hers to hold onto. She was young, but vengeance was something that would fester and grow, like a flower.

"Just let me go, and…I'll take him too," the former gunman offered, pointing at his colleague, "and I…please, just let me go," he pleaded remorsefully. "I want to see my family, I–"

The masked one brought his index finger to his mouth again. This time around, the hint was picked up. "You want to see your family?" He asked. "She did, too."

The masked one approached the window. The crony crawled away from it, careful to avoid him. He pulled the window open and stepped through it, straddling the window sill.

Vanessa stared lovingly and regrettably at her parents. She did her best to keep from crying again. It was difficult for her to see her parents taken away so suddenly, so violently…she wished she could overlook it. She wondered why this happened. She wondered why she didn't tell them she loved them one more time. She thought people didn't exactly think in those terms.

The masked one held his hand out.

Vanessa was hesitant. It was clear he wasn't going to hurt her. If there was a way out, she needed to take it. She'd figure out tomorrow later.

She snatched her parents' watches off the nightstand, and then took his hand. He pulled her close. She wrapped her arms around his neck from behind, and wrapped her legs around his torso. He turned his palm up, and revealed a few buttons. He pushed one of them and dropped out of the window, placing his hands and feet on the wall outside the hotel.

For several floors, he effortlessly climbed down with Vanessa on his back. She never thought for a moment that he struggled. Although he took his time, he didn't have the look of a novice, to her. As long as they didn't fall, she wouldn't ask questions.

She looked down below her while the wind blew lightly on her face. The ground was so far away. She pinched her eyes closed and held on tighter and said, "It's not too late to drop me. I pointed a gun at you, you know."

"I remember," he said to her. "I just think it would defeat the purpose of you trusting me."

Vanessa nodded. "Quite the observation."

When her savior finally touched solid ground, Vanessa slid off his back and looked around. She was in an alleyway. He was a man of his word; he didn't hurt her.

He faced her. She looked into his eyes again. There was something about him that was more than just a masked man saving her. She couldn't pinpoint how she felt, but one thing was for certain.

"Sir, I don't know who you are, but thank you," Vanessa said. She moved backward slowly, trying not to look so obvious. She was failing. "I just have to go. You have to understand, I'm really scared. A lot of things just happened a few minutes ago, I just…I just…"

She ran away from him, hard and fast, with no destination in mind. She didn't have a clue about the city she was in. This was supposed to be a vacation. She was too busy grabbing keepsakes to remember to grab her phone. She needed to find a place to go.

It wasn't long before Vanessa found herself alone in another alleyway. She stopped and caught her breath. She looked to the sky and closed her eyes again. Her back skidded against the wall as she lowered herself. She folded her arms and buried her head, her cries nearly silent. Despair never felt so apparent in her life.

Back at the scene, the masked man pulled the inside of his wrist up to his mouth.

"Find me."

Within seconds, a two-door, black sports car with sleek blue detailing pulled up to the curb. It looked like a Lamborghini, but it wasn't. It looked heavier. The engine was as loud as a whisper. He entered the car and shut the door, with one more command.

"Home."

The car pulled forward and accelerated out into the street. It tightly weaved in and out of traffic, passing up nearly every car. Around fifteen minutes later, the car neared its destination, where "home" was.

"Proximity Check."

Inside the car, a grid popped up on the screen, where the car's stereo should be. He examined a few key points, concluding that the coast was clear. The car accelerated again. Everything he saw out of the side windows whizzed by. He kept both hands tight on the steering wheel.

As the car approached its destination, the ground opened up. It lowered to reveal a ramp. The car hit the mouth of it and shot down with the speed of a bullet. In his rearview mirror, the ground return to its previous look. The car drifted to a stop in one of the vacant parking spots, sitting idly in the humongous garage.

"Off."

His prompt killed the engine. He took his mask off, rested his head on the headrest and sighed. He hoped the girl was okay, wherever she ended up. "You did the right thing," he assured himself. "She's safer than she was in that hotel room."

He fully trusted and condoned his actions, in the end. When the time came, he hoped she would, too.

Chapter 2

A month passed.

A month passed since Vanessa's run-in with her masked savior, one that coincided with the tragic death of her parents. Vanessa only knew sorrow and poverty during this time. The days were long when there was nothing to look forward to and nowhere to go.

She fended for herself the best she could. By day, she looked for jobs, but she assumed no one would want to hire a girl that looked as if she'd been without a shower for weeks.

As it turned out, she was right.

By night, she was a thief. Vanessa burglarized the homes of wealthy Texas citizens, taking only what was necessary for survival. The remorse grew more intense by the day, only suppressed when she thought about how long she'd gone without eating. She didn't feel *that* bad.

On this day, she was headed to Pay 4 Play Headquarters – P4P, for short. It was the largest adult accessory distributor in the world. Just a year and a half ago, P4P was the largest distributor in

Texas. Six months after that, P4P was the largest in the United States.

They were at the top. The 2nd-leading distributor was light years away.

From what she read, the difference between first and second was Markus Doubleday. He had a great mind, and not just for business. Vanessa decided against applying a million times, chickening out at the last minute.

Some of the most elite business minds worked with and for Markus. The people Vanessa saw leaving that place blew her mind. The cars they drove, the clothes they wore and the things they talked about…Vanessa thought she was way out of her league. Everything these people had, Vanessa couldn't dream of legally acquiring.

From the research she'd done in her spare time, P4P had all the gadgets and clothing to make nights unforgettable for singles, couples…the whole lot. Everyone spent money at P4P. Vanessa noticed. Currently, the company held open interviews for a personal assistant to Markus Doubleday.

The sun was out early on this day, and Vanessa found herself gawking at the enormity of the Doubleday-owned building. She observed the hundreds of windows, and imagined all the offices and elevators inside. There was definitely a mystery about it.

"I'd be good at this. It can't be *that* bloody difficult, can it?" Vanessa asked herself. "Look good, answer good, and smell…presentable, I suppose." She raised her arms as if she were stretching, and inconspicuously sniffed her armpits.

"A grade below, but it'll do."

The air was filled with different perfumes. The mixture gave her a pungent kick in the nostrils. She could only imagine the smell on the inside. Just based on the smell, she was a long shot to get this personal assistant job. It stunk, but it still smelled better than her. She wondered if someone would be willing to look past her appearance.

"Confidence…Confidence…Confidence…" Vanessa repeated those words as she strode to the front doors of the building.

When she opened the door, it was definitely a rude awakening. With one quick scan, Vanessa saw several beautiful women, obviously dressed to impress Markus. It was overwhelming.

"So *that's* where all the perfume went," Vanessa murmured.

The smell outside paled in comparison to the smell inside. The women in the waiting room gave Vanessa a terse once-over and went back to filling their time with random conversations, phone-fiddling and straightening out their shorter-than-short dresses to make sure they were noticed, amongst other things.

Once the candidates took one look at Vanessa, they were visibly more confident. She was dismissed in their collective minds, one less woman they had to worry about. Their hiring chances increased, just from her being in the room.

"I don't belong here," Vanessa said quietly to herself. Everywhere she looked there were giggles, snickers, and nasty looks. She was surrounded by Mean Girls; it reminded her of middle school. She straightened out her clothes again, in a fit of nervousness. She ran her fingers halfway through her hair. That didn't bring comfort.

This had to be the stupidest thing she'd done in her short life. She was outdressed, outclassed and – judging by the way these women were built – outgunned.

She wanted to blame someone, but she was really mad at herself. If it weren't for the murderous bastards that took her parents, she wouldn't be in this situation. On the other end, she concluded that these were great life skills to learn.

There was no time like the present. In the present, she was leaving.

At that very moment, Markus Doubleday – in his office – watched the happenings unfold from his computer screen.

"It has to stink in there."

Markus shook his head incredulously at the security screen. He wished he could point at his next assistant. He quickly counted 18 women waiting for their interview. Most of them eliminated themselves, thinking the high-profile gig was unattainable. Most of them were right.

Markus narrowed his eyes at the security screen. He picked up the phone and punched a few numbers, waiting with the phone close to his ear.

"Yes, Mr. Doubleday."

"Joyce, stop the young lady that's leaving and bring her to my office, please."

"Right away, sir."

“Thank you.”

Markus hung up the phone and sat in his plush leather office chair. To others, comfort was overrated. Not to him; he spared no expense for relaxation.

A couple minutes later, Joyce opened the door and poked her head in after two knocks. “Sir, I have her.” She brought the young woman inside Markus’s office.

“Ms. Vaughn, the Wizard of Oz,” Joyce said with a smile. Markus furrowed his eyebrows slightly.

“Oh, she *definitely* wasn’t meant to repeat that,” Vanessa stammered.

“Thank you, Joyce,” Markus said.

Markus Doubleday was a couple inches taller than Vanessa, who stood 5’10”. He was handsome, clean-shaven. His hair was light brown, and closely cropped on the sides and back; the top was a bit longer and casually styled. He was in his late 20’s, and looked like he never missed a day at the gym. The suit he wore fit his body perfectly, but Vanessa’s favorite part was his dimples.

After Joyce left, the two remaining in the room were silent. Markus sat while Vanessa stood. He took a small amount of time during the silence to make sure that everything would be worded properly. He gave Vanessa a look that told her that he didn’t see the amusement in the nickname she’d given him.

“Wizard of Oz, huh? Hmmm…I’ve never been called Wizard of Oz.”

“Wow. Needless to say, I’m beyond embarrassed,” Vanessa said. “I haven’t the slightest idea how to apologize, either. I can see they don't allow a little gossip inside these walls. I think I've said enough. I'll just stand here."

"All right," Markus said. "Let me ask you a question, and be honest: are you afraid of me?"

This could make or break her. She didn't know if there was a right or wrong answer. She decided to go with the truth.

"Absolutely not. If it's not a bother to you, may I ask you a question?" Vanessa asked.

"Sure, go ahead."

"If you take away the notoriety, all the money, all the lavish things that you're into…well, what do you have?"

"I'm Markus Doubleday."

"Are you afraid of whom you'd be, without all that?"

"You can take away all the things you mentioned and it wouldn't matter. Nobody can take away what's in your heart."

Vanessa watched Markus intertwine his fingers and place his hands on the table. He leaned forward. There was more silence between the two. They were deep in thought, digesting the words and philosophies thrown about.

"Let me ask you a couple of questions," Markus said. "Where are you from? Your accent is a dead giveaway."

"I was born in the United Kingdom. London," Vanessa answered.

"You came here to interview to be my assistant, correct?"

"Yes."

"I assume you've been working. You didn't bring a résumé for me to look at. You really didn't come with anything."

Vanessa's body became rigid. Her posture changed. She was at a loss for words. She didn't want to lie to him, or tell the truth.

"Well, sir, I have an explanation. I'm not sure you want to hear the truth. It may be too much."

"For who, exactly?"

Vanessa sighed with her mouth closed. She had to tell him now.

"Okay, the truth it is…I'm afraid of what I've become," Vanessa said candidly. "Everything's been taken from me. Everything. I'm jobless and homeless. I even nicked this pantsuit," she said, pointing to her attire.

"Nicked?" He asked.

Vanessa said, "I'm sorry. Like 'stolen.' Anyhow, I've been sleeping in different places, eating when I can. I'm doing what it takes to survive, but I plan on giving back to the people I took from, in some way, shape or form. That's the truth."

A look of concern swept over Markus's features. He raised his eyebrows slightly at Vanessa's words. Usually a stoic man, it was hard to hide his reaction.

"If you don't mind me asking, why have you been homeless?" He asked.

"No, I don't mind you asking," Vanessa said. "My parents passed, about a month ago. I checked to see if they left money, anything…there was nothing. I've been briefly feeling the effect of poverty; it's going quite well, if you haven't noticed."

Vanessa's quip made light of a very serious situation. Markus took his hands off his desk and leaned back into his chair. His fingers intertwined and rested right below his stomach.

"Last question: there are almost two dozen beautiful women in the other room, waiting just to talk to me. Why should I hire you?" Markus asked.

"I've always fancied myself a hard worker before, but now, there's no better motivation than the predicament I'm currently in. I also think I'll appreciate the opportunity more, if we're to be honest. I don't want to be your assistant so I can propel myself using your name."

"It *does* have its perks."

"I agree wholeheartedly, but that's not my aim. I don't want to do this because it'll sound good at a party, or something; I want to be your assistant because…well, I need a job. I don't know if you want some sort of elaborate answer. I simply don't have one, at the moment."

Vanessa laughed at the simplicity of it all. Markus laughed very lightly.

"We'll call you," Markus told Vanessa. "You have a phone, right?"

She reached into her pockets, pulling them out for Markus to see. She shrugged. "No, I sure don't. Still having a rough go of it, I'm afraid."

"Be in the P4P lobby at 7:37 a.m. tomorrow, and not a second late. At that time, you'll be notified of your job status."

"O-okay. I shall." She turned to leave.

"Oh, and Vanessa?"

She turned back.

"Talk to my secretary, Joyce. She'll drive you anywhere in the city. Also, I'm going to arrange that you stay at the hotel of your choosing, just for taking the time to interview with us. Is that okay?"

"Yes, sir. I'm appreciative of your generosity."

"Take away everything and what do you have, right?" Markus asked.

"Right. Well, thank you."

Vanessa shut the door behind her and rested her back against the wall. She breathed a sigh of relief and took the moment in. She'd never met Markus Doubleday before. She'd seen him in magazines and on TV. Why was he being…

Maybe that's just who he is, she thought.

On her way to the waiting room, Vanessa thought about how much Markus relaxed her. Understandably, it was hard for someone in his position to trust people and their motives. Even though she didn't feel she would trust another soul for the rest of her life, it was refreshing to come in contact with someone who meant well.

"No need to go back in there," Joyce notified, upon Vanessa arriving at the waiting room. "How do you think the interview went?"

"Well, I didn't set the world on fire, but hopefully, I did enough to merit some consideration. Judging from the sound of the room," she said, pointing with her thumb, "those ladies are still waiting patiently to impress Mr. Doubleday."

"Well, Mr. Doubleday isn't impressed by a nice dress and perfume. In fact, I would say he's not easily impressed, in general."

Vanessa smiled. It confirmed her assumptions about Markus, if nothing else.

"Joyce, Mr. Doubleday said you'd take me anywhere," Vanessa told her.

"That is correct."

"Can you take me to a motel that's close and, at least, moderately safe? Would that be all the same to you?"

"It would be my pleasure. I know just the place."

Joyce took Vanessa to the cheapest, closest and safest motel she knew about. Vanessa wouldn't try to break Markus's bank, though she didn't think it was possible. She longed to stay in a half-decent place, with a bed, a toilet and a shower. Those were three things she didn't find consistently, living on the streets.

"Thanks for everything, Joyce," Vanessa said. "Please thank Mr. Doubleday for me when you see him?"

"Absolutely, dear. Take good care of yourself," she responded. She handed Vanessa the motel room key.

Vanessa took it and said, "I shall do my best." She walked around the back of the car, and watched it pull away.

The motel sat in a quiet neighborhood. Vanessa didn't have any money, so her options were limited. When she opened the motel room door, everything in the room looked fresh and clean. She hadn't felt this safe since the moment before her parents were murdered. It felt good to slow down and gather her thoughts.

She plopped down on the bed and turned the TV on while she undressed. *All right, I need to wash my clothes in the sink, take a shower, and rest as much as possible before I meet up with Markus tomorrow*, she thought. A knock at the door broke her of her thoughts.

Vanessa's heartbeat raced. "Coming!" She pulled her top back on and slowly walked to the front door, exhaling a few times to calm her nerves. She stopped just short of the door and looked around the room. There was nothing she could see to aid her, in case she was being set up. The best idea she could come up with was to take one of her shoes off. She was good for one hard swing, but after that…she didn't know.

"Okay," she said. She slowly cracked the door and looked outside. There was a man with numerous boxes. She barely saw his head peeking over.

"Ms. Vaughn?" He said.

"Yes?" She answered.

"All of these pizzas are yours."

Vanessa's features softened, somewhat, and her body became less tense. To say she was on edge was an understatement. She was about to assault a pizza deliveryman!

"Oh, did ummm…" she hesitated, clearing her throat. "Did someone already pay for that?"

"Yes, they did." The deliveryman pulled the receipt out of his pocket and checked it. "P4P. That's who the card's name is under."

"Oh, well…okay," she said. The deliveryman handed her the pizzas. "I'm sorry I don't have a tip for you."

"It's cool. Also taken care of," the deliveryman said. "Have a good one."

Vanessa kicked the door closed and walked over to the bed, placing the boxes down. There were six. One by one, Vanessa opened them. She was surprised to see six different pizzas. She couldn't eat it all – could she?

"There's no way Joyce could possibly think I would eat all this," Vanessa said, walking back to the door. She locked the deadbolt and the chain, now that her hands were free to do so. She couldn't tear her eyes away from the pizza. "I *am* a bit peckish, though. I've had a great carb deficiency lately. It's only proper."

She partook in a slice. She figured to stop once she was full, and then have one more slice. She closed her eyes and chewed. "God, it's so good!" Vanessa confessed between chews. The smell and the look of the food made her laugh. She had a mound of pizza in front of her. To her, she'd won the lottery.

Back in his office, Markus studied the women in the waiting room.

"This should be good."

A few of them adjusted their dresses. He'd heard them say things like, "Yeah, I'm still waiting" and "I don't know what's taking so long" from the audio of his security screen. With a remote control, he muted the audio.

Not long after he turned down the TV's volume, his Head of Security, Justin Stratton, walked into the waiting room and spoke to the women. While he spoke, Markus watched as some women shook their heads in disbelief. Some threw their hands up in frustration, some pointed a finger in the burly man's face, and some even stomped their feet. Markus was not the least bit interested in being directly involved in that.

Gold diggers, blood suckers…no difference, he thought to himself.

Markus knew Justin's short spiel like the back of his hand: in a dull voice, he'd let the contenders know the position had been filled, and they were free to fill out applications for other posts. The notoriety wasn't as good. Naturally, the women were livid.

Markus so badly wanted to be reminded why he didn't hire these women. Judging by their character, Markus made the right decision.

The sun rose the next morning. Vanessa could've slept another 12 hours. She snuggled in the warmth of the comforter and moaned. She resembled a tightly-wrapped burrito, the way she'd rolled herself up. Only half of her head peeked out. For the first time in forever, she felt safe.

It was as if something – or someone – watched over her.

Vanessa rolled toward the clock. Her eyes widened and her eyebrows shot up at the sight of the time.

7:42 a.m.

"Oh, bollocks!" Vanessa exclaimed. She threw herself back in frustration, the back of her head hitting the pillow. She looked at the ceiling. Her only way out and she blew it! She was sure she set her alarm. *I must've turned it off. I was sleeping so well.*

Vanessa threw her clothes on as fast as she could, scrunching up her nose and squinting her eyes when she felt the damp fabrics settle on her body. She looked in the mirror; her hair and face were a mess.

Mr. Doubleday would notice all of this. Would he point it out? Would he send her home? What kind of excuse could she come up with? She wasn't far from P4P…there had to be something she could think of between now and then. Instead of wasting time thinking in the hotel room, she'd think on her way to P4P.

When Vanessa opened the door, she let out a high-pitched shriek and fell to her butt, landing with a thud. She looked up quickly, observing the man looking down at her.

Markus Doubleday.

"I have *completely* bodged this meeting," Vanessa said, "but the point of it all is, at least I'm extremely awake now."

Markus held his hand out. Vanessa laid her hand in his, felt his pull. He looked strong, but he felt stronger than that. She didn't know what he was working with underneath his suit, but she made a mental note to figure it out in her dreams.

"I'm glad you're awake," Markus said. "You're late, but you're awake."

“How’d you know–”

“That’s the beauty of registering things in your name,” Markus interrupted, “they’ll tell me where I’m staying.” He smiled warmly.

A light went off in Vanessa’s head. Of course, they’d tell Markus where he was staying. He was smart. She thought about how much she could trust him. How much would she be interacting with him after this day, anyway? She was late. The window of opportunity was shut.

“Listen, I know it’s not the best impression, to wake up late for a second interview. I know I set that damned alarm before I went to sleep, but…it’s just…I guess I overslept. I understand if you want to sack me, even though I’m not employed by you, but…I’m more embarrassed than anything. I feel like such a slag right now.”

Vanessa turned her back to Markus.

“I’m not quite sure what a slag is, but I assume it’s bad,” Markus admitted. “I do have a couple of questions for you, however.”

Vanessa turned back to face him, her face ripe with shame. “Sure.”

“First, can I come in?”

“It’s your room,” she said, with an attitude and a shrug.

She sat down at the edge of the bed, still in disbelief at how badly she mishandled the situation. Markus sat in a chair in the corner of the room, adjacent to where Vanessa settled. As he did the day before, he intertwined his fingers and rested his forearms on his legs.

"I'm going to give you this job, Vanessa."

Vanessa looked at Markus with skepticism. Was he kidding? She was late – prompting Markus to come and check on her – and even gave him attitude. By his grace, she found herself employed.

Her face lit up.

"I'll be on my best behavior!" She assured. Her cheeks turned a slight red. The sparkle in her brown eyes returned. "I'm happy to be employed, but…I guess what I'm trying to…well, what will you have me do?" She tripped over her words, able to recover at the end.

"Well, you're my personal assistant, you just…assist me in anything I need you to assist me with," he said plainly. "All of it will be work-related. I'm not going to have you getting a bunch of things I couldn't get myself. However, I have two eyes, two hands and two feet. I can only do so much."

Vanessa nodded.

"If there's something that I haven't gotten to, you will take care of it," he continued. His tone was sterner now. "Make sure you keep me in the loop; there's no worse feeling than doing a job someone's already done. I'm not into wasting time. If you were before, you're not anymore, starting today. Time isn't always money, but time has a value."

"Right. I can handle that," Vanessa said.

She thought to herself as she blankly nodded at Markus's words. *He's forceful at the right times, but he doesn't come off like a total git. I could understand someone else thinking that. He's not in his current situation by sitting idly.*

"Here is your card."

Returning back from her thoughts, Vanessa took the thick credit card from Markus's grasp, looking it over. It was heavy, much to her surprise. She'd seen a few of these cards in her lifetime, but she'd never held one, nor had her name on it.

"The balance currently on your card is your signing bonus. It has no bearing on your salary," Markus informed her. "I want you to report for work tomorrow on time, if you can manage it," he said smartly.

"Okay, I definitely deserved that," Vanessa confessed.

"First things first: I need you to make sure these projects get done before you report to work."

"I'm all ears, Mr. Doubleday."

"It's still early. I want you to take this day to find a place to live and some form of transportation. Go shopping, buy yourself a new wardrobe. There's a full day ahead of you, and every second counts."

Vanessa dropped her eyebrows. *My signing bonus was THAT much?!*

This was a plateful of information. She was awake for less than 20 minutes, and her world was flipped upside down. She had so many ideas flying around, her head spun.

The only coherent thing she could say was, "I can't thank you enough." Her grin was toothy. "I can't believe this. I promise not to spend recklessly. I'll get what I need and you can have the rest back, and–"

Markus put his hands up. "I'm the last one that needs it…it's yours to keep. Signing bonus, remember?"

Markus planted his hands on the arms of the chair and pushed himself to his feet.

"I almost forgot," Markus said. "Before you do anything on your list, I want you to do one more thing for me: I want you to go to every house you took from and compensate them. Replace what you took, with interest."

Vanessa felt hesitant. Markus basically wanted her to go back to the houses she stole from and turn herself in. He said she had to compensate them, but didn't say how. He probably did that on purpose. She'd think of something while she was out and about. She contorted her face into a smile – more like a grimace – and nodded yes at Markus's orders.

"Vanessa, I know you'll do a good job. I'll see you bright and early tomorrow. Welcome to P4P."

"I swear I'll be there bright and early tomorrow. Everything will get done on the list, I promise."

"I know," he said.

Vanessa's confirmation came with lightness in her voice. Markus exited the hotel room, having put his stamp on the conversation.

Muted moments passed. Vanessa sat at the edge of the bed. She opened her hand, looking at the card again. It said her name. She was really Markus Doubleday's personal assistant. In less than 24 hours, she would have a place to stay, a mode of transportation, and clothes. This had to be a dream.

She was downright giddy!

Vanessa walked to the door and opened it. She looked down the hallway, first to her left and then, to her right. The coast was clear. She shut the door behind her and let out a squeal of delight. She couldn't hold it in anymore.

Even though she just got herself a "big-girl" job, she was still a kid. She ate pizza in bed, still liked boy bands, and was up-to-date with all the trends. Even still, she ended up with a small measure of success. If only her parents could see her now.

Like a child, she jumped on the bed and danced with glee. It was like Christmas.

Chapter 3

The alarm was loud. Jonathan Deadmarsh's hand came down like a hammer, knocking it to the ground. He was adamant about missing work. He didn't sleep well; he tossed and turned all night, but couldn't get comfortable.

Jonathan was a punctual detective. However, the morning was always a disaster. His bedroom was an unkempt living space. The only thing missing was his mother telling him to clean up. If someone came over, he'd surely throw everything under the bed and in the closet and presto…one clean room.

He blinked his eyes open and grunted loudly.

"If only they made hours of operation from 12 p.m. to 8 p.m. I would work the crap out of that shift. A swing shift, methinks?"

Jon rolled to his side and stepped one foot out of his bed. It sat roller-less on the floor. With his other foot following onto the cold wood floor of his apartment, he walked gingerly to the bathroom.

The only reason I'm getting dressed is because it's cold in here. Not because I have to work, or pay bills or keep my livelihood. It's the temperature, I'm sure of it.

Jon brushed his teeth with his Batman-designed toothbrush. hardly something a 22-year old man should have. His pearly, perfect whites were made possible by his parents' insistence on braces, which only made his adolescent life more difficult. He was already a nerd; the kids didn't need more ammunition.

One of their favorite picking points was Jon's love of comic books. He possessed so many useless facts about them that it would make anyone's head explode. He itched to talk about them, but the opportunities for engagement were few and far in between. However, it didn't stop him from hoarding information.

"Oh, what the heck?" Jon shrugged in the mirror. "What's the worst that could happen if I went to work? Oh, right…all the heckling and ridicule I thought would stop when I graduated grade school. Not everyone grows up, I guess." He examined his Batman toothbrush. "Oh! Sweet irony!" He smiled in the mirror and washed his mouth out.

After he got cleaned up, Jonathan left his apartment with an apple in his hand. He couldn't recall ever buying an apple, but it looked good on the outside. There was no telling what was on the inside of that thing. He didn't care; he was starving.

One short drive later, Jon exited his Nissan Pathfinder, a graduation gift from the parents. He walked up the steps and through the front doors of the police precinct, wearing a suit and tie. He wasn't the "tough" type, and he embraced that. He didn't own a leather jacket – like the 1% that did his job – and never would.

"Top of the morning!" Jon said cheerily, busting through the doors of the department. Everyone looked at him like they were fresh out of a funeral. It was only Monday morning, hardly anything to be sad about. Not everyone was as whimsical as Jon; he felt it in the room.

"Good morning, douche," Detective Willis said. He was Jon's main tormenter in the precinct. An older, slightly overweight fellow with a terrible-looking mustache, Jon knew that this was one of the ways Willis overcompensated for his low self-esteem. Never mind that he reminded Jon of Super Mario.

"Read any good comic books lately?" Another detective asked. Chuckles filled the small department.

"I'm just wondering, do you think that's a good character representation of you two?" The young detective asked.

Willis stood up.

"Oh no!" Jon exclaimed lowly. He strode over to his mentor's desk, Detective Daphne De La Rosa. He looked behind him a couple times before he made it to his "Home Base," of sorts. Today, she was dressed in jeans.

She was rough around the edges – much tougher than he was – but very good at her job. Naturally cynical, Daphne could rip a hole in a story faster than one could snap their fingers. She told him that it was a curse more than a blessing. She'd lost friends and become jaded over time because of her "gift." One thing he knew: he wouldn't want to cross her in a dark alley.

On the other end, Jon was a free spirit. He wasn't trying to change anyone, or look at them through a thin telescope of expectation. They were who they were, to him.

Once making it to De La Rosa's desk, Jon sat down on the edge of it. "And good morning to the best gosh darn detective in the universe!"

"Cut it." Daphne chopped the air with her free hand. She blinked long and hard, continuing to fill out paperwork.

"Ummm…okay?" Jonathan said. The statement sounded more like a question. "You seem more grumpy than usual. What are we working on?"

"*I* am working on this Masked Maniac case. Slippery," Daphne said. "I went to the hotel. Two lowlifes were ranting and raving, going on about a masked guy that assaulted them. They think they're safer in jail."

"Any fatalities?" He asked.

"Two bodies," Daphne said, putting up her index and middle fingers. "The ID's on them were inaccurate. We can't properly identify them. John and Jane Doe: two of my favorite people."

"Oooooh…you think maybe they were spies?" Jon offered.

"Spies…"

Jon shrugged. "Maybe, it was just a thought."

Daphne's words flew off her tongue with great speed. "Well, it was a dumb thought. What kind of world do you live in? The world isn't like your comic books. You're aware of that, right? Spies?! You're kidding, right?! Those haven't been around in *how* long?"

"Agents? I don't know. I'm thinking in extremes, but they're still around, Daphne. Wudking for thell cunthrees!" Jon said with a laugh. His Russian accent was horrendous, but he found it humorous.

Daphne looked up from her paperwork. "See, I thought I said cut it. I don't want you to take this the wrong way–"

"Well, how could I possibly do that, since you said that?" Jon interrupted.

She ignored his last comment. "You can be really annoying sometimes, especially: A) When I haven't had my coffee, and B) when it's the morning. That's double trouble. Just take it down a notch. You think you can handle that?"

"You're right. How could I take *any* of that the wrong way?" He stood up and took the few steps required to return to his desk. He turned on his computer. When the desktop screensaver popped up, it was a sizeable picture of the *X-Men* logo.

Embracing nerdiness, indeed.

Jon logged onto his computer. As he did every day, he opened up multiple pages and read different articles, forums and blogs about *him*. They didn't have a name for the hero, but it wasn't the Masked Maniac. He wasn't, like some portrayed him.

Jon understood why people viewed the masked man in that light. On one hand, there were people that applauded his assistance to the police; on the other hand, there were people that thought he should be minding his own business.

He figured Daphne fell on the latter side.

While he read the information on his computer, the feeling of someone creepily looking over his shoulder settled in. He stopped all of his cyberspace navigation and sighed, looking at the reflection in the computer screen. Daphne usually made her way over to his desk when there was research to be done on things she considered outside the box.

"It's no surprise that you've come to see what I've been researching," a brash Jon said.

"It shouldn't be. I'm your supervisor."

"Okay," Jon said listlessly, rolling his eyes as he brought his attention back to his actions. After it was apparent Daphne wasn't going anywhere, Jon stopped what he was doing again. "Would you feel more comfortable pulling up a chair, or something?"

"What's this?" She picked up a sheet of paper off his desk, skimming the written words while failing to acknowledge his question.

"It's the Superhero Code."

"What's that?"

Jon gave her a quizzical look. "You don't know what that is?"

"You know what? Forget I asked."

You are squandering an opportunity to share your craziness with someone that's actually asking about it! Don't screw it up! Jon thought. He turned around in his chair as Daphne walked away. "Wait! Okay! You win! I'll explain it to you, but you have to come back over here."

She returned to Jonathan's desk, planting her rear end on the edge of it. "Okay, lay it on me."

"Okay, this is what I have so far." Jon examined the paper. "This guy…"

"Or girl…"

"Well, from the stories I've read, it's implied to be a guy. It seems the majority of bloggers and internet pundits think it's a guy. It could be a girl, but not likely."

"I stand corrected, even though I'd prefer an actual expert," Daphne admitted, "but go on."

"Okay, so this guy, he's got a strict code. For someone that had the chance to kill these two guys and didn't, I would say he has some kind of moral code."

"And what makes you think this person didn't kill the two in the hotel room?" Daphne questioned.

"No fingerprints, remember?"

Daphne nodded her head. Jon knew she habitually jumped to conclusions, in an attempt to prove people wrong. She picked up a couple sheets of paper with Jon's writing on it and skimmed while he spoke.

"The fingerprints we have belong to the two guys. They said a girl was in the room but nobody can find her. Her fingerprints don't match anything, and none of the other sets of fingerprints we tried returned any results."

Using the reflection of the computer screen, Jon observed Daphne nodding.

"I don't see these guys coming in and stopping this girl from killing her associates, given their lengthy criminal records. It doesn't sound right. I could see it being the other way around. I'm profiling, I know; but hey, if the shoe fits…"

"They killed these people and she tried to stop them?" Daphne asked.

"With some more-than-obvious help," Jon said. "I think our man helped our girl in her moment of need. Those two knuckleheads came out with injuries, but no deaths. There's a moral code in play here."

"Maybe these guys tried to shoot your hero guy and missed. Is there more?" She asked him.

"I don't have concrete evidence, but I don't think that's the case," Jon said. He understood; she didn't want to leave any stones unturned. "And yes, there's more. This masked man is scary-good at protecting his identity, like he's leading two lives."

"Well, isn't he?" Daphne asked.

"Somewhat," Jon answered. "Usually, it's two extremes. Whatever they stand for in the daytime, it'll be the opposite at night, or they'll be exactly what they stand for, whether it's day or night."

"Interesting," Daphne said.

"The toughest thing about people like this: if they don't want to be found, they will take the proper precautions to make sure they aren't found. There aren't many superheroes out there that are dumbasses. Excuse my language," he said.

"You truly are the salt of the earth," Daphne said. "So…who do you think we're looking for?"

"My hunch is that it's someone who may hold themselves to a higher standard than most, a millionaire playboy, like Bruce Wayne."

"Like Batman," Daphne added.

Jonathan said, "Yes. He's probably someone who has lost something of importance, if we're going to be all cliché. At this point, it could be anyone. That's where I'm kind of stuck. No one really comes to mind when I lay it out like that."

Daphne nodded.

"Speaking of billionaire playboys," Jon said, "Markus Doubleday is having a big to-do tonight. He's one of the few on this planet that can throw a party on a Monday and have everyone show up, dressed to impress. I wonder if he does stuff like that on purpose, you know, as an ode to his cavalier status."

"That's good information," Daphne said. "What should we wear?"

"I think everyone's going to be dressed in things that cost more than my car and apartment combined," Jon replied.

"Or both of ours, combined."

Jon looked up from his computer. He turned around and faced Daphne. "Wait…did you ask what I thought we should wear?" He asked, almost at the level of a whisper.

"I think we should go," Daphne opined. "I believe this one's open to the public, so why not?"

"Fair question, and don't get mad: do you own anything besides jeans?" He asked. He grinned ear to ear.

Daphne glared at him like she was ready to rip his head clean off his neck and punt it out the window. Blood would squirt everywhere, in Jon's twisted fantasy. It grossed him out.

"I'll start my apology now," Jon said, half-cowering. "Is the 'cowered in fear' look working for me?"

"Just meet me outside Doubleday's house at nine tonight," Daphne ordered. "Dress nice so you don't stick out. No time for mingling. We have a job to do," she said, standing up from the desk and walking toward her own desk.

"Hey, is this a–"

"Deadmarsh, don't kid yourself."

"Ouch."

Jonathan felt the coldness of Daphne's words while she typed away at her keyboard. She didn't know it – or never mentioned it, if she did – but she was extremely attractive. He assumed she was sensitive about it, despite her tomboyish choice of clothing.

Jon heard that Daphne got a lot of flak over the years – and still did – for not only being a woman in the department, but for being perceived as someone who used her looks to get ahead. He assumed she felt she had to work hard every day, or there would be a recurrence of rumors and comments.

He respected her for that.

Later on, Jonathan returned to his apartment early, to look for something to wear to the Doubleday gala. He was rummaging through his closet when his phone rang.

"Oh, what could it possibly be now?!" Jonathan frustratingly picked up the phone. "Hello? …Okay…Okay…Yes, I…You know, you don't have to talk to me like that…Yes ma'am…"

She hung up on him.

"How rude, Ms. De La Rosa!"

He looked at his phone screen. "Call Ended" flashed on the screen a couple times, then disappeared and returned back to the main screen. He tossed the phone on his bed and continued his search. After a few minutes, he finally happened upon tonight's ensemble.

"Okay…"

He studied the garments he pulled out. He'd keep it simple: a gray sweater vest with a dress shirt, a black tie and dark slacks with a pair of dress shoes. That was as simple as Jon got. When Jon finished dressing, he looked in the mirror.

"Good…I'm pretty sure De La Rosa isn't going to be a knockout or anything," he assured himself. "Yeah, I don't think she will."

The problem when he saw her? De La Rosa looked absolutely stunning. He couldn't believe it.

She was wearing a short dress and high heels, showing off every ounce of her robust figure. As far as he could remember, Jon had never seen De La Rosa's legs. She was showing more than *anyone* was used to. He blinked a few times and rubbed his eyes for dramatic effect.

"Wow…" Jonathan stammered. "You look…you look…"

"I look…like someone who could give a rat's ass about what you think I look like?" Daphne said.

"Well, that's not quite where I was going with that."

Daphne lightly tugged at her dress, and then smoothed it over. Even though she always wore jeans and pulled her hair back, here she was, doing the opposite. Her hair was full, a product of a couple hours at the salon. What stood before him was visual proof that Daphne cared about her appearance more than she led on.

“Well, I think you look pretty. For fear that you might claw my eyes out, I’ll leave it at that,” Jonathan said as quickly as he could, afraid of De La Rosa’s wrath. He made sure he wasn’t within striking distance, should she decide she’d had enough of his compliments.

De La Rosa said, “Trust me. I have a soft and chewy center, just ready for someone to tap into. My attitude is just a front.” She snaked her arm around his and walked. Deadmarsh followed suit. “I’m just waiting for that nice guy to sweep me off my feet.”

“How much of that is true?” Jon asked.

“None of it. On the hop,” she commanded.

Jon walked with her until they landed at the front of the house.

“Holy cow.”

He’d underestimated the size of it. The heavy black gate that led to the front door was four cars wide. In the middle of the roundabout in front of the house was a low-sitting fountain. The grass smelled freshly cut. The house itself looked custom-built. The music thumped inside. The windows were darkly tinted. Jon’s eyes shot up to the top of the house. It looked like two levels.

His gaze scanned downward and stopped. His focus was now on a man that undoubtedly towered over the two.

I’m a solid 5’11, and I feel like a baby, next to this guy. Good Lord, he’s gargantuan! Jon presumed.

"We...are here for the party. I hope we're appropriately dressed," Jonathan laughed nervously. He was actually concerned about that. He'd never been to a party of this stature, where the price of his whole wardrobe equaled some of the scarves he saw. Jon felt self-conscious, being surrounded by the rich. If his assumptions about Daphne were correct, he wasn't alone.

"You're good," the burly man grumbled, using his thumb to quickly motion for them to keep moving.

"I guess they're just tallying," Jonathan concluded.

He and Daphne strode through the doors.

She shook her head at him and mumbled, "Shut up. It doesn't matter."

Jon noticed Daphne's face twist into a grimace. He narrowed his eyes, anxious as to what words might follow the look she gave him.

"And you look...fine."

"Did that physically hurt? Better yet, did you just say I look fine?" Jonathan asked. His ears perked up. "Wait, what's that mean? Fine as in, 'Boy you be lookin' fine,' or fine as in...not good and not bad, just average?"

"Fine as in...fine," Daphne said. "Don't over think this, Deadmarsh. It was just a compliment. They'll be few and far in between, so...you know, don't get used to it."

Jon smiled. If that was as close to a compliment as he would get, then he would take it. De La Rosa was heavy on sass and critique, and very light on compliments.

Jon cruised around the house, once inside. He wanted to laugh. Markus Doubleday had an obscene amount of money. As Jon moved about, he heard conversations being had over the music, and clanging glasses. He'd never seen so many beautiful people in one place.

While it appeared Markus enjoyed social gatherings, the rumor was they had a hard stopping time. Markus Doubleday's people would immediately help the partygoers vacate the premises…it was quick and efficient. He hoped to still be at the party when it happened. He wanted to see it, up close and personal.

"Nothing good goes on after midnight anyway," Jon muttered.

"What?" Daphne said.

"Nothing…well, I was saying to myself that nothing good happens after midnight."

"You're right. Nothing, except things that *shouldn't* be happening."

"Right…well, right. Nothing good. What are we doing here, again?"

"We're here to see how the upper-class plays. You were talking about a person that might hold them self to a higher standard, right? Well now, we have a house full of suspects."

"That's a great point," Jon acknowledged.

"Why don't we have a few drinks, mingle and maybe…just maybe, this guy will fall into our laps. Hey, maybe Markus Doubleday is the Super Vigilante."

Jon gave the look of someone that smelled something foul. “The what?”

“The uh…Super Vigilante?”

“No…that’s a really dumb name, I’m sorry. Heroes and villains usually have pretty cool names like Rogue, Wolverine or the Punisher. Super Vigilante just doesn’t sound right.”

Jon laughed. Daphne didn’t look amused. He surmised she didn’t like to hear that one of her ideas was dumb, but also, he was being a comic book snob.

“Do you have a better name for this guy?” Daphne asked.

“Or girl?” He raised his eyebrows playfully, reminding Daphne of what she said earlier.

“If you don’t…”

“Okay, okay! I have a name. Well, a couple names.”

Jon placed his free hand up to inform her to settle down. He waved a white flag faster than he waved hello or goodbye.

“I’ve been playing around with a couple names, but I really like them.”

“And I’m still waiting,” Daphne said as they approached the bar.

“I like the Answer, but from what I’m reading in the forums, the users on the boards like the Sound.”

“Those aren’t *that* much better than Super Vigilante. You know that, right?”

“Maybe to you, but–”

He noticed Daphne looking at him like he had three heads. It wouldn't deter him from saying what he had to say.

"I connect with those names because…well, I've been looking for things about this guy. The perps we've brought in, they all say the same thing. They say he–"

"It might be a girl, remember?" Daphne said. Jon heard the blatant sarcasm in her tone.

"It's a guy, detective. I'd be willing to bet my first-born that it's a guy. Let's just put the gender to rest, and we can move forward. Is that okay?" Jon proposed.

"Sure. I'll humor you."

"Thank you for humoring me," Jon said, just as smartly as Daphne had before. *God, she thinks she knows so much. Just give me this. I'm not asking for much, just that you take ONE thing I say seriously!* He thought.

"Anyway, they say he made a couple of sounds to alert them of his presence. From there, he took care of business. Because of that, I understand why the Sound is a popular go-to."

Daphne nodded.

"And I chose the Answer because…well, call me simple but I feel like…you know, he's the Answer. How can we rid the streets of crime? The cops? We can't get to everything. Try as we might, we can't. But him? He's there to help us. He's the Answer. The only reason I'm leaning towards the Sound is because the Answer already exists, in comic books."

"Well, I've got an answer." Daphne leaned in. Instinctively, Jon slightly leaned away from her. He had a personal bubble, just like most people. "What happens to people who take the law into their own hands? They get brought to justice. That may not be the answer you're looking for but it's the right one."

"Yeah, but–"

"They get *brought*...to *justice*."

Through Daphne's interruption, Jon felt she banged her point home while half-scolding him, for trying to speak after she'd made a conversation-defining point.

Jon stayed in his own head while he stood at the bar with Daphne. *How would I act if I ran into this Answer or Sound guy? As much of a fan as I am, he's not above the law. Daphne probably has other ideas. She'd throw his butt in jail, the first chance she got. She wouldn't let a fanboy like me slow her down.*

"Something hard," Daphne said to the bartender.

"Something hard," Jon repeated. He nodded his head in agreement. "Sea Breeze? Is a Sea Breeze hard enough?"

He wasn't a huge drinker. He was the type to take one Sea Breeze and stretch it out over the course of the night. He'd have two, at the most. When he left the Doubleday estate, he wouldn't be buzzed at all. He'd be okay to interact, drive and apprehend.

"I really wanted a Shirley Temple," he confessed.

He received his drink. Daphne rolled her eyes and quickly downed hers.

Chapter 4

Marissa Buchanan was fresh off the plane from France, where she modeled and designed clothes. She had long days of work and even longer nights of partying, which left little time for sleep. That was the way she liked it, to live life at breakneck speed because, well…why not?

She would sleep when she was dead.

One of the reasons she found herself back in the states so often was because she missed her parents. As an added bonus, she caught wind of a party that Markus Doubleday was having. Marissa felt like they'd been best friends forever. She thought the odds of a relationship working out were good. How much would actually change?

We'd get to kiss, the hugs would be more meaningful and we could possibly…oh, stop thinking like that, Marissa! She thought to herself, on the way to Markus's party.

She loved him, and was in love with him. All the little flings in the past, they only passed the time. Nothing ever came to fruition, and she didn't want it to. She'd been on dates, sure. She'd slept with a few, but none had captured her heart like Markus. He was mentally stable, handsome and – most of all – had a huge heart.

Marissa remembered the day he received his inheritance from his parents' passing. She remembered how he tirelessly researched properties and eventually funded a few schools that lacked resources, relaying any and all decisions through a figurehead. He remained anonymous through it all.

Marissa was always impressed with the way Markus kept his ears open when he walked the streets, how he knew so much about current and past events, paying off the houses of people on the verge of losing them, how he just…

The world needed more people like him.

So, dressed in a blue halter top dress cut a few inches above her knees, the olive-skinned model pulled her black, two-door BMW around the roundabout and parked in front of the house. With one hand, the valet helped her out of her ride. With the other, he reached for her keys. Marissa willfully handed them over. She gave him a simple nod before he landed in the driver's seat and pulled off.

The dazzling brunette took her time walking up the driveway. She smoothed her dress out, and rubbed her palms together. When she happened upon the front door, the *Magnetism* fragrance pulled the well-dressed doorman's attention away from his clipboard.

"Miss Buchanan…it's great to see you," Justin said cheerily. "Is Mr. Doubleday expecting you?"

"Great to see you, and no, he's not. He has no idea," Marissa responded. She turned a full 360 to show herself off to Justin. "You think this is something he might like?" She raised her eyebrows in anticipation of his response.

"I don't see how he wouldn't," Justin said.

“Can you do me a solid and keep my arrival a secret? I feel like it’s been forever since I’ve seen him, and I want it to be a surprise.”

“Your secret is safe with me.”

Marissa flashed a smile. “Justin, you’re a godsend.”

She lightly pecked the doorman on the cheek, careful not to smudge her lipstick, and passed him up on her way to the festivities.

Meanwhile, Markus Doubleday was on the list of hosts who were never on time. He didn’t truly enjoy hosting parties, but it was a good way to look normal. He felt “reclusive billionaire” was a label that didn’t suit him. In his bedroom with Vanessa, his head was cocked slightly upward as he listened for voices.

“If noise is any indication, there are a lot of people out there,” Markus said.

“Do you want me to go down there and shout at them to quiet down?” Vanessa asked.

“Don’t be silly. They’re having fun.”

Markus smirked at his shiny new assistant. “Are you nervous?” He asked. “It’s your first party and all.”

“No, not really. Just hordes of people I don’t know,” she replied. “Shouldn’t be too overwhelming.”

"Just so we're clear, I don't expect you to do much tonight. I don't think it would hurt to branch out and be a part of the human race again."

"Is that an order?"

"If it'll make you do it, then yes." He crinkled his eyes when he smiled at her. He turned back toward the mirror. "I'm looking myself over for the twelfth time. Does everything look okay? Did I miss anything?" He asked her.

Vanessa walked slowly around him with a careful eye. Even in his suit, he was toned to the bone. Along with his strong jaw line, he smelled good enough to take a bite out of. Vanessa understood why Markus got so much attention.

She hadn't known him for long, but she wanted to pry. She wanted to ask him why he kept such loose relationships. She wanted to know why he hadn't settled down yet, as most people of his standing do. She thought he came off as aloof. She wondered if he actually enjoyed company, or if he simply did it because "that's what rich people do."

She'd finished inspecting Markus. She said, "Not that I can see, no. You didn't miss a thing."

Vanessa faced him and smiled. With a delicate touch, she slightly adjusted his collar. Seldom sporting a tie, Markus wore an open-collar shirt, with slacks and a suit jacket. It was a simple – but expensive – ensemble.

"All's clear, sir."

"Thank you, Ms. Vaughn." Markus gave her a quick nod and walked towards his bedroom door.

"Um, Mr. Doubleday?"

He stopped at the door, his back still turned to Vanessa. "Yes, Ms. Vaughn?"

"Call me blunt for asking, but…"

"But…"

"Never mind."

"See you downstairs."

He slowly walked down the stairs that led to the main level of the house. Some eyes made their way to him. Some clapped. By the time he made it to the last stair, he heard clapping from all the partygoers, with some whistling mixed in. He waved and winked at everyone he could. He looked around the room and nodded his head at the countless people. When the clapping died down, Markus addressed them.

"Welcome to Casa de Doubleday. Eat, drink, and be merry. It's on me."

Markus's words drew scattered laughter. He thought it was mostly pity laughter. He was good at a lot of things, but telling jokes wasn't one of them.

With one quick motion from Markus, the party started back up, and people returned to mingling. Markus slithered through the crowd with an air of confidence, shaking lots of hands and doling out lots of fake hugs and air kisses. The upper-class thought of this as mingling. While not enjoyed, Markus was adaptable.

Vanessa remained a moderate distance away from Markus at all times. He assumed she didn't know anyone; she said she'd been living on the street after her parents' passing, after all. She appeared to be adjusting well, despite the tragedy. She never really opened up to him about it.

While lost in thought, he bumped someone.

"Oh, I'm sorry. I–"

Marissa Buchanan standing in front of him was the best surprise anyone could ask for. Her bumping him was no accident. She'd been gone for too long, only visiting for a pixie's breath before disappearing to another country to live her life. Now that Marissa was here, how soon would she leave again? Being a businessman, he couldn't help looking into the future.

"It took you long enough." His arms opened. He was more than ready to welcome her.

"I had to build suspense. I wanted you to actually start missing me."

"Come here."

Markus squeezed her like she never should have left. She hugged him back like she never wanted to leave. He closed his eyes, feeling one of his cheeks press against hers. She was home.

To him, she looked as beautiful as every other time he'd seen her. She wore his favorite color. He was excited about her being there, right in front of him; however, his facial expressions weren't making that known.

Marissa's voice was a whisper when she said, "Nice to see you, stranger." They stayed close to each other after breaking their embrace. Markus used the raucous crowd as an excuse.

"I should be saying the same thing," Markus quipped. "You're on quite a few magazine covers. That's a little time-consuming, don't you think?"

"Good point." She twirled the bottom of her hair with one hand. "New shirt?"

"You noticed. You like it?"

"Love it. You know what it's missing, though?"

"What's that?"

"A woman's touch." Marissa stepped a couple inches closer and subtly fixed Markus's collar. After admiring her work, she said, "There, all done."

The two had a chemistry that couldn't be questioned or matched. The problem: he lived here and she lived there. Neither would risk what they'd built.

"How did that last date go?" Marissa asked. "Didn't you say something about a date, about a week ago?"

Markus sighed. "That was a fail."

Marissa frowned, sincere concern on her face. "Another? What was wrong this time?" She questioned. His list was extensive.

"It wasn't you."

Markus's face was solemn when his words came out. Marissa's green eyes softened, as she continued to maintain a pouty look. Then, she laughed. She couldn't take it anymore. Markus followed suit. Call it an inside joke.

"No…all joking aside, it was her toes."

"Toes?! I can't take that seriously, Markus. You can't honestly tell me that *toes* were the reason you stopped talking to her."

"You don't want to know. Onto better things. Date life?"

"Oh come, now…not in France. All they want is a nice American woman they can bed. If she's hot…well, that's just a plus. Although the occasional one-night stand never hurt anyone, it's just not the life for me."

"Something you learned or something you heard?" Markus asked.

"Learned…heard…who's on trial? Like, if I took a guy home, it'd be feeding a stray dog," she said, stealing a champagne flute from a passing waiter.

Markus smiled momentarily at this information. Deep down, he was protective of Marissa. He was there during most of the rollercoaster she called her dating life. During those times, he had conflicting thoughts about doing what was smart vs. doing what was right.

"So…where are we headed next?" Markus asked.

"Mexico," Marissa answered. "Rome, Australia and back to France. A few shoots, and back to my villa, I go. Ho hum, right?"

"Ho hum," he agreed.

Markus was enjoying his time with Marissa so much, he didn't see *her* coming.

Johanna was a Spanish model and freelance photographer that was in Texas, for the time being. She was an ambitious woman, but Markus's interest needle for her stayed between "slightly" and "not at all." She served to pass time, nothing more.

The slender Spaniard now stood by Markus's side. He noticed the unfriendly way Johanna looked at Marissa. She'd always known about Marissa, but didn't know she would be at Markus's party. Johanna was committed to protecting her investment. She coiled her arm around Markus's and said nothing

Marissa felt the awkwardness in the air. She wanted to let Johanna know that her "mean face" only worked on intimidating little girls. She wouldn't acknowledge it, because it wasn't worth her time. She wouldn't get into some altercation because of this woman's obvious trust issues.

"So…speak again soon?" Marissa said to Markus.

"Yes, definitely," Markus responded.

"Ciao."

Marissa sent a smile and a wave Markus's way. She could feel Johanna's jealous eyes on her, like a sentinel. She would head away from this devil woman. She knew Markus would deal with Johanna more than she ever would.

Markus's eyes followed Marissa as she walked away. He thought about the way Marissa took care of him, the way she looked at him, the way she touched him…

"And what the hell are you looking at?!"

Johanna's accented anger brought Markus back to earth in record time. Her eyes were bugged, her shoulders shrugged with palms out. She was confused and angry.

"You are looking at me like…like…like you haven't cancelled on me the last three times!"

Markus couldn't come up with an excuse on the fly, so he stayed quiet. He wasn't sure he wanted to come up with a story. The scene had the potential to escalate. Never mind they were in a public place.

"You are being really loud. It's embarrassing," Markus commented. His voice was lower than normal. A couple people had already noticed Johanna's tone. Her antics brought Markus unwanted attention.

"I don't care!" She pointed at him. "Are you going out tomorrow night?! Yes!" She answered before he could come up with a response. "Yes, we are going to dinner at Abacus tomorrow night. Make reservations. Pick me up at 8?"

"Sounds dynamite."

Dejection filled Markus's words. He finally gave Johanna the eye contact she craved. He took in her features. She was beautiful to him, but he didn't feel the same way about her as she did him. She wasn't even close to being the one.

"Jesus! Imbécil!" She scolded, her tone now lowered. As if it never happened, her demeanor changed completely when some paparazzi wandered over to snap pictures.

"Turn for the camera, please." Her voice was docile, all of the sudden.

Being a photographer, Johanna loved pictures, naturally. Of course, she also loved the attention. She may have gotten a following through modeling, but it was different when getting your picture taken on the arm of a billionaire. That screamed "every magazine" material, as opposed to "modeling magazine" material.

While Johanna smiled for the camera, Markus stayed in his own head.

If Johanna's yelling at me, she's effectively tuned out. My attention is on my only true friend. She doesn't want anything from me but my friendship, and I appreciate that. Not my money, not my notor–

He cut his thoughts short. His eyes scanned the room until he found Marissa. Her eyes made their way to him, despite the crowd. He raised his eyebrows slightly. She gave him a weak smile. Right now, it was not their time. Or was it?

Markus pulled his phone out.

"What are you doing?!" Johanna asked. "That's rude! We are taking pictures!"

"I'm a businessman, Johanna. Business doesn't stop just because we're at a party."

Let's face it: you wouldn't give me the time of day if it wasn't for my status, he thought. He punched a few keys rapidly and slid his phone back into his pocket, back and posing with Johanna in no time. He'd sent a quick text to Marissa.

Meet me at the Crooked Tree. 12:30?

The Crooked Tree was a 24-hour coffee shop that Markus could occasionally be found at. The CT was a low-key place for Markus to decompress from the day. He even had a certain table he sat at.

Between snapshots, Markus slyly watched as Marissa looked down and checked her phone. She smiled while she rapidly punched keys, sliding her phone back into her purse. She looked up at him again and raised her eyebrows.

"Are we done here?" Markus asked. He'd lost patience with all of the pictures. "I'm very eager to mingle with my guests and I think it would be rude to continue this photo shoot. Agreed?"

Markus gave the paparazzi a nod to let them know that it was less of a question; he was trying to be polite while letting them know they were done. The picture-takers didn't have much to say. It was his house. He made the rules.

Markus was so interested in getting the paparazzi to stop taking pictures that he failed to notice Vanessa standing next to him.

"What would you have me do, sir?" She asked him.

"They can stay on the premises, but their cameras need to be put away for safekeeping. Leave them with the door man, the valet…it doesn't matter. The cameras need to be out of their hands for the duration of the night."

"Good, sir." Vanessa stalked away from the fray, leaving Markus with Johanna.

Johanna didn't look happy. Markus had no idea why she wasn't. She got what she wanted. What could she possibly be upset about? To him, she was just a miserable woman, simple and plain. If she wasn't complaining about something, she wasn't happy.

"Where'd you get her, the Whore Store?" Johanna smirked as she trained her eyes on the tall, golden caramel-skinned woman walking away. Markus bit his tongue, mindful of his expressions. He didn't want to cause another scene.

Instead, he leaned toward Johanna, as if readying for a candid conversation. The paparazzi would call them priceless, if they had their cameras. Johanna smiled. She loved when Markus got close to her. She took in his cologne, good looks, and sometimes, the way he'd look at her…

"She's my assistant. Her name is Vanessa Vaughn. I want you to remember it, because the next time you forget it, I'll forget your number."

He kissed her on the cheek and adjusted the lapels of his jacket. Johanna gave a look of surprise.

Markus had never talked to her like that before. A part of her was turned on by it. Sometimes, she said things to get a rise out of him; it was also a very rare event that he would "set her straight." She wanted a man to be a man; gender roles were important to her.

"The business relationship I have with Miss Vaughn is in its infancy, but I refuse to let anyone disrespect her in any way."

Markus quickly developed a soft spot for Vanessa. In his mind, Johanna knew her boundaries, no matter how aggressive she might come off. Feeling a buzz in his pocket, Markus pulled his phone out and read the contents.

You drive a hard bargain, Doubleday. Your sweet Mare needs her beauty sleep.

Markus smiled after he read Marissa's message, punching in a few keys and putting his phone away.

We're not THAT old. C'mon. It'll be just like old times.

"Are you done with your little phone?!" Johanna asked Markus. "You've been playing on that thing since I got over here, and I need some attention sent my way! Are you done?!"

"Almost," Markus said, placing a single index finger up, in an effort to keep Johanna at bay. He pulled his phone out one more time.

You know I can't say no to you. See you at 12:30. Xoxo

Markus wished those hugs and kisses Marissa sent were real.

"I'm done now."

"Good," Johanna said. "Maybe you can make all of this up to me tonight? Your behavior has been kind of embarrassing."

"Not tonight. I'm early to rise tomorrow and I'm going straight to bed as soon as this party's over. I don't think I'll have the time or patience for more company. I'm tired right now, as it is."

Part of his words was true. He wasn't too tired to meet Marissa for coffee.

"Then you better make it up to me tomorrow night! I mean it! No more excuses!" Johanna told him coldly. "I want you to myself for dinner, and if you're lucky, dessert." While Johanna had her seductive moments, she wasn't Markus's preference.

He wasn't completely sure about Marissa's feelings on the matter, but he thought they were meant to be together.

Chapter 5

Midnight struck.

Some had already left the party, preferring not to stay for the midnight deadline of a Markus Doubleday blowout. The manner in which people were ejected was comical for him, but not so comical for partygoers. Markus would make an announcement about the party's end, and just like that, people were timely flushed out the front door.

Marissa was gone. Johanna left in a huff, about an hour before. Most that stayed were either all about attention, or trying to sell Markus one of their products. Either way, Markus wasn't buying.

Daphne and Jonathan found themselves still at the party, having a little trouble getting out the door.

"Stop it! Stop it! I'm a detective!" Daphne shouted at one of the bouncers as he inched the belligerent brunette toward the door. "And I detect…that you have little pebble-y cojones. Tell me, when's your next cycle?" She mocked.

A smile from Daphne immediately followed, much to the bouncer's chagrin. She wasn't walking fast enough. He was just doing his job. More than likely, he'd heard worse.

"De La Rosa, what do you say we just go?" Jon bargained with her. She was picking a fight with a bouncer and Jon wanted no part of that action. He didn't want to break a fight up; he also didn't want to be directly involved in one, either.

"What do I say? I say I wanna know if I detected right. Actually, I want to know two things: when his next cycle is, and how small his cojones are."

The bouncer crept closer to his tolerance level while Daphne laughed like a maniac. It was written all over his face. A man of his stature could have his manhood challenged for only so long. Jon could only assist the bouncer; hopefully, all of this would go on without incident.

It's time to diffuse the situation. Let's see if this will help, Jonathan thought.

"Listen," he said, "I'm with you. It's none of her business, how big your co– …junk? Whatever you want to call it, it's none of her business. I want to make your job easier, sir. I'm sure you're a good man with no felonies. You don't have any felonies, do you?"

"No."

"Let me continue, then! You look like the type of guy that's always been bigger than everyone, but has a really sweet heart. Just a shot in the dark."

The bouncer stopped and looked at him intensely. Jon gulped and blinked rapidly for a moment. He thought maybe he should start apologizing.

"I've seen *The Notebook* before."

Jon's eyes lit up. "How *good* was that movie?!"

"Cried like a baby."

"I know! I did too! But we have to keep that inside, or we're leaving ourselves vulnerable to judgment. We should hang out sometime and have a movie night, or something. What do you think?"

The bouncer scowled. "I don't think so."

"And it might not be the best time to ask something like this, something that can be taken *completely* the wrong way. You're just trying to do your job. I get that. Can you thank Mr. Doubleday for his hospitality, please?"

The bouncer nodded. He gave one last nudge to Jon and Daphne before walking away to herd other lagging strays. As they walked down the driveway together, De La Rosa took Jon's arm for balance. She was glad he was there. She didn't know how she would've fared if she left the house, alone.

"That push was totally unnecessary," Jon said. He didn't understand the need for roughness. Forgetting about the bouncer's actions for the time being, he focused on slowing his pace down to help Daphne keep up. "And, you know, we could've left that house in *much* better standing. What if Markus Doubleday saw how you were acting toward one of his hired gorillas?"

"I'm sure he doesn't notice little people like us. I'm sure we don't even register on his radar. We're not even close to his tax bracket. He'd probably laugh if someone asked him about us."

Jon opened his passenger's seat door for her and helped her into the seat. For a few moments, Jon watched Daphne struggle with buckling her seatbelt. He shook his head and used his sober hands to intervene. When he finished, Jon locked the passenger door and shut it. Moments later, he appeared in the driver's seat.

"I don't know what they put in those drinks, but they were strong!" Daphne said. Her words slurred. "I don't know how I got this drunk, but damn it, I'm drunk. Thanks for driving me home. Will you drop me off at my place?" Daphne asked.

"That was my plan," Jon responded.

"Do you mind picking me up in the morning and dropping me off at my car? I'm not asking too much of you, am I? I'm being such a burden, I just know it. You don't have to, really, if you don't want to."

"I don't mind, Daphne."

"Thank you…you know, for driving me back to my place."

"Oh, don't mention it. What are friends for, right?"

"Right. Don't get too happy, Deadmarsh. It's not like I'm asking you back to my place like that. Just get me back alive, okay?"

"Yes, ma'am."

Jon felt like a babysitter. Daphne leaned the side of her head against the passenger window and sighed a few times during the duration of the trip. She was tired and sick, to say the least. She should've stopped after a few drinks, but she didn't. She would pay for it in the morning.

Time passed, and the two sat silently parked outside Daphne's house. Jonathan's face remained forward while he looked out the windshield and down the street. Daphne slowly peeled her head off the passenger window, blinked hard, and turned her head to face Jon.

"Thanks a lot, Deadmarsh," Daphne said. "I don't know where I would be without you."

"You might take your keys and try to drive home, I would think. You could be in a ditch, you c–"

"Stop talking."

"Okay, great." Jon kept his gaze out the windshield and looking into the night.

"If anyone ever asks about this, I'll deny it," Daphne warned. "There are a lot of jerks walking around in that precinct, okay? Most of them want my job. I don't want to regret saying this, but you're the only one there that I'm even *close* to trusting, and I appreciate everything you do, and I just…"

She leaned over and placed her lips on Jon's cheek. He closed his eyes for a moment, smelling the rum and coke she swilled all night emanating from her pores. He was sure her lips tasted the same. He was sure she was the prettiest girl to ever kiss him. She was the only girl to ever kiss him.

After she pulled back from the kiss, Daphne cautiously stepped out of the car, shut the door, and didn't look back. Even though she stumbled up to her doorstep – and unlocked her front door, after repeated attempts – she wasn't too drunk to know what she just did.

After another successful party at his home, Markus pulled up to the Crooked Tree in his car for the night – his blue Aston Martin, aptly called "Blue Steel." He opened the coffee shop door and stood just in the doorway, allowing the door to touch his back, to quietly close it. *Where is she? Where…oh, there she is…*

His eyes met Marissa's. It wasn't common practice, but she showed up earlier than him. He couldn't believe it. He also didn't recognize how slow time moved, once he and Marissa agreed on a meeting time. He never wanted people out of his house so bad. He checked his watch constantly, so his night wasn't all it could've been.

Markus smiled as he slid into the chair across from Marissa. She was wearing a tight pair of jeans and a tight t-shirt. They were on the same wavelength when it came to attire, occasionally. "Stating the obvious, but you're earlier than me."

Marissa grinned. "What can I say? I was literally *dying* to hang out with my best friend. There's only so much superficiality I can stand before I want to grab a pencil and stab myself in the eye with it. By the way, nice shirt. The boots are a nice touch, too."

"Thank you," Markus said, raising an eyebrow. "You're very morbid tonight. Something bothering you?"

"No…well, kind of."

Only after Marissa pondered all her thoughts about the subject did she decide to backtrack and tell Markus the truth. If she could help it, she wouldn't lie to him. Best friends could tell each other anything, she thought.

"Markus, why are you with Johanna? I mean, if you want to call it that. You two are…I'm trying to find the right word for it…"

"Well, it's kind of complicated. I–"

"Not right for each other! Take it from a friend. Friends know better, right?"

"Usually…but I can't 100% agree that it's just that ea– …"

"Johanna's a B, with a capital B. And you know what's worse? There's no reason for it! I see her on the modeling circuit all the time. The way she treats people she deems below her…she's just…actually, I won't say the word I think suits her, but it starts with a C."

Before her emotions got the best of her, Marissa bent her elbows, placed her hands up. She needed a quick time-out. She closed her eyes and exhaled a couple deep breaths. She opened her eyes again.

"You know I care about you and your feelings, Markus."

"I know you do, Mare."

"I think you can do better, if my opinion matters."

"It's always mattered," Markus said. "Johanna gives me a level of comfort. She fits into my busy schedule, chock full of late nights. No relationship pressure…it works for me right now."

It got quiet between the two while they sipped the drinks they received minutes ago. Hers was hot; his was cold. Fire and ice. Marissa peered at Markus over the cup she sipped from, attempting to read him. Ultimately, she came up with nothing.

"I want to ask you something," Marissa proposed, breaking the silence between them.

Markus shrugged and looked back down into his drink. "Shoot."

"Do you even *want* that stuff? A different life, I mean."

Markus's gaze slowly found its way to Marissa. "What do you mean?"

Marissa rubbed her rapidly perspiring palms on her jeans. She wasn't sure if she wanted to keep going on with this conversation. Her mother once told her something that stuck with her all these years: shut up while you're ahead. If she listened to all the advice given to her, she didn't know where she'd be. Her mouth now dry, she took a sip of coffee and pressed on.

"I mean…well, marriage…kids…the whole shebang. I'm talking about doing something besides 'work-work-work,' you know? There has to be time for other things."

"Well, what do I need to be doing?" Markus questioned. "If you have something on your mind, Mare…just say it. It's too late at night to try to read between the lines."

She thought to herself, *don't play dumb, Markus. Your smile isn't helping your cause, either. Okay, maybe a little bit. I'm going to have to say this if I want to get my point across.*

"All I'm saying Markus, is that…I know I can't keep doing what I'm doing forever. The parties and the little flings, and–…the party has to end sometime."

"I agree with that. Parties don't last forever," he said.

"Right. Eventually, I'll want to settle down. Maybe retire from modeling and design clothes for a living. Have a nice house, have some kids…I don't know if that sounds enticing for your future, but that's my little slice of heaven. I just can't wait to meet that guy."

She bit her lip. She'd already met that guy. She wanted him to ask her out. Marissa fell quiet, using both her hands to sip her coffee. She had to use her hands, or she'd fidget. Because her words came out quickly, she figured it was a lot for Markus to digest. Her eyes barely peered over her cup again.

"Honestly Mare, I haven't given much thought to it."

Marissa's shoulders dropped slightly. Although very subtle, it was something Markus noticed.

"I don't have much downtime. The time I do have, I sleep. I don't get to do that a lot. I might get about four hours a day, at the most. How about this? The next time I go on vacation, or get more than an hour to myself, we can revisit it."

"Or maybe we can talk about how you don't get much sleep? You know as well as anyone that sleep is important. I don't see how you do it." Her words were snippy and quick, coming right after his.

"Success before rest. That's how I do it." Markus smiled warmly at Marissa. With a shake of the head, Marissa returned the gesture – with less warmth. She placed her lips back on her cup. She wasn't drinking anything; she was trying to stall. She was going to do something brave, even though every feeling inside of her told her not to.

"Markus, I want to share something with you, and I just want you to listen."

His smile faded. He took another sip of his drink. He wasn't prepared for something like this. He loved preparation, and hated surprises. This would bother him later on, stick in his craw for a night, maybe *nights*.

"Markus, I was there when your parents passed. And-and…you know, there's a reason why I'm bringing this up: you holed yourself up in your room, wouldn't see anybody but me.

You had tons of homework sent home. I brought that to you. I didn't do that for friendship, Markus. I *wanted* to be there."

Markus remained tight-lipped. He knew she was right. His stomach turned as he fought from tipping off his emotions. He controlled them as best he could. Stoicism was his choice for the conversation.

"You buried yourself in work from then on. Understandable; I get that. You had a school built. You give to charity anonymously. I know about all of that. You have a good heart – scratch that, *great* heart. You deserve that kind of life, the life I talked about earlier. You deserve the nice house, the kids, to retire…"

"Doesn't everyone?"

"Yes, but–"

Marissa stammered. The conversation was at a crossroads. Would she tell him how she really felt? Or would she choke up, like she'd done so many times before? She pondered for a few moments, gripping her coffee cup with both hands. If Markus Doubleday deserved anything, he deserved the truth.

Delicately placing both her hands on the table, Marissa said, "Damn it, I'm just going to say it."

As she was about to speak, she heard a loud bang. She let out a loud and quick yelp. Her eyes grew wide when she turned away from Markus and watched two men enter the coffee shop. Armed. Dangerous. One locked the door.

"Everybody put your hands on the damn table! Now!" The other screamed.

Markus calmly placed his hands on the table. He looked around and saw a lone exit door, through the kitchen. He brought his eyes to Marissa's.

In a very low tone, he said, "Breathe. Keep your eyes on me. Count to three and breathe. You can do this. Everything will be fine. Count to three and breathe."

Marissa nodded yes. She fought the urge to shake. She established a consistent breathing pattern while training her eyes on Markus's steely blues. He seemed so calm in the face of danger. Marissa took a few seconds to glance around the room. People had their hands on the tables, just like her and Markus. They looked afraid, just like her. Light murmuring, not loud enough to understand.

1…2…3…Breathe…1…2…3…Breathe…1…2…3…

Markus turned his head slightly to get a look at the masked men. One of them noticed. He jammed the barrel of his gun into Markus's temple and pushed. Markus tensed his neck muscles to keep his head steady. Marissa's breathing picked up, and her fingers stretched.

"Eyes on each other, Big Shot. Mind your own business, if you know what's good for you."

Markus nodded yes. The gunman pulled his gun away from Markus's head and moved on.

Markus's eyes returned to Marissa's. He said, "I'm sure you want to be somewhere else now."

"As odd as it sounds…no, I wouldn't," Marissa whispered. "I enjoy your company." A small smile crept onto her face. She felt her nervousness steadily decline with every word shared between them.

Markus knew that, as forgetful as Marissa could be sometimes, she wouldn't forget the conversation they were having. Too much was said, on her end. She was no stranger to clearing her conscience, and even more so, if she cared about the topic.

Everyone remained quiet while the masked men pilfered the money from the registers and the safe, leaving them largely empty. To Markus, they were petty criminals; they didn't want to make a grand scenario or kill anyone. All they wanted was money.

"Thank you for your time," one of the masked men said. "Wait five minutes, and then you're free to go. Have a good night."

The two men disappeared through the kitchen. After the coast felt clear, most everyone in the shop collectively blew out a sigh of relief. While everyone made their phone calls, shot their texts and gave their well-wishes, Markus and Marissa's eye contact endured.

"Let's get you home, Mare."

The simplicity of Markus's words was calm. While the masked men shook up the coffee shop, Markus thought about how much time he spent with Marissa when they were in college. Even though everything was – supposedly – platonic, it didn't feel that way.

He'd never made a move, even during the countless movie nights they spent together. When Marissa was too tired to go home, he'd always give up his bed for her. He'd sleep anywhere else, even on the floor. It may have ruffled her feathers, but she was worth it, to him.

On her end, Marissa felt like she had to spell it out for Markus. He wasn't picking up on any of her cues – and it irritated her to no end – but he was worth it. She justified his behavior with those words, anytime doubts about him arose. In her mind, the pros outweighed the cons of taking their relationship to the next level.

"So…here we are," Markus said. "I think everything is clear."

Marissa bristled at those words. "I don't think everything is clear, Markus."

Markus's body stiffened. Marissa noticed Markus got this way when it came to affairs of the heart. He wasn't that way when someone waved a gun around and threatened people. Was he more comfortable with a gun to his head over feelings?

As quick as Markus's body hardened up, it looked to relax. "Mare, be careful. Your adrenaline's still pumping. It might be nerves, from what happened. I think it's a delicate time."

Marissa crossed her arms across her chest. "We're about to argue this, because I think it's worth it. I have to say something."

"Okay, Mare. Go ahead."

"Frankly, I think it's funny that you've been acting oblivious to this whole thing. You have a Dartmouth education and you can't figure out that someone is just…*tired* of being your friend? You didn't notice, in college, the way I acted when you said you had a date? And you were just fine, I assume, when I went out on dates with other guys?"

"Well–"

"Please, just be honest."

"Well…no. But we're friends. I don't want to–"

"Forget friends, would you?!" Marissa interrupted. She was infuriated. "I need you to do something, right here, right now. Just throw caution to the wind. I know this…this isn't something you scheduled, but just…"

"Mare, I– …I want to tell you the truth, and I want you to just let me talk. When I'm done, I want you to be okay with it."

She prepared herself for what could end up being the worst. *Hurry up and talk…I'm kind of holding my breath, here!*

"I'm absolutely in love with you, without a doubt. When I go to bed, you're the last thing I think about. When I wake up, I know I would've slept longer, better, if you were there. My quality of life would be better, if you were around. You're the perfect example of someone I'd spend the rest of my life with. There is no doubt about this. However…"

Marissa shook her head no in frustration. Her nostrils flared and her arms tensed; her lips pursed while she blinked numerous times. She'd cried in front of him before, but it was never from his doing. "I knew you would say that. Damn it, I knew you would say that."

"However…" Markus repeated, his words fighting through hers. "We've been through too much as friends. There are a lot of moving parts in my life right now, Mare. I don't know if that's something you can handle."

"Then why not leave it up to *me* to make that decision?! You don't think I can handle it? Fine! But let *me* make that decision, Markus! You can't just chalk it up to what you think without giving me a say!"

"Marissa, let me just make the decision."

"What could possibly be holding you back?! What's your reasoning?!"

"I dress up and terrorize the night," Markus said lowly, his eyes on hers. "It's hard for me to find the time for a steady relationship."

Marissa's eyes softened, her eyebrows rose. Was he serious? There was no way. She furrowed her eyebrows. She couldn't tell if he was lying or not. Markus wasn't giving anything away. He had to be kidding, she thought.

She couldn't help but laugh at Markus's words. He was so good at calming nerves.

"Wait…what? Where did that even come from? Okay, so you're like Batman or Bane, or something? Can I be Wonder Woman?"

She placed her hand on his chest and patted it. "I want to be mad at you…you just make it hard."

Markus shrugged. "Well, you know...anyway, you should get some rest, Mare. Get home safely. Hey listen, if you're around tomorrow, let's do lunch."

"Definitely. Hey listen, I–"

"No, *I'm* sorry." Markus pointed to himself.

Marissa didn't understand how Markus couldn't pick up on her cues, if he knew her well enough to cut her apology off. She concluded that her emotions were all jacked up from the robbery. She also concluded that the topic of their relationship would be revisited, probably when emotions weren't running so high.

Marissa let Markus take her hand. She squeezed his tightly a few times.

"Everything will be fine," Markus said. "Be patient. I promise I'll get there."

"Well, you know what I believe."

She let his hand go and slid into her car. Markus tapped Marissa's hood twice as she backed out of her parking spot. They both waved to each other as she pulled away from the coffee shop and into the night.

On another side of town, someone was running.

His arms and legs pumped; his feet smacked the pavement. His breathing became heavier, over time. He heard footsteps behind him while the perspiration bled from his body.

Though he knew the streets better than the man chasing him, he ran, anyway. He didn't slow for anything, even fatigue. He saw his house in the distance. As he ran, the house got closer and closer. Relief washed over him, even if he was running too hard to show it.

As he approached his front door, the stranger fumbled his keys. He let out a grunt of frustration during his short stretch of three failed key tries. When he finally fit the right key in the keyhole, he burst through the door and quickly shut it, locking the deadbolt. No one would get in.

Through shallow breaths, he said, "I need to…call the… police."

Another voice said, "Hello."

The man whipped around to face his living room, where he found another man settled in a recliner. His fingers intertwined, he looked comfortable. He was about six feet tall and dressed in nothing but black: turtleneck, cargo pants, boots, a thin trench coat and gloves. He wore a black mask with a white skeleton face, a large designed crack at an angle towards the top of the mask.

He'd seen the Broken Skull before, and ran from him then. He was now trapped. Defeated, he looked at the Broken Skull for something, any semblance of forgiveness. He was frozen against the door, unable to move or speak.

"You've made noise…I've heard your noise. You knew this night would come. There is no reason for fear, at this juncture."

The delivery of the Broken Skull's voice was slow and deliberate. The man was still frozen against the door, his eyes on the Broken Skull's every move. The Broken Skull slowly rose to his feet and approached the man. The man's eyes rolled and bulged. His focus spread evenly on the masked man's imminent approach.

The Broken Skull was mere inches away from his shorter, more heavyset counterpart; so close, he clearly heard wheezing. The two met eyes, one looking up as the other looked down.

"Sooner or later…everyone pays what they owe."

After he read him his last rites – of sorts – the Broken Skull reached out and snatched him by the throat. The man's feet barely left the ground, just enough to stop him from bracing himself. He fought for air. He looked directly in the face of his perpetrator.

"You have to understand…this is something I have to do…but it's also something I *want* to do."

At a snail's pace, he guided the man to his back. Though the man resisted, the Broken Skull was too strong. As he lay on his back and fought for air, the Broken Skull stood over him, using both hands to increase the pressure on his throat. He beat on the Broken Skull's hand and wrist. While the man clearly struggled, the Broken Skull stayed calm, almost relaxed.

"While you struggle to stay alive…I want the last things on your mind to be of your two small children. They'll surely miss you. Your wife…she will miss you. Think of all the people that you are currently letting down. That you have…let down."

His eyes squinted shut from the Broken Skull's pressure.

"And understand…this would have all been preventable…had you been a man of your word." The strikes to his arms and wrists were slower, more childlike. The Broken Skull continued without missing a beat. "A man is only as good as his word. And you've shown the world that your word…means…nothing."

The man's hands dropped, his eyes still open. The Broken Skull stood up.

"And now…you're not in this world."

The Broken Skull unlocked the man's front door and opened it. Two men stood in front of him, looking down at the handy work, nodding in approval. The Broken Skull nodded.

"For the Cause."

The two men across from him smiled, also nodding.

“For the Cause,” they said in unison.

“Make it look like an accident, if it’s not too much trouble. Thank you.”

The two men parted to let the Broken Skull through. The side door of a parked van opened. He stepped in and the door closed behind him, the van slowly pulling away from the curb. A cell phone rang. One of the passengers handed him the ringing phone and he hit the “Accept” button, placing the phone to his ear.

“Hello…No, I’m not busy. I’m here with you.”

Chapter 6

The night of the robbery, Markus and Marissa retired to their respective abodes. Marissa stayed with her parents when she visited. She didn't own a house; she rented villas or hotel rooms. She viewed it as a place to stash her things, a more stylish storage locker.

As much as she wanted to stay with Markus, it wasn't happening.

When Marissa left the coffee shop that night, she maintained a stiff upper lip while he turned down the chance at a relationship with her. She wouldn't do it in front of him, but on the way home, she cried. When she got home, Marissa sat in her parent's driveway and wiped away tears with one hand. She had to let some of her feelings out.

"I know what I want. Because Markus has concerns about it all, it's just…not going to happen?" She asked herself out loud. The reasoning didn't make sense to her.

"And, to no one's surprise, I'm coming in late, so I don't get to say goodnight to Mom and Dad," she said as she got out of the car. She shut the door and made her way into the house. "Somehow, I'll make it up to them in the morning…if I wake up before them."

After she locked the front door, Marissa walked to her adolescent bedroom and closed the door. After she undressed, she looked through her bag to get to more nighttime-y clothes. She hadn't made it around to emptying her bag, to set up her stay. After sifting through her bag like a raccoon through trash, she finally found some night attire.

She dressed and knelt down by her bed. She bowed her head, intertwined her fingers and closed her eyes.

"I don't know what you have in store for me, but you know what I want out of life. I try to be a good person…I want what's best for everyone. I just pray that you help Markus find what he's looking for, even if it's not me. I can be happy enough, knowing that he's happy. I know that I deserve a good life, and with your guidance, I'll get it. Amen."

Marissa slowly rose to her feet and slid into bed, disappearing under her comforter and surrounding herself with pillows. Faith moved Marissa far in her life. She had no intention of changing her approach.

Just as she settled into sleep, Markus dropped to a single knee.

Inside his head, he said: *Protect me, as you've done every night. I ask for guidance. I don't feel I'm the man Marissa deserves. Please reveal to me what's needed of me to accomplish my goals. Help me let go of the anger I harbor for my parents' death, and achieve peace of mind. Amen.*

Markus swiped up his mask and slid it atop his head, pulling down the bottom until it covered his face and connected to the rest of his suit. He dressed in the familiar black and blue suit he'd donned nightly for years now. He started the engine and revved the motor. He remained focused as the ground opened up, the ramp leading into the garage ahead of him.

He punched the accelerator. The tires screeched, their shrill sound filling the area. The car pushed past 60 miles per hour within seconds. The vehicle hit the ramp and accelerated through the open space. When the car passed through, the ground quickly closed behind him.

Early the next morning, Markus planted his feet on his room's Berber carpet. He stretched upward, and then ran his hands down his quads, knees and shins. His silk pajama bottoms were so soft. He looked out the window to see yet another day in a quiet, neighbor-less neighborhood.

He yawned when he walked down the stairs, still tired. He had a meeting today. It covered important topics, such as the evolution of the company, something he was very interested in.

Markus scratched the back of his head when he hit the bottom step, looking the house over. There were things displaced, not as clean as usual. He'd already scheduled cleaners to work in his absence. It worked better that way. They could do their job without worrying about if they were disturbing him. He thought the way to maximize work was to leave people alone to do their job; less distraction equaled more work done.

Markus looked at the blank TV screen.

"TV…on."

The TV flipped on.

"Local news."

The channel flipped to Markus's request.

He caught the news anchor at the beginning of her speech. "And now, a different story: the Crooked Tree was robbed last night. In a bizarre twist, the money stolen was returned. The robbers were apologetic, even though an arrest was made. Someone must have scared the bejeezus out of them."

Markus grinned. Late last night, he ran into the robbers, just as they finished knocking off another establishment. Instead of confronting them right away, he followed them to a place where they felt safe.

When he finally confronted them, he ran his right index finger over his left index finger as if to say, "Tsk, tsk." Since he rarely spoke – if at all – when he was masked, they took his cues as words. He kept his distance while he watched the robbers return the money and turn themselves in. No harm done, no violence.

I feel refreshed. I usually come in banged up. I could get used to this. Sure, I have technological and chemical advances when it comes to recovery, but this is different. Waking up every single day without even thinking about it is like a dream.

For a moment, he thought about Marissa's words.

Am I ready to accept a world that includes Marissa, but not the mask? It's not like I've been masked my entire life, but it feels like it. Even when I'm hurt, sick or both, when everything in my being is saying no...I'm out there, taking chances.

On the other side of the coin, he wondered if Marissa would accept him if she knew about his "night job." Would she overreact and change her mind? Would she end up finding out before he had a chance to tell her? Would he tell her outright, to avoid problems?

He didn't know. That was something he'd give more thought to. For now, he would get ready for his meeting.

As part of his daily routine, Markus showered, styled his hair, checked for bruises and injuries, and got dressed. A few sprays of his favorite cologne – *Sophisticated Gentleman* – and he was good to go.

While Markus readied himself at his house, Marissa was also awake, her mind racing. She had a crisis on her hands. She didn't want to tell Markus all she told him, but she was known for being bold, especially when it came to sharing her feelings.

"Did I really act like that last night?" She asked herself. "Did I let myself become *that* vulnerable? Dumb, dumb, dumb! Well, another fine mess you've gotten yourself into, Marissa!"

The brunette blew the hair out of her face. Her hair fell to the sides of her head as she looked up at the ceiling, buried in a huge bed with numerous pillows. The way she handled the situation last night was akin to a teenager who blabbed about what they thought or felt about something: no tact involved, just talking. She looked at the digital clock on her nightstand.

10:32 a.m.

She rolled over toward the nightstand and grabbed her cell phone, pulling it back into bed with her. She opened up the main screen. She saw a message from Markus. A wave of nervousness hit her. She felt like she was back in high school. What was it going to say?

I hope you slept well. Talk tonight?

Not as bad as she thought. She wondered how that talk would turn out. What would they talk about? How she made a complete fool of herself? She didn't want to relive that. Her response was the best she could muster, in a matter of moments.

Late night. I'll actually be working on something. Maybe l8r than usual?

She wanted to see him, but on her terms and, in a place where she felt comfortable. All the things they talked about the night before was in a coffee shop, hardly the place to share feelings. Marissa made mistakes, but not such an obvious one. She kicked herself all night about it.

Sure. See you then.

Marissa laid back and let her head hit the pillow again. Meeting with Markus again gave her more incentive to finish up her commitments. Hopefully, they could come to some kind of understanding. Well, she hoped they could.

Markus's board meeting struck in the early afternoon. In his personal elevator, he looked at himself through the reflection of the buffed stainless steel doors. His blue wool suit and leather shoes looked good and his arguing points sounded great. He was ready for this quick – but probably painful – meeting.

Not everything presented to him was as simple as a yes or no. However, he treated the board like walking suggestion boxes. Markus had final say over what happened with and to P4P. Nothing went forward without his endorsement.

The door to his elevator opened at the top floor. Markus confidently strode out. He pushed one of the office's double doors open and shut it behind him, his eyes observing the men and women huddled in the board room. Vanessa waited in a familiar spot, right beside his chair.

"Mr. Doubleday, the statistics are here, as you asked," Vanessa said, pointing to a thin stack of papers encased in a binder.

"Thank you, Ms. Vaughn."

Markus thought Vanessa was loyal, despite the small amount of time she'd worked for him. It was the only job she ever had; if he had anything to do with it, it would be the only job she'd ever want. Since she'd started working for him, Markus found himself with more time for other projects.

Markus sat down at the head of the table. As he shuffled through the bound papers in front of him, he stopped and looked up at the board members. He felt like the room was glaring at him.

"I'm assuming everyone's doing well?" Markus asked.

There was little chatter. Most of them opted to nod yes. Some of them opted to kiss Markus's ass. There was a tone they used, a tone he picked up on as soon as he took control of the company. In Markus's mind, there was a difference between asking how someone was doing, and asking in a nasal-y, fake voice.

Markus closed his eyes for a moment. When he opened his eyes, he said, "Look, we all know why we're here. People, this isn't about reinventing the wheel; this is about putting out great products. Is everyone in agreement?"

The board unanimously nodded yes.

"We're going to take the next step."

There were a couple gasps and negative head shakes amongst the group.

"Like adult movies?" One asked.

"We're not peddling smut; get that out of your heads. Everything we've ever done has been tasteful, and porn's never been what we've been about."

"Some people like the smut," one of the other board members said.

"And I completely understand that," Markus retorted quickly. "Nobody told California to stop distributing or to change the way they're conducting business. I'm just taking another step forward in the way *we* conduct business."

The board members nodded.

"Your average guy comes home and watches smut. What's he getting? He's getting a woman that performs a multitude of acts with multiple partners. Your average woman is not okay with a lot of this stuff."

"So what are you saying?" Another board member asked.

"I'm saying that, in most cases, people who watch this are getting an inaccurate and unrealistic depiction of your average scenario: altered body parts, shoddy acting, and a general misconception of what the actual act is about. Let me ask you all a question: what do people crave the most in this world?"

"To be loved."

"Absolutely," Markus said, pointing to the voice.

The board members looked at Vanessa. They were old-school; they believed assistants were better seen and not heard. Some of them wondered why an assistant was in there at all, but they wouldn't question Markus. She looked down at the clipboard she held. She may have been out of line for what she'd just done – and she'd apologize later – but she understood his message.

"So, simply put, we tastefully put out products that promote what it's like to be loved," Markus said. To him, the board still looked skeptical. He would have to do more persuading.

"I don't know about you, but nobody I know wants to introduce their family to a significant other that's been with hundreds of people. For some reason, it doesn't sit well," Markus said sarcastically. "They want to be able to say, 'This is me, and I'm in love with so-and-so.' People in the world want the opportunity to say that. You know it, and I know it."

The board members nodded positively with Markus's words. He continued.

"This is just another dimension to P4P. Yes, there are perverts everywhere, but there are more people out there whose emotions don't involve your standard adult movie. We will be successful. I've never invested in something that wasn't worth it. Guys…this is worth it."

The board members unanimously agreed with Markus's proposal. It wasn't because it was the right thing to do; it was more about a great way to make money. The board wouldn't agree with something that would cut their vacation time down or make them wait an extra week to purchase nice things. The company's bottom line mattered more than Markus Doubleday's feelings.

"Thank you for your time, ladies and gentlemen. Let's get the right people on the 'brainstorming' front, shall we? See you again next month," Markus told the board. "Vanessa."

Vanessa followed Markus out the door.

"I don't really know how these things are supposed to go," Vanessa admitted. "The board members seem skeptical. Not that you need it, but if my opinion means anything, I think it's a good idea," Vanessa told Markus.

"So you're saying that, if you didn't think it was a good idea, you would tell me, in front of the board members? You'd embarrass me like that?" Markus replied.

"Well, I-I…"

"No, you would."

He brought Vanessa's stammering and stuttering to a swift halt. He opened the door to his office and used a hand motion to invite Vanessa along. He shut the door behind her and took a few steps forward, facing her again.

"And I want you to do that. If you don't think it's a good idea, tell me." He pointed out the door. "Those old blowhards won't. They're all about saying no without really thinking about it, and you have a level head. You don't make as much money as they do, but with time, you'll end up making more."

"How do you know that?" Vanessa said, "I mean, with all due respect."

"You do more. You're asked to represent me, in some cases. They've all been in their position for years, and they're nothing more than figureheads set to say no at any and everything that involves change. They're like gargoyles with opinions."

"I understand."

"They did well in the beginning, but this is not my parents' company anymore. So, if it's all right with you, you'll learn and grow and develop. Are you ready for something like that?"

"Yes," Vanessa told him confidently. "I'm sure I'm for the job."

"Good. Should be a good night. Meet me at my house tonight, around nine o'clock. I'm out for the day."

"Very good, sir."

Markus boarded his personal elevator. He slid his hands into his pockets and kept his gaze on the elevator's floor.

When the doors closed, Vanessa sported a smile that could melt the universe. His words to her sounded like a promotion. She wanted to be good at her job. She would readily admit that she wanted Markus's attention and his approval.

After all, that was all she had left. Markus mattered more than he thought.

Just as Markus left his office, Jasper Kane walked into his.

Dressed in a suit with a purple turtleneck, the therapist sat his six-foot-one-inch tall frame down at his desk and leaned back. He stroked his neatly-trimmed Balbo beard while he read the newspaper.

He was the masked maniac they talked about, that murdered someone.

He remembered his victim's fading grasp vividly, the look in his victim's eyes while his life slowly drained from him. How his body went limp. Taking. That was a feeling of power like no other.

Jasper remembered when a man told him that the people in his profession were often the ones that needed the most help. Jasper laughed it off at the time. On the next night, he ended that man's life. He needed help, and he knew that. Until he faced the demons of his past, he would always need of help.

Lorraine, his secretary, rapped on the door lightly before opening it.

"Mr. Kane, your appointment is here."

"Good. Send her in," he said.

What brought Jasper out of his own head was a woman walking through the door. She shut the door behind her and took a seat on Jasper's couch. She was wearing a pair of jeans, a short t-shirt, and a jacket. Her hair was pulled back into a tight ponytail.

It was Daphne De La Rosa.

She'd been going to Jasper to deal with her anxiety issues. She wasn't a fan of seeing psychiatrists and doctors; being in her line of work, she knew mental health was important. The department also took it seriously. Her parents had their own ways of fixing things, something she hated.

She will make a beautiful victim…when it's time. "Hello, Daphne. It was good that you called last night."

"Yes, I was…feeling a little anxious," Daphne said. "Thank you for taking my call."

Jasper's smile was warm. "Oh, don't mention it. Get comfortable. You look tense. This should be a place of relaxation, not for stress. You're in a safe place."

Daphne apprehensively rested on the couch. She used a pillow to prop her head up, wiggling her feet out of her flat leather sandals and crossing one leg over the other. She intertwined her fingers and placed them on her stomach, letting her elbows hang while she looked up at the ceiling. She slowly lost herself in thought.

"Is there anything new in your world?" Jasper asked.

Daphne was ripped from her brief thoughts with his words. "No. Yes. Well, kind of," she stammered. "Some new developments, with feelings. I have this guy I work with–"

"You know how you feel about workplace relationships," Jasper reminded. His chair stayed in a relaxed position while he spoke. "They don't always work out the best, and then, you have to continue to work with them, for them."

Daphne didn't want to hear that. "Yeah, I know. He's a kid, you know? He looks like he's still wet behind the ears, for God's sake! I don't know what I'm thinking!" Her words were filled with excitement as she peeled her fingers away from each other and halfway reached up to the sky. "But Jasper, he's genuine. He's just so genuine, in his words and actions."

I wonder what it's like to have a genuine relationship with someone. I've never had one, not a memorable one, at least. Lorraine is the closest, and if she ever crossed me, I would kill her. I wouldn't think twice about it. I know that's not normal. I just don't care.

"Daphne, if this means as much to you as I'm hearing…perhaps it's not out of the realm of possibility to crave a connection with a man that's wet behind the ears, as you put it."

"I don't know if I can risk it," Daphne said.

"If it's worth it, it will be," Jasper countered. "You've had a few bad relationships in your time on this earth. Who hasn't? They shouldn't scar you forever. It shouldn't hold you back from taking the requisite steps towards a better quality of life. You are better."

"I am better. Right. Listen, don't–"

Jasper listlessly pointed out the window. "I know you're tough out there, and that's respectable; admirable, even. You have to be. You don't have to put on a facade in here. Remember, this is a safe place, Daphne. You're free to let your guard down."

Daphne agreed with Jasper's words. She wasn't ready to let her guard down completely, but she was definitely interested to see how much damage was done by some of her past relationships. At the moment, she felt insecure.

"There's only so much somebody can take, Jasper. So much of someone telling you that you're worthless, you know? Telling you that…that you don't deserve what you got. The day I found out I was promoted to detective, my boyfriend at the time, he asks me, 'Who'd you sleep with?' He was a very jealous guy."

"I know the type," Jasper said.

Daphne smirked. Her gaze rested on the ceiling again. "He wouldn't dare put his hands on me. He's not dumb. He knew about the badge and gun, so it never came to that. I can't write him a ticket for being a jerk, I…I should've just left. It was one of those things where I loved him and we'd been through so much together that I just…I didn't want to give up. Do you have a type for that?" She turned her head toward Jasper's desk. He nodded yes. She looked at the ceiling again.

"So yeah, I know I should've skipped out."

"There had to be something else stopping you," Jasper said.

Daphne hesitated. It needed to be said. She thought it might make her feel better, in the end. If she was going to move forward with her life, she felt she needed to talk, bounce her insecurities off of Jasper. Who was better than someone that was legally bound to hold onto her secrets? No one, she thought.

"My father bothers me about this," Daphne started. "He talks about how our people stay until the end, through good times and bad. Stay and support. Stay and support."

"Because of your Hispanic heritage?"

"Of course. So, I thought I was doing the right thing. He tells me all the time about how I can't keep a man in my life, about how I voice my opinion too much, and that scares them away. I'm strong but not silent." Daphne laughed inaudibly.

"I don't know how much your therapist's opinion matters to you, but…be who you are," Jasper said. "If this is who you are, find people that appreciate that. There are people out there that are going to positively feed off you, and vice-versa. They'll accept you for you and won't try to change you. Sure, someone may think you talk too much, but the guy whose wet behind the ears, he might be just right. Does that make sense?"

"Yes, it does. That felt good." Daphne sat up from the couch.

"You needed to get that off your chest. Everyone needs someone to talk to, Daphne."

"You're right. Thank you, Jasper."

"My pleasure."

He wanted things to work out for Daphne, just like any other patient that came to see him. When it came to his profession, he wanted everything to work out. He was – arguably – the best, in his line of work.

His nightly activities were a different story.

There was a knock at Markus's front door. He was dressed in his default silk pajama bottoms and a silk robe that tied at the waist and stretched to his knees. He opened the door and saw Vanessa in the doorway, dressed casually. She looked at him. He looked at her.

"You made it," Markus said, "and 15 minutes early, no less."

"I did. I told you I'd be here. You should have known I'd be early."

Vanessa walked past Markus and into the house with a sly smirk. She examined the house for moments, familiar with her surroundings. She liked to get lost in just how nice his house was.

"I meant to ask you this earlier: did you design this all on your own?" Vanessa asked.

Markus feigned offense. "What's *that* supposed to mean?"

"All on your own," Vanessa repeated. "Did you design the interior all on your own?"

"Gotcha. No, Marissa helped me. She picked out some of the things you see on the walls around the house. The technology you see in the house, however, that's something I'm good at. You know that."

"Of course I do, but…we didn't come here to talk shop about interior design, did we?"

"Am I that transparent?"

"Sir, I've been around you for a little while now. I won't hold you up with mention of house design. You're straightforward, as it is."

It was apparent that Vanessa paid attention to Markus, studied him, even. She knew when something was on his mind. That was enough to get her far, as his assistant. Markus was straightforward about everything, except his more-than-strong feelings about Marissa Buchanan.

"You're absolutely right," Markus admitted. "Hey, speaking of meaning to ask things…do you mind telling me what happened to your parents? You told me they passed, but we never really got into it."

Vanessa visibly froze. She hadn't talked with anyone about this, and didn't know if she wanted to. Could she trust Markus with information about her parents? What was he going to do with it? Would he use it as leverage against her in the future?

"I-I…"

"I want you to listen to me," Markus interrupted. "You told me you wanted to learn, right?"

"Yes."

"You told me you wanted to grow, right?"

"I did."

"Here is your chance to learn and grow."

Markus's words cut like a knife. He slowly rubbed his hands. He didn't know what to do with them. The situation had grown tense; he didn't want to cross his arms and make a tense situation tenser.

"Well…"

She had to think back to the night her parents were murdered. She didn't want to revisit that, but as Markus said, it would help her grow.

"I was in a hotel room with my parents, and–" Her eyes welled up as she fought the urge to be reduced to a blubbering mess. "We'd come back from somewhere. My father was showering, because he fancies a shower first. My mother and I were on the bed talking when there was a rap at the door. We thought it was room service, someone to come and fluff pillows with no sense of time, I don't know."

She looked at and to Markus for guidance.

"It's okay. What happened next?" His words were soft and assuring.

"Well, my mum, she didn't know who it was. She thought it was room service, but she told me, just in case, I should get under the bed. I did that really quickly, and when she saw that I was safe under there, she opened the door. I heard a sound. Real quiet sound."

Vanessa paused. Markus gave her a knowing nod and mouthed, "It's fine." It barely relaxed her, but just enough. She pressed on.

"It sounded like…when someone hits another in a pillow fight. That's what it sounded like. Barely notice it if you're just passing by."

"Gunshots," Markus said.

"Yes sir." Vanessa thought about what happened next before she spoke. This was uncharted territory.

"I saw my mum's eyes. They had a little life left in them. I remember looking at her from under the bed. She didn't look scared at all. She just had a look like, 'I can't believe I made a mistake like this.' I heard another sound, and she was gone. Her eyes were open, but she was gone."

Vanessa blinked. A single tear ran down her face.

"And your father?"

"Sir, I need a minute, if you could spare one."

"You may not have one. You came to learn and grow. I need you to do this before we continue to grow."

Vanessa stared at Markus, her face full of surprise. He was straightforward, sure, but he'd never pushed like that before. She wasn't fully comfortable anymore. She had no idea what she'd gotten herself into.

"Okay, ummm…well, my father…they knocked on the door and when he opened it, they shot him. He probably thought it was me or my mum, trying to use the bath. It wasn't."

She wiped another tear away and smiled. Markus smiled back at her, albeit very briefly. He didn't want to give off the impression that he thought any of this was funny; it wasn't. Some of the things he'd seen in his life were more grisly, by comparison.

"And then…this man showed up."

"And then this man showed up," Markus repeated after Vanessa's words, "to help or hurt?"

"To help. A masked man. I couldn't see his face. He wore a blue and black suit. It was quite tight. He was very impressive, really. Well, from the sound of it."

"Really? Well, I'm quite skeptical," he said, mocking her. "Are you sure you saw something like that?" He asked, cocking his head to the side.

"Sir, please don't ask me if I'm sure about something of that nature. These are my parents we're speaking about. I know *exactly* what I saw," Vanessa snapped.

"Point taken," Markus remarked. "Go ahead."

"Anyhow, there were two men. This masked man, he was so precise. He stopped them from doing more harm. At a quiet point, I crawled out from under the bed and grabbed one of the guns on the floor. Those guys were all sprawled out, and the one with the mask, he was up."

"Wow," Markus said.

"I wanted to kill those men for what they did. That man, he took the gun I picked up and dismantled it in maybe…less than two seconds. He offered me his hand and I just…I went with him."

"Where'd you go?"

"I went…he took me down the outside of the building with him. He crawled down while I hung on his back, like a baby koala. As soon as we made it to the ground, I dropped to my feet and took off. Probably the fastest I'd ever run in my life, I was so scared."

Markus remembered that night. *No kidding. I watched you run away. Nobody I know runs that fast. I wouldn't be able to catch you.*

"So after that, I just kind of…ran amok," Vanessa said. "You know the rest of the story: I was homeless, and broke into houses to take what I needed, and then you gave me a job. Are you happy?"

"I am. That took tremendous courage, Vanessa. You didn't have to tell me what happened to your parents, but you did. I appreciate and respect that."

"Thank you, sir."

"Now, I have one more question for you: what would you say if I told you I knew where your parents' murderers are?"

Vanessa recovered from her emotions quickly. Her sniffles disappeared and her posture improved. "With all due respect, I would demand to know where they are, and I wouldn't take no for an answer." Her words were forceful. She looked at Markus with fire in her eyes. She refused to blink, she was so enraged. She wanted to find those men and make them pay dearly for what they'd done to her parents.

"No."

Her mouth stood agape, along her now enlarged eyes. "No?! You're telling me you have information about my parents' murder! Not death…*murder*! You're withholding information from me about this?! Why?! Why are you doing this?! Are you mad?!"

Vanessa stared at him, the fire in her eyes burning brighter. She was highly upset. She felt like she couldn't control it much longer.

"Because, you have potential. I want you to harness it. I don't want you solely as my assistant at P4P…I want you to be my assistant in the field."

Vanessa's eyes shuttered. She didn't understand what he meant by "in the field." She wondered what field he was talking about. "So you want me to be able to harness and control my potential in a field?"

Markus nodded no. "*The* field, not *a* field."

"And do what with it? Twiddle my bloody thumbs?" She asked abrasively.

"I don't want this project to be for the sole purpose of a vengeance mission," Markus said sternly. "This is more like a life choice. It all comes down to how much you care about your fellow man, even when your fellow man doesn't seem to care. Let's call it…a public servant in the shadows."

Vanessa laughed, which caught Markus off-guard. "You couldn't possibly be serious. Like, what you see in the comics? What you see on TV?"

"Yes."

"That's all fiction! The people that actually *try* to do things like that get killed!" Vanessa's laugh was condescending and unbelieving. Markus's demeanor never changed. Even though Vanessa was practically laughing in his face, Markus remained steady.

"I was reading the news one day, and it said that someone dressed up like a vigilante and got his bloody nose broken in a fight! The funniest thing I read that day!"

Markus raised his eyebrows. He knew who she was talking about. He'd helped the guy out before. Markus remembered the guy's clumsiness, and his lack of secret identity. In his mind, that put a huge bull's eye on him and anyone close to him.

"Do you want to continue giving me your opinion or are you ready to move forward? I feel like you're wasting my time," Markus said. "My time is important."

Vanessa immediately stopped laughing. She sensed his seriousness, now that she was paying attention.

"I'm sorry, sir. I'm ready."

"Good."

Markus turned toward the door that led to the basement and placed his hand on the sensor. A green outline of his hand showed, blinked and disappeared. "Confirmed: Markus Doubleday," the sensor box said. The door clicked numerous times and opened. Markus walked through it, Vanessa in tow.

Vanessa was apprehensive about the scene. She didn't think that was a normal door. She believed to have heard 10 clicks, maybe more.

Markus stepped on an escalator-inspired platform. Easily able to fit four, it moved faster than a standard escalator. His hands lingered in his robe's pockets while Vanessa kept one hand on the rail, while the other rested by her side. She made a note to pinch herself when she got home. This was too good to be true.

"Jesus…"

When the platform landed, Vanessa feasted her eyes on Markus's massive underground facility. It went on forever. Vanessa performed a slow pirouette; everything her eyes laid on, she took in. She would have never thought that Markus's house had all this space underneath. The space looked bigger than the stadium the Dallas Cowboys played at.

"We're a go," he said.

"What? We're a go? What do you mean we're a go?" Vanessa repeated.

Vanessa's mouth opened wide. The whole room changed. Multiple flat screen television screens rose from the floor, along with a large steel desk with multiple computer keyboards. Two rows of cars – at least 15 – all ranging from large to small, "everyday use" to "maybe once a week." Vanessa walked around in amazement before her momentum was stopped. It felt like she'd run into a wall.

It was Markus.

Vanessa took a few steps back, her gaze moving up to find what he was looking at. *That black spandex suit…the upside-down triangles for eyes…blue on the shoulders…black and blue gloves…no way…I can't believe what my eyes are showing me.* "You? That was…you?"

Everything came flooding back to her. She'd seen glimpses of Markus's lean physique. She noticed how much attention to detail he had and the way he carried himself. It all made sense now. The man she assisted in the day was the man that assisted her that night, the man that kept her alive. "Oh my God. This *has* to be a dream." Vanessa's words were barely heard.

"It's not a dream. Are you ready to learn now?" Markus asked without skipping a beat.

"Yes," Vanessa said. She nodded yes vehemently.

"Come back tomorrow. When you show up to work, I'll know you're in and committed. If you don't show up…"

"If I don't show up?"

"Then I'll know that you're not in and you're not committed," Markus said. "But the things you saw tonight, Ms. Vaughn…you can't unsee. I want you to remember that while you mull over your options all night."

"How do you know I'll do that?"

"Trust me…you'll mull."

"Then…I suppose I'll mull. Is that all you require of me tonight?"

"Yes. I'll lead you back up to the top."

Markus stepped foot on the platform of his escalator. Vanessa joined him. He kept his hands in his robe's pockets. Vanessa placed a hand on the handrail.

In Markus's mind, he didn't have reservations about Vanessa returning. In Vanessa's mind, her handful of reservations was enough to make the pendulum swing.

When the two made it to the top, Markus placed his hand on a wall sensor, similar to the sensor that led them inside. Once the sensor confirmed Markus's handprint, the door unlocked. The two walked through it and were in the living room again. Something told him she'd already made a decision.

"I will definitely let you know tomorrow," Vanessa notified.

"I understand. Goodnight, Ms. Vaughn."

"Goodnight, Mr. Doubleday. Wait…"

"Yes, Ms. Vaughn?"

Vanessa's lips curled into a smile. She stepped forward and wrapped her arms around Markus's neck, pulling him into a tight hug. She rested her chin on his shoulder. She felt his chin on her shoulder, as well. She exhaled. "Thank you for saving me," she said, speaking directly into his ear.

Markus wrapped his arms around her torso, patting the small of her back with one hand. "You're welcome," he said.

Vanessa pulled back from the hug and left Markus's side.

"I won't mull," she said to herself as she heard Markus's house door shut. "There's not much to mull about, anyway. I don't have the slightest idea of what he's talking about."

After she found herself back at home, Vanessa found herself exclaiming, "He's insane! He knew I would mull!" She didn't want to admit it, but he knew her about as well as she knew him. "Okay, I guess I'm mulling, then."

Vanessa grabbed a glass out of the cabinet and poured herself a glass of water. She got comfortable on the couch. Usually, Vanessa watched trash TV after work. However, she knew she couldn't think about Markus's proposition with that noise in the background. She took a sip of her water.

"He saved my life, for starters. That's a heck of a place to start. He's doing this out of the kindness of his heart, I'm led to believe. He has too much money, too many resources and is too important to this world to do it simply because he's bored."

She took another sip.

"What if I don't take him up on his offer? Will I lose this job? Will I lose everything and be back out on the streets again? He's not fickle like that, is he? Good God, he's a billionaire…aren't they *all* fickle? Whatever's in front of their face is what's good in the moment."

She took another sip.

"But he's different, right? He's been different from the moment I met him. Perhaps his eccentricity is how I know he's genuine. He doesn't lie, that I know of. Maybe I should sleep on it? I've seen a lot today, probably more than my noggin can handle, at this point. Yes, best get ready for bed."

Vanessa stood up from the couch, placed her unfinished glass of water on the kitchen counter, and headed to bed. She decided it was best to sleep on it. She'd have a better time with it in the morning.

Chapter 7

"Hey! This is Marissa Buchanan…Yes, for real. Listen, I– …Yes, it's really Marissa Buchanan, but I need you to listen. I'm looking for some fabric, and everything is closed. I know it's late, and I know you're about to close, but–…You will?! Okay! Thank you so much! I'll be there shortly."

Marissa hung up her cell phone and slid it into her pocket. The Texas weather was warm, even at night. Sometimes, tensions ran high because of the heat. The reason Marissa's tensions were high: she found a place still open that had the fabric she was looking for. She had to get there.

And, there was that pesky Markus Doubleday situation.

I'm going to give him one more chance tonight. I've thought about it all day, and even though Johanna is a B – with a capital B – the love I have for him is requited. What I want to know is…what's holding him back?

She brought her thoughts with her on the way to the store. They kept their doors open a few minutes past their closing time. A few minutes wouldn't hurt and, it was their chance to meet Marissa Buchanan.

Try as she might, she wouldn't deny it: being a celebrity had perks. In her mind, celebrities used their status to get in and out of things. She wouldn't be able to get away with it forever, so she would strike while the iron was hot.

Maybe I could be a celebrity forever if I got my fashion line off the ground? I don't want to model forever, that's for sure. There's a cap on that profession! Let's face it: there's a fresh new face made every minute, and a "Flavor of the Month" every second. I'll be sure to attribute my future successes to my present paranoia.

Marissa grabbed a book, stepped out of her parked car and shut the door. She looked around. The store was in a seedy part of town. Dimly lit and eerily quiet. She'd be in the store 10 minutes at the most, not nearly enough time for possible danger to crop up. She'd be in and out.

"It'll be fine."

Marissa's mind filled with forced assurance as she happened upon the store door. She knocked lightly on the door and waited. After a few seconds, an awestruck young woman let her in. About 18 or 19, Marissa guessed. She looked too nervous to say anything to Marissa. Her smile made her look like she was in pain.

Marissa smiled politely.

"What's your name?" Marissa asked.

"Cindy," she said.

"Okay, Cindy. Good to meet you. Here, maybe you can help me?" Marissa said to her. She opened the book she carried in with her and pointed a few places on the pages. "I'm looking for these colors in these fabrics."

"Sure, Ms. Buchanan. Right away."

"I'm also sorry about coming so late," Marissa apologized.

"Not a problem!" Cindy called over her shoulder.

Marissa walked around the store, running her fingers along the different fabrics offered. Her mind jumped to the different ways she could utilize them. She opened up her notebook and jotted down notes.

After a few minutes, Cindy had retrieved all the fabrics Marissa requested. Marissa had several different dress and skirt ideas. In her mind, what she wanted to put together was going to be big and successful, come hell or high water. All she had to do was get some believers out there, and the products would sell themselves.

Marissa knew she was meeting Markus late again. She didn't have time to go home and improve her look. Markus had seen her in worse shape, from a "looks" standpoint. She thought the Crooked Tree was a good place to meet, when it wasn't being robbed.

After Marissa paid Cindy for her fabrics, she left. The store's lights went off almost as soon as she walked out the store. She turned back to the store's window. She didn't see anything.

When she brought her head back around, she noticed a stranger leaning on her driver's side door. She wondered what this guy wanted. Her heart raced. She narrowed her eyes slightly, as if to notify the man to move, and fast.

"Excuse me. That's my car. Do you mind moving?" There was a hint of attitude in Marissa's words as she pointed to the car parked in front of hers. "*There's* a perfectly good car to lean on. I'm just trying to leave, that's all."

Marissa looked the man up and down. He was dirty-looking. He also wore a jacket with his jeans. It was still warm – despite the time of night – so Marissa had no idea why he was dressed in such hot clothes.

He said to her, "I think you better watch who you're talking to. I've hurt people for less."

A sound caught Marissa's ear. She looked down. The small knife instantly grabbed her attention. He kept the blade barely visible. She quickly became aware of how her night could go. She didn't want to end up dead in a ditch. She regretted not telling someone of her whereabouts. *I have to get out of this*, she thought.

Marissa said, "Look at me, in a blonde moment…and I'm not even blonde!"

"Walk down that alley right over there. Act like nothing's wrong." The man motioned with a quick head nod; his words were stern and plain.

"O-okay?" Marissa nodded her head yes, with a confused tone. *What does he want from me?* She slowly headed into the alley behind the store. Before she got too deep into the alley, she pieced the scene together: he was going to do something to her, and it would be too late if she screamed.

Marissa took her chances and raced down the alley. Another stranger appeared on the other side. As Marissa neared, she thought this one looked cleaner than the other, a little taller than her, with dreadlocks.

"Help!" Marissa's voice was loud and clear. "There's a man chasing me, and-and…"

"Calm down. You're safe," he said. "Just calm down."

Marissa heard footsteps slowly approach in the dimly lit alley. Moments later, the man's face shone. His small knife still in-hand, he drew near.

"There he is!" Marissa exclaimed.

As she tried to move away, the man whose arms she'd run into were now holding her captive. She'd been set up. She was trapped. No one knew where she was. She looked up at the man holding her momentarily before she looked back at the man with the knife. She didn't know what to do.

"I'm sorry for talking to you that way about my car," Marissa said to the man.

"*Now* you want to apologize? *Now* you want to say you're sorry, now that you don't have anywhere to run, now that you have a knife in your face?"

"But you can't kill me!" Marissa argued. "Do you know who I am? I'm in the media! I'm on the covers of magazines! I'm not someone that you can just lay waste to! Every cop in this city will look for you!"

The man didn't say anything.

"All I'm saying is…just think about what you're doing, okay?"

That was her natural reaction: to throw logic in the conversation to sway their opinions, but she didn't know if it helped or not.

"I've thought about it," the man with the knife said. "I think I'm going to do it anyway."

The grip on Marissa's arms tightened. She tried to pull away from her attacker's dreadlocked accomplice, but he was too strong. "I'll pay you anything, just let me go!" She practically yelled at both of them.

When the knife-wielding man took a step forward, a sound rang in the air.

Tap…Tap-Tap-Tap-Tap-Tap…Tap-Tap

"What was that sound? You hear that?" The knife-wielder asked his partner.

All three people in the alley looked around. They all heard it.

Tap…Tap-Tap-Tap-Tap-Tap…Tap-Tap

The knife-holder's eyes widened, like he'd seen a ghost. He tried to discreetly motion to Marissa's captor. A second later, her captor buckled. He used Marissa to try to stay on his feet. His weight pulled her down. She let out a quick yelp.

The crusader jumped over the fallen two and attacked with a combination of lefts and rights, until the man hit the ground. The clang of the knife rang in the alley.

The dreadlocked one that previously held Marissa scrambled to his feet and placed his hands in the air. "I'm sorry, man! Please, don't–"

The masked man's baton connected with his hand. The thug let out a blood-curdling scream, and scurried into the night.

The knife carrier was alone now. He attempted to find his bearings. The punches rattled him. The masked man positioned himself between Marissa and the threat. *He's protecting me*, she thought.

While on his hands and knees, the dirty one looked up and saw the mask. When he did, he crawled backward to make space between the two. With his baton, the hero pointed out of the alley.

"Go. Now."

The man pushed off the pavement with his hands and ran away, sharply turning the corner. When the masked man turned and faced Marissa, he sheathed his baton, locking it onto his belt. He offered his hand. Marissa took it. He pulled her to her feet with ease.

When he let her hand go, he tapped his opposite wrist with his index finger. He then used the same index finger to wag back and forth at Marissa, as if to tell her she knew better. She scrunched her nose. *The hell was that about?*

Her hero cocked his head up when he heard sirens fill the air. She looked at him.

"I don't really know how to thank you. I don't even know who you are." She turned around to see where the sirens were coming from. "Hey, is this going to be like *Spider-Man*, where you raise your mask so I can kiss you?"

She turned back to face him. He was gone. She looked up and caught just a glimpse of the stranger pulling himself over the top of the nearby building. Back to the shadows he went. Marissa was left with a knife in the alley, two departed attackers, and a small scrape on her elbow.

Marissa was checking her arm when she heard tires screech to a halt. She looked up. A few police cruisers had arrived. A handful of officers rushed down the alley to tend to Marissa. Everything soon became a blur. They asked her what she saw, if she could identify anyone, and what stopped them.

She couldn't recall much. Everything happened so fast. Marissa told them that a man with a mask helped her. She heeded the cop's reactions: annoyance and disgust. In their minds, they didn't need any help. These people were vigilantes, menaces to society. Their thoughts echoed a colleague of theirs.

"Detective De La Rosa," one of the cops said, "it's another Masked Maniac story."

Daphne cocked her head up. "Great." She pointed at Marissa while looking at the attending officer. "She doesn't know much, does she? She looks disoriented."

"No, she doesn't," the cop said.

"Make sure she gets home safe."

The cop nodded and turned to leave.

"Hey…"

The cop turned back.

"Is that Marissa Buchanan?" Daphne mouthed to the cop, pointing at Marissa again.

He nodded yes.

"Find out who accosted Ms. Buchanan, but we also have to find this vigilante. Whoever it is, we need to get them off the street before it becomes a big mess, and innocent people get killed because someone wants to play dress-up."

The cop nodded again and headed toward Marissa. De La Rosa looked around the scene, looking for clues to tip her off on this vigilante's whereabouts.

No matter how she felt about Jonathan Deadmarsh and his attempts to push the Superhero Code on her, she was still a cop with a job. She wasn't very flexible on matters. She would bend minimally, but never break. She was more by the book than most, with an aggression to her. If she came in contact with this vigilante, she'd give him a piece of her brand of justice.

Later on, Marissa found herself at Markus's. She told the cops she refused to go home. She was too shaken up. She didn't tell them where she was going when they asked. It was none of their business. She felt safer with Markus than she did with her parents.

Happening upon the gate, Marissa hit the brakes abruptly. Her car jumped forward, and then stopped. She pushed the button to the intercom and forcefully chirped into the speaker.

"Hey, Markus! It's me! Please open up!"

A soft, robotic voice said, "Confirmed: Marissa Buchanan."

The gate opened and Marissa drove her car through. The gate was completely closed by the time Marissa parked her car. She got out of her car and slammed the door shut, scurrying to Markus's front door. She knocked rapidly, the knocks becoming louder and more frequent as time passed.

Around a minute later, Markus swung one of the big steel doors open, rubbing his eyes. "Mare, what's up?" He asked.

"I can come in, right?" Marissa asked, stepping through the threshold without waiting for an answer. She looked frazzled. She paced.

"Mare…what's wrong?"

"Well, that's a loaded question! Let's see: I went out late to get some fabric on the wrong side of town. Dumb! Then, I was chased into an alley and thought there would be at least one reputable person. This guy said he was going to help me and didn't. Imagine that, right?! Story of my life! This other guy tried to stab me, and–"

"And…" Markus dropped his eyebrows. He feigned ignorance to the whole thing and it was killing him.

"And then some guy showed up and whooped up on them!" She said excitedly. She threw a few short, wild punches. Markus looked at Marissa like she wasn't making sense. "Everything just went so fast!" She continued. "They were gone, ran off, whatever the hell they did…they weren't there anymore." She waved her hands to signify that that wasn't the point. "One thing I noticed, though."

"What was that?" Markus asked.

"His eyes were extremely blue, like yours. Do me a favor: do your hands like this," she ordered, mimicking the masked man's actions from earlier, when he nonverbally scolded her.

"There you go, seeing things again." His words bled skepticism. He did what Marissa asked him to do, performing the task a different way, more lazily. "There…is that okay?"

Marissa wasn't sure. "Yeah, I guess. Do you remember when you said you fight crime at night?"

"Yes. It wasn't that long ago. That was like, last night, right?" He asked.

"Yes, it was. You don't…you don't really do that, right?"

Markus shrugged – with his palms out – and grimaced.

"Marissa, come on," he said. "Me? I get pedicures. I travel a lot. I'm running a billion dollar company. I don't know if the question should be if I terrorize the night; the question might be: would I even have time to?"

She closed her eyes and waved her hand dismissively. "I know, I know. It sounds stupid. Maybe I just need some sleep, I don't know. Mind if I stay here tonight?"

"No, not at all," Markus said quickly. "It sounds like you've been through a traumatic experience, and two nights in a row," he smiled, placing his arm around her shoulders, "I'll take care of you."

Marissa placed her arm around Markus's waist and walked up the stairs with him. With her free hand, she took his occupied hand. "I'm just glad I have a friend like you to count on."

He would make sure her stay was as comfortable as possible. There was a bed in every one of his bedrooms, but they weren't as big or as comfortable. When the two made it to the top of the stair, Markus relinquished his hold on her. He gave a quick nod and began walking down the hall.

"Hey, where are you going?" Marissa asked.

"Is there something you need? I'm going to the other bedroom. You know me. That's just what I do."

"Are you sure you don't want to come in here, with me?" She asked, hopeful.

"I'm sure. We both need our rest, I think. It's been a stressful night. I'm just glad you're alive, and in good spirits. I think you'll find my bed comfortable enough to sleep through two nights, at least."

She wouldn't let her disappointment show.

"I'm sure it will. Goodnight, Markus."

"Goodnight, Marissa."

Markus retired to one of the guest rooms. He shut the door behind him and stood in the dark. A few moments later, he heard the door to his bedroom shut.

Markus sighed. "What am I doing?" He muttered to himself.

He knew what Marissa wanted. Sex didn't come to mind; he knew she wanted to be comforted, considering the circumstances. He held back. He was scared to death of two things: how he acted in defense of her, and that he'd eventually get her involved in something they wouldn't be able to get out of.

However, there was just something about tonight.

While Marissa lay in Markus's bed, she took in his essence. It was all around. He smelled good, even when he worked out. Even though she would enjoy the rest, she didn't enjoy the fact that he was in another room. She wanted him there, with her. She was scared. She remembered back when that masked man showed up. When she looked at him, her heart slowed down.

It had to be him, she thought to herself. With her whole heart, Marissa believed it was him.

Marissa rose from the bed. She wasn't in it long enough to get comfortable, anyway. She thought it'd be a good idea to share her feelings with Markus. She couldn't sleep. She wouldn't pretend she could. No matter how much she tried, she couldn't shake the certainty that she was in love with him. He wouldn't get away so easily, this time. Nothing – short of a home invasion – would stop her.

Marissa half-confidently strode to the door and swung it open. She took a step back, pulled her head back slightly. Unexpectedly, Markus was right in front of her face. She took a couple steps forward, inches from him now. She tilted her head up slightly, looking at him.

She pointed at him. "I have a bone to pick with you, Markus. Listen, I–"

He kissed her.

He must've read my mind. Marissa received Markus's kiss fully, parting her mouth slightly and slipping her tongue in his mouth. He repaid her actions. Their tongues swirled around while their lips played nicely with each other. It wasn't aggressive or raunchy, but she found it to be the sweet kiss she wanted from Markus for years.

On his end, Markus had wanted this for some time. He thought about her night and day. At the current moment, the mask was far back in his mind. He had full confidence in his decision less than 24 hours ago, but no longer.

Marissa lightly clutched the back of Markus's head as they kissed, feeling his hair in between her fingers. Markus wrapped his arms around Marissa's torso, pulling her in tight. Their bodies were close. They could feel each other's heartbeats.

Marissa thought a first kiss was supposed to be this way, not some awkward event. It had to feel right, and be done for the right reasons. Marissa let out a small moan through their kiss. She never felt so alive.

She did things to make her feel alive: she took chances in life; she knew about the thrill of the chase. She knew how much the pursuit of an individual made the pace of her heart quicken. Up until now, once she'd been caught – or did the catching – she would lose interest by the end of the honeymoon stage. She never lost interest in Markus.

On the other end, Markus dreamt about a scenario that ended like this. The "harlequin romance novel" in him wanted to ravage Marissa. She was a beautiful woman, as many pointed out. He didn't care about their opinions and always thought she was beautiful since the day they met.

He followed her lips as she backed up. Her feet slowly took her into Markus's bedroom. They moved in rhythm to make it to the bed. When the back of her knees hit the foot of the bed, Marissa slowly lowered herself. Markus continued to follow her, lowering as well.

Markus ran his hands along Marissa's thighs. She let out a giggle, barely heard. She had very ticklish quads and hamstrings. Marissa cocked her head back so far, she could see the pillows piled up at the head of the bed. He was so warm. As he slid up toward the top of her body, Marissa ran her hands along the sides of his sculpted frame.

Marissa looked at Markus.

"I don't…we don't…"

"No, we don't. I just want to appreciate you."

She nodded her head yes as he lowered his lips and met hers again. Things between them were definitely about to change.

The next morning, Markus – predictably – woke up early. It was still dark outside. He stared at the ceiling. They slept wrapped in each other's arms all night. He hadn't gotten a good night's sleep like that in a long time.

"You know, the nights I would come over to study, it wasn't really to study."

Marissa yanked Markus from his trance. She lay on her side, the big and heavy comforter covering up her body, snugly beneath one arm while the other arm propped her head up.

Markus smiled. "I know. When we studied together, it felt like spending time together. When you weren't looking, I would steal glances at you. I wondered what it would be like to do what we did last night."

"You mean kiss?"

"Yes."

Marissa smiled shyly. "Well, I also stole glances at you. I never cared about who you were dating; I always asked so I could get an update. A little bit of me would celebrate inside, every time I heard of something not working out. I know that sounds screwy."

He took her hand in his. "It doesn't sound too screwy, or we're both screwy, because I would do the same. I was too afraid to go past friendship but I didn't want you to find someone that wasn't me. I know it sounds extremely selfish and self-centered."

"But we were thinking the same thing," Marissa countered. "I think it's just a simple case of two people not having enough guts to say something."

Markus nodded in agreement.

"So what do you want to do, now that we know what we know about each other, about ourselves?" She asked.

"Well–"

"I know my opinion matters just as much as yours, in this situation. I don't want to go backwards. I want to keep moving forward. I want to wrap up my overseas obligations and come back here, and just…just see where it goes, you know?"

She was dreaming right now. Considering the last two nights they had, a conversation like this didn't seem close to realistic.

"Well–"

"What do you think?" Marissa interrupted again.

Markus smiled. "I'll tell you what I think, just as soon as you give me a few seconds to talk."

Marissa smiled back. She couldn't help her excitement! When she was really excited or nervous, she had a tendency to ramble. She was excited *and* nervous, so all bets were off.

"Listen, we both understand business. This is a long-term investment," Markus said.

Marissa nodded yes.

"Here's what I think: you should wrap up your commitments overseas. I'll wrap things up here. When you get home, I want to see where this goes. I don't think we can go back, after last night. Frankly, I don't want to."

"And that's what I always liked about you. Loved, even! You are so confident when your mind is set on something."

"Do you know what I love about you? You're confident, somewhat out of necessity. Tasteful, intelligent…I could go on and on about your qualities. I guess the old saying is true: well-behaved women rarely make history."

Marissa blushed at Markus's flattering words. A candid moment they could share was a moment cherished.

This was also a first-time conversation for them. Marissa wouldn't take the social media avenue, where couples relentlessly expressed their love to each other. Marissa was of the opinion that moments like these were the memories that would last forever.

"Hey, listen…I'm going to have to make a plane in a couple hours. Not everyone can have their own jet," Marissa teased.

Markus chuckled. "I know. All good things must come to an end, I suppose. Hey, if you want to use my jet–"

"No, I'm good. I like to take these trips. It keeps me grounded. As important as people make me out to be, I use the same planes as everyone else. I pay a little extra for the plush chairs, warm towels and other perks, though," she giggled. "But, if you're not busy, I would love for you to take me to the airport. I mean, if you have something to do–"

"No, I would love to take you. I don't usually go into work until late morning. I'll follow you back to your parents' house and help you pack up your stuff. Sound good?"

"Sounds dynamite. Hopefully, there won't be many more robberies or attempted murders in our futures." She'd officially stolen a word that Markus liked to use. Everything looked so different now, in both their eyes.

Not everything was right, however.

There was a churning in the pit of Markus's stomach when the words "robberies or attempted murders" came out of Marissa's mouth. If he didn't tie up the loose ends on his side, there very well could be more robbery and attempted murder in their future. He looked away, but felt safe in the darkness.

"Okay, you just got really quiet. Did you fall asleep?" Marissa asked. She barely heard him breathing.

"No, I'm here. I'm just thinking."

"About what?"

"About the future, and how bright it looks for the two of us. I just…if you would've told me that all this would happen in the last 48 hours, I wouldn't have believed you. Mare, this has been a whirlwind. I'm speechless."

Marissa kissed him on the forehead. "I know. It's crazy, but it's real. You know what I did this morning, first thing? I pinched myself. Yeah, it's real," Marissa gleamed. Though it was a dark room, Marissa felt like a million-watt light bulb. She couldn't stop smiling.

"I'm going to give us 20 more minutes and then we have to get up and get ready," Markus announced.

Markus and his schedules. Marissa broke off of her hand support and laid her head on Markus's smooth, solid chest. He wrapped an arm around her. She placed a hand on his chest and got comfortable. Twenty minutes would be over quick, and she'd savor every second.

On another side of town, James – the vigilante Markus referenced earlier – rested in his one-bedroom apartment. He'd finished another night of attempting to keep the streets safe. No wife, no kids. His face was still swollen, and he found it difficult to breathe after his nose was broken in a fight the other night.

James, an average-sized man – maybe 5’8 or 5’9 – had a beard and some scars. His goal was not notoriety. He helped bring justice to the city. He armed himself with a can of mace and handcuffs, a bulletproof vest, and open-fingered combat gloves.

He simply called himself a Guardian Angel.

James quietly locked the apartment door behind him. He walked over to the cabinet and pulled out the cleanest shot glass he could find, and placed it on the counter. The bottle of liquor he poured from had been open for days. He downed a shot immediately.

James closed his eyes and shook his head from the disgusting taste and moved to the bathroom. He got into a tussle earlier tonight, resulting in a small cut above his eye. He needed to clean his face. He turned the bathroom light on and ran warm water in the sink. Antibacterial soap came first, then lather, then rinse, then alcohol to help with the swelling.

I don’t know how much longer I can do this. Maybe I need a vacation.

He wet his hands and rubbed soap onto them, and then massaged his face with it. He looked in the mirror, observing his soap-soaked, weathered features. James lowered his head into the sink and pushed warm water onto his face, washing the soap away. As he slowly rose to face the mirror, James caught a glimpse of a masked man behind him.

He moved to turn around. A hand found the side of his head, smashed half his face into the bathroom mirror. The loud crash filled the bathroom. The side of his head caught the edge of the sink.

James rested on his hands and knees. He panted like a dog. Blood dripped on the floor. His head felt fuzzy. He shook his head. He barely focused. His eyes caught sight of a pair of boots. He placed one of his hands on them. It moved away from him. James's hand touched the floor again.

"The Broken Skull," James said.

"You're familiar with my work?" The Broken Skull replied.

"I've heard the name." James stalled to snatch his bearings. Blood crept into his eyes. He couldn't locate the broken glass lodged in his face.

"It seems as if you have some kind of…death wish," the Broken Skull said, "which is ironic, for someone who has adopted the name of the Guardian Angel. You've been making trouble for the Cause…"

James confusedly said, "The Cause? Why are–… what is this?"

The Broken Skull grabbed the back of James's vest and pulled him to his feet. "I'm here to expedite the processing of your request. You make yourself quite accessible to the public. You made it easier to track you down. Why this wasn't done earlier to you…is beyond me."

"Because nobody had the guts," James told him.

The Broken Skull slowly placed his hand on James's throat, pressing him against the bathroom wall. "For someone to be so…blatant about their intentions…you knew this day would come."

James's words were a slight whisper when he said, "Take it. I have nothing but this."

The Broken Skull laughed. "And through it all, you still believe you *have* this?"

The Broken Skull unloaded a vicious shot to James's ribs before he could respond. He tightened his grip on James's throat. James wanted to crumple to the ground. The fact he was being forced to breathe while upright was killing him. He struggled with his enemy's grip.

"You're fearful," the Broken Skull diagnosed. "I can feel it. It courses wildly through your veins. This is not your Fight or Flight kicking in, friend. The need for survival consumes you. That's not the Guardian Angel I know. Perhaps it's the first time opposed by your better."

"You mean…my equal?" James barely got out.

"No…I don't."

A flurry of ruthless punches pounded James's ribs. James wanted to yell out. The pain was intense.

The Broken Skull's tight grasp obstructed his breathing. He continued to strike James until he felt James's ribs break. The Broken Skull studied his counterpart. He slightly let up on James's throat, but kept him upright.

James could feel blood rising up from his insides.

"You have nothing…you *are* nothing." The Broken Skull's words were frank.

With all James could gather, he spit blood on the Broken Skull's face.

The Broken Skull laughed. His grip loosened more on James's throat.

James crumpled to the ground. He clutched his ribs and slowly writhed on the cold floor. Blood ran from the man's mouth. He felt himself fading.

"I will wipe this blood away and my life will go on, as will my never-ending ride of terror. You…you will die here…in this bathroom, alone. Do you still feel brave?"

James's light grew dim. His eyes flickered as he looked up at his attacker.

"As you approach the end…will you look back with regret? Will you wonder what could have been? Of course not…you're just trying to breathe."

James's eyes froze. The Guardian Angel was no more. The Broken Skull studied him for a few moments and then looked around the apartment. James died quietly, without much of a fight.

The Broken Skull craved competition, but wanted to eradicate the weak. At heart, he wanted to be killed by someone that was worthy, not someone like the Guardian Angel.

And when the time came, the Guardian Angel lacked execution. This led to his own execution, at the hands of the Broken Skull. The streets were safe no more.

It was just the beginning.

Chapter 8

"Are you ready?"

"I am."

The black Mercedes-Benz SUV hummed away from Marissa's house. She and Markus had the opportunity to clean up and eat breakfast together. They also had the opportunity to realize that they couldn't return to being friends, even after they tied up loose ends. They couldn't rewind that kiss.

Marissa called it magical.

She wouldn't use another word. To her, magic was real sometimes. She felt magic last night. She also felt other things. No fault of Markus, his reaction was more emotional. She turned him on. She wouldn't apologize for human nature.

It went without saying: he turned her on, as well. The way he took care of his body…junk food was foreign to him. He was chiseled from head to toe, like a Greek god. He looked like a living sculpture, like Michelangelo's *David*. He had a short haircut, a face shaved clean, ocean-like eyes *and* her parents loved him? As Marissa asked herself on many an occasion before this day, what wasn't to love?

So, with confidence, Marissa took Markus's hand while he drove down the road. He accepted hers, squeezing her hand a couple times while he kept his eyes on the road.

Markus was a little bothered by his inability to go out last night, but he was doing something much more important. He was building a more-than-friends relationship, something he hadn't cared to do since his parents passed. All the flings and different "girlfriends" he had were purely cosmetic. With Marissa, it was real.

Eventually, I'm going to have to tell her about the mask. That, or I could retire, and I won't have to, he thought.

Marissa felt extra peppy today. Even though some things went wrong, what went right eclipsed it all. She was leaving town with a goal in mind. She was motivated beforehand, but the latest progressions motivated her even more.

"I really enjoyed my time with you, Markus."

"I enjoyed my time with you, Mare."

They looked at each other momentarily before Markus returned his eyes to the road. He loved her company. When she was excited about something, he enjoyed it that much more. She would surely ramble at some time during the trip to the airport.

"I wish we had a time machine, honestly," Marissa said. "I mean, it'll just motivate us toward our goals, I think, but I wish I could just hurry up and get back here, just to see if…you know…if we can make it work. I mean, I know a little bit about what would happen between us, but…"

Markus continued to focus on the road. A small smirk escaped. She knew he'd like that. He was enjoying Marissa's thought process, just not verbalizing it. Markus put his right hand into Marissa's left. She caressed his hand as the car rolled down the highway.

The two didn't talk much more on the way to the airport. Markus was stuck in his own head thinking about any and everything while he assumed Marissa was doing the same. She would have a lot to work through on the long plane ride back home.

My home won't be overseas much longer. A year could go by so fast if I busy myself and take care of what I'm supposed to. I wish I could get it done in one day! Ah, I guess I can be patient, although it's something I really don't want to do. What I want to do…is not appropriate.

As they pulled up to the airport, Markus parked in a space reserved for drop-offs. He let go of Marissa's hand and stepped out of the car, calling for help from one of the check-in clerks.

"We're going to need a…" The word escaped him. He used his hands to describe what he needed. Marissa had more bags than she or Markus could carry. As the baggage clerk unloaded Markus's SUV, Marissa alternated between looking at the bags leaving Markus's SUV and Markus.

"Please shut the back when you're done," he told the clerk, who nodded.

Markus slid his keys in his jean pocket and took Marissa's hand to walk her into the airport. Marissa felt warm inside. She could see the near-future coming: goodbyes were hard. They were always hard. Even when they were friends, it was hard. With these new developments, she didn't know how she would react.

Marissa pulled one of her credit cards out and ran it at the boarding pass kiosk. She grabbed the freshly printed slips of paper and placed it in her backpack. She always took a backpack with her when she checked in. It was a "comfort" thing. It was more than a purse could ever handle.

Marissa smiled at Markus. "Okay…I guess that's it. You have to understand, though…I'm not trying to be sappy right now. I just want to get out of here without ruining my makeup," she laughed as she felt her eyes sting. She told herself she wouldn't.

"Here we go." She shook her head no lightly, her lips pursing. Marissa exhaled and fanned her eyes. She didn't want to be seen crying, especially when people were taking pictures. It was Marissa Buchanan; naturally, people tried to get pictures, especially the paparazzi.

Even when Marissa tried to catch an early flight, they knew about it. It wasn't the best time to invade her privacy, but she was used to it. She made them invisible. She wasn't going to let the paparazzi ruin her goodbye.

"Okay, come here," she said quickly. She motioned with her hands for Markus to come forward. She hugged him tight, held his body close to hers. She didn't want to let go. He hugged her back; he wanted it to last until she returned. He closed his eyes. She did too.

I want this memory to last, what he looks like, what he smells like…everything.

"I'm sorry for the rainstorm," she apologized. Her tone was low. She rested her forehead on his chest. "But this is *not* goodbye, Markus. I'll be back. I want you to understand that. We can just call it a business trip, okay?"

Markus rubbed Marissa's back, in their embrace. "I understand. I'm going to miss you, Mare."

Forty-eight hours turned his thoughts completely on their head. Markus was convinced he wouldn't feel this way, if they were just friends. There would be less to lose. Markus was hesitant to call it a relationship, but it was what it was. He and Marissa may not have wanted to admit it, but they were on their way to one.

"I want you to Face Time me when you get home, all right?" He requested.

"I will," Marissa assured him, pulling her forehead away from Markus's t-shirt. *I can't feel his heartbeat anymore. That's sad. It helps me sleep. There's just something about him that calms me; it's been that way, since the moment we met.*

Without thinking twice about it, Marissa looked into Markus's eyes and leaned in. She kissed his jaw line before meeting his lips. They held it a few seconds before she pulled back. She pressed her lips against his one more time. When she pulled back again, her eyes looked into Markus's ocean blue eyes.

"It's not goodbye," Marissa repeated.

"It's not. It's 'until next time.'"

Marissa nodded her head yes. "Until next time. Right."

The brunette let him go and headed toward the metal detector. She turned around and waved at Markus, who returned the favor. She then turned back and gave the clerk her flight credentials. In a flash, she was gone.

Speaking of flash…

Markus was blinded by multiple flashes as soon as he turned around. Two paparazzi flashed pictures of him. It caught him completely off-guard. He wished he had his baton with him. He would smash those cameras into little pieces. The utter lack of respect for privacy was something he'd never get used to. Even after all these years, it annoyed him.

"What's Johanna going to think about this?" One of the cameramen asked.

"Are you and Marissa Buchanan an item?" The other asked.

"Come on! Give us something!" The first asked.

"We're just talking," Markus answered. "A friend taking a friend to the airport. A friend in need is a friend, indeed. Nothing wrong with that, right?"

"Right, but that kiss..."

"I think Johanna's going to be mad," Markus smiled. "But the reality is that we're not together. We've been seen together a time or two, but I'm an eligible bachelor. I can kiss who I want."

As Markus walked through the sliding double doors, a few thoughts came to mind.

I need to call Johanna first. She'll be mad, probably pick a fight. She'll tell me I'm good for nothing, and that I'm like every other guy. I'll remind her that I know she's around for what my name brings hers. She'll resort to insults, from my haircut to the size of my manhood. I won't respond. She'll become frustrated and hang up. I'll be fine with that.

As he pulled away from the airport, Markus stayed in his head.

How much longer will Marissa keep modeling? Will she want to start her own company after? Does she have the means, or does she want a partner? How quickly does she want to get married?

Have kids? How quickly will she assimilate into a relationship once she returns to the states?

Lots of questions swam through Markus's head on his way to P4P. He had other things on his mind, like the conclusion Vanessa came to.

Back at her apartment, Vanessa popped her head out from under her comforter, stretched and sleepily rubbed the side of her face. She didn't get much sleep the night before; maybe because of all the time she spent thinking about Markus's proposal? There was a lot to think about. Vanessa looked at the digital clock on the nightstand by her bed.

"Oh, bollocks."

Vanessa slid out of bed and trudged into the bathroom. She flipped on the light and turned the water on in the shower. It warmed quickly, just the way she liked it. She looked in the mirror.

I'm sure he's waiting for an answer. I want revenge for my parents' murder. I'd like to learn how to effectively snuff those bastards out; as of now, I don't have a snowball's chance in hell. I don't know if I care enough about this city to train for more than a one-time mission. Markus explicitly said that if I decided to go through with this, there was no turning back. How could he police that? It's not even my city.

She undressed and stepped into the shower. She started her maintenance routine.

How could I go back on my word? I have two options: keep quiet and stay out of the whole thing, pursue these men with no formal training and more than likely be killed, or I could follow Markus into the abyss of the unknown, stand a chance in it all, and help others in the process.

After she finished showering, she dried off and tied the towel around her body. She walked back into her room to look for clothes.

What about my own goals? Would a relationship be in the cards? What if I want children in the future? Do I even have a future? Ah, I suppose I do. I'll take my life on the path I think is best.

Vanessa sat her clothes out. There was still more time to mull, to use Markus's words. A second wouldn't be wasted.

On the same morning, Jonathan received an early phone call at home to investigate a crime scene. After hastily putting himself together for the day, he found himself approaching the scene. His vehicle rolled to a stop. He placed it in park, stepped out, and took in his surroundings.

The apartments looked newly made, maybe in the last few years. They had two levels, with stairs at the top of each respective pathway. It looked like a ghost town. Jon noticed that people weren't coming out of their houses, but wanted to know what was going on. Endless eyes peered through the slits of window blinds. He wouldn't bother with them. Either they legitimately didn't know anything or they did, and weren't talking.

Jon didn't feel very optimistic as he followed the police tape to an apartment with an open door.

"He's in there, in the bathroom," one of the officers told Jon, pointing him the right way.

"Well, at least we got the gender out of the way," Jon said.

The officer ignored Jon's quip and returned to his work. The young detective made light of the death he encountered while on the job, the part he hated most. Looking for criminals, questioning suspects and everything else were things he liked; it was seeing dead bodies that bothered him.

Jonathan looked around the apartment. A shot glass was on the counter, still wet on the inside, along with a bottle of alcohol. Dishes were piled in the sink, and the counters were dirty. No pictures on the wall or the coffee table. The living room was somewhat clean. Shrugging lightly, he walked down the hallway to the bathroom, where he saw Daphne, who was crouched down by the body.

"Guy looks fine," Daphne said.

"Well, no," Jonathan said. "There's that broken glass lodged in his face and some blood. Other than that, he looks fine, I guess. He picked up a lot of enemies on the way. This is the Guardian Angel."

Daphne looked closely at the deceased's facial features. "Looks like he needed one. This is James Caldwell, according to his bills and his ID. That was the name he answered to, when he wasn't busy on the streets."

Jonathan frustratingly shook his head. "Yeah, but he was the Guardian Angel at night. He helped a lot of people. He didn't ask for anything in return. All he wanted was harmony in this world, and–"

"How do you know all this?" Daphne asked. She turned her head toward him slightly, with a look of dismay and annoyance.

"Because I've talked to him before. Because I believe in what some of these guys…people…are doing. It's not just us, anymore. We're not alone in this fight. These people…"

"Die for nothing," Daphne said coldly.

"Die for something," Jonathan corrected.

Daphne stood up from the body on the bathroom floor and motioned out. "Come with me."

"Well, where are we going?" Jonathan asked.

Daphne continued to aggressively nudge Jon until they made it into – from the looks of it – James's bedroom. She shut the door. Jon tried to read Daphne the best he could. She seemed upset, and he had no idea why. The past couple days had been a little off. She paced.

"Look, I understand that you love comic books. I understand that you love the look of a superhero, people you think help us, but in reality, they don't! If anything, they make our jobs harder! You may not want to live with that reality, but *I* have to, and I'm reminded of it every time you bring it up! You have the worst case of hero worship, and I'm sick of it!"

Before Jonathan had a chance to say something, Daphne did. Her voice remained raised. "I'm the lead detective on these cases. Do you understand that?! So when I come here, I don't need some kind of…"

"Superhero apologist?" Jonathan asked.

"You're on their side!" Daphne exclaimed. She was trying not to yell but it was increasingly becoming difficult. "If it's so glamorous, if it's so rewarding…then why don't *you* do it?!"

Jon calmly said, "Because I don't have it in me."

Daphne felt something for his words. She meant what she said to him, but she didn't want it to come to this. She still had feelings for Jonathan, feelings that hadn't quite yet been straightened out, but that wasn't the only culprit.

"What do you mean you don't have it in you?" Daphne asked. Her voice was more subdued. She wouldn't have done that for anyone else, save a supervisor.

"I ran cross country in college. I don't have those kinds of skills. I'm not brave like that. I'm not going to stand toe-to-toe with whoever did this to the Guardian Angel. I do a job that pays me to put my life on the line. James Caldwell didn't get paid for what he did. Whether you want to avoid it or not, he helped us."

"You can't work these cases," Daphne told him plainly. "If it's going to hit you hard every time one of your heroes die, you're no use to us. This is your job. Your job is not to worship these people. Do it on your own damn time. You're an adult now, Deadmarsh. Act like it."

Jon nodded, finally looking at Daphne. He started to say something, but stopped. It was better this way. He shuffled out of the room quietly, avoiding eye contact with Daphne, like a scolded puppy.

Daphne looked up to the ceiling. She placed her hands on her hips, sighed and closed her eyes. She felt she may have gone too far, but she also felt that Jon had to be told something about his behavior. She wondered if he'd been told before. She wondered if she was just rubbing it in. *I'll leave him to work it out,* she thought.

After Jon left the room, he left the apartment. Daphne's tone embarrassed him, and he surely wouldn't stick around to hear the snickers and jokes from the other officers. He got into his SUV and sat, reflecting on his and Daphne's conversation. He reclined his seat and looked at the ceiling of his vehicle.

I can't help but believe. I won't let it go so easily. Sure, I'll come back to my car and collect myself. At the end of the day, I believe in how they help law enforcement. I won't stop helping them. If push comes to shove, I'll keep my beliefs to myself. Supporting them is the right thing to do.

"Who would do something like this?" Jonathan questioned aloud. "Someone who is stronger than the normal man, I guess. It didn't look like they had help or anything. There was only one set of footprints that weren't consistent with his…"

Jonathan racked his brain for ideas, running a short list of scenarios in his head. A loud bang on his driver's side window made the young detective jump, sending him into a panic. He quickly looked out the window.

It was De La Rosa.

Jonathan rolled his window down and stuck his head out. Short of breath with a half-crazed look in his eyes, he said, "Geez-o Pete! What's wrong?"

Daphne said, "I want to…I want to know more about this stuff. I may not like what's going on with the Masked Maniac situation, but some knowledge is better than no knowledge. I'm sorry about what I said."

“I accept your apology.”

“I guess…do you want to just take a walk and talk? Get some fresh air? It was pretty intense in there, after all.”

“I think that’d be good…Jesus.”

Daphne smiled coyly as Jonathan got out of his vehicle. He held his chest and took a deep breath, and then exhaled. The two started their walk around the apartment complex. “Off-topic, but I have a name for our mystery man. The Sound is what I’m going with, over The Answer. What do you think?”

Daphne pondered the name. As much as she didn’t want to entertain or engage in this talk, she wanted to remain informed. It was in her, to remain educated. She wouldn’t let those jerks at the precinct pass her, and she knew they were too macho to follow up on something like this.

“I uh…I think it fits. It’s better than The Answer…I guess.”

Okay! She’s attempting to act interested or maybe she’s legitimately interested? From what I know about her, she’s genuine with her intentions. I’ll always respect that about her.

“Listen…”

Daphne looked at him.

“I’ll bring these comic books to work, if you want me to. I have a few ideas to help you out with this, in case it gets confusing. You can read them and kind of see…”

“Why don’t you just come over for dinner?”

Her words came out nonchalantly. On the inside, she couldn’t believe what she said. How would he react to the information? During the silence between them, Daphne thought about taking her words back. In her mind, if someone had to think about it, they were trying to find a nice way to say no. She'd taken a chance, per Jasper's request.

"Sure," he said.

On the inside, Daphne took a big exhale. She tingled. It was too early to be completely truthful about her feelings toward Jon. It would be a tremendous burden off her chest, but right now, she couldn't see herself telling him anything along those lines. *Wait, does he think this is a date?*

"Dinner, I mean, to discuss the–"

"No! Right! Right!" Jonathan placed his hands up in submission. "This isn't some kind of–"

"Date? Oh, no-no," Daphne shook her head no. "It's so we can get a better grip on what's going on here. It's education for the job."

"Okay, which is what I was thinking," Jonathan said. When he got home, he would rummage through his comics to find the best ones for the case. Finally, he had a friend at work.

Daphne stopped walking.

Jonathan stopped with her. He turned her way. "What's going on? Why'd you stop?" She didn't say anything. He followed her eyes and looked forward. A guy was making eye contact with Daphne from 50 feet away. She knew him.

"He's going to run," Daphne warned.

Daphne's words puzzled Jon. "He's going to run? Why would he–"

He ran.

"I told you he was going to run!"

Daphne was in a full sprint in no time. Jon ran after Daphne, who ran after the man, who ran towards something. He seemed to know the apartments well, from the detectives' point of view.

Soon, Jon caught up to Daphne. In a second, he passed her up.

As Jon gained on his target, he wondered what he would do when he caught up to the perp. He wasn't the physical type, so roughing him up was out of the question. If anything, he would serve to – at least – slow this man down so De La Rosa could catch up. Jon kept his pace up as the man's pace faded. As fast as the man ran, it didn't seem like an everyday activity for him, much less, a competitive one.

"Police! You have to stop!" Jonathan called out.

When the man felt he was about to be caught, he stopped, placing his hands up. Moments later, De La Rosa arrived.

"Why…why are you running?" She asked him. She struggled to catch her breath.

"Man, because…I know you gon try to rough me up…take me to jail or somethin'. I ain't even do nothin'."

The man locked his fingers and rested them on his head while he grimaced. He was tired and cramping. Soon after, he took one of his hands off his head and dug his fingers into one side of his body. Jon wasn't tired. He still trained, despite being out of college.

"If you didn't do anything, why'd you run?" Jon asked innocently. His breathing had already regulated. His hands rested at his waist.

"Because I know this lady here…she gon try to get some information from me! Watch!" He said. He pointed at De La Rosa. The man pressed harder into his side. "And I didn't see nothin', either! Please believe me, Ms. Lady Cop! I didn't see nothin'!"

Both De La Rosa and the perp caught their breath around the same time. "My name is not Ms. Lady Cop. It's detective De La Rosa. And this, detective Deadmarsh, is Leonard Robinson."

Leonard Robinson was in his late 20's. He was about six feet tall, a shade darker than mocha and slender, with dark brown eyes and a styled five o'clock shadow. He was dressed in a pair of jeans with a red plaid short-sleeve button-up shirt and a pair of black Chuck Taylor's.

"He's a snitch."

Leonard looked at De La Rosa like she just slapped his mother. He placed his fingertips on both sides of his chest.

"I am not a snitch," Leonard corrected, dipping his head slightly and widening his eyes. "I am an information salesman. Don't get it twisted; snitches tell whoever, whenever. Me? I ain't telling nobody a damn thing unless I'm getting something in return. And speakin' of…you are looking *extra* spicy today, detective." He smiled. He laid it on thick.

"Cut it," De La Rosa said. "What did you see?"

"What do you got?" Leonard asked.

"I got a gun," De La Rosa said. She raised her eyebrows. "And I would love to pull it out and have it go off accidentally."

"Man, you see the way she talks to me?" Leonard said. He turned Jon's way. "I don't know you, but you look nicer. I'll talk to you."

"O-okay…talk, I guess," Jonathan said, putting on his "tough" look.

"Man, did you *not* hear me two seconds ago?" Leonard asked. "What…do…you…got…man? I need to know. What are you givin' me?"

Slowly, he pulled his watch off. De La Rosa looked suspiciously at the young detective. She couldn't believe he was giving this lowlife something of actual value. Most of the time, Daphne threatened to pin something on him, take him to jail for the night. She couldn't believe Jon was feeding the monster.

"That's a nice watch," Leonard said to Jon. He then looked at Daphne and shook his head yes. "That's a nice watch." He was pleased with his take; a watch like this deserved good information, something that could actually help the detectives.

"Okay, there's a dead dude in there y'all lookin' at."

The two detectives nodded in agreement.

"I seen a dude comin' out that apartment late last night. He was wearin' a trench coat and a black mask. Mask looked like a damn…like a skeleton face. I can't get into all the details because it was dark and I wasn't right up in his face. Man, this sure is a nice watch! You really came through, my man!" Leonard again diverted his attention to the watch Jonathan gave him.

Daphne sighed. "Leonard…"

Leonard stopped in his tracks. "Okay! So anyway, I didn't see that dude go in there but I saw him leavin' out. That's a damn shame, too. James was a good dude. I may dabble in some seedy things, but I ain't gonna mess with nobody tryin' to do the right thing."

"Do you know any vitals at all?" Jonathan asked. He looked at Daphne, who looked as if she was about to ask the same thing, but maybe more abrasively.

"Vitals?" Leonard asked.

"Yeah, stuff like height? Build?" Jon replied.

"Learned somethin' today," Leonard said. "Maybe about my height but like I said, it was dark. If that dude went in there and did James like that, I ain't messin' with that. Y'all shouldn't be messin' with that, neither. That's all I got. You gon have to keep me out of this one, detectives. That's a job for y'all."

The two detectives nodded at each other. She then looked at Leonard. Her words to Leonard were quick.

"Thank you."

Leonard smiled. "What was that? I'm sorry…I just never heard that from you before. Can you repeat that again?"

"You are pushing your luck," Daphne warned. She started towards him.

Leonard quickly walked away, making more space between him and her. "So hostile, man!" Leonard muttered as he walked away.

"Well, now I don't know what time it is." Jonathan tried to diffuse the situation. De La Rosa laughed. "On the bright side, we have some kind of suspect, even though it's a small part of the puzzle. I wonder how we're going to find him; it's not like people just walk around with masks on."

"Like finding a needle in a haystack," De La Rosa said.

"We gotta keep the faith."

"*You* keep the faith. I'll keep plugging away. We're going to find this guy, Deadmarsh. We have to stop him before this happens again."

Jon nodded his head in agreement.

"Do you like lime chicken?"

"I've never had it, but I'm willing to try."

"Okay. I'll see you around 7 or so," De La Rosa said. "Bring those…your books."

Daphne made sure she was clear out of Jon's sight before she smiled. She didn't want Jon to see her smile, but she knew what comic books were. She hadn't cooked for someone in a long time. She usually made dinner for one. *This isn't a date, Daph. It's just two colleagues with a shared zeal for stopping what's wrong with the world.*

Jonathan chose to leave entirely. He had to get home and search through mountains of sleeved-up comic books. He had some that were worth more money than his yearly salary, but he decided to hold onto them. He wouldn't tell about their worth.

Technically, he was off the case, even though he and De La Rosa continued to work together. He wouldn't argue her decision. While he was at home searching through his comics, he would also work on his approach toward special cases.

Markus turned the knob of his office door and pushed it open. Vanessa hadn't arrived yet, and he was starting to worry.

He was also feeling the effects of Marissa's exit from the country. Her plane wouldn't land for several hours. He stopped back by his house to change before he went to work. He hardly ever showed up to P4P in plain clothes. The room smelled like Marissa's perfume. He made a mental note to get the room cleaned as well. That smell would drive him mad, over time.

He didn't want to be constantly reminded of the void Marissa left. He had other reminders, but he would control what he could control – like cleaning his sheets.

There was a knock at the door.

Maybe it's Marissa? She'll tell me she couldn't leave, and that she wants to start our future. It would start with us having a "closed-door meeting" at my house, and that would last for days, with our phones off.

Markus opened the door. It was Joyce.

"The papers you asked for, sir."

She handed Markus the papers he'd forgotten about. He was too self-involved at the moment to remember a request he'd made before he came into work. He sighed. "Thank you, Joyce."

"Is she gone?"

"Yes, she is."

"So *that's* why you look like such a sad puppy dog." Joyce smiled warmly at her boss.

"I would love to get into it but it upsets me, honestly," Markus said.

"Well…she'll be back. You two are drawn together."

Markus nodded and his mouth curved into a smile. Joyce winked, and then left Markus to his own devices. After his office door shut, Markus was back in his head again.

I can't let this get me down. I have to pull myself out of this funk. Life has to go on for the both of us. I want us to be able to come home and have a conversation about our day. I'm not about to complicate things.

There was another knock at the door. Markus grabbed the doorknob, but paused. "Well, here's to getting my hopes up." He opened the door. He looked at her. She looked at him.

"May I enter?" Vanessa asked.

"Sure."

Markus opened the door wider to give Vanessa enough room to slip by. He walked over to his desk and sat at the edge of it, one foot still on the floor while the other leg was raised. "What can I do for you, Ms. Vaughn?"

I don't want this to come out negatively. I want it to come out the right way, but I also hope everything will work out in my favor, somehow, some way.

"I do have an answer for you, but I wanted to get something off my chest, if you'll allow it," she said.

"Absolutely. Go ahead," he said.

"Okay." Her chest heaved up and down one time, and then she continued. "I have fears, sir. I have a fear I'll die, doing what you're asking me to do. I fear I'm never going to catch my parents' murderers, no matter what I do. I have an absolute fear of what will happen in the future. I don't even know if I *have* a future, sir."

Vanessa didn't cry often, but her words and thoughts were so emotional and truthful, it was overwhelming. Just the thought of her slain parents was overwhelming, in itself. Yet, she stayed strong. She wouldn't let it get to her, like some of the other nights she cried alone in her apartment.

"But, with that being said, I want to try. I understand your concern, over whether I would stop once I found my parents' killers. I will tell you, I won't stop after that. You've been doing this for quite some time, and you've brought more peace to this world than many. I want to do that, because–"

She needed to push the words out.

"There could be another little boy or little girl that ends up like me. And if I have a breath in my body, I want to help prevent that."

"Then…how can I say no?" Markus asked Vanessa, drawing a smile from her.

"What happens now?" Vanessa asked.

"Well, since you've made your intentions clear, I'm going to put you through an extensive training regimen. Report to my house. I will have your credentials within the hour. Do you remember how I gained access to my basement?"

Vanessa nodded yes.

"The same credentials will apply to you, now."

Vanessa's heart raced. She was excited and afraid, at the same time. She wondered if she would freeze up when she had an opportunity to go out and fight crime, like Markus. She was putting a lot of trust in his expertise. She would do her best to trust in his training.

"I want you to meet me at my house, at say…two o'clock," Markus said. "Everything will be explained to you then. I want you to take this time, Vanessa. After two o'clock, you won't see things the same again."

"Right, sir." She headed to the door.

"Oh, and Vanessa?"

She turned around.

"Try to bring workout clothes, if you can."

Things were definitely about to change.

Chapter 9

Two o'clock came fast.

Vanessa was 10 minutes early. She stepped out of her car – a white Kia Optima – wearing a sports bra with spandex pants that made it down to the middle of her shins, and cross-training tennis shoes. Her light brown hair was pulled into a ponytail and her caramel-colored features were devoid of makeup.

"All right. Confidence…Confidence." Vanessa placed her hand on the sensor by Markus's front door. The sequence ran through, outlined her hand in green and blinked.

"Confirmed: Vanessa Vaughn." The sensor spoke her name and the door unlocked.

Vanessa turned the knob and pushed the door open, making a beeline over to the basement. She placed her hand on a second sensor, right beside the basement door. When the confirmation played through, she opened the door, careful to shut it behind her. She stood on the platform and descended to the lower level as she heard all the locks engaging behind her.

She had butterflies the size of bald eagles in her stomach as the bottom level drew near. This was it. Once the platform reached the bottom, it locked in place. Vanessa stepped off. Her eyes quickly caught Markus, who stood with his back turned to her. He was rapidly manipulating holographic documents.

She took him in while he worked. He wore a tight t-shirt with tight spandex pants, and a pair of cross-training tennis shoes. While he worked, she noticed the tendons and muscles, and how they worked in harmony. His back and forearm muscles showed the most. His biceps and triceps, his finely sculpted calves and rear end, he was something to look at.

"Nice to see you made it," he said. Markus didn't bother turning around.

His words interrupted Vanessa's train of thought, which was getting naughtier with every passing moment. To Vanessa, Markus seemed like everybody's type. Maybe she was biased because she knew him. Maybe she should pay attention.

Vanessa watched Markus effortlessly shift holograms around. "All right, well…what might we be getting into today? But, I believe a better question is: are you reading *any* of what you're moving and discarding?"

"Yes, I am."

Markus answered her question quickly. From what Vanessa caught, the holograms were full of news stories and various information outlets. The way he ran through it all blew Vanessa's mind. She couldn't read that fast, not even close. He ran roughshod over the information, and moments later, there were no more holograms. Markus turned around and faced Vanessa.

"Maybe we can find time to learn how to throw a punch correctly."

She laughed. "I do most certainly know how to throw a punch!"

“I mean…like, a real punch. I just want to make sure that when you go out there–”

“Oh, I think I’ve got the gist of it,” Vanessa said confidently. She feigned cracking her knuckles.

“You see, I’m not sure you do.” Markus turned his back to Vanessa once again. “Computer: I need some imagery.” The computer in front of him lit up, ready for his next command. “I need to see…” He pondered his words. “I need to see the hotel room, from the night Vanessa Vaughn’s parents were murdered.”

Within seconds, the room changed, right before their eyes. Markus was used to this; Vanessa wasn’t. A few seconds more and she saw the bed she hid under. Her parents weren’t in this room, but everything she saw looked so real.

The feeling of fear took over. She was so afraid that night. She may have told Markus she wanted to kill those men, do unspeakable things to them. In reality, she was afraid. She was afraid of what those men were capable of, afraid of the moment. She felt like she was hyperventilating.

“Turn around,” Markus said.

When Vanessa turned around, she found herself staring down the barrel of a gun. Vanessa fell on her backside, her palms slapping the ground as she rapidly crawled backwards. She put as much space as she could between her and the gun barrel. While she crawled backward, she was stopped by something sturdy. She looked up.

It was Markus.

He extended his hand. Vanessa placed her hand in his and allowed herself to be pulled up by Markus’s firm touch. Out of nowhere, she reared back. Markus caught her wrist right before she made impact on his face, looking her squarely in her brownish-green eyes.

Her eyes welled up. "Are you insane?!" Vanessa yelled. "How could you do that?! Why would you?!"

"I needed to know where you were, in accordance with your training. Now, we know the truth: everything isn't so rosy when there is a gun in your face. We'll–"

"I can't believe you did that!" Vanessa interrupted. Markus let go of her wrist and she dropped it by her side. She was so incensed, she couldn't see straight. Her adrenaline was at the tippy-top. "You could've just asked me!"

"There's no telling what you would've told me," Markus said truthfully. "At first, you told me you were ready. I knew it was a lie, but I let you believe it. You told me what you would do if you were faced with these men again, and you lied. From now on, I want you to tell me the truth about everything, and that's not up for discussion. If you're afraid, say you're afraid."

She sniffled. "Are you afraid?" Vanessa asked, wiping her eyes free of the tears.

"Not anymore," he replied.

"Then teach me," Vanessa said. "I don't care how long it takes. The way you handled yourself in the hotel room, the way it looked as if you weren't afraid of anything they could've done, I want to learn all of that."

"If you want to learn, you'd be best served working on your physical and your mental conditioning. We won't learn how to throw a punch until both of those are on par with your program," Markus said.

"My program?"

"Yes, your program," Markus replied. "I have it all laid out for you, how you'll learn, what you'll learn. Some days will seem long, some won't. It will be extensive; we have to make sure we cover everything."

"Everything?" She questioned.

"Everything. I won't send you out there ill-prepared. That will defeat the purpose. Even if I'm outnumbered and outgunned, you won't go out with me until I feel you're ready."

"Right," Vanessa said skeptically. As much as she thought she was ready, this was a wake-up call for Vanessa. She felt like she had a long way to go. She hoped Markus would bring her to where she needed to be, put her in a position to stop some of the injustices of the world.

Jonathan pulled up to Daphne's house, using the directions texted to him earlier in the day. *She's got a pretty nice house, for having a cop's salary.*

Jon pushed his hand under the comic books that sat in the passenger's seat and placed his other hand on the top of the stack, pulling them out as carefully as he could. They were like his crown jewels. He got out of his SUV and bumped the car door shut with his hip. He made the short walk to the front door. Once he found the doorbell, it occurred to him that he was using his hands to keep the comic books in order. He frowned.

"Of course, it would play out like that."

Moments later, the door swung open. It was Daphne.

"Wow. You look beautiful." He sucked his lips into his mouth and shut it, his eyes widening. He couldn't believe he'd thrown his opinion out there so carelessly. *There I go, talking without thinking again!*

"Okay…thank you. Ummm, come in." Daphne said. She wasn't great at taking compliments, especially from people she liked. When she was younger, she got something along the line of, "Nice boobs," "You got a fat ass," or her personal favorite, "What are you doing tonight?" As she got older, the prospects at a bar or random party became less appealing.

Daphne faced away from Jonathan, taking a short moment to appreciate his compliment. Even if she wasn't great at taking them, she liked them.

"Put those comics down. I'm going to give you a tour," Daphne announced. Jonathan placed the stack of comic books on the couch, nestling them between the arm and back cushion, so they had support. "So, you really care about those things, don't you?" She asked him. "I see some of them are wrapped in plastic."

"Oh yeah, I care about them a lot," Jon said, following her into the first room. "I'm definitely going to keep those things more in order than say, my closet." He looked around the room. Awards and pictures hung from the walls, with an old desk that a laptop sat on top of. "Using my damn fine detective-ing skills, I'm assuming this is your office?"

Daphne giggled. "Yeah, this is it," she said. She extended her arms like she was showcasing the room.

"This is awesome," Jon commented. "So, you're proud of your work, we just don't get to see it."

"I'm very proud of my work," Daphne said. "I feel like this room is where I can go to recharge my batteries. If I have a bad day at work, I can kind of…I guess…look at all the things I've done and know that it'll get better."

"I see," he said.

"All right, keep it moving," she pushed.

Jonathan followed Daphne to the next room. There were boxes inside, four stacks of two boxes, and the carpet looked vacuumed. "Storage room?" He asked.

"Yep," she said. "It's a three-bedroom, two-bathroom deal. It's not that big, but it's better than an apartment."

"Well, yeah," Jon said, "I live in one of those, a crappy one-bedroom. Who am I to throw stones? I would just love to not be able to hear *every* little thing that goes on with my neighbors."

"I would probably shoot someone," Daphne joked. "Let's go."

She then led Jon to the master bedroom. When she opened the door, it smelled of the fragrance Daphne was currently wearing. She had a bed, a dresser, and a nightstand in there. The closet was closed. It was a very simple room. It looked kept up and clean.

"You're a well-organized woman," Jon said candidly.

"I like things to be nice and tidy," Daphne said. "A clean home is a happy home."

"Then I have a clinically depressed home," Jon said, shaking his head. "Just about everything is everywhere. If you came over, you would think there were definite signs of a struggle. I could stand to learn a lot from you."

Daphne didn't respond to Jon's words, but her body language responded to his charm and playfulness. "Are you ready to go?" She asked. "There isn't really much to see here, it's just a regular old room."

"Yeah, sure," Jon said.

She nodded and led him to the kitchen. "Well, that completes our tour. The lime chicken's ready, so I guess we can eat and talk."

"It smells perfect. It was nice of you to make dinner, anyway."

"I hope it's good. I haven't cooked for another person in a while."

"I'm sure it'll be good. I'll eat anything."

Jonathan was sure he should've taken more time with his response. He felt like backtracking. The two were silent for a moment.

Daphne had grounds to tear into Jon, but decided to use her energy to scoop pieces of chicken out of the slow cooker. She placed a single breast on Jon's plate before placing a breast on hers. She then shoveled some seasoned rice and vegetables – a medley – on both their plates. She was satisfied with how the food came out.

Daphne led him to the couch, and pulled up and unfolded some wooden TV trays. The dining area was too cramped, so she rarely ate there. The two placed their plates on their respective trays, and sat on the couch. They pulled the trays closer to themselves. Jon immediately took a bite.

"Oh, this is good! This is *really* good!"

Jonathan shook his head yes exaggeratingly. He was a terrible cook. Sure, there were recipes on Facebook or Pinterest, and some things could be found using a search engine. Try as he might, cooking wasn't his strong point. Daphne outdid herself.

"Don't kiss my ass, Deadmarsh," Daphne said impassively. "You're just saying that because you know I can choke you out. If I couldn't do that, you would talk about how terrible this food is."

"Don't put words in my mouth! Put more of this chicken in my mouth!" He pointed at the chicken before he cut another piece off and chomped on it. He closed his eyes and looked up. "Seriously, Daphne…I haven't had a meal like this in a long time. There are only so many Ramen and TV dinners I can eat."

While Daphne maintained a rough exterior, at heart, she wanted to please the ones she liked. She liked Jon more emotionally than professionally, at this point; professionally, she'd eventually come around. She still wasn't a big believer in his comic book references, but he was intelligent. He had a bright future.

The key was staying optimistic in an occupation as dreary as detective work.

"Okay, so tell me more about these books."

"Oh! Oh!"

Jon realized he hadn't moved the books. He turned around to extend his arms to grab the comics, but stopped short. He nabbed one of the paper towels given to him by Daphne and thoroughly covered and rubbed the tips of each individual fingertip, cleaning them as well as he could. He wasn't eating with his hands, but he could never be too cautious when it came to his babies. Jon scooped up the comic books and laid them on the carpeted floor.

Daphne cracked a smile at Jon's handling of the books. He acted as if they would break. They looked pristine, unlike his desk. "I know you're excited, so let's get to it," she instructed.

"Okay…okay. Let me grab a few." Jon grabbed a few comics and placed them between the two of them, spread out like playing cards. "I know they're from different companies, one from Marvel and one from DC. DC is Batman and Marvel is Iron Man, two of my favorites."

"They made movies about these guys, right?" Daphne asked.

"Yes, they did," Jonathan answered. He was surprised that Daphne wasn't into the movie versions of these heroes. Most people were. "A lot of comic book nerds have something to say about the movies because they're not always accurate to what happened in the comics. I don't mind, and I'm about as 'fanboy' as they come."

"Fanboy?" Daphne asked. "Okay, what the hell is that?"

"Kind of like…you know, when little girls scream about One Direction? I scream about something that happens in the comics or if I'm at Comic-Con or something like that, and I see an actor that played a character from the comics in a movie, or something like that. That's the only way I can really explain it."

"So, you have some kind of man-crush on these guys?" Daphne asked.

"No! Okay, yes, kind of. They're just awesome…maybe it's because they can do things I can't, maybe it's because they're larger than life, I don't know."

"So, who do you go with first?"

"We'll start with Batman. You know the story, right?" He asked.

"Ummm…not really."

"Okay, well his parents were killed when he was a kid. He had no other family but the butler."

Daphne continued to eat but nodded to let him know she was listening.

"The death of his parents shaped him and he becomes this crime fighter that keeps the streets of Gotham safe. He has all these gadgets, and different people try to destroy the city, but Batman is always there to foil it, somehow. In the comic book world, he's one of the smartest and richest people."

Daphne nodded again.

"Iron Man is kind of a different story." Jon took a bite of his food. He got excited when talking about this stuff, but the food was too good to forget. "This guy, Tony Stark, he gets kidnapped and critically injured while performing some weapons demo for the government."

"Wow," Daphne said.

"He has something like an artificial heart installed into his body, something to keep the shrapnel he was hit with from piercing his heart and killing him. He makes a suit of armor and just kind of…fights injustices around the world. I think it's more of a vanity project for this guy, though. He's got a *massive* ego."

Jonathan laughed. Daphne didn't know what he was laughing at, so she nodded. Though there wasn't much information, Daphne was comfortable hearing him talk about something that was more in his element. Jonathan wasn't always confident, but when he spoke about comic books, he exuded it. The guys at the station would be surprised.

"Where do you think the masked man falls?" Daphne asked. "Since you know so much about the comic book world…is there someone out there in that universe that we could compare him to?"

"That's a good question," Jonathan acknowledged. Daphne smiled. "No."

Daphne frowned.

"I've never met or seen him. I don't know what his motives are…I don't know how he dresses, if he's using anything besides his hands to subdue criminals. I'm going to need more information, when it comes to that. I will tell you what I noticed, though."

Daphne's ears perked up. She leaned in.

"There's altruism to this guy. He's not in it for notoriety, that's for sure. He's not parading himself around, saying, 'I'm so-and-so, and I'm here to save the day!' What he's doing is righting wrongs and fixing things, all while staying in the shadows. He doesn't want to be noticed. He's even risking his life anonymously."

It dawned on Daphne that it wasn't just hero worship with Jonathan; there was something deeper there, an admiration that was warranted. As much as she wanted to proceed by the book, she couldn't help but give some respect to anyone that helped law enforcement out.

"What about the dead people we're finding?" Daphne asked. "I noticed that it's forceful, the way they're being murdered."

"I noticed the same thing," Jonathan said, "very blunt, too. He clearly imposed his will. If I had to guess, this person is conspicuous about it. He wants to prove a point."

"What, no he or she?"

Jon smirked at Daphne's attempt at humor.

"Since you brought it up, I think it's another guy. The style of murder would suggest it's a male. I think it's too blunt to think a woman did this. I think a woman would be a little more cunning; she'd make up for her lack of strength with her mental aptitude. You'll have to forgive me if that sounds chauvinistic."

"Kind of, but I get what you're saying," Daphne said. "Go ahead."

"Okay…I think this guy, whoever he is, took a page out of the Book of Psychopaths."

Daphne looked at him skeptically. "Okay, you lost me. What are you talking about?"

"Look at the two murders we've investigated recently: one criminal, one vigilante. He saw enough in those two to do something painful and violent, and he had to have known them. There were no signs of a break-in, and little to no signs of a struggle. I don't have all the facts, but if someone is out there doing extreme good, like our masked friend…you can bet your bottom dollar–"

"Someone's doing extreme bad," Daphne finished.

"Right!" Jon explained. "And he's not differentiating, either. Good or bad, he's wiping them out."

That caught Daphne's attention. "If we have a chance to stop this person, this lunatic…"

"We have to stop him." Jonathan finished Daphne's sentence. He looked into her eyes.

She looked into his.

They shared a moment. Both their minds raced. Jon thought about how he would help Daphne out, if she was targeted. Daphne thought the same thing.

Daphne said, "Close your eyes."

Jon furrowed his eyebrows. "What? Why?"

"Close your eyes, Deadmarsh."

"O-okay."

Jonathan's words came out stammered. His eyes apprehensively flickered shut. He held them closed and waited.

Moments later, he felt lips on his.

Daphne, the more experienced of the two, kissed him slowly and sensually. Her lips sucked on his bottom lip for a flash. Finally, Jon's lips puckered awkwardly. It was good enough to accept a kiss, but also, return the favor. Daphne returned to a more traditional kiss for a few moments, and then pulled back.

One of Jon's eyes opened, shortly followed by the other. He had to make sure it was okay to peek. "That was nice," he said softly.

"I don't want you to get all 'puppy-dog' in the face," Daphne said. "It was just a risk I took. I'm glad I did it. I don't want you to think you're getting laid or anything, but–"

"Oh, no! No! I-I wouldn't even think of it!" Jonathan stuttered. "We only just kissed, Daphne. I'm not looking to do anything like that."

"Let me ask you something, Deadmarsh: are you a virgin?" Daphne asked.

Jon's body language changed. Her words were deflating. His words were low. "I am, but I'm totally okay with it. That was my first kiss on the lips. I consider you a cherry-popping kisser, I guess."

He smiled weakly.

"I just always wanted to wait for the right girl to come along before having an affair between the sheets. Sleeping around never interested me. My parents just kind of…stressed the importance of abstinence."

Daphne laughed.

"My parents did, too…but that didn't stop me," she said. "I did some things that I'm not exactly proud of. I fell for the guy that told me I was pretty. I had some self-esteem issues. I still have them, but I'm working on it. Everyone's got problems."

Jon shook his head yes. "Yes they do. I have tremendous self-esteem issues! I don't mean to turn this into a peeing contest, but which excuse do you think is worse: the 'funeral' one, the 'wash my hair' one, or the 'take your small sibling somewhere' one?"

"Well, you've definitely had it worse than me," Daphne admitted. "I would say a funeral, but hair? Come on."

"That's what I said!" Jon told her.

"You know, you're not so bad, Deadmarsh. There's something cute about you, maybe the inexperience, I don't know. Those girls missed out."

"Thank you. That means a lot. I think a lot of people missed out on *this* Daphne, the Daphne that's caring and thoughtful, can cook a mean lime chicken…your secret's safe with me, though. Nobody needs to know about this."

"Good. That's what I wanted to hear."

Daphne placed her hand on Jon's jaw and kissed him again. He gently placed his hand on her wrist and kissed back, using his free hand to keep his balance. The two of them slowly leaned onto the back cushions of the couch. The dinner and comic books shared between them quickly became a distant memory.

Chapter 10

Marissa was back in her comfortably uncomfortable surroundings. In the daytime, she was fine; she kept busy. At night, the loneliness hit her. She wasn't stateside for very long, so she couldn't wrap her head around why she was so down. Her conclusion: new(ish) love did things like that.

Speaking of time, Marissa's alarm went off at 4:30 a.m. Paris was six hours ahead of New York time, where Markus would be going on a late night talk show.

The host's name was Jackie Reed, a former stand-up comedian and TV show writer. He had the top nighttime show, his quick ascension due to his charm and wit. He was in his early forties, with slicked Jet-black hair and a styled five o'clock shadow. His delivery was always on point, the product of note-taking from past hosts and comics. It was all about delivery, with Jackie.

She flipped on the TV and walked around the room, to wake herself up. Jackie's monologue went on in the background. Marissa usually recorded Jackie and watched when she was more awake, but Markus was on. *I would NOT do this for anyone else. Marissa needs her beauty sleep.*

Marissa washed her face free of sleep and slipped back into bed. She positioned her back against a pillow that lay against the headboard. She pulled her comforter up to her waist and patted her quads a couple times, rubbing them a few times before she settled her focus on the TV.

"Okay, my first guest is the CEO of some place called P4P, if you've ever heard of it. He's doing lots of good things. Please help me welcome Markus Doubleday. Come on, Markus!"

Jackie stood up from the chair behind his desk, motioning for Markus to come out from behind the curtain. Jackie's house band played Marvin Gaye's "Let's get it On."

Markus emerged from behind the curtain. The studio audience cheered even louder once they laid their eyes on him. The touch on the song choice amused him. He didn't take himself too seriously. Markus looked out into the small studio audience and waved, his grin becoming wider while he indulged the crowd.

Markus boldly strode over to the couch by Jackie's desk and shook Jackie's hand firmly. The host smiled big after Markus leaned in and said a few quiet words.

While Jackie was well-dressed every night, there was something that caught Marissa's eye when Markus wore suits. He may not have loved the "tie" part of a suit, but when he wore them, it did something for Marissa. This night, he went simple: a blue open-collar shirt, a black jacket and slacks. Clean-shaven, with closely cropped hair.

"Yummy!" Marissa covered her mouth, allowing herself to giggle like a schoolgirl.

"Good to see you. Good to see you," Jackie said. The crowd wouldn't settle down.

Marissa wanted those women to calm down. Her preference was for them to shut up. She understood how handsome Markus was, and that he would attract the opposite sex, like he had since she met him.

"Good to be here," Markus said. The crowd finally settled down.

"You have a heck of a grip," Jackie said, shaking his hand out. "Lots of stuff to cover; good thing you got out here early, so I can have you all to myself."

The studio audience laughed.

"Now…you are the CEO of a place called P4P."

Markus nodded.

"You run that place. Tell us about it."

Markus was quick with his response. "Sure. This is what we do: we sell adult accessories, apparel and fragrances…a lot of things that are bedroom-related. At the end of the day, what we really sell is bedroom positivity."

"Bedroom positivity," Jackie said. His tone was plain and skeptical.

"Bedroom positivity," Markus repeated.

"Please explain. I'm intrigued."

"Good! I'm glad you are," Markus said. "As a society, I believe we're repressed. We don't want to openly talk about bedroom topics. The problem is: it's more social than it's ever been. By the way, I'm glad you're on late night," he smiled, "because I'm going to give you some details, if you don't mind."

"Oh, no! I don't mind at all! You guys don't mind, do you?" Jackie asked the crowd.

The word "no" scattered across the audience.

Jackie was about ratings, and Markus rarely – if ever – gave interviews, formally or informally. He had an agreement for this exclusive.

"You look excited to talk about this! That makes me excited!" Jackie said.

"I am," Markus said. "The opportunity to teach, the opportunity to learn…it excites me. Not many better things in the world."

"I like your attitude. So, tell me more about bedroom positivity."

Markus smirked. "You got it." He rubbed his hands together, settled them near his crossed legs and leaned in slightly. "So, sex has a lot of negative connotations. Some view it as a means of procreating. Here's the reality: we're all just waiting for the opportunity to shout from the rooftops, that…you know…when it feels good, it feels good."

"Wow," Jackie mouthed. He fanned his face with his hand, raised his eyebrows and looked at the camera. He then blinked a few times and returned his gaze back to Markus.

"P4P promotes safe activity and positive consent, first and foremost," Markus continued. "After that, I think it becomes about pleasure calibration."

Jackie pointed at Markus. "That's a great point. I think I get what you're saying."

"In a nutshell, it shouldn't be bad," Markus said. "As people, a lot of the time we say, 'No, I don't like that,' and wave different things off, and we have *no* idea what it really is. Who's to say that we won't like it?" Markus questioned. "I'm about to speak in generalities here, so please forgive me."

"Forgiven."

Markus went on. "We grow up, but with certain things, we keep an immature mentality."

Jackie nodded. His audience was hooked to every word coming out of Markus Doubleday's mouth, powerless to his engaging personality. He would add himself to that group.

"When you have some free time, sit around and think for two minutes," Markus continued. "Close your eyes and think about what you like in the bedroom. After that, think about the things you want to try, and don't give yourself *any* restrictions. Ask your partner, as well."

"Can I share something with you?" Jackie asked Markus.

"Yes. Sure."

Jackie held back laughter. Markus snickered at Jackie's facial expression, a grin forming on his face. "Not only did it get hot in here, but I feel like getting online and cleaning out *your* inventory. We'll be right back with Markus Doubleday. You don't want to miss this. Stay tuned."

The audience burst into laughter and claps as the show went to commercial.

Between the confidence when he speaks and that build he's been blessed with...I'm smitten. By all accounts, Jackie Reed's straight. Maybe not, after tonight, Marissa thought.

She closed her eyes and daydreamed about what Markus pushed everyone to do. She fought the urge to think further, but she was slipping. The sound of Jackie rebounding from commercial ripped Marissa away from her dream world.

"Hmm…" She sighed with frustration. She had a head full of ideas and an empty bed.

"During the commercial break, our audience was excited, but that's because I told them that they're all getting $200 dollar gift cards to P4P. Let's see if they take your advice."

The crowd enthusiastically cheered, happy for another giveaway. That was one of the consistent things of his show: people came empty-handed, but they wouldn't leave that way. Markus looked out into the crowd and gave a mischievous smile.

"I need to keep this audience under control," Jackie sarcastically admitted. "It's getting too sexy in here."

"I agree," Markus said. "Maybe a segue would help?"

"Can't argue that," Jackie replied. "So, I understand you're a very generous man?"

"I try to be."

"Why is that?"

Markus stammered on the inside. He knew they would get into some personal things, but Jackie promised to keep it tasteful. Markus would get over it eventually, but he didn't like to talk about his philanthropy.

Markus took a deep breath and exhaled. "Well, both my parents died around the time I was finishing college. They were killed in a head-on collision. Drunk driver. My father died on impact. My mother was alive for maybe 15 minutes after that. I didn't get there in time to see her in her last moments. I was…probably 2, 3 minutes late. I remember sitting in this big, empty house for weeks."

Jackie's face was more serious. "That's really terrible."

"Finally, one day, I decided to pack the house up, clean it and put it on the market."

"What happened then?"

"I sold everything in the house. When I finished selling everything, I divvied up the money and sent it to a handful of well-researched charities. I wasn't homeless, but I didn't have my parents anymore. I wasn't underprivileged, but I was without. I know there are a lot of people out there that work with less than I do, so I try to help out the best I can."

"That's really good of you," Jackie said.

Markus nodded. "With the inheritance my parents left me, I had a house built from scratch. It took about three months, from permit to completion. I also took over the day-to-day operations of P4P. It was a middling establishment when I took over, enough to be considered rich, but not wealthy. And obviously–"

"It's not middling anymore. Not even close," Jackie interrupted. "In fact, I wouldn't even mention that word again. Now's not the time to be modest, Markus. You turned P4P into a juggernaut."

"Some say I've cornered the market. There are multiple companies trying to replicate in California what I'm doing in Texas. I always said that I wanted to be the best option for this retail, and I am. I turned a million-dollar company into a billion-dollar company. Is that going to bring my parents back? No. I know they would be proud of what I've done, what I'm doing, and will do."

The crowd clapped loudly. When they calmed, Markus continued.

"So, what's your message?" Jackie said. "Your overall message, if you have one?"

Markus pondered Jackie's question before responding, "The most important things in this life are the hardest to get back. I'm a billionaire, Jackie; that's just a matter of fact. The talks I had with my father, or the things I shared with my mother, the warmth, the loving environment…I can't re-create that, no matter how much money I have. The memory is there, but it's not the same."

Jackie and the audience listened intently, hanging on every one of Markus's words.

"So, I try to give back," Markus said. "I do extensive research on social issues in the most need of my resources. I anonymously take care of them the best I can."

"Why anonymously?" Jackie asked.

Markus smiled. "Because some charities, they don't agree with the way I make my money, which is fine. They're entitled to their opinions, and I respect theirs. They can't do anything about anonymous donations, so that's how I beat the system. I don't want to be lumped in with the recognizable face that loudly gives. I don't want or need the fanfare."

"You employ volunteers?" Jackie asked.

"I do," Markus replied.

"Tell us about that."

"When I have time, I'll go and volunteer, myself. When I don't have time, I collaborate with a handful of people, and we bring supplies and anything places need. Every place has specific needs, and we work to make sure they don't go without."

"Do you ever sleep?" Jackie asked, drawing laughter from the crowd.

"No," Marissa said to the TV.

"Sleep? Yes," Markus said. "When I have the time. My father always said, 'success before rest,' and I just kind of…took that to heart. I make sure I find some level of success before I turn in for the night."

"You are interesting. I don't know if you get this a lot, but I feel like I could talk to you all day," Jackie said.

"I've heard that before," Markus said.

"Okay, I have one more question for you, and you'll probably kill me for this later. We have to address the elephant in the room and I, Jackie Reed, am here to help you." He pointed to himself with a balled-up fist and a protruding thumb. He then pulled a picture out from under his desk, showing it to Markus.

"What are your thoughts about this?"

It was a picture of Markus and Marissa kissing at the airport. The minute the crowd saw that, they reacted accordingly, making the sounds a sitcom studio audience would make during a passionate kiss. That was one of the rare moments people saw when dealing with Markus.

"Oh my God!" Marissa covered her mouth, her hands formed like an oxygen mask. Her eyes swelled to the size of silver dollars. If she didn't want anyone to know about this, she was screwed. Then again, if she wasn't prepared for people to know, she wouldn't have kissed him. Still, her heart dropped into her stomach.

"Um, yes," Markus smiled coyly. "That happened very recently at the airport."

"Now, here's the *real* elephant in the room…are you two an item?"

Markus waited for a moment while the suspense built. He felt every eye in the crowd on him. The light that shined down on him was white-hot. The masses wanted to hear a clear answer. For as evasive as Markus could be, he didn't mind being vocal and matter-of-fact when it came to his feelings for Marissa.

"I wouldn't go that far," Markus said, "we're just two friends that kissed."

"If you don't know Marissa Buchanan, I think you've been living under a rock. I'll explain anyway: she recently became the top-rated model in the world, an entrepreneur and this year, cracked the top 5 of *John and Jane's* '50 Most Beautiful People.' Am I missing anything?"

"No. She's a good person." Markus's words were quick. He looked directly at the camera and gave a little wave, directing his wave solely at Marissa. "I don't want her looks to get caught up in the scrum," he winked at Jackie.

"I will tell you this: it's been a pleasure to have you on and talk to you. I'd love to have you on again sometime, if that's okay."

Markus smiled. "Fine by me. Thanks for having me on."

"The most interesting man in the world!" Jackie announced. Markus waved to the crowd, amid cheers that doubled in decibel level from his entrance. "Markus Doubleday! For all our friends at–"

Marissa turned the TV off. She was fuming. Ripping the comforter off her legs, she jumped out of bed and paced.

"Friends?! We're just friends?! What the hell is that?!" She asked herself out loud. She looked at her phone. "You better text me back, Markus! I mean it!"

She'd sent a simple message to Markus, and that was to text her back. After what seemed to her like hours, her phone buzzed. It was Markus. She opened her phone and checked his message.

Hey. I'm kind of busy. What's up.

She wondered when he got too busy to answer her calls. She punched several keys with her thumbs and replied back quickly.

That was a great explanation on Jackie. We're just friends now? What changed?

She continued to explore the space of her bedroom until she heard back from him.

I'll explain later. Right now I don't have the time.

What was his whole thing with time?

You seriously don't have two minutes? Seriously?

She waited.

No, I don't. Talk to you later Mare.

That wasn't good enough, to her. She immediately replied to his text.

So that kiss didn't mean anything?

Marissa waited. She stared at her phone, waiting for it to light up, but it didn't. When she finally got around to looking at her clock, an hour had passed, and nothing from Markus. She'd gotten plenty of messages from other people during that time, but didn't respond to any of it.

She'd been fuming since she heard Markus's proclamation of their friendship, but the hurt was settling in. She thought they had something; apparently, she was wrong. Also, Marissa thought Markus was being very secretive. She wanted to know what was going on. She looked at her phone for a moment.

"I'm going to do it," she said. She hit a couple buttons and held the phone to her ear. Her grip on the phone was suffocating. There was a click.

"Hello, you've reached Markus Doubleda–"

"Seriously?!" She shrieked. She hung up the phone and flung it against the wall. "That's it! I'm through, Markus!"

She put herself back in bed. She grabbed one of her pillows and covered her face, clutching the sides of the pillow tight. She screamed as loud as she could, pulling the pillow down harder on her face to muffle the sound.

Markus's generosity couldn't be questioned. Every time she learned something new about what he did for people, she fell for him more. He was an ambitious man, filled with ideas and drive; it drew Marissa to him. She wondered what he was waiting for.

Back stateside, Jonathan Deadmarsh was becoming very generous, talking at the precinct. After the night he had with Daphne, Jon felt good about everything. It was plastered all over his face on a day that Daphne hadn't made it in to work yet.

"What's going on Detective Douche? What are you so happy about?"

"Nothing! Just feeling good!" Jon beamed. "Also, I don't think you really care about how I'm doing, since you just referred to me as Detective Douche. I'm just pointing something out, I don't want you to get mad, but I'm just throwing that out there."

"Well, I want to know…well, *we*."

Detective Willis motioned for the other detectives to gather around. They ambled over to the detective's desk, waiting to hear a story. "Consider this a rite of passage. Did you get laid, or something? You have that glow about you, and I know a thing or two about that glow," he laughed as he nudged one of the other detectives.

The other detectives nodded in agreement. Jon thought about what he could say to people that clearly didn't have his best interests in mind. He really wanted to fit in at the precinct, but he remembered the conversation he and Daphne had.

"Yeah-yep, that's exactly what happened!" Jon said. He nodded yes and cocked his head to the side. He could feel the detectives' eyes on him. People loved stories, especially when they were out of the ordinary. For this kind of story to come out of Jonathan's mouth was out of the ordinary. "IIII totally got laid. And you'll never guess with who."

The detectives threw out different names from different departments, and even started in with their own department. Jon continued to shake his head no; they weren't even close.

"De La Rosa?" Jonathan heard.

He hesitated for moments, vehemently shaking his head no. He gave it away, and he knew it. The detective's faces changed.

They'd figured it out. They were detectives, after all. As it turned out, his poker face needed some work.

"That's a stretch, but you have to talk now! It's De La Rosa!" One of the detectives said.

Jon hesitated again. He knew it was wrong, but it was an opportunity to be accepted. He desperately wanted that. It drove him crazy that he wasn't accepted in this coven of law enforcers, and now, he was too deep in the conversation.

"Well, nothing happened. Guys, I really don't even know her. That's the truth." He shrugged, trying to be as nonchalant with his words as possible.

The detectives' faces turned white.

"What?" Jon wondered.

All the gatherers dispersed, either going back to their desks or finding someplace else to go, anywhere but where Jon stood. They were acting as if their conversation didn't happen, deliberately distancing themselves from him. Suddenly, he could feel heat on the back of his neck.

"What's going on?"

When he turned around, Daphne stood in front of him. She appeared out of thin air. Jon didn't say a word, too caught up in the moment.

"Come with me." Daphne's words were stern, direct and demanding.

"Okay."

Jonathan walked behind Daphne. She shuffled to her office quickly. The walk they took was like a funeral procession. After he made it into Daphne's office, Daphne slammed the door, causing Jon to jump. She closed the blinds.

"Are you out of your mind?!" Daphne asked angrily. "What the hell is wrong with you?! Did you say something?!" She piled on the questions.

"Okay, I would love to apologize to you. I didn't say anything about us, but they figured it out. I came in here with a smile on my face, and if you hadn't shown up, I don't know how much longer I would've held it in. As many times as I've seen that happen with sitcoms, I wouldn't have handled this situation the greatest. I also shouldn't share anything with those guys, I–"

"Damn right, you shouldn't!" Daphne snapped. "They don't like you! You're easy to manipulate! Since you like sitcoms and comic books, let me paint a picture for you."

"You know, I would rather you not, but–"

"No, I think you need to hear this." Emotion wrapped around Daphne's words. "I work hard for what I have. I told you this. It's not the rumors you were about to start that bothers me; that's not the first time that's happened at this precinct. What bothers me is that we had a *talk* and we *agreed* that nothing like this was going to happen."

Jon kept his eyes locked on hers while she spoke.

"In that fantasy world you live in, even then, the geek doesn't fit in with the jocks. They use the geek for a good laugh, a resource for homework, whatever the hell. You thought that trying to fit in with them was somehow better than respecting our time together, and that's a shame."

Jon knew what was coming next. He slumped slightly, his shoulders dropping, even though he stood face-to-face with Daphne.

"So, we can't do this. 'Don't tell anyone' means just that. I can work with you on other cases, but that's it. I refuse to be the next rumor."

Jon was frazzled. She'd just stomped his heart out like a fire, and he didn't know what to say to make it right.

"In sitcoms, the girl usually slaps the guy, or something," Daphne continued. "Why don't I just tell you that you're not worth the time, and you just get the hell out of my office? Do your job and keep your mouth shut. Do you think you can handle that?"

"Y-yes ma'am."

"Get out."

Daphne's words were frigid. Jonathan quickly made an exit, shutting the door behind him. She plopped into her chair, her hands shaking. She wanted to hit him so badly. She wanted to treat him like a criminal, bust him up for breaking the law. How could something so promising go up in smoke so quickly?

He's out of chances, she thought. De La Rosa was too rigid. Maybe that wasn't such a bad thing, not when it came to her emotions. She wouldn't allow herself to be hurt, not again.

Chapter 11

"Are you ready?"

"I'm ready."

Markus pointed to different words on a hologram screen with a laser pointer. Vanessa was expected to read the words clearly, carefully and without error. The problem was that every day people that talked to her knew she had an accent. In the field, she would have to hide it. If she spoke while she was out there, there had to be a difference.

Speech pathology was the answer.

As Markus pointed at various words, Vanessa spoke.

"How now, brown cow? Markus, do I really have to do this?" She whined. She didn't want to learn how to speak like this; she liked her English accent just fine. "I'd rather be training. Wouldn't that be more prudent?"

"What would be more prudent is if you learned this first," Markus said. He pointed to more words with the laser pointer. "I'm compromising with you right now, when you think about it. We do class work and mix in physical work. You're getting the best of both worlds."

I don't know why I'm questioning him, anyway. I don't know if Markus has ever trained anyone to do something like this, but he was trained...right?

"Who trained you?" Vanessa asked.

Markus stopped pointing with his laser and raised his eyebrows when he said, "What?"

"Who trained you? I need to know more about you, if we're to be working together."

"Yes, I agree," Markus said, somewhat hesitantly. "To answer your question, I was trained by the Black Diamond. He was one of the city's first vigilantes. He thought it was his calling. Nothing traumatic happened."

"Interesting, because it seemed there was a story a minute on the Black Diamond. What ever happened to him?" She asked.

"Everything came crashing down," Markus said. "One night, Black Diamond was apprehended by police while out in the field. He was hard to catch, but not impossible. I don't want you to go out in the field and think you can't be caught. If they want to catch you, they will."

"Aren't you leery about eventually being caught, should the department turn their attention to you?"

"Leery? Yes. Afraid? No. It won't stop me from going out."

Vanessa nodded at Markus's words. What he was doing was brave, but who was protecting him? "Did they just run Black Diamond down, or something?" Vanessa wondered aloud.

"The police department did, yes," Markus replied. "Daphne De La Rosa arrested him."

Vanessa raised one of her eyebrows. "Who?"

"Daphne De La Rosa," Markus repeated. "She was at the party I hosted, with a younger gentleman. I don't know that they were just having a good time. They were looking for something."

"What makes you say that?" Vanessa asked skeptically.

"Detectives look for things."

Markus smiled at her. She smiled back, caving to his charm. He said simple things without being "holier-than-thou," the condescending way that most people in his position came off. There was warmth to him, a willingness to educate, rather than denigrate.

Vanessa didn't know who Daphne De La Rosa was but, from what Markus said about her apprehension of Black Diamond, she should steer clear of the woman. De La Rosa clearly wasn't on their side, unless something changed.

"His name was…is Irving. He's a normal person, like you and me."

"You'll have to excuse me, but I hardly think we're normal." Vanessa chuckled. She stopped when it was obvious Markus wasn't joking.

"He worked a normal nine to five job," Markus continued. "In the evenings, he trained me. He didn't have all the technology available now, but he taught me lessons."

"Like what?"

"Well, once…" Markus laughed, "He left me in an alley with a ski mask and half a broomstick. He told me to find what I was looking for."

He shook his head.

"I was hardheaded. I rushed to get out there, like you want to. The difference between my training and your training: he did that to me, even when I clearly wasn't ready. The lesson was to take his guidance, no matter how ready I thought I was. I want you to take my guidance. The game is to stay alive. The longer you stay alive, the longer you can impact the world."

Vanessa nodded in agreement. "It makes sense, I suppose. Back to the task at hand; what are the next words?"

Markus used the laser pointer to point at the next sentence.

"My car is broken down. Can you help me?"

"Not bad. Concentrate a little more," Markus instructed. He pointed to another slew of sentences.

"Will you concentrate a little more?" The photographer, Brian, implored.

He was past testy. Marissa Buchanan was being difficult, trying her best to pose. It wasn't working well. The interaction with Markus was still bothering her.

"Concentrate on what?!" Marissa yelled. "The fact that I don't want to be here?! That's what I'm concentrating on, Brian."

Mark bristled at her attitude. "Would you like to do this on another day? We're already late with this shoot."

Marissa's hands became rigid. She closed her eyes, and breathed in and out a few times. "No, let's just…let's just do it now." Marissa channeled her inner professional and posed for the camera. Her eyes became intense. Her poses became more deliberate.

"There she is…I like that," Brian said. The numerous snaps of the camera filled the warehouse room. "Let's take it to the bed."

Marissa walked over to the bed and lay down. She decided to give Brian everything she had for the day; when she got back to her villa, she was free to do what she wanted. In the model world, time wouldn't stop because a model was upset about something.

She simply pretended to be somewhere else.

Propping her hand on the side of her head and resting her elbow on the mattress, her eyes met the camera. Mentally, she'd checked out. Marissa was making plans for the rest of the day and week. She had a large calendar hanging on the wall in her villa, where she would mark down the days before she headed back to the states, until she could talk to Markus, face-to-face. Face Time wasn't the same.

"Okay, now lie on your back," Brian said. Marissa obliged. "Hang your head off the bed…tilt back…look at me…"

Marissa took all of Brian's commands willingly. She needed to talk to Titus, her personal assistant. She needed to tell him what to add to her itineraries, but she also confided in the young man for some girl talk.

That's exactly what I'll do when I get home, come to think of it. I'll dress down, watch some TV and have a nice, long talk with Titus about Markus. I need to get it out to someone, and the truth is: I don't trust everyone with my feelings.

"Looking good, looking good." The rapid snaps of the camera stopped. His voice brought Marissa out of her inner thoughts.

She blinked a few times and set her brain to "conversation with photographer" mode. "I think we're done here," he announced.

"You got some good shots, right?" Marissa asked innocently.

"Of course," Brian said. "You're still Marissa Buchanan, even if you're a little down."

That was a great compliment; some models couldn't handle adversity. She was the consummate professional, and a lot of up-and-coming models looked to someone like Marissa for guidance. Not everything Marissa did was perfect, but she was exceptional, from start to finish.

Later on at her villa, Marissa was dressed down, with Titus over for dinner. Titus Williamson was a short young man, around 5-foot-6. He was mocha-colored, slender and lean. All of Titus's veins in his arms were easily seen. Marissa described him as "vein-y."

Walking through the door dressed in a flannel button-up shirt with the sleeves rolled up and a pair of jeans, Titus shut the door behind him and plopped down on the couch, sitting on one side while Marissa sat on the other.

"So…how was your trip?" Titus asked.

"Well, it was–"

"Girl, tell me everything!"

He didn't want to hear about the little things Marissa did while she was in Texas; he wanted to hear about what happened with Markus. They had plenty of time to talk about the things she ate or the shopping she did, but M&M – Titus's nickname for the two – was the top priority.

"Okay!" Marissa laughed playfully as Titus pulled one of his legs onto the couch and turned his body toward Marissa, who did the same. His foot just barely hung off the couch. "So…my time with Markus was a little up and down, but let me tell you this other thing that went on, and then we'll get back to Markus."

Titus sighed. "Waiting…with baited breath."

"Okay, so I went to grab this fabric on the wrong side of town, right?" Marissa said. "In my defense, it was the only place that had what I was looking for, that late at night."

"Ooh, dangerous…go on," Titus said.

"When I was leaving, there was some guy leaning on my car. Rude, right? So anyway, I told him to get off. He started running his mouth, making threats, the whole nine. So, I tried to get away from him, I tried to just…create space between me and this overly aggressive guy. I wasn't thinking…totally ran down a poorly lit alleyway."

"That's something a blonde would do in one of those camp-y slasher films!" Titus said animatedly, using his hands when he spoke. "What were you thinking?!"

Marissa let out a faint laugh. "I don't know! So this guy, he had his hands on me, telling me everything was going to be fine, but it wasn't…he was working with the guy that chased me down the alleyway! I mean, do you recognize the plot twist?!"

Titus's eyes widened with suspense. "To think, my friend, in dire straits!"

"So anyway, out of nowhere, this guy shows up," Marissa said.

"Another guy?" Titus asked.

"Yes, another guy. He had a mask on, and the garb you would look for in something like a comic book, I don't know."

"Holy comic books…girl, I think you're delirious," Titus said skeptically.

"Titus, this happened. I'm serious. I saw him kick their butts six ways to Sunday. He looked like a professional…butt-kicker, I guess," she said.

"Everyone loves a butt-kicker!" Titus said. "So then what happened? Or is that the end of the story?"

"It's almost over. Let me tell you what he did to me after all of this."

"He ravaged you?"

"No. He waved his first finger in the air at me, like this!" She showed Titus. "What am I, like, five?"

"Um…*rude*! Girl, you are *not* five! That dude had no business doing that to you!"

"I know! The next thing I know, he's gone, like he vanished into thin air!"

"Oh, so now he's a magician. Now, he's Houdini." Titus said dryly. He knew better than to doubt the things Marissa said. Since they'd been friends, she'd given him every reason to believe what she said.

"You could say he pulled a Houdini. I don't want to purposely get myself in trouble but I want to know this guy's story, Titus. It was like…it was like, like he showed up out of nowhere, and then *poof!* Gone. It felt like he knew to be there, or something. It was the weirdest thing."

Titus thought on Marissa's words for a few moments. "What about Markus?" He wondered. "Where was he at, through all this?"

"Who knows? Home's my guess. I was obsessed with getting that fabric, Titus."

"And he's like a knight in shining armor, isn't he?"

"He's better. He's not looking to save me. That's the difference. He's everything you would want in a Prince Charming. I don't have that…Wicked Witch, Wicked Stepmother or whatever…I don't have that drama going on for him to swoop in and save me. I'm just…"

"Girl, you're–"

"In love! God, Titus…I'm in love with him!"

Marissa glowed. She had the largest smile on her face she could muster. Titus ate it up.

"Gotta love a happy ending, especially when it's not all generically manufactured," he said. "M&M are meant for each other!"

"I'll tell you, Titus: he was the first person I thought of, the one person in the world that I just…I don't know, feel safe with," Marissa explained. "So, I went to his house, without thinking of anything else. He's never screamed 'butt-kicker' to me. I think he's more of a lover than a fighter, personally."

"Can we get to the good stuff?" Titus asked. "We get it! You're in love with him! Go on!"

"Okay! So anyway, he gave me his bedroom and went off into one of the guest rooms across the hall. I wanted to be next to him, and he was still playing the part of gentleman. Now, I wasn't sending the heavy 'Do Me' vibe or anything, but honestly, Titus…my adrenaline was pumping from what had just happened, I…I was a little turned on."

"Ooh, stop!" Titus warned. "You were turned on by all that?"

"If you ever feel your life flash before your eyes, why don't you tell me how *you* feel after that?" Marissa posed.

"You got a point. So, what else happened?"

"So, I'm in his bedroom, lying in this big and comfy bed, and he's in another bedroom," Marissa chuckled. "I'm lying there and I'm thinking…what would he do if *I* made the first move?"

"Inner crisis," Titus quipped.

"So, I get up. I'm like, on a mission," Marissa continued. "I open the door and…"

"And?! And?! Girl, you better tell me!" Titus interrupted.

"He just…kissed me." Marissa's words were a level above a whisper. Her words brought her back to the night Markus kissed her as if it would be the first of many kisses that had an element of longing to them.

"He kissed me like I've never been kissed before. I know it sounds cliché but he literally took my breath away, Titus. He kissed me, I kissed him back, we went in his bedroom and just…I know it sounds really 'high school,' but we just had a *really* good make-out session. He was a gentleman, didn't try anything…he just…held me, all night."

Titus smiled.

"People still do this!" Marissa laughed. "Excuse me." She wiped away a stray tear. She was emotional. Even though Markus wouldn't commit to a relationship, she still missed him. She remembered how sweet that gesture was. He wasn't fishing for something more than what he gave her, and that was a lost art. "His touch was electric, I–"

"Girl, you're about to make me tear up," Titus said. He feigned wiping away a tear. Both Marissa and Titus could think about some reality TV stars that mastered this. "That's one of the sweetest stories I've ever heard. Congrats on making me jealous," Titus said, half-jokingly. "So what do you two do now, then?"

"Did you watch Jackie Reed?" Marissa asked.

"No. Why?" Titus answered.

"Well then, he turns around and says that we're just friends, on live television!" Marissa exclaimed. "Here I am, thinking I would just finish my overseas modeling contract, and he would finish up whatever he needs to finish up, and then we would get together. Apparently, I was wrong."

"Wait…does that mean you're trying to move stateside?" Titus asked. "If you are, I'm instantly depressed. If you go stateside, what am I going to do?"

Marissa smiled and sent a wink Titus's way. "You'll have options, I think." Titus's ears perked up. "Who knows? You could meet the man of your dreams out here, for all we know. A year is a long time. I also know you have an eye and a heart for fashion, so…I was wondering…"

Titus waited patiently for the words to leave Marissa's mouth.

"I was wondering, since I want to go with my own line of clothing in the near-future, if you wanted to continue working for me? You're an up-and-coming designer, Titus; most of all, you're my dearest friend. I know talent when I see it, so…"

Titus hugged Marissa tightly. Marissa hugged Titus back and closed her eyes.

"To work for a hot name like yours would be an honor. I'll work for you until you kick me out," Titus assured. "We're gonna have some fun!"

"I think we will," Marissa said sweetly. "And hopefully make a profit to write home about. Are you ready for food?"

"I'm famished. Let's eat and celebrate new beginnings!"

On the other side of the world, the Broken Skull looked for more work.

His next victim had taken refuge in a house. He easily picked the lock and entered the house, locking every exit door he came across. He understood how difficult it was for someone to open a locked door when rushed to do so. It also alerted him of their whereabouts. The Broken Skull walked slowly through the house. He laughed to himself.

"Come out, come out, wherever you are…" He continued his slow walk through the one-level house, quietly opening a door. "Olly, olly…"

He heard a sound.

"Oxen…free."

The Broken Skull heard movement. "Hmmm…"

Every step creaked on his way to one of the bedrooms. The bedroom door was already open. He entered the room. When his eyes rested on the closet, he was certain of the noise's origin. He peered at the closed closet door. He didn't hesitate. He slowly turned the knob of the closet and opened the door, staring at the woman in front of him.

Her bare heels dug into the carpeted surface. The look on her face spoke volumes. Her elbows bent, her fingers dug into the floor. Her eyes trained on the Broken Skull, watching his every move. While he moved, she didn't. She was too afraid to.

The Broken Skull's arms outstretched. "The fear is everywhere. It speaks through these walls, in the streets, in your wildest dreams. Hopefully, your last words are memorable."

The woman spoke through sniffles when she said, "They will be."

The Broken Skull smiled through his mask. He was sure she'd plead with him, anything to motivate him not to kill her.

She wiped her eyes free of tears. "My dear, sweet Patty Cake…was that good enough?" She inquired. Her demeanor changed; her mouth formed a smile as she looked past the Broken Skull. He'd been had.

The Broken Skull heard clapping.

"Splendid. Bravo. Worthy of the highest award bestowed on an individual." The voice behind the Broken Skull got closer. The Broken Skull looked at the woman, the smile still plastered across her face. The man that spoke about awards walked into the room. Three was definitely a crowd.

"Patrick, do you think he's realized he's not alone with me anymore?" The woman's tone resembled a damsel in distress.

Broken Skull finally turned his head barely, silently acknowledging there was company.

"Emma, if he hasn't realized it yet, we could always spell it out for him." The man's suggestion came with a smirk. The moonlight showed through the blinds. His tone was upbeat; he was eager to teach a lasting lesson.

"With our hands and feet?" Emma asked Patrick.

"I prefer to call them *fists*, but absolutely. My sentiments exactly," Patrick said.

"Can I talk you two out of what you're thinking of doing?" The Broken Skull asked. "It's your last chance."

"You see, we like trouble," Emma said.

"But we hate chaos," Patrick added.

"You represent chaos," Emma added.

"And we can't have that." Patrick shook his head no.

"Patrick, would you like to do the honors?" Emma asked.

A three-punch flurry followed Patrick's words, blocked cleanly by the Broken Skull. Patrick reared back and threw one more desperate haymaker at him. Broken Skull smacked Patrick's arm down with one hand, and stiffly clotheslined him with his free arm.

Patrick's back smacked the surface immediately. He rolled over to his stomach.

The Broken Skull turned his attention back to Emma. She was legitimately afraid now. She'd depended on Patrick's brawn for so long; she'd never seen him wasted so easily. While her companion had a chance to recover from what the Broken Skull did to him, Emma wasn't so sure about the outcome anymore.

The Broken Skull confidently spoke to Emma. "There is a lesson in everything, a learning opportunity. Who am I to deprive of you of this gift?"

Emma sneered and pushed off the floor to her feet. She threw a kick at the Broken Skull's head. He caught Emma's foot. In one motion, he elevated her leg and sprinted forward. She hopped a couple times, but not fast enough. He launched her into the clothes, shoes and racks that inhabited the closet. He slammed the door shut and kicked the doorknob, jamming it.

Patrick struggled to grab hold of his faculties. The Broken Skull reared back and kicked him in the ribs. He rolled a full revolution. He clutched his ribs and lay in the fetal position.

"I tried to warn you!" The Broken Skull called to Emma through the closet door. He watched Patrick barricade himself in a corner, bringing his knees up to his chest. The Broken Skull knew it would be hard for Patrick to breathe.

"You hate chaos, do you?" The Broken Skull asked Patrick. No answer. He wasn't able to. "I *am* chaos. I will show you."

He methodically approached Patrick while the beats from the closet door got louder and louder. The Broken Skull fell silent. Patrick said nothing.

Emma stopped beating on the door. She couldn't hear anything on the other side. She was afraid of what happened to her twin brother.

"Patrick! Are you okay?!" Emma yelled through the door. She was panicked and frustrated. As much as she struck and kicked the door, it still wouldn't budge. She continued on; she wouldn't give up so easily.

Patrick had been reduced to a quivering mess as he listened to the Broken Skull's breathing. He looked up at the mask, not sure what to expect next. *He's skilled. I can't compete with him. I'm completely outmatched*, Patrick thought.

"Patrick?! Answer me!" Emma yelled through the door.

Suddenly, the Broken Skull unleashed a flurry of closed-hand strikes to Patrick's arms, as hard as he could, and for several seconds. Patrick covered his head and body up. He felt his muscles being brutalized. His bones rattled with every shot. The Broken Skull grunted with every devastating blow.

Patrick couldn't hold his arms up any longer. The Broken Skull sensed this. He punched harder and faster. The pace was impossible for Patrick to keep up with.

With everything in her being, Emma punched, pushed and kicked the door. No more time. Guttural screams emerged from the closet as Emma violently beat on the door. She felt progress.

The Broken Skull heard the sound of shattering wood behind him. The closet door flew open. He turned around. Emma was breathing hard. She shook her hands out. Without notice, she charged her captor and gave everything to the punch she threw. He blocked it and flung her against the wall. Her limp body left cracks in the plaster before falling and slapping the floor.

Emma and Patrick were tired, battered, bloody and broken. The Broken Skull stood over the two. He breathed normally, as if he'd just walked into the room.

"I've seen your…potential. The both of you…and I'm fascinated."

Emma pulled herself up from her lying position. She brought her knees up and rested her back against the wall, alongside her brother.

"Does this feeling…feel good?" The Broken Skull asked. They both nodded no. "Do you wish to continue feeling this way?" They nodded no again.

"Consider yourself invited. What if I told you that…you would never feel this way again? That you would always be in control, that you would be more powerful than your wildest imaginings?"

Patrick's head barely rose up. His eyes focused as well as they could on the Broken Skull. "I want to learn from you," he said confidently.

Emma looked at her brother. She usually went along with Patrick's ideas, but this felt like insanity. "He doesn't speak for me," Emma said breathlessly. She was defiant. "What are the other options?"

"I could kill you immediately," the Broken Skull said quickly. "Sizing you up, I would say you're not strong enough to defend yourself at this point, not even adequately. Your body is beaten. It would be a lopsided defeat for you."

He continued.

"But I have chosen you. I want to break you of your bad habits, your weaknesses…I want to rebuild you, mold you. After your training, you will be able to take the control you crave."

Emma struggled to her feet. She held her hand out for Patrick to take. Patrick took it, and allowed himself to be helped to his feet. Patrick gritted his teeth, his other arm holding his ribs.

"I want you to teach me," Emma said.

"Teach us," Patrick added.

The Broken Skull reached into his pocket and pulled out a piece of paper. He unfolded it and handed it to Emma. "We will start here, with her."

"Who's this?" Emma asked.

It was a photo of Daphne De La Rosa.

Chapter 12

Daphne and Jonathan were out on their lunch break, discussing the aftermath of their conversation a day ago.

"It's good that we're continuing to work together," Jon acknowledged. "I'm glad we came to that conclusion."

"Yeah, *I* did," Daphne told him, "but thanks for taking some credit. It's a lot easier to work on cases without the thought of a relationship hanging above our heads."

"Do you think you would ever reconsider?" Jon asked.

"Not that you're not making it really weird right now during lunch or anything, but–"

"Daph, it's a fair question," Jon said. Before she had a chance to say anything else, he said, "Okay, I'm sorry. I know we already talked about it, so I'm sorry."

"*Are* you sorry?" Daphne asked sarcastically. "Just stop, before I get worked up again."

"Okay, I'm sorry," he said again.

"God, I hate you," she said.

"No you don't. Changing the subject as quick as I can, I'd rather eat donuts than this," Jon said. He plunged his fork into his Asian salad. Dressed in a gray suit, Jonathan had his black tie thrown over his shoulder.

While his fork was full of lettuce, he used his other hand to pluck a crispy noodle from his plate, and popped it into his mouth. It stuck out like a toothpick while he slowly chomped away.

"Donuts don't sound very good in the middle of the day," Daphne said, taking a bite of her Caesar salad. On this day, she wore tight jeans and a v-cut shirt, the sleeves stretching to her forearms. Her badge was attached to her hip.

"They should! Isn't that when people need their boost?" Jon questioned. "People talk about being tired at 2 p.m. Why wouldn't they have a donut and get a little sugar rush, instead of doing it in the morning and crashing later?"

"I guess it beats crystal meth," Daphne joked, poking her fork into her salad and taking a bite.

Jonathan already had a bite in his mouth when the comment was made. He stared at her, amazed at her dark sense of humor. *Cynical, sarcastic and dark, just the way I like it!*

"What?" She asked.

"You're just funny," he said.

"I like you too. Now finish your food; bad guys don't go to lunch at the same time we do."

"Yes, Mother," Jonathan said dully. He raised his eyebrows sarcastically and took another bite before he dropped his napkin into his food. He grabbed his jacket and slid it on while Daphne straightened out her clothes. They left a few bills on the table and ventured off into Daphne's vehicle.

The two pulled out of the restaurant and into the street, on their way back to the police station to recuperate and pick up a few things. They hadn't talked about the Guardian Angel's assailant in a while.

"Do you have anything on that guy?" They both said in unison. Once they realized they said the same thing about the same guy, Jon smiled.

"You go first," he insisted.

Daphne hid her smile. She didn't want to look like a pre-teen with a crush. "I didn't make any headway with this case. I did a little bit of comic book-reading and I came to a grand conclusion; I don't know if you'll agree or not, but–"

"I don't think it matters," Jon said. "We're just spitballing, speculating about someone we know next to nothing about. There's nothing wrong with ideas."

"Okay, well…you're the comic book professional in this partnership, so excuse my dummy-ness: do you remember how we were talking about extreme good and evil?"

"I do."

"As big as this city is, this city is small," Daphne said. "You never know who you know until…you know…you know them."

"That's a mouthful. Try saying that five times fast," he joked. Daphne acknowledged his joke, but knew he understood the severity of her words.

“All joking aside, though…who says they haven’t run into each other before? Who says they’re not about to run into each other? Who says we won’t get caught in the middle of all of this, these two extremes?” She asked. She hoped Jon would be able to shed a light on this questioning, just to clear her clouded mind.

“You know, as much as I read comic books and find that world intriguing, that’s the part I try not to think about. When two people are on opposing sides of the extremes, from two worlds destined to collide…the results can be disastrous,” Jon warned. Talking about it caused the hairs on the back of his neck to rise. “It’s intriguing, but it also scares me.”

“Is there something in particular that scares you about this?” Daphne asked. She cared about him and his emotions. This was a case, yes, but a case that seemed close to the heart.

“Yes…someone is going to win, and someone is going to die. It reminds me of a Daredevil comic. Not that I want the conversation to take a somber turn, because I don’t, but it needs to be talked about. I think this is only the beginning.”

Daphne let the words sink in. Jon continued.

“The guy on the good side, it’s imperative he keep his identity secret. He will do whatever it takes to keep it under wraps. He may have acquired things to lose, like human relationships. Maybe he has a girlfriend, boyfriend, wife, husband or best friend, something.”

Daphne nodded her head while keeping her eyes on the road. “That makes sense.”

“Now, on the other hand, our villain might start revealing himself. Look at the way he’s getting rid of people. It’s more like an outright extermination than killing. He’s imposing his will; he wants to show how strong he is, what he's capable of. Sooner or later, if you get away with things of this magnitude, it won't be about slipping up and being caught; it will be about daring people to oppose you."

"That also makes sense," Daphne agreed. She pulled up to the station. "I can't believe this is real."

"Well now, you have to. We're in the middle of it."

Daphne turned the key, turning the vehicle off. "How are we in the middle of this?"

"Maybe not right this second, but it's coming," Jon said. "We're going to have to stop this. We're the police. This guy can't run wild in the streets, unchecked."

"Pick the side of the police. It's safer," Daphne said. The authoritarian in her voice and posture came out.

"You've said that before."

Daphne sighed and said, "Consider it a friendly reminder. I care about you and I want the best for you."

"But you have to do your job. Got it," Jonathan said smartly as they both exited the car.

"And this is why it wouldn't work between us."

They walked side by side. She didn't want to pull that information out but she felt the need to let him know where she stood emotionally. He stopped. She stopped too.

"*This* is why it wouldn't have worked between us?" Jon quizzed. "Because of my love for comic books? Because I believe in doing the right thing over some rules made before I thought about being a police officer? Get off your high horse, Daphne."

He left her at the steps of the police station doors. He pushed the doors open without thinking of turning back. She didn't call after him, either. Sometimes, it was best to say nothing until two people were comfortable. Things were obviously uncomfortable.

Markus sifted through different holograms while in his office.

"Hmm."

He quickly read through and discarded things. He was so into his search, he didn't notice someone enter his office. He cocked his head down and sniffed lightly, then went back to his activity.

"What can I do for you, Ms. Vaughn?" He plowed through information quicker, discarding it almost as soon as he pulled it up.

She wondered how he knew it was her. Maybe it was because he knew her schedule like she knew his.

"I think you're quite mad," Vanessa said. "I still can't believe you can talk to me whilst sifting through all that rubbish. That's just…mad."

"If there isn't anything pressing at this very moment…I would find a good reason to be in here right now," Markus said. He continued to read and discard.

"What exactly are you looking for?"

"Door: lock."

The door locked, and Vanessa immediately felt concern. Why did Markus want the door locked?

"Are you planning on giving me a stern talking-to?" Vanessa smiled half-heartedly. She couldn't tell what kind of mood Markus was in. Just because he was looking for something, didn't mean he was in a bad mood. He seemed busy, from what Vanessa could see. She prepared for the worst, nonetheless.

"Depends on how you look at it. You need to see something."

Holograms stayed afloat above Markus's head. Vanessa had no idea what she was about to look at, but she was excited for the opportunity to be shown something by Markus. It had to be important. "I'm all for it. Whatever you feel the need to show–…are you listening?"

Vanessa stopped in her tracks. She stood beside Markus and focused her eyes on the screen. She looked for what Markus was looking for. It didn't take long. A face showed up, a man wearing a skeleton's mask. Two others stood by him, clearly in the shadows.

"Good evening, citizens. Allow me to introduce myself. I am the Broken Skull. The two behind me are members of my family." His voice was ominous. He took a moment to breathe.

So did Vanessa. Markus didn't.

"I can't enhance this picture enough to see who's flanking him," Markus said.

"As you can see, my army is growing…slowly but surely. First there was me, now there are three."

"Clever choice of words," Vanessa snickered.

"Shhh," Markus snapped.

"We plan on changing the way you look at the world, inside and out. We will render the police…obsolete. When my vision for the city comes to fruition, there won't be enough to stop us.

Embrace it. Only the fittest will be hand-chosen and offered a place by my side."

Vanessa looked to Markus for guidance. None was provided. His eyes hadn't left the screen since the video started playing. All that Vanessa could do was move her attention back to the screen. Markus wasn't saying a word.

"And for my special friend at night, who scours the streets of wrongdoing…I can't wait to meet you. And I will. Soon, friend…soon."

The video went blank, and the news anchor began to speak.

"Off."

All the holograms that Markus moved around disappeared. Markus furrowed his eyebrows. Crossing one arm across his body, his other arm pointed upward, his thumb and forefinger rubbing his chin. He dropped deep into thought.

Who is he, and who did he have with him? In this city, I'd say there were a few million people. If this man doesn't want to be seen or caught, he doesn't have to show himself.

"Are we going after him?" Vanessa asked. "Tell me you're taking the training wheels off, Markus. You're going to need more help than just you. Do you get what I'm saying?"

Markus slowly turned his head and looked at Vanessa. Her eyes met his. He said, "I can't risk it." His response was quick as he pulled his fingers away from his chin and walked over to his desk. He sat down, placing one arm on his desk flat while he used his other arm and hand to prop his chin up, his elbow planted.

Now, they were both annoyed.

"How can you say you can't risk it, when clearly, I can help you?! So, you're just going to…go out there, without help?" She asked, her voice rising. "It sounds like *he's* looking for *you*, not the other way around!"

Markus stared blankly at Vanessa; she might as well have said nothing.

"Markus, I'm begging you," Vanessa pleaded with her boss.

"I've made an investment in you," Markus said. "I can't just recklessly throw you out there in the field with limited knowledge and feel comfortable. You are my responsibility, no matter how you look at it."

"So I don't get a say in this?"

"No, you don't."

"Markus, I–"

"That will be all, Ms. Vaughn."

Markus looked down at some loose papers on his desk to distract from looking at Vanessa. He wouldn't argue with her; he knew more about the streets he prowled than Vanessa did, plain and simple. In the end, he would make sure she knew more than he ever would.

Vanessa gazed at Markus. While doing so, she was in her own mind. *I understand his point, but…will I ever be truly ready for this? Even if I got all the training in the world, people are unpredictable. If I mess up in the field, it could cost me my life.*

She softly said, "I understand. You know where I'll be." She left Markus's office.

After a few moments, Markus looked up. The coast was clear. "Computer: everything you have on the Broken Skull."

He leaned back in his chair and kicked his feet up on the desk, intertwining his fingers and resting them on his stomach. The holograms started up again, overlapping each other for Markus's view. He would be as prepared as he was going to be.

Markus sighed. "Are you ready for this?"

"Of course I'm ready for this, Dad."

Marissa was on FaceTime with her father. She missed him terribly. Despite a huge time difference, Michael Buchanan stayed up to talk to his little girl. That's the way she would always be, to him. It sounded preposterous to him that she wanted to date, but Markus? Michael was more okay with him than some bozo.

"He seems like an awfully busy man," Michael said. "Do you think he'll have time to have children and be a good husband?"

"Stop it," Marissa said quickly.

Michael shrugged. "Can you blame me?"

"Yes, as a matter of fact, I can!" Marissa laughed. "You can't arrange some kind of marriage. We haven't dated one day and you're already talking about marriage and babies!"

Secretly, she'd thought about marriage and children with Markus, but she wouldn't parade her feelings around for everyone to see and hear. It was just a shame that he wasn't ready for those kinds of thoughts.

"Well sure. Take your time, if that's what you want. Your mother and I, we kind of grew on each other with time, hated each other at first," Michael chuckled.

The elder Buchanan thought back to when he first met Pilar. They met through mutual friends. Over time, they happened to be at the same places. What started as "talking every once in a while" turned into dating. They fell in love, and the rest is history.

"Markus has grown on me since day one," Marissa confessed to her father. "He's a good guy. We're just friends, Daddy. Good guys don't grow on trees, you get what I mean?"

"I do, and I agree," Michael told her, conceding to her words. "Have you been reading the local news?"

"No, I haven't. Why? What's wrong?"

Michael paused for a moment, and spoke. "It crossed my mind, when you mentioned good people. There was this man on TV, the Broken Skull."

"Sounds kind of dumb," Marissa quipped. She popped a small piece of celery with peanut butter on it into her mouth. It was one of Marissa's guilty pleasures. "The Broken Skull? Really? He couldn't come up with a better name?" She snickered. "Did he even come up with that name?"

"Marissa, this is serious stuff," Michael said. "Fun and games are fun and games, but this is serious. Even though you're grown and doing your own thing, that doesn't mean I don't worry about you. You're still very important to me, young lady. I mean that."

"Daddy, I know," Marissa said. "I'm fine here. I have Titus with me, I'm working, I'm eating celery and peanut butter…I think everything is going just the way it's supposed to." Marissa's words brought a smile to Michael's face.

"I don't think this guy and his people are going to show up out of the country. People like this are everywhere, Marissa, they just haven't shown their face yet," Michael pointed out. Marissa nodded. "I know you'll be back in the states again soon, but I just wanted to give you a head's up. We still haven't found the guys responsible for your little scare the last time you were here."

That took Marissa back to the night she was stalked and nearly assaulted. That night, a man saved her, proof there were still good people in the world.

"Just leave them alone," Marissa ordered. "It'll be fine. You don't need that karma. I'm sure you have other things to worry about, don't you? Isn't business good?"

"Yes, very well. Business is always going well," Michael answered. Her plan to change the subject proved successful. "Sales are up, we're getting rid of what doesn't work…it's proving to be a very efficient machine. Anyway, it's late. Mother sends her love. You know her, early to bed and early to rise."

"And you'll be up for hours, thinking about business and or money."

"She knows me!" Michael threw his hands up in defeat. "Goodnight, Honey."

"Sweet dreams, Daddy."

The screen went blank. Michael leaned over and kissed his sweet wife while she slept.

"Are you going to work?" She asked wearily, snuggling up to her pillow.

"Yes."

"Be safe."

"As always."

Michael left their bedroom, walking down the stairs of their expansive abode. Dressed in a suit, Michael checked his watch once he made it to the bottom level. 12:54 a.m. He turned the knob to his door and opened it. There was a man there that looked as if he were about to knock.

"I beat you to it, Dwight," Michael said.

"Good. I didn't want to wake Pilar up with my Cop Knock." Dwight had a hard knock, just like the police were known for.

Dwight Durant was 15 years Michael's junior. Michael was tough, but Dwight was muscle, something Michael would always need. Everyone thought twice about throwing their weight around, when Dwight was factored in. He was the kind of guy that, based on his physique, made you think twice.

Dwight was mixed with Black and White, 6-foot-4 and a chiseled 265 pounds. He played football in high school and college. Going undrafted to the pros, Dwight got a job unloading trucks. Michael spotted him and offered him a job working in a shoe store he owned, schmoozing with the rich and famous. After a year, Dwight was running the place.

One night, Michael offered him an avenue to make extra money on the side, while keeping his hands clean. Why would Dwight turn him down? He'd given him the first real job he ever had, taught him everything he ever knew about business, and – most importantly – been a man of his word. He got to provide for his family, while still getting a taste of the physicality he craved.

As far as Dwight was concerned, he viewed Michael as a mentor and a father figure.

“We found those guys,” Dwight reported.

“Did you?” Michael’s ears perked up.

“Yeah. Wait until you hear *this* story,” Dwight warned.

Michael’s job was around 15 minutes away, a mostly silent ride. He owned different businesses but the business where he performed all of his shadiness, was in the back room of the shoe store Dwight ran. The only shoes sold were expensive, so there weren’t many clients. Not new ones, anyway. They closed around 6 p.m. Around 1 a.m. is when his real work began.

Stepping out of the black sedan with Dwight, the two walked to the back door of the store. He unlocked it and walked in. Dwight followed closely behind. He looked to his left; two bound men, with another man watching them.

“Nice to see you.”

Dwight stepped behind Michael, and helped him wiggle free from his jacket. Once it was off, he held it.

“Thank you, sir,” he said to Dwight, who nodded. Michael unbuttoned his cufflinks.

“This is an uncomfortable situation. See, my daughter, God bless her…she believes in karma.” Michael rolled his sleeves up to the ends of his forearms. Dwight’s laugh could be heard in the background. The other man – the man holding the two men hostage before Michael and Dwight came – stayed off in the shadows, not saying a word.

“I don’t.”

Michael paced. “So I’m going to give you an opportunity. I’m going to let you explain to me what happened that night…and please, guys…make it genuine. As it stands right now, I don't need a reason to swell up my knuckles on your face. I'm just asking that you give me a reason not to."

"Do you want to tell him?" One said to the other in exasperation.

"Y-yeah, I'll tell him," the other said. "Listen, Mr. Buchanan…honestly…it was dark. I didn't know it was your daughter, at first." Michael crossed his arms across his chest. "When I saw it was her…I-I panicked. I'd already gone too far."

"Gone too far? You know that sounds worse on you, right? That means you found out it was my daughter and you *still* kept with the plan."

"Which I'm sorry for," he said. Regret cradled his words. "So, this guy comes out of nowhere."

"What guy?" Michael questioned. He was more skeptical than ever.

"He had a suit on, but not like you…like a superhero suit. Mask and the whole thing."

"Excuses."

Michael clenched a fist and started his walk towards the man, about to tee off on his face. The man's eyes widened with horror. He dipped his head down, in an effort to absorb the pummeling he would surely get.

"No! Stop! I'm telling the truth! Seriously! Tell him I'm telling the truth!" He ordered to his accomplice.

"He's telling the truth!"

Those words stopped him. "You don't know how bad I want to make good on my threat. A man in a *superhero* suit came and did *what*?"

The man's chin dipped back up slightly. He looked up at Michael. "Cleaned house. He just…attacked. We couldn't say anything, we couldn't do anything. Just…skills. Skills all day. Every time he swung, he hit something. He had this baton thing. Did work…it was overwhelming. He stopped us, Mr. Buchanan. We're sorry, a thousand times, we're sorry. It'll never happen again."

"Stopped you from doing what?" Michael queried.

The man's eyes widened again. It dawned on him that he'd made a mistake. He didn't want to tell Michael the truth about what he wanted from Marissa. It definitely wasn't something you would tell the father of a victim.

"Stopped you from doing what?!" Michael asked again, his anger rising.

"I didn't!"

"But if this superhero guy hadn't shown up…if he hadn't cleaned house, as you put it…what you're saying is that you would've, right?"

The man remained tight-lipped.

Michael nodded. "That's what I thought. I wonder if you properly said goodbye to your family today. You're the kind of scum I don't like, the kind of scum that makes me sick. You get off on stuff like that, don't you?" He pulled a hammer off the shelf. "Do you paint me as a man that likes to do things like this?!"

"No! I just–"

The man stammered as he tried to find the words to apologize. His eyes welled up. He knew what was coming. He would be bludgeoned in the back of a store room, and dumped somewhere. He wasn't immune to what Michael Buchanan was capable of. He was about to become a victim of it. The elder Buchanan was very sensitive about his family, and this man made a mistake.

"You just what?" Michael wondered. "I don't suppose it matters. One less scumbag to worry about."

He raised the hammer above the man's head. There was a knock at the door. Michael stopped and looked at the back door. Dwight looked at him. He tossed the hammer to Dwight.

"See who it is, would you?"

Placing the hammer behind his back, Dwight took a few steps to the door and cracked it open. It was a younger lady, petite. Brown hair, brown eyes; a sight for sore eyes, indeed.

It was Emma Starks.

"Excuse me…maybe I'm lost," she said, her perfectly-crafted doe eyes sucking Dwight in. She pouted her lips and batted her eyelashes a few times. A bit overboard, but it was for effect. Emma knew her beauty could distract the strongest male. She was a modern-day Delilah.

"Do you mind giving me directions?" She asked.

"I'm sorry, we're closed." Dwight opened the door more and looked her up and down. He liked what he saw. "I'm sorry." He slowly closed the door on the young brunette. As he started to walk away from the door, there was a knock again.

"Lady, I told you…"

Dwight swung the door open. There was a sound and a gasp for air. Dwight flew away from the door, hitting the opposite wall and slouching down. The hammer fell out of his loose grip.

"What the hell?!" Michael exclaimed. He was without a weapon right now, and he couldn't see who caused all the commotion.

"I'll huff…and I'll puff…" A man's voice was heard as he stepped across the threshold. It was the Broken Skull, flanked by Emma and Patrick. "Apologies to you, young man. We tried knocking," the Broken Skull said. Dwight was still collecting his senses.

Patrick laughed at the Broken Skull's words.

"He looked like a sucker," Emma said sweetly to the Broken Skull. She took another look at Dwight. *He's cute, no doubt. He's not very smart, but cute*, she thought.

"This isn't the guy, is it?" Michael asked the bound men.

They both nodded their head no. They were too mesmerized to take the scene in. Michael turned his attention back to the Broken Skull.

"I saw you on TV earlier. What, am I supposed to be scared of that Halloween costume?" He was old school, too tough for someone to push up so easily on his dealings. "What is the meaning of this, some kind of shakedown?"

"My dear Michael," the Broken Skull said, "I will explain it all to you. Patience is a virtue, friend."

"You don't get things done with patience."

"All good things come with patience. I'm afraid you've been misinformed."

Michael Buchanan wouldn't stand for being talked down to. He pointed at the Broken Skull.

"I want you to listen to me and I want you to listen better than you've ever listened to anyone: nobody disrespects me. I won't stand for that. Do we understand each other? I'm not afraid of you. I've dealt with tougher.

No response.

"Do we have an understanding?!" Michael repeated.

"Sure," the Broken Skull said. "I meant no disrespect to you, Michael. I just want to make you an offer."

Dwight struggled to his feet, rubbing the back of his head. As he took a couple steps towards the group, Patrick popped his head in between the Broken Skull and his sister.

"I wouldn't do that if I were you," he grinned.

"I didn't ask you," Dwight said.

"I feel like you should have," Emma said, mirroring the same grin as her brother. She exchanged looks with Dwight. She was a beautiful woman with natural charm that conveyed the words with her eyes.

"We mean you no harm," the Broken Skull said. "We will only react when there is action. Do you understand?"

As Dwight thought about the Broken Skull's words, he looked to Michael for direction. Michael subtly placed his hand up. Dwight backed off.

“I’ve seen your work before, and it impresses me,” the Broken Skull told Michael. “There is no shakedown I’m looking for; we can work for each other, with each other. I want you to join my family.”

“How insulting. What the hell do I look like, a follower?”

“I’m not asking you to follow me. We can work together.”

“I still don’t get it. You’re speaking in riddles. All I want is an explanation.”

“Of course. The two with me tonight, we work for each other. I have their support and they have mine. You have valuable resources, as do I. All I ask of you is the opportunity to merge.”

The Broken Skull finally had Michael’s attention. “Keep talking.”

“You’re in the midst of ruling the city. Slowly but surely, you’ve spread like a virus. You have a flair for simplicity. We have that in common. I want to provide you with the final push you need…I want you to realize what you can achieve. You’re family-oriented; all I’m looking to do is fit in with your current structure.”

“And what do you want from me?” Michael asked.

“When I make decisions, all I need is for you to stay out of the way. A silent support, some would call it. Rest assured, I will do nothing to hurt you or your business…ventures.”

“How do I know you’re as trustworthy as you’re trying to come across right now?”

“Pilar goes unmolested.”

Michael's emotions were further stirred up by the two flanking the Broken Skull. They both smiled carefree, and he knew the smiles were directed at him. They were trying to provoke him. "Is that a threat?" He asked.

The Broken Skull was frank. "Simply a matter of fact. I know you're family-oriented. If I wanted to go after you, I would make victims of the ones closest to you. The love of your life would be a great place to start…if those were my intentions. Perhaps you need a few days to think about this?"

Michael nodded.

"As far as I can see, it makes sense, but I still need to mull over this. This is big."

"You've handled it so far," the Broken Skull pressed. "For instance, what do you have here?" The Broken Skull motioned towards the bound men.

"We have two that violated the rules of the game. They tried to do things to my daughter. They say it was an accident, but even after they found out who she was, they went on with it. Only reason they stopped is because a masked guy showed up…like you."

"Not like me," the Broken Skull abruptly corrected, waving Michael's words off like gnats. "He stands for something else. I stand for something better, real justice."

"Real justice," Patrick repeated. Emma nodded her head yes.

"They broke the rules. You shouldn't have to take care of this," the Broken Skull said. "As an olive branch of trust and peace…we insist on handling this."

Patrick hugged one of his fists with his other hand and cracked his knuckles, a big smile on his face.

"We've been waiting for some action," Emma said to Michael, also smiling a toothy grin. She briefly looked at Dwight. She was currently overlooking what she thought about him before – that he was big, dumb muscle – and viewed him for his physical gifts. Dwight returned the favor.

"Very well, then." Michael raised one eyebrow. "We have a deal." He strode forward, extending his hand to the Broken Skull. Michael's counterpart took his hand and shook it tightly, holding for a few moments before the two let go.

"Dwight…"

Michael walked away with Dwight. Without turning around, he spoke to the man that stayed in the shadows. "Lock up when they're done." He left out of the back door, Dwight on his heels.

When the door shut, the three turned their attention back to the two bound men, who looked as scared as ever.

"Who will save people like you two?" The Broken Skull asked. He pointed to one of the men, then the other. They broke down, almost immediately. They thought about their families and their lives, along with their unmet goals and expectations. It was too much.

"You've terrorized people, but…who will step in when things of this nature affect you?" He asked them. "Your eyes have tears in them, as though someone will miss you. No one will miss you, I assure you."

Both of the men's heads dropped.

"I will do what someone should have done a long time ago," the Broken Skull notified the two, who degenerated into a blubbering mess.

"You're garbage," Patrick said.

"The worst kind," Emma chimed in.

"It will be quick," Patrick said with a positive nod.

"But *very* painful," Emma finished with a nod and a big smile.

As Michael raised his leg to step into the sedan with Dwight, he heard two distinct screams, then nothing. Michael smiled as he entered the car. The black sedan pulled off into the night. Michael still wasn't completely sure about the Broken Skull, but he felt he gained an asset tonight. The city would soon be in the right hands.

Chapter 13

Because of the circumstances involving the Broken Skull, Markus was forced to expedite Vanessa's training. They'd been training for months, but the last few weeks, they'd been going two long sessions a day. Vanessa was involved in speech classes, combat and strategist training, with mental skills and situational training sprinkled in, as well.

Blood, sweat and tears was real. It wasn't just a catchphrase.

So far, Markus's work wasn't affected. If he didn't want to go into work for a day – or several – he didn't have to. He would go out tonight, even though he was extensively involved in her training.

Vanessa wanted nothing more than to be out in the field, but she trusted Markus. If he wanted to, he could cut her training off. He could cut ties altogether, and if she told anyone about his secret identity, it wouldn't go well. To her, the public wouldn't believe it. She had to thank him for not recklessly putting her out there.

"Positive thoughts…positive thoughts," Vanessa coached herself. She placed her hand on the pad. The door unlocked. She walked through the door, took a deep breath and headed towards the basement.

She was dressed in tights, with a tight t-shirt that left some of her midriff showing. Vanessa made sure every door shut behind her. Markus was adamant about making sure the basement door stayed closed. To Vanessa's knowledge, only she and Markus had been down there.

While she was on the platform that brought her to the basement level, Vanessa thought about ways to fast-track her training. She would have to go harder and faster; everything had to be more precise than she was used to. Attention to detail was the preeminent theme. After all, she was a 19-year old girl, about to embark on a journey that would most likely kill her.

More than enough incentive to be focused.

When she landed at the bottom of the stair, Vanessa noticed the bright lights. Everything was functional. Markus emerged from the Sound's signature black car. Vanessa always thought he was handsome. Even when he was teaching her something, she couldn't help but avert her eyes sometimes. She didn't want to be accused of staring.

"Good to see you again," Markus acknowledged.

"Always a pleasure."

On Markus's end, he was very protective of her during this process. Even as his personal assistant, she'd become more responsible. No longer was Vanessa the girl who came in late twice a week, but a woman that was 10 minutes early every day. Markus would like to think he had a hand in her maturation. He was thankful she listened.

"So, what's on the platter today?" Vanessa wondered. "Essay? Something in the classroom? No hitting, right? Are we not going to hit anything? As usual…"

She muttered the last two words to herself.

"We're going to learn how to hit people today. We're going to learn the how, the where, the how much…it's going to be very intensive. Are you ready?"

Vanessa squealed on the inside, gleeful for the opportunity. "Of course! I've been waiting for this day for months!"

"Okay, then," Markus said, "you know what to do."

Nodding, Vanessa grabbed a small ear piece and placed it in her ear. Markus walked over to his computer and jabbed buttons with his fingers, typing rapidly for a few moments. He turned and looked at Vanessa and smirked.

"You're on your own," Markus said. "Good luck."

"Never heard of it," Vanessa murmured to herself, a smirk of her own forming.

Moments later, her surroundings changed to an alleyway. Dirty stairways, rickety trashcans and metal fences constructed around her. She turned a full 360 degrees, witnessing Markus's garage turned into a run-down alley before her eyes.

People go missing and get hurt in alleys, Vanessa thought.

She was completely out of her element. She'd worked striking independently, but the feel of this was different. The last exercise she went through scared her half to death, reliving the hotel room where her parents were murdered.

"I guess we'll see what we're made of now, won't we?" Vanessa said as she slowly crept through the alleyway. As she crept, confusion settled in. "What in the bloody hell am I meant to do, here?" She asked herself out loud.

Vanessa was now faced her objective: a mountain of a man across from her, easily a half-foot taller. He was 10 feet away. He was one hell of a threat to start with.

It's where you hit, how you hit. Not how many times…not how many times…

She coached herself, repeating the words over and over in her head while she sized up her massive adversary, looking for a weakness. She had to act fast. He approached. It wouldn't be long. Someone had to make a move.

Well, the best defense is a good offense…I can't wait on him.

As her opponent drew near, Vanessa swung at him and connected. He staggered back and disappeared, an obnoxious buzzer going off for seconds before stopping. She plugged her ears with her fingers and grimaced while all the buildings, fences and foliage disappeared. The lights came on. Vanessa spun around again, confused.

Markus rose from the computer and stalked towards her.

"This is why you're not in the field yet. The man did nothing."

"He was coming at me! I didn't know what to do!" Vanessa cried. She tried to explain, but Markus would have a better outlook. It was his program.

Vanessa's excuse wasn't good enough, to him. He frowned and asked, "So, the first thing you do is swing at someone? What if he was asking for directions?" Before Vanessa could answer, Markus spoke again. "What if he was offering *you* directions? There are numerous scenarios, and next to none end in you striking an unarmed man. He wasn't a threat."

"He wasn't a threat, was he?" Vanessa argued. "How am I to know that? Big burly bloke, dark alley and twice my size…I thought I was meant to hit him! What kind of training exercise is this?"

"It was a test, and you failed," Markus said bluntly. "This isn't just about hitting people; this is about helping people, saving people. I don't know if you're ready to do something like this, since you're so easily excitable."

"Excitable?! Am I a puppy?! As if you've never made a mistake before, Markus. Oh, come now."

"I've never hit the wrong person. Not once. I wasn't roaring to hit someone or something. That may be what your problem is. You need to get some aggression out, and I have no problem with that. So…I guess that we're going to learn about scenarios later and just get to fighting."

He pushed Vanessa forcefully, planting both hands on her chest. It sent her reeling to the ground, her rear end landing first. She angrily looked up at Markus.

"Have you gone mad?!" Vanessa asked. "What do you think you're doing?!"

"If you want to fight, then we're going to fight. You need to get some of your pent-up aggression out, and if anyone's going to help you do this, it'll be me. The first thing you have to do is get up."

The news hit Vanessa like an anvil. Was she ready for this? She wanted to take her aggression out, yes, but on Markus? Didn't he have to go out tonight? Wasn't he the boss? Would this make their relationship awkward?

She slowly rose to her feet. "Well, you asked for it. Aren't you worried I might tire you out?"

"No. In fact, if you can hit me, then you can go out with me tonight."

Vanessa's eyes lit up.

"All I have to do is hit you…is that what you're saying? I can go out with you tonight if I hit you, just once?"

Markus nodded yes. "Just one time."

Without warning, Vanessa threw a punch. Markus dodged and passed her attempt, and pushed her in the back. Her body crashed to the ground again. She looked at her surroundings while she lay on her stomach. Markus's style was frustrating.

Even though it was the two of them, she felt embarrassed. P*ut it together, Vanessa. One time*, she thought.

Vanessa returned to her feet. Markus's body language stayed the same. Vanessa threw a series of punches, high and low. Markus met every attempt with a slap on the wrist. It resembled the scolding of a child. Vanessa threw more punches. Markus's slaps became more thorough. He moved his feet to evade her.

Markus's actions were frustrating in the beginning, but now, they were annoying.

"Little bugger!"

Vanessa stopped and faced the source of her pain. She rubbed her wrists. It stung more than it hurt. The sting wasn't going away. She felt like Markus could've slapped her wrists harder, but wasn't. He smiled at her. That pissed her off even more. The sting on her wrists didn't sting anymore.

"Right, then."

She threw another punch. She put everything she had into it. Markus passed Vanessa's attempt one more time. He grabbed her by the wrist on the way past, and took it downward. The force made her front flip. Her body crashed to the ground.

She was past the point of frustrated. She couldn't handle it anymore. She felt helpless and hopeless. It reduced the young woman to tears.

"It's over now."

Markus's words came with the extension of his hand to help Vanessa up. Reluctantly, she grabbed it and allowed herself to be helped to her feet. She looked at Markus.

"Do you like the way this feels?" He asked.

"Oh God, no!" She laughed as she wiped away a couple stray tears from her face.

"My goal is to make sure you never feel this way again. I didn't bring you in here to break you. I brought you in here because I believe you can do this…you just can't do it when you feel like it. Do you understand?"

"Yes, I suppose."

Even in defeat, Vanessa was stubborn. That was one of the things Markus liked about her: she may not have possessed all the skills needed at the moment, but when she did, she would be a force to be reckoned with. He didn't doubt that. He was willing to be patient and watch her grow.

Was she?

"I think I'm losing my patience, Titus," Marissa notified.

"With what?" Titus wondered. "With who?"

"It's more like 'what' than 'whom'…I think. I just miss Markus, that's all. I also miss my parents, as well. It's not just about him."

"But it *is* about him, isn't it?" Titus asked.

Marissa smiled. "Well…like, yeah. It would be good to see my mom and dad again, go back to the states…but I would really be going to visit him. Probably out to lunch or dinner a few times with the parents, go shopping with Mom, but I know Markus's schedule would magically open up if I were there."

"Aren't you all Ms. 'I-know-what-kind-of-power-I-have-over-a-man'?" Titus chuckled. Marissa joined in. She loved Titus. He was one of the funniest people she'd ever met. She truly enjoyed his company.

"Not just any man, Titus," Marissa corrected, "Markus isn't just any man. I wouldn't even try to get another man to open up his schedule, it's just…"

"It's just…"

"He's like, busy all the time, Titus. Like, I didn't know someone could be so busy. He's got to be the busiest guy in the world."

"Could you say 'busy' one more time?"

"Busy!" Marissa mocked. He dared her and she accepted. "But seriously, Titus: I don't know if the man ever sleeps. When does he have time? It's like he's always gone, always doing something."

"Well, being busy never hurt anybody," Titus opined. "Maybe he loves what he does?"

"Maybe," Marissa said reluctantly. "I mean, I love modeling. I love to travel the world, I love to have people wearing my stuff, and I love to speak at events, but just–…doing it 24 hours a day, seven days a week? Titus, doesn't that seem like overkill? I think all that work would kill someone. Am I wrong for thinking this?"

"I don't think you're wrong for thinking that," Titus said. "But…I've kind of been wanting to ask you a question since you got back."

"What's that?" Marissa questioned.

"After that stuff with Jackie Reed, are you okay with being his…friend again, I guess?" Titus couldn't figure out the right words to say. "That romance ain't dead, but it might be on life support."

"I'm not giving up, if that's what you're asking," Marissa said. "I'm concerned with how busy he is, but I always felt – and still feel – that he's always made time for me, no matter what. I don't want to mess with his routine, but I want to be a part of his routine, you know what I mean?"

"Well, like you said, Markus isn't just any man. Everything is going to be fine, girl! Every time you come around, he's making time for you, so where's the issue? Don't talk yourself out of an opportunity to be happy. Now, can we talk about some *Real Housewives*, or something?"

He smiled.

"Thank you…you know, for being you," Marissa said.

"Yeah, yeah," Titus responded.

"Yes," Jonathan Deadmarsh said. He looked in the mirror. He gave his face the once-over, turning to one side, then the other. "Do you look like Burt Reynolds?" He asked himself. He formed his thumb and forefinger in the shape of a gun and shot the mirror.

"Yes."

Jon had a fake mustache. It was part of an undercover prostitute sting. He and De La Rosa were going to make some busts tonight.

"A mustache always works." Jon spoke those words into the mirror propped up on the wall of the hotel room. "I already said Burt Reynolds…Dangle, from *Reno 911*!…Inigo Montoya…the list goes on and on. True strength is here," he pointed at his prop, "in a mustache."

"Then why don't you actually grow one?"

De La Rosa emerged from the bathroom. She was dressed in a streetwalker's uniform: something to push up her breasts, a tight skirt cut in the middle of her thighs, high heels, and neatly styled hair and make-up.

"I'm still young. There's still time," Jonathan said. "You, on the other hand, look like someone I'd pay a thousand dollars to sleep with."

Daphne feigned offense. "Is that all?"

"I'm on a cop's salary. I'd be all tapped out by then. I think a thousand dollars is a lot, for something of that nature."

"Some are pretty high-end," Daphne said. "You have to take them to dinner, take them out somewhere. I'd be the one that gives a definite happy ending, as opposed to an actual escort, where you're just paying for their time."

"You sure know a lot about this."

"What are you saying?" Daphne said quickly. "That I know a lot about it because I do this all the time?"

"No. I'm saying you know a lot about this. That's all," Jonathan responded. "You're very knowledgeable about things that pertain to your job. Imagine a world, Daphne…imagine a world where people give you a compliment without any insinuations."

"I imagine a world where it's becoming increasingly harder to work together," Daphne said.

"We don't have to! That's the beauty of it! If this is something you can't handle, or something you're not going to let me get over, then maybe it's in our best interest to go our separate ways. I don't want to be made to feel bad every time you do. Let's just get this over with."

"I agree. Let's do that," Daphne added.

Jon sat on the bed. "Have fun."

"You know, you–…you know what?" She asked. She closed her eyes and clenched her fists, bringing them up like she wanted to use them. "It's not worth it. It's not worth it, it's not worth it." She turned away from him, opened her eyes and left the hotel room, slamming the door behind her.

"Just stop liking her!" Jon pleaded with himself. "It's that simple, right?"

Jon knew Daphne was afraid of her feelings, but he was also afraid of his own. He never had a relationship to fit into his adult life. The thought of it freaked him out. Even though he was highly skilled when it came to the human response, human error was expected.

While Daphne walked the streets, she thought about how Jon adored her. She thought he would do anything for her, but she always found a way to mess it up. She had to get over it. She thought if she kept treating him like this, she'd have herself another enemy.

"Excuse me, Miss…do you need a ride somewhere?"

The voice was familiar. It was her psychiatrist, Jasper. He stopped his Mercedes near the sidewalk and rolled down the window. She walked up to the car and bent over slightly, resting her forearms on top of the car door. She stayed true to the role she played.

"This isn't a second life," Daphne assured Jasper. "Seriously, I'm working on a sting operation. We're out arresting bad guys that pay for the deed. I'm telling you that because I'm assuming you don't partake."

Jasper smiled at Daphne. "Or warning me."

Daphne smiled and shrugged lightly.

"Well, you certainly look the part, and I mean no disrespect by that." He looked her over one more time. She was certainly beautiful. She had an exotic look to her, very welcoming for a gentleman caller, the kind of paying customer Daphne would attract.

"You just look…stunning."

Daphne was caught off-guard by Jasper's compliment. She blushed. "Thank you."

"Why don't you talk to me for a bit, and when a paying customer comes around – something better, I assume – I will let you go about your business. You have to keep the streets clean, after all, detective."

"Sounds like a plan," Patrick said to Emma.

The picture of Daphne De La Rosa was still fresh on their minds as they knocked on the door.

"Place looks run down," Patrick said.

"How would they lure their prey back, dear brother?"

Emma looked at Patrick with a childish grin on her face. Patrick did the same.

"I don't know what I was thinking," he said.

The two waited for a few moments. A head poked out from behind the door.

"Um…hello? May I help you?"

Jonathan had no idea who these two were, or what they wanted. They didn't look like room service.

"Um, yes…we were looking for Carrie?" Patrick said with a concerned tone. "I was told she was staying in this room."

"Carrie? I don't know who you're talking about," Jonathan said. "No one is in this hotel room by that name. I'm sorry."

Patrick and Emma looked distraught. While Emma huffed, Patrick feigned consoling his sister. "I know…I know…it's going to be all right." Patrick hugged his sister tightly. Her head rested on his chest.

There wasn't a Carrie at Jon's precinct or personal life. There was no way to help this situation. He needed more information, and the two weren't sharing. They looked out of sorts, the way they took the crushing news.

Then, without warning, Patrick popped Jon in the nose. His mustache flew off. Jon fell to the ground. His eyes welled up quickly. He struggled to see. The young man rubbed his eyes free of tears with one hand, while creating space by rolling away from his attackers. He didn't want to be in the vicinity of another punch.

The two cackled as they stepped inside the hotel room, shutting the door behind them.

"Sometimes, it's just too easy," Patrick said.

"You know…if you finagle the last two letters in 'hello,' you can make a P," Emma said with glee.

"She's too smart for her own good," Patrick acknowledged. Emma beamed at her brother's compliment. "Anyhow, I think 'help' is more appropriate for you."

Jon was never more afraid in his life. Nothing was more terrifying than the unknown. He didn't know what these two were capable of. He looked up at the two, made mental notes about their appearance.

They had a lot of confidence in their ability, since they came in with no masks on at all. Jon thought their intention was to kill him. They were blatant about showing their faces. That scared him the most.

“Come on. Get up,” Patrick commanded. Jon scrambled to his feet, still keeping his distance between the two, wary of what would happen next. His head felt cloudy. His eyes had just recently refocused.

“Don’t be afraid,” Emma said.

“Why shouldn’t I be?” Jon asked.

“Because we haven’t done anything to you, silly,” Emma said.

“Yet,” Patrick added.

Emma approached the young detective. She had an allure about her. She was the calm between herself and her brother. She could soften up a rock with a single look. Understandably, someone as soft as wet toilet paper – such as Jon – would be no match for someone like Emma.

“Sweetheart…you’re going to have to relax,” Emma said. She stroked Jon’s jaw line. Her smell was intoxicating. “You’re a cute boy, but anxiety will age you horribly,” she smiled sweetly at him, using her other hand to run it from his shoulder down to his arm, down to his hand, where she took his in hers.

“We just want to ask you a couple questions…after that, we’ll be on our way,” Patrick guaranteed. “My sister, she’s a great judge of character. If she thinks you’re lying, there’ll be consequences. That’s fair, in our judgment. Sound good?”

“Okay, sounds good,” Jonathan replied nervously.

“Let’s start simple: what’s your name? Well, full name?” Patrick queried.

“What?” Jon said.

"It's the easiest question," Patrick said. "You look like you're in your twenties. Do you not know your name?"

"Jonathan Edward Deadmarsh," he responded.

"That's him," Emma said.

Patrick nodded. "Do you know Daphne De La Rosa?" He questioned. Emma let go of Jon's hand and took a place by her brother's side. Jon looked at the two of them before he answered.

"Yes."

"Good. Off to a good start," Patrick said. Emma smiled at Jonathan.

"Here's the toughie: do you like Daphne De La Rosa? I mean like the 'relationship' kind, just so we're clear." His eyes widened at Patrick's question. Emma widened her eyes, in an attempt to look into Jonathan's soul. She really wanted to know how he felt about the detective, if this would all be worth it.

"I would."

They asked for the truth. He didn't know who they were or why they were asking but he was told to be truthful or the consequences would be dire. He didn't deal well with dire consequences. That's not what he wanted for himself.

"I mean, I do."

"You see, that's where we're confused," Patrick said.

"Puzzled, I'd say," Emma chimed in.

"Even better. We don't know how she feels about you. Don't you want to know? It seems like it would be pretty important, right?"

"Well, y-yeah…" Jonathan stammered.

"And you know as well as anyone that people deserve to know these things. No reason to sit in the dark about it." Emma said. Her head cocked to the side with curiosity.

"I believe they do," Jon said.

Patrick smiled. "Good. I knew you'd say that. Well, we're going to help you find o–"

He threw a vicious punch at Jon's jaw, the same jaw Emma's fingertips stroked minutes ago. Jon careened into a nearby wall. The back of his head hit the hard surface, and he slid down the wall. He toppled over to the side, face-down and unconscious.

Patrick shook his hand free of the sting of bone-on-bone contact.

"Hmmm…hard jaw," Patrick said. He slowly flexed his fingers. "Well, shall we ransack the place?"

"We're not monsters, Patrick," Emma said. "I believe we've made our point. No need to accumulate motel room costs."

Patrick smiled at his sister as they both exited the hotel room. If Jon was lucky, his partner would find him. She was busy dealing with the delightfully debonair Jasper Kane.

In the distance, Jasper noticed Patrick and Emma approaching. They gave him a nonverbal cue to alert him of their completed mission as they passed up his car. He nodded and looked at Daphne.

"Well, it's been a pleasure talking to you. I'm sorry I have to cut this so short, but as you know, duty calls…for me, and for you."

Daphne enjoyed her interactions with Jasper so much that when they were over, she felt somewhat disappointed. He was someone that was easy to learn from, but hard to emulate. If he ran for President of the United States, he'd win in a landslide.

"Yeah, duty calls," Daphne said solemnly. "Well, as usual, it was good talking to you, Doc."

"Always a pleasure, Daphne," Jasper said warm heartedly. "Take care of yourself out in these streets. You never know what might happen."

"Will do," Daphne assured.

She turned on her heels and walked away from the car as it pulled away from the curb.

While she didn't lure a customer back to the motel, Daphne felt her internal clock go off. She needed to get back to the motel to check in. She didn't think she was out for very long, but 20 minutes in Jasper's company could be easily lost. She'd be back out on the street soon enough.

"I've been doing this job too long," Daphne grumbled to herself. She hated the way she had to dress during these stings. It got the job done, however. She didn't like high heels, but she would wear them, if that meant getting scum off the streets.

As she trudged up the motel stairs, she thought about how she was done doing stings for a while, after this one. Her feet and lower back already hurt – they weren't used to the punishment of walking with high heels on the pavement.

"Hey, Deadmarsh, why don't we..."

Daphne was horrified to see Jon lying on the motel room floor.

"What?" She whispered. She rushed over to him. She dropped to her knees near his head. "Deadmarsh? Are you okay?" She stroked his face lightly. She didn't want to move him. She didn't know the extent of his injuries. After several seconds, she watched him slowly come to.

"Oh man…"

That was all Jon could get out. His eyes blinked rapidly. He tried to rid the cobwebs from his head. He got knocked into next month. Jon had never been hit that hard in his life, much less, been hit. "That guy…"

"That guy? What guy?" Daphne questioned.

"I opened the door, and–"

He didn't know if he should tell Daphne the whole story. His head was fuzzy, but he still remembered the questions he was asked about her.

"Some guy hit me, like some kind of home…motel invasion."

"Are you okay to move?" Daphne asked.

Jon slowly moved his appendages, and then slowly moved the rest of his body around. He lazily nodded yes. He grunted and started to get to his feet, but Daphne grabbed him. She wrapped an arm around his waist and the other arm took his near arm to help him.

"Let's get you up. Not too fast," she directed.

She knew Jon would be put under the "Gatherer" category, if posed with the question of whether he was a Hunter or Gatherer. Some people weren't built to hunt.

Jon sat at the edge of the bed and rubbed the back of his head. He wondered if he needed to be out in the field, if this was the end result. Right now, he felt like a liability.

His hands rested on his knees. While he understood that there was nothing he could do about it, it didn't stop him from being highly upset. He fell for the looks of the girl and the brawn of the guy.

"You wouldn't get knocked out so easily," he muttered. "Your paranoia wouldn't have let them–… that guy in."

A stray tear fell off his face. He couldn't hold his emotions in anymore. He was disappointed in himself. At this point in time, he didn't know what he wanted for the future.

Daphne thought his brain was scrambled. "I think you should lie back and relax for a second." She placed one hand on his back and let him slowly lower himself onto the bed. "Do you need me to call an ambulance?"

"No, just some ice for my jaw, if there is any," he answered, sniffling a tad, using his palm to run up the bottom of his nose, like a child.

"Okay, just sit tight and I'll grab some ice for you," she said. She moved to get up. He grabbed her forearm lightly.

"Well, no…it's not that bad," Jon pledged. "Honestly. Maybe I just need some aspirin and some rest. Maybe that's what the doctor ordered?" He smiled weakly at Daphne. There wasn't a proper way to tell her he was scared out of his mind.

It made sense to her that he didn't want her to leave. She wouldn't push the issue. She looked into his eyes. He was afraid of what might happen if she took too long to get ice. It wasn't far away from their room, but Jon was clearly shaken up over this.

"Yeah…maybe you just need to rest. I'll make some phone calls," Daphne notified. Jon nodded and rested his head on one of the pillows. He stared at the ceiling. She grabbed the remote on the nightstand and flipped the TV on. She turned the volume down, just in case her partner had a headache. She didn't know if he was concussed, but she knew to keep him awake for a while.

It would be a while.

Chapter 14

After a night of conversation, Daphne gave Jon a ride back to his apartment. They showered and changed the night before, so they wouldn't have to go back out in public with their disguises.

The ride back to Jon's apartment was silent. Daphne's eyes remained on the road while Jon looked out the window. His headache from last night lingered, but he would try his best not to let that slow him. He was self-conscious over the tears he shed the night prior, but he couldn't change what happened. It was out there.

Daphne pulled up to Jon's apartment building. She finally looked his way.

"Okay, well thank you," he said. He cracked open the car door.

"Wait…"

Jon stopped from completely opening the door. He turned and looked at her.

"I– … I just wanted to tell you: you were brave last night. I'm glad you're safe. Maybe when you're comfortable doing this again…I'd like to keep working with you, is what I'm saying."

Jon was surprised by Daphne's words. "You'd like to keep working with me? But…am I not a liability?"

"Everyone's a liability, in one form or another," Daphne explained. "Your job is to make sure you're not viewed as a general liability. You may not be as strong or as fast as everyone, but I've never worked with a smarter detective," Daphne said. "Just get healthy," Daphne ordered.

Jonathan nodded minimally, rubbing one side of his temple with two fingers and opening the car door. He grabbed his bag from the floor of the passenger's side and shut the door. He didn't look back.

As he walked away, Daphne placed her hands on the steering wheel and sighed. She felt for him. She thought about how, if she was in that situation, she could've been overpowered, as well.

Bringing herself back to reality, Daphne pulled away from Jon's apartment once she saw he was safely inside.

As she pulled away, another car pulled up to another house. A black four-door sedan stopped in front of the Buchanan household.

Marissa emerged, and listened for the pop of the trunk. When the trunk door rose, she pulled the bags out and used one of her arms to shut the trunk, tapping it a few times to signify she was done. When the car pulled away, Marissa walked up the driveway. The front door opened.

"Well, if it isn't my big-time model daughter?"

Pilar Buchanan had just finished her yoga session. "I'm just trying to get my Buchanan Body back." Pilar smiled.

Marissa hoped to look that good, 25 years down the road. When the model stepped through the doorway, she dropped all her bags in the foyer. "Mommy, it's so good to see you!" Marissa proclaimed.

"I'm sure you'll get those up later," Pilar said, dropping Marissa a hint about cleanliness. "We don't have a maid around here, so that should be up by the time you go upstairs for bed."

"Can I get a hug from you before you tell me where my bags go?" Marissa laughed as they both hugged each other tight. She wondered when her mother would stop bossing her around, but it was her mother: that was her job, as long as she lived.

The two broke their embrace. "Where's Dad?" Marissa asked.

Pilar scowled. "Dad is doing business, as usual. He's been busy lately, very busy. He's been in and out, these past couple of days. One thing you know about your father, he'll be busy until he dies."

Marissa understood everything her father did. From the day she witnessed his seedy dealings, she understood. It was a family thing. She wouldn't be forthcoming with any Michael Buchanan-related information to authorities or otherwise. No matter the rumblings, Marissa knew the real Michael Buchanan. He was a good man and a faithful provider to his family who never missed an appointment.

"How's Markus?" Pilar asked.

Marissa blushed when Markus's name came up. She glowed. Just the thought of Markus made her smile. She wondered if, when he had a break at work, he thought the same thing.

"Not too loud, Mom! I want it to be a surprise that I'm here. I want to see him tonight. I know we're just friends, but...I want to show up at his house and just…surprise him, Mom. I'm very excited to see him, even if it's for a weekend."

Pilar grabbed Marissa's hand and led her to the couch. "I know. Young love. We can sit and talk for a moment and then, maybe you can join me for the second half of my work out?"

"I'm going to pass on the workout," Marissa notified. "I'm going to take a little nap. I'm tired. That flight wasn't exactly an hour. How about a long shopping day? I'll eat lunch with Markus, and then I'm all yours for several hours. We need to catch up, anyway."

"I'll take that offer," Pilar replied.

Meanwhile, Markus sat in his P4P office. He missed Marissa. He wanted to spend time with her. He thought about the things they could do and see. It was fun for his company to make money while he daydreamed for a few minutes. He snapped out of it and shot Marissa a text.

I know it's about 3 a.m. where you are. On the off chance you're up, what are you up to?

"Computer: look up Marissa Buchanan's last photo shoot for me, please."

It took less than a second for Markus's computer to throw several holograms of Marissa's last photo shoot into the air. They settled at eye level. Pictures upon pictures, the shoot was so big. All of her photo shoots were big, to him.

As Markus studied Marissa's pictures, he noticed she had a distinct look about her. It couldn't be copied. Her smile was one of a kind. Light smile lines and full lips. Her teeth were as white as the keys on a brand new piano. Her skin had never been pierced by a tattoo needle. She was also clear of scars. It wouldn't surprise people if Marissa told them she'd been wrapped in bubble wrap and delivered at her current age.

"Computer: enhance." Markus commanded. The picture of Marissa he stopped on zoomed in slowly. "Stop."

The picture showcased Marissa's irreplaceable features. She wasn't photo shopped or airbrushed. Markus remembered a company that took enormous hits for two things: naming a color for women after a massive animal, and manipulating body parts to make women look skinnier.

Markus definitely had an opinion on the subject: Marissa's body was a popular pick. Her stomach was nearly flat, her chest was full, and her hips rounded out perfectly. He also understood that not everyone shared – or preferred – the same body type.

Markus's phone buzzed.

You know, just sleeping :) What's going on?

Markus smiled at the message. He finished his thought, thinking about how models like Kate Upton got so much flak over not being the standard model, the "skinny *everything*." Upton had some meat on her, and that wasn't a problem, to Markus. He never understood how the "skinny *everything*" look was accepted to be America's general opinion on body types. Markus sent another text back to Marissa.

I was just checking up on you that's all. Nothing going on.

He went back to studying her features, but was interrupted by a quick message back from Marissa.

Okay. Maybe I'll see you soon?

Markus sent another quick text back.

Sounds good. I'm glad you're doing okay. Get some sleep! :)

Markus placed his phone face-down on his desk. He started to study Marissa's features again when he heard a knock at the door. Markus discarded the holograms, crumpling them up like paper. He threw them in a hologram trashcan. The coast was clear.

"It's open," Markus notified from his desk. The door slowly opened and from behind it, Vanessa popped her head in.

"Sir, may I come in?" Vanessa solicited.

"Yes. As I said, it's open," Markus smiled. Vanessa slid through the door and shut it behind her.

She was decked out in white: white dress pants, white heels and a white blouse. It barely showed her cleavage – Vanessa wasn't one to accentuate things like that – but it showed off her unmistakable hourglass shape. Markus also thought Vanessa had a beautiful body type as well, though he wouldn't admit it to her.

"You look great today," Markus praised. A big grin appeared on Vanessa's face.

Don't act so surprised that he noticed, she thought. "You look…quite normal," Vanessa returned. "Just another ho-hum day being Markus Doubleday, I assume?"

He laughed minimally at her humor. "Yes, just another ho-hum day. What can I do for you, Ms. Vaughn?"

Vanessa's mind ran away from her with thoughts about what he could do for her. He could show her the ins and outs of the streets. She could show him the ins and outs of kissing. She also wanted to know how he sculpted his body, but she wanted a full demonstration from him.

"Well, I would love to go out with you tonight, but I know it's not going to happen," Vanessa said, pouting inwardly.

"That's a slippery slope. Do you mean go out, as in, on a date?" Markus teased.

"Oh, you know exactly what I mean, Markus!" Vanessa laughed at her boss's quip.

"Well, you know the deal we made. You didn't hold up your end."

Vanessa stopped laughing. She didn't want her failure pointed out, even if it was far from one. She thought it was asking too much, when he wanted her to hit him.

"How many times have you been hit by anyone, really? And tell the truth," Vanessa inquired. "And not just hit; I'm talking about being kicked, stabbed, shot, thrown…all those things, not just hit with a fist."

Markus didn't think Vanessa would ever ask that, so naturally, he was surprised by it. Markus pondered for an instant, thinking back to how many times he'd been hit by anything during his years-long expedition.

"Twenty-six," Markus said.

"Twenty-six?" Vanessa said.

"Twenty-six."

"Let me get this straight: since your inception…you've only been hit 26 times?" She asked, flabbergasted by Markus's revelation. "That's unbelievable. It's crazy to me, how good you are at this."

Markus furrowed his eyebrows.

"Well, isn't that the point?" Markus grilled. "To hit people and not get hit? Ms. Vaughn, you're smart enough to know the rules of the game. I try my best not to get hit and when I do, it's imperative to recover quickly. I've been hit pretty hard before, but it can't stop me. If you look invincible to your opponent, chances are, they'll fold."

"I'm sure you're not speaking much whilst out in the field, coupled with your air of indomitability make for one tough customer," Vanessa said. "The scariest ones are the ones that don't seem fazed by anything."

"Hey, I wanted to ask you what you thought about Ivory Fox, for a name. You need one, out in the field. That one makes the most sense, to me."

"How in the blue blazes did you come up with that?" Vanessa asked harmlessly. She wanted to know Markus's thought process. Then again, she always wanted to know what Markus was thinking.

"Well, I've been thinking about it since I recruited you. I see you wearing white, all white…a suit similar to mine."

Vanessa nodded. "And a suffocating mask like yours?" She asked.

"No. Something like, old-school Catwoman, or The Lone Ranger, something similar to that. The mask looks black, in my head."

"Oh…right," Vanessa said. "I'm sorry, go on."

"My thinking behind it is this: I want these guys to know who they're dealing with – a woman that's a force to be reckoned with. The sex appeal is still there, the style, the elegance…everything that makes a woman attractive, but you'll overwhelm them with your skills. The beauty is only a perk."

"You think I'm beautiful?" Vanessa asked.

"Well…yes, there's no doubt about it."

Markus's truth-telling caused Vanessa's face to warm. She hid her teeth with her ear-to-ear smile. When a handsome man like Markus threw a compliment out, people ate it up. It came from a good place.

"One thing I want you to keep in mind: if a person wants to do bad things, there's no amount of beauty in the world to stop them," Markus advised. "So, make sure that we keep that in mind at all times. Are we clear?"

Vanessa nodded.

"We are clear. So…Ivory Fox is my new name. I love the idea. Ivory Fox," she repeated, nodding positively while she thought of the possibilities. No wonder he had such a successful company.

"Mr. No Name and Ivory Fox, ridding the streets of evil, risking their lives so that you can rest easy at night…right, that just sounds fantastic," Vanessa said proudly. "I can't wait to hit you!"

Markus narrowed his eyes, furrowing his eyebrows in confusion.

"So I can go out?" Vanessa corrected. Her words were in question form. "If I hit you, I go out, right? Is that deal still on? Or was that just a one-time thing?"

"Well, I've been thinking…"

Vanessa's eyes widened, in anticipation of what Markus was going to say. It was hard to read him when he spoke, since his voice didn't get too high or low. He never got too excited about anything, as long as Vanessa had known him.

"You should come out tonight…with me."

"Really?!" Vanessa said. The excitement in her voice was unmistakable. She'd been waiting to go out, since day one. Now was her chance! She was beyond motivated, and more than enthusiastic. "I would love to, sir! I hope you're not yanking my leg on this."

"Of course not. I wouldn't lie to you."

Vanessa nodded again. "I can't believe this. You just made my day!" She shrieked. She was doing a horrible job of keeping her emotions in check. She loved to lend a helping hand to Markus in the office during business hours, but during his *real* job, she would relish the opportunity. "I'm going to go…work, I guess, but my day has gotten infinitely better. Oh my God…"

She left Markus's office. When he heard his door close, he took a moment to smile at the situation. He remembered how full of vigor he was, in the beginning. He just wanted to make an impact on the world. Nowadays, he viewed it more as something he *had* to do, not just something he wanted to do. Right now,

Vanessa was in the "want to" phase. It also invigorated him. He'd go out tonight feeling like a new man.

There was another knock at his door.

"It's open," he called again. The door slowly opened and from behind it, Marissa's head popped out, just past the door.

"I was just thinking about you." Markus pushed away from his desk and stood up from his chair, making his way towards Marissa to greet her. "When did you get in?"

"A few hours ago," Marissa answered. "I figured since I was in the area, we could have lunch together, if you're not too busy for a friend."

Markus noticed how tight Marissa's jeans were, along with that apricot lipstick he'd fallen in love with a year or two ago. She always wore it light. It was a nice touch. So was the loose bun she enjoyed sporting atop her head. Markus liked lunch, as well as her look.

"No, I'm not too busy," Markus said.

Marissa closed the door behind her. When she turned around, Markus was less than a foot away from her.

In a low tone, she warned, "You have to stop sneaking up on me like that. I swear, you're like a terribly handsome ninja."

Marissa smiled as Markus leaned in. She cocked her head to the side, closed her eyes, and leaned in. She didn't feel anything. Marissa opened her eyes, and there Markus was, still standing in front of her. He didn't kiss her. They leaned in one more time, but this time, it felt awkward.

"If you want to, just do it," Marissa said. "I don't see what the problem is. Well, maybe I do: is it because you told Jackie Reed that we're just friends? Or is it because you haven't really been returning my calls? Maybe a mixture of both?"

"I've been legitimately busy," Markus explained, even though he knew that that wasn't the best explanation. He'd made time for her before. "I know I probably shouldn't have said that…I probably shouldn't have said anything, I guess."

"Well, I'm not going to push. I'm sure there's a good reason, on your part. I don't understand, but it's not for me to understand, I guess."

"We're doing a lot of guessing."

"Yeah. Maybe we're better off eating lunch?"

"Yeah, maybe."

Markus grabbed the bag of food from Marissa and walked to his desk. She followed him over, sitting in the middle chair of the three that sat on the other side of his desk. With the size of Markus's desk – and the fact that there was always next to nothing on it – there would be more than enough room to accommodate their lunch.

Marissa brought food from their favorite place, a hole-in-the-wall bar called Coleman's. Their food was very good; they weren't popular enough to be featured on various foodie shows but popular enough for locals to know where to get a good meal.

"Coleman's?"

"Yes. The top one is yours."

Markus grabbed the container and placed it on his side of the desk and pulled out Marissa's container. He placed hers on the side nearest her. He also pulled out all of the napkins and utensils, and placed them in the middle of the desk.

"Not bad, huh?"

He opened up his container to reveal his food: a rib-eye steak, grilled medium, with two helpings of grilled asparagus. "Looks good, all of it. Thanks, Mare. I appreciate it."

Marissa smiled. "No thanks needed."

She opened up her container, definitely the lighter of the two: an effortless crispy chicken salad with a couple sides of ranch dressing. Some fat mixed with some lean. Marissa didn't see how people dieted all the time. She wasn't big on "cheat days," either. If she wanted some ice cream, someone would lose a limb if they tried to stop her.

As Marissa drizzled ranch dressing on her salad, she started a conversation. "So anyway, I'm in town for the weekend, and I was wondering if you had plans? If you could spare a night, I was thinking we could have a slumber party? It sounds good to me, I don't know about you."

Markus smiled at the thought of spending the night with Marissa. The last night they spent together they made out a little. Before the thought could completely invade his brain, he remembered how he promised Vanessa he would go out with her on her first night out.

His neck muscles tensed slightly. He pursed his lips into a grimace.

Marissa knew exactly what that meant. She frowned. She said, "There has to be a good reason for you to pass this up, I just know it. Massage, candles, light music in the background, no paparazzi, just me and you…"

"Okay. I give up," Markus relented, laughing. "A night in sounds good, but you have to leave at a certain time. You know how I like my schedules. There are some things I needed to get done a long time ago, so I'm kind of pressed."

He tried to fight Marissa's come-ons. She was persistent. He was powerless. He had to compromise. How would he manage to have a quiet night inside? He couldn't let Vanessa go out by herself, could he?

"I'm going to change the subject. How are your mother and father?" Markus queried.

"My father and mother are well, thank you for asking," Marissa responded. "Dad is always busy working. You know how it is. You guys are kind of cut from the same cloth, so I'm sure you two would understand each other way more than I ever will."

Markus nodded while he cut his steak up. He and Michael had similar work ethics. They could work hard and for long periods of time, as if nothing else existed.

"Mom is Mom," Marissa continued as she took a bite of her food. She covered her mouth lazily and maintained the conversation. "She's busy too, but she's busy in the 'latte-drinking-yoga pants-wearing-trashy-TV-watching-housewife' kind of way," she giggled.

"Good to hear," Markus admitted.

Markus always loved Pilar, but Pilar wanted to be taken care of. Michael didn't have a problem with the "old school" way of doing things. Markus was accepting, but he preferred more independent partners. Marissa was independent. Markus couldn't keep her at home, even if he wanted to.

"How are things on your side?" Marissa took more food into her mouth.

"Things are great. Business is booming. We're trying to continue evolving and tie up loose ends, sharpen or round the rough edges," Markus winked. "We're trying to get better, every single day."

"Nice interview. I'm glad I got that gem out of you," Marissa deadpanned. "The ol' company line…thank you for your time, Mr. Doubleday."

"That's what we're doing!" Markus argued jokingly. "I just threw it all out there on the table, just for you!" He mimed laying things out on his desk. "That's all we're doing, just trying to get better."

"Okay, let me ask you this: has your net worth increased since the last I saw you?"

"God, Mare…"

Marissa smiled. "It's just a simple question, Markus. It should be easy to answer."

"Yes." Markus spoke with defeat in his tone and a roll of his eyes. He exhaled.

"Then you're doing more," Marissa said finally, taking the last bite of her salad.

Marissa hardly ever had leftovers when she ate. She hadn't reached "garbage disposal" status with her eating habits, but she got just enough to fill her up. Usually, if it was too much, she would split the entree with Titus and get an appetizer to share. As an added bonus, it saved money.

"You truly are a conversationalist. One of my favorites, actually," Markus admitted. He took the last bite of his steak, having already finished his asparagus. "I'm looking forward to seeing you tonight. Maybe tomorrow, we could have a nice, relaxing lunch?"

Marissa frowned again. "Lunch?" Marissa cried. "Are your nights *that* busy?" She asked with a hint of attitude.

He would have to amend this somehow, and the only way he could do it was with time. Not money, not jewelry, not cars, none of that. The only currency Marissa Buchanan accepted was time. If Markus's nights were busy, then he had two choices: long breakfast, long lunch or both.

"Yes they are," Markus said. He threw a few used napkins in his food container and closed it. "I'm a busy guy, Mare. You've known this for years now."

"I can accept that, but one of these nights needs to be for us. You know, for our friendship," Marissa said curtly. Markus nodded yes and disposed of the containers. He let the to-go bag rest on his desk.

"I understand that, and I hope in the future that this isn't an issue."

"Excuse me?! An issue?!" Marissa questioned. She narrowed her eyes and shook her head no fervently. "You're kidding, right? Aren't you the boss? Can't you set your own hours?" She wondered aloud. "I don't understand what you're getting at. You need to spell it out for me."

"I did set them, actually," Markus corrected. "That's my schedule. I'm a night owl, so most of my work is done at night. You know this, Mare. I don't know why you're reacting like this."

Marissa's eyes opened up even more. "I'm reacting like this because I'm in town for like, three seconds, and you're busy for two of them. That's why I'm reacting like this, just so we understand each other."

"Marissa, let's have a good night tonight," Markus dismissed, refusing to engage in the conversation Marissa was trying to have. He didn't bite when it came to fights. There was no good reason for them, so he wouldn't involve himself in them. It was hard to get under Markus's skin, or get him to raise his voice.

"I l–…have a good day, Mare."

She leaned in and kissed him. She felt hesitation from him at first, but he came around. She closed her eyes again. It felt so good. She couldn't help it. As they kissed, Markus held her hands.

"Okay-okay…"

Markus pulled away before they got carried away. Marissa feigned anger, wrinkling her eyebrows as she looked at him.

"That's not going to work every single time," he said. "Granted, it has so far…but maybe the next time, it won't work as well."

"I think I'll keep playing the odds," she said.

Markus smiled slyly. The two of them exchanged cheek kisses. She loved to kiss him. If there was a day she couldn't kiss their problems away, it would remain as the highlight of his day.

"I love you Markus, even though you're afraid of what might happen if you say it. Have a good day," Marissa told him. "I'll see you tonight."

With that, she left. She sauntered towards the door, one leg past the other, purposely changing her walk so Markus would have something to remember her by. It would definitely be etched in his mind.

He thought he'd be better than Houdini ever was, if he could pull off going out with Vanessa while hosting Marissa.

Chapter 15

Markus stood in his basement, thinking about what the night would bring. How would he be able to share the night with Marissa? It seemed so distracting. He looked at his black and blue night suit, settled in a large, metallic holder.

You have to manage your time, that's all. That's all you have to do. Don't over think it.

The basement door opened. He heard his platform start up. Moments later, Vanessa made it to the bottom of the stair. She saw him dressed in his silk pajamas and tight t-shirt. She wondered why he was dressed like that, if they were to go out.

"Are you properly psyched up?" Vanessa asked Markus. She was dressed in nothing but tights: tight t-shirt, tight spandex bottoms and running shoes. Markus was dressed more for bed than outside activity.

"Is that what you fight crime in? You have to be the most comfortable crime fighter on the planet."

Vanessa was in a joking mood. Markus hesitated for a moment. "That's funny. No, the problem is that I'm hosting Marissa for the night, but I told her she had to leave in a few hours because I had some work to do."

Vanessa laughed quietly to herself. "Of course…always a girl," she smiled. She figured something like this would come up, she just didn't know when. "Well, I don't know about you, but I believe you have to view a partnership like a relationship. I think we're getting off on the wrong foot."

"Well, I believe you should wait," Markus ordered. "I don't think you should go out by yourself, this being your first night."

"There's the suit!" Vanessa said. She completely disregarded Markus's words. She looked at the suit encased right by his. His wouldn't be coming down right away, but she was eager to get hers down. It sat so high, jumping to grab it wasn't an option.

"How do you get it down?" She asked.

"Just say the word," Markus said. "But I'm going to warn you one more time: I don't think you should be going out there by yourself. It's more dangerous than you think. I still want to look out for you, I–"

"So, what are the words?"

"Are you sure?"

"So, what are the words?" Vanessa repeated. As soon as she saw the suit, she didn't hear a word Markus said. Her sole focus was to get that suit out of its holder. Markus made his decision for the night. She was done discussing it.

Other than physically, Markus couldn't stop Vanessa. Some people learned differently than him. Where he would've waited until he was comfortable and ready, Vanessa was willing to take chances and go out there with a *clear* lack of experience.

"The words are: Peace First."

The case holding Vanessa's suit lowered. While it did, Markus spoke.

"I want you to remember why you're doing this, every time you go out," Markus replied. "It's easy to get lost in the allure of wearing a suit and doing the things we do. I want you to keep perspective. There's always a way out, Vanessa."

As much as she roared to prowl the streets, Vanessa was also being trained and mentored by the best to ever do it, a man who didn't have superpowers, but managed to stay alive. She knew he charged himself with keeping her safe, sane and sound. The least she could do was be respectful while he spoke.

"Are there any explicit instructions you have for me?" Vanessa asked.

"Yes. Always be safe," Markus said. "Always give them a warning and a way out. Some will turn themselves in, some will turn and run and some will stand and fight. I want you to be ready for all three."

"Right," Vanessa said. She grabbed her suit off the holder and headed to the bathroom a few feet away.

The bathroom in the basement was the same size as a few master bedrooms, with everything anyone could ever want in there: vinyl flooring, a neck-deep stainless steel tub, a shower with a sitting and sauna option, stainless steel dual sinks, and an individual room for the water closet.

The clicking sound of the motion-activated lights filled Vanessa's ears as she walked into the now-illuminated bathroom. Holding her garments in her hand, Vanessa looked in the mirror. In her mind, she was ready to go. In her heart, she knew she wasn't completely ready.

“I can do this,” Vanessa told her reflection. She nodded her head yes a couple times before she undressed.

Meanwhile, Markus stood in a big, empty room. He looked around at everything built. Some of the things, he could take credit for. He didn’t build everything. He was thinking figuratively. His brand was out there, had been for years. He didn’t think about retiring anytime soon, but Vanessa had quickly become an important part of what was being done in the fight against crime.

She’s part of the solution, not the problem, he thought.

Markus heard the bathroom door open. Vanessa emerged, dressed as the Ivory Fox. Wearing white, her outfit clutched her curves, just like the suit intended. She didn’t have her mask on, but she walked confidently toward Markus, who was very surprised as to just how well Vanessa’s outfit fit.

“So, what’s the news? How do I look?”

Markus didn’t say anything.

“That bad, huh?” Vanessa said.

“I’m sorry, you just look amazing. These people might fall in love with you before you have the chance to apprehend them.”

The side of Vanessa’s mouth curved a little. She wondered if he was hitting on her. He had a tendency to call it like it was, when it came to compliments. To her, he lived by the old mantra, “If you don’t have anything nice to say, don’t speak.”

“Well, thank you,” Vanessa said. “It’s quite the shame you’re going to miss my first capture.”

“Don’t count me out completely.”

Vanessa smiled and placed her mask on her face. She felt the light adhesive on the inside of her domino mask.

"What's with the glue?" Vanessa asked.

"If you get hit, your mask isn't going to go flying off. It also won't rearrange and blind you. With proper maintenance, that mask will last you for a long time.

"Can you tell me a little about this suit? Like, what does it do? Is there anything I should be aware of?" Vanessa questioned.

"Your suit is like mine: it's light, bulletproof and highly resistant to attacks. It'll take a lot to hurt you when you're in it. You have a belt like mine. On your belt, you have little vials that, when smashed, cause disorientation and grogginess. They're made for if things get too dicey. Are you with me so far?" Markus asked.

Vanessa nodded yes.

"You have boots similar to mine. They look heavy, but as you've probably felt by now, they're not."

"They feel like a pair of tennis shoes."

"Right. Light like tennis shoes, but provide all the support of a boot. Look on your side."

Vanessa's eyes followed Markus's finger to her hip.

"Hmmm…a Taser?" Vanessa questioned. "I'm going to be rearranging someone's muscular functions?"

"Yes, just make sure you know how to use it," Markus warned. "If you don't know how, don't. That's a general rule. You want to look like you know what you're doing, not someone who is wondering what a certain button does while they're getting punched in the face. Does that make sense?"

"Of course it does."

"Now, look over here."

Vanessa peered down again. She followed Markus's finger to the other side of her hip. It looked like a small pipe.

"And what's this?" Vanessa asked skeptically, one of her eyebrows rising.

"It's a bo," Markus answered.

Taken aback, Vanessa asked, "What am I supposed to do with this?" She preferred the Taser over this bo, as Markus called it. "Maybe I can play the part of the third Super Mario Brother?"

"Just take it off your belt." Vanessa heard the impatience in Markus's tone. She obliged, taking the bo off the latch.

"Whoop-de-do," she said smartly. She twirled it in between her fingers and whistled. Not only was this thing light but it was thin. "How am I to protect myself with this thing? Markus, if it's all the same to you, I don't think I even need th–"

The bo quickly shot out from both sides. She yelled and dropped it. The acoustics in the basement were tested; the sound of the bo hitting the ground filled the area. This pipe-like weapon turned into an actual staff. It scared her half to death. She looked clumsy as ever. She picked it up and rested one end on the ground, holding onto the other end at the very top. She guessed the staff was nearly six feet tall.

"Quite embarrassing, really…I believe mine's bigger than yours."

Vanessa's comment made Markus shake his head. He couldn't help but be amused by her. She had a sense of humor that was on-time, most of the time. For someone who experienced so much unexpected tragedy, she still managed a joke or two. It motivated Markus. It took him a long time before he could laugh again.

"If you want to latch it back on your belt, bump it on the ground," he explained. "You activate it by turning it; just try not to drop it next time."

Vanessa mouthed "ha-ha" to him as he continued.

"You asked what you were supposed to do with your Bo," Markus said. "Stop threats. It's made out of the same stuff my baton is made out of. It's light, but doesn't feel that way when you hit someone."

Twirl to activate. Bump it on the ground to holster it again. Right. "Okay, will that be all?" Vanessa said quickly. She bumped the Bo, and it shrunk back to its normal size. Vanessa holstered it.

The two looked at each other. A moment of silence came, where Markus understood that she had to learn her craft. On the other end, Vanessa understood that, while she was afraid, she knew she could do it. She had to.

"Your vehicle is over there."

Markus pointed over to a motorcycle, a black and white Suzuki Hayabusa. He didn't know if Vanessa knew the bike could reach 200 miles per hour, but he hoped she wouldn't have to find out. A sticky situation on the first night was not his goal.

"Voice-activated, like my car. Just tell it what you want it to do, and stay balanced. If there are any bugs you encounter, just tell me."

"Good, then," Vanessa said. "Will that be all?"

"That will be all, Ms. Vaughn."

Markus broke eye contact with her, looking away momentarily.

"I should go…Marissa will be here soon, and–"

"I know. All's fine," Vanessa reminded, shaking her head yes to his words. She walked away. As she headed towards her bike, Markus walked towards the door leading up to the main level of his house. He stopped.

"Vanessa?"

Vanessa sighed and turned around. "What is it?"

"Be careful."

"Right."

She opened her leg, mounted the bike and settled in on the seat. She bounced a few times. She watched Markus place his hand on the sensor, the door opening. He walked through without turning back. Vanessa knew Markus felt bad about not being able to accompany her on her first night out, but she was stubborn. She wanted to go.

Crime wouldn't wait, would it?

"On?" Vanessa said. She skeptically raised an eyebrow at the small, blank screen on her bike.

The roar and rumble of the bike gave it life. She was surprised by the sound as she grabbed one of the handlebars and revved the engine.

"Wow! Wait, how do I get out of here?" She yelled over the sound of the bike.

Markus missed something. That never happens. Maybe a garage door opener is what I'm looking for?

Vanessa peeled out in her parking spot, and sped towards the entryway. As she sped past on her bike, lights on either side of the wall lit up, creating a pathway for her to follow. She saw an opening just ahead. With an excited grin, she increased the speed.

This was happening.

Her heart beat faster. Her hands perspired inside her gloves. By the time she got to the mouth of the entryway, it was completely open. She hit the main street at well past 100 miles per hour, turning the corner tight and heading out into the city.

Markus got a look out the window just as Vanessa turned the corner.

She's going pretty fast. Markus quickly shoved those thoughts from his brain. Vanessa was well-trained, more trained than he was on his first day. Minutes later, he watched Marissa's car pull up to his house.

"It's worth it. It's worth it. Mind on Marissa, not the other stuff."

Markus coached himself up as he relaxed and waited at the door. When he heard a knock, he opened the door quickly. It scared her, if the look on her face was any indication.

"Wow! Were you right by the door?! You had to be right by the door!" Marissa said breathlessly. Markus made her heart skip a few beats, in a bad way.

"I was just passing by the door," Markus answered. He gave Marissa the once-over. Her hair looked the same as before, but her clothes were different. Tight jeans and a tight t-shirt. She also had a pretty good-sized bag with her.

"What's in the bag?"

"It's an overnight bag, silly!" Marissa walked through the door. She brushed him on purpose, just to feel his hard body against hers. He knew what she was doing. It was unspoken between them. Flirting wasn't dead. "We might stay up late, I might get tired…not everyone is a night owl like you."

Markus said he would be busy later on, but it didn't seem to faze Marissa. She was bound and determined to stay at his house. She wouldn't tell him this, but sometimes, just being in the same room with someone – even if they were busy – was enough.

On the other hand, Markus was a very detail and schedule-oriented person, so something like this could throw him off. He refused to look at this situation as a bad one. He wanted to be around Marissa. Even the way her perfume hit his nostrils, he could sleep soundly.

Markus led Marissa toward the kitchen. She purposely stayed a step or two behind him, just so she could check him out from behind. Even when he wore pajamas, she could see the curvature of his rear. He usually wore a suit jacket, but there was nowhere to hide. The clothes he was wearing were virtually transparent.

What a fine piece of man!

The two finally happened on his kitchen, where Marissa found herself in love, over and over. One thing Marissa loved about Markus's house was the kitchen. Not the house-sized rooms, not the bathrooms that resembled guest houses, not the basement…the kitchen. Everything she could ever want was there. Every top-of-the-line appliance was featured.

It was a chef's dream.

She knew Markus didn't cook much. He had a chef come in every few days and make sure his food was cooked and stocked. He only needed to reheat it. This was further proof there weren't enough hours in his day.

If we ever get together-together, we need to have a talk about getting rid of this cook. I don't want – or need – anyone else in here.

"Coconut water?" Markus asked Marissa.

Before Markus could completely open his frig, Marissa pushed it shut. He looked at her. She looked at him. Devious smiles came from both of them. The intensity for each other in their eyes showed like nothing before. They loved each other, but the lust they shared was obvious and intentional.

As to be expected.

Their bodies blasted against each other as their lips embraced. In a big and empty house, something like kissing and heavy breathing was easily heard. Garments of clothing were lost on their bodies, now found on the floor.

"This is not a booty call."

Marissa kissed Markus sweetly. She looked to the sky. He laid his lips on her neck, destroying all her senses. His hands planted firmly on her sides, right above her hips. He continued to map something out on her skin with his lips and tongue. She laughed delightfully.

"Absolutely not," Markus said between kisses. "You mean more to me than that."

And here, Markus thought they'd have a late dinner. It was now a multi-course dessert. Marissa had just a bra and a pair of unbuttoned jeans on. Markus sported his pajama bottoms.

Markus kissed on her bare skin. His tongue ran the length of her bra strap on one side, then the other. Her hand found the back of his head and massaged it. She loved how soft his short hair was.

"I don't want to do this here…I love your kitchen too much to dirty it up. Let's go upstairs."

Marissa's words were music to Markus's ears. He stopped kissing her and looked deeply into her eyes; she could've sworn he saw into her soul. She was helpless. He'd never looked at her like that before. The emotion of the setting made her eyes well up, the sensual nature of the moment keeping her from crying. She would reflect on this later.

Markus slowly led Marissa up the stairs. He had no reason to rush; it was something both of them had been waiting for. Just the anticipation was enough to push her past excitement. She felt slightly light-headed; she could pass out, and still be happy.

She'd hold on, though.

Speaking of holding on, Vanessa sped through the streets on her bike, smoothly weaving in and out of traffic.

This doesn't seem so bad. I quite enjoy being a smidgen above the law, she thought.

She was riding through the street so fast, she almost missed something. Angling around, the screech of her tires filled the air as she made it back to a wide and dimly-lit alleyway. She looked at the screen on her bike.

"Off?"

The bike powered off. Vanessa kicked her leg back high and exited off the bike. She brought the kickstand down and let the bike rest at an angle.

Vanessa said, "This doesn't look sketchy in the least." She heard a loud bang in the alleyway. She took her time investigating the noise; she wouldn't run headlong into it, whatever it was. It could be a few cats at odds, for all she knew. She proceeded with caution.

She wondered what Markus would do in this situation. Would he even waste time in this alleyway?

Vanessa crept closer and closer to the sound's origin. Her eyes scanned up, down and around for anything out of the ordinary. She gulped down the saliva in her mouth. Her hands formed in front of her as if she was about to chop something. She felt very awkward.

"This is a *lot* scarier than I thought it would be," Vanessa said in a faint whisper.

She heard someone say, "Do you have the stuff?"

She heard another voice say, "It's all right here."

Vanessa couldn't make out the faces. By the time she happened upon the two gentlemen, they hadn't noticed her presence yet. Vanessa loudly cleared her throat. The two casually-dressed men were jolted by the sound. They faced her.

Vanessa placed her hand in the middle of her chest as if she'd just finished coughing.

In her new American accent, she said, "Excuse me…I didn't mean to interrupt you two, it's just that it sounds like shady dealings."

"And what if it is?" One of them asked her.

They both appeared surprised at Vanessa's get-up. They also appeared unintimidated. They didn't try to run. That was a bad sign, more or less. Markus warned her that if they didn't try to run, they would stand and fight.

With that in the back of her mind, she said, "Well, if you are, then I'd have to stop you."

"You mean *try*?" The other man asked. "You're not going to stop us, little girl. You can't."

"I'm almost six-foot tall, and you call me little. That's rich."

Those words got under Vanessa's skin. She wasn't going to *try* to do anything. She was going to do it, plain and simple. *When there are two, keep them separated. Run to create space, if need be*, she remembered.

"Six-foot tall or not, it ain't just us you have to worry about."

Two more men emerged from the shadows. She wasn't prepared for four. She saw a lot of running in her near-future. She was up for it, but the thought of testing herself tugged at her. She was eager to see how she measured up.

Vanessa feigned bewilderment. "My, has it gotten hot in the kitchen! Four? That's a little overwhelming, if you ask me."

"Are you afraid you can't handle all of us?" One of the men asked.

Vanessa formed a smile. "Actually, no. I'm afraid all of you can't handle me. I have a feeling you're going to have a story you won't be in a rush to tell, getting beaten up by a girl, and all."

"You're not going to have a story to tell at all," one of the men said. "You're going to be dead."

They approached. Vanessa readied herself. This wasn't a necessity, but she felt the need to have something to grade.

"I got her."

One of them reeked of confidence. He took quick steps toward her. The other three stayed back. Vanessa studied his movements. He led with a right jab. She dodged. He came around and swung with his left. Vanessa dodged again.

Then, Vanessa noticed his eyes widen and teeth gnash. She mocked his look. The other three couldn't see what the culprit was until their associate dropped to the ground.

A Taser.

She pushed the Taser's button twice to show them what she did. The man she electrocuted flinched a few times while he lay on the ground. The faint smell of urine was recognized when she inhaled. The Taser was more powerful than she ever imagined.

"Is that all you got?" One of the remaining men said.

"What else do I need?" Vanessa asked them.

"More power," the man said.

The three rushed Vanessa. Six arms flew at her from different angles.

Dodge what I can. Strike to stop the threat. Nothing lethal.

She blocked what she could. Some punches came in clean. She threw a front kick, knocked one of her attackers backward. She bought herself a few moments. Both of the remaining men simultaneously threw a punch. Vanessa ducked. The two hit each other and staggered back.

All four men passably recovered. They looked at her. She looked at them.

She darted through the small crowd. She heard commotion behind her, the pitter-patter of footsteps gaining on her. She jumped and grabbed onto a stair on the side of an apartment building.

One of the men grabbed one of her feet. He grunted while he tried to pull her down. She held on tight. She looked down at him. She brought her foot down hard, on his face. She felt him slipping. She raised her foot and fiercely came down on his face again. He fell and smacked the pavement. She climbed faster.

She gained her footing at the top of the building. She peered down at her enemies for a moment before she sprinted away.

"We know where she's going. We'll catch her."

Back on Markus's side of town, it was late. Marissa was fast asleep; Markus was wide awake. He looked at the ceiling.

Is this too much for her? Is it just enough? Is she using blunt force? Lethal force?

Markus quietly slid out of bed and walked to his bedroom door. Three of his senses were engaged: he tasted Marissa's kiss on his lips, he smelled their lovemaking, and he heard his heart beat at a breakneck pace.

He shut the door as softly as possible. The minute it shut, he became very rigid and single-minded. His walk and eyesight changed; the intensity he possessed with Marissa was replaced with a different intensity.

When he got to the bottom of the stairs, he heard a voice.

"What are you doing?"

Markus turned around.

"I'm just going to work in the basement for a bit," Markus told her. "I'll be back up soon."

Sleepily, Marissa said, "Okay." She slowly headed back to the bedroom.

She agreed, too tired to argue about Markus coming back to sleep. She understood: they had fun when they spent time together, but she knew he was a workaholic. His work ethic wouldn't magically go away, even if the one he loved dearly was in town. It bothered her, but not enough to make a conversation of it.

When he heard the upstairs door close, Markus finished his walk, landing at the basement entrance. Markus took a few moments to appreciate the green light that shined in the dark, while he listened to the door unlock and pop open. He turned around again, finding no sign of sounds or people. He shut the door behind him.

Once in his garage, he rode the platform down to the bottom of the basement. He looked around. It was dark.

"We're a go."

The basement lit up. His suit pushed out of the wall and lowered. His cars rose from beneath the ground. He walked over to his suit, pulled it out of the case, and got dressed.

While working into his night suit He started to work his body into his night suit.

"Computer: can I get a GPS on Vanessa Vaughn's whereabouts?"

The computer threw a hologram up, a few feet above Markus's head. He glimpsed at the location while he slid his arms into the sleeves of his suit. Judging by the location, Markus knew it wasn't anywhere she wanted to be. The white dot indicated she was moving fast. Either she was chasing something, or something was chasing her.

That worried him.

"On," he said to the inside of his wrist. His car started. He zipped up his suit and stalked towards his car, mask in-hand. He looked in the mirror that sat at the top-center of his windshield. His eyes shone in the mirror.

"I'm doing the right thing. It's Vanessa."

He slid his mask on, feeling it lock in place. There was no turning back now.

Chapter 16

Vanessa found herself atop the apartment building. She breathed in and blew the air out, hands on her hips. She walked around in a circle. While the men made their way to the top, she would use that time to devise a game plan. The first one didn't work so well.

Divide and conquer…divide and conquer…divide and conquer…

A nearby door was forced open. The four men filed through. They didn't waste time spreading out and surrounding her when they saw her. She turned every which way slowly, unsure of where the threat would come from first.

"We're done playing games," one of the men said.

"And so am I," Vanessa responded.

With a defiantly determined look, Vanessa stood pat. The more she ran, the more they would chase her. She took her abbreviated bo off her belt and twirled it. The two sides shot out. She tightened her grip.

Vanessa stared at the man in front of her. She felt the heat of the two on either side of her, while she listened for the man behind her. She stood in an attack stance. She wouldn't let them dictate her actions.

She heard footsteps behind her. With an ounce of quick-thinking, Vanessa jammed her bo backward. He dropped to his knees. She jammed the bo behind her again, cracked him square in the forehead. He collapsed. She turned back towards her attackers.

Vanessa told them, "I told you I was done playing games. I want to give you a warning, if you'll let me: walk away from this whilst you still can. I will give you time to ask your friend, the one that's lying on the ground, possibly brain damaged." She smirked.

The hurt one grabbed her boot. While she tended to him, the other three rushed. She popped the prone man in the ribs with her staff. She turned to face the other three. One hard push sent her flying out of the prone man's grasp. Her staff hit the ground.

If not for the suit she wore, the push would've been much worse. It provided a thin level of padding. It protected her, but only so much. Not long after she landed on the concrete, the three that remained stood over her.

"I told you we were done playing games," the man said.

They kicked Vanessa repeatedly. They didn't spare any limbs. With the force absorbed, she was sure they were trying to break bones. They wanted to send a message. She stood in their way. They would destroy her.

Vanessa balled up in the fetal position. *This was a bad idea. This wasn't the way it was supposed to go.*

After a few seconds, all the action stopped. Vanessa stretched out, her breathing heavy. She was nervous and hurt…she didn't plan adequately for this situation. A part of her wished she would've listened to Markus.

Vanessa heard her staff being picked up in the near distance.

"Damn it." She breathlessly pushed the words out.

"Just a little overhead action." He raised Vanessa's staff up high. Vanessa closed her eyes.

She heard a high-pitched sound that swallowed the air around it. She opened her eyes. She saw Markus, in his black and blue night suit. He was on a single knee, with his baton raised to block Vanessa's staff. She had to be dreaming.

The staff thief was amazed. The other two were amazed as well, while the fourth man stirred and struggled to his feet.

Markus stood up, easily overpowered him. His attacker's downward motion rose. A quick kick to the staff thief's chest sent him backward. Markus caught the staff from the air and tossed it back to Vanessa. She cleanly caught it. She scrambled to her feet and dusted herself off.

Now, it was fairer. No more quips or cute jokes. It was time to stop the threat.

Markus moved to the left. Vanessa moved to the right. He slowly swung his baton at one of the men on purpose. The man ducked. Markus's knee sprung up and met his face. The connection made a loud slapping sound. He fell to his back, out cold.

Markus latched his baton at his side. He wasted no time with the man in front of him, peppering his adversary's mouth and cheeks with rapid, urgent jabs. The threat resorted to covering up, falling into the fetal position to avoid more damage.

Vanessa dazed her opponent with a spin-kick. She smacked his chin with one swing of her staff. He staggered back, his eyes to the sky. Vanessa spun herself and her staff toward him. She latched on hard to one end and swung it as hard as she could. The other end of the staff struck across his face. He spun in the air and hit the ground, moaning.

Vanessa stood over the man, placing her staff right above his throat. "Done playing games, are you?"

Vanessa wanted to show him the same courtesy he showed her. He had no regard for her life. She just wanted to return the favor.

"All I need to do is drop this staff and put my weight behind it. It'll jar your throat, absolutely," she notified. "I can watch you choke to death. Sounds about fair, right?" She asked him.

She felt a calming presence behind her. She looked down and saw a gloved hand on her staff. She needed to keep the peace between control and insanity. It wouldn't take much to go to the other side.

He tugged lightly at the staff. Vanessa felt herself being backed up with his pull. She was a few feet away from the man now, just enough space for him to recover without the fear of more violence.

Vanessa bumped her staff on the ground, made it retract. The young heroine latched it back onto her belt. She positioned herself to face all four men while they helped themselves – and each other – up.

"I just want you to know, this isn't over. The Ivory Fox is here to clean up this city, as well. Make sure everybody knows that from now on…"

She pointed at Markus.

"He's not alone."

The group nodded, as a whole. The two heroes walked toward the entry door to the stairwell. They walked past the men and were halfway to the door when they saw it forcefully kicked open. Vanessa jumped.

"Police!"

Markus and Vanessa found themselves literally staring down the barrel of a gun. The two stopped, placing their hands in the air in surrender. They'd been caught. The two authority figures approached. Markus spoke to her as quietly as he could.

"On three, run. Push the button on your right wrist, right before you jump off this building."

"Are you crazy?!" Vanessa blurted out, louder than expected.

"Keep your hands up!" The two figures commanded loudly, as they cautiously continued their approach.

"One…"

The officers crept closer.

"Two…"

The officers just stepped into the light.

"Three."

Markus stepped in front of Vanessa and turned his back to the two gun-toters. She darted away, fast and hard. The two guns opened fire while she fled.

Without hesitation, she jumped off the building. In mid-air, she pushed the button on her right wrist. She felt herself being pulled toward the wall.

She used the side of her face to brace her landing.

Vanessa let out a solid groan, but gave herself no time to slow down while she climbed down. When she got to the bottom, she used a little muscle to pull herself away from the wall. She had to get out of there.

But wait…

She heard a litter of gunshots while she ran, while she escaped, untouched. She wondered if Markus was okay. He told her to run, and she did. She wondered if there was anything she could do to help him.

Seconds after Vanessa landed, the sound of something slamming against a dumpster made her yelp out. She looked up. There he was, standing on top of the metal container. He coolly hopped off the trash receptacle.

"Find your bike and meet me back at the house. It's easier to use the transmitter on your left wrist. Tell it to find you."

Vanessa nodded and ran out of the alleyway, pulling her left wrist to her mouth.

"Find me!"

She heard her bike rev up in the distance. She wouldn't just stand in one place and be caught. She just wanted to feel safe for two damned seconds. As she turned the corner, Vanessa almost plowed into her bike. It stopped, just short. She quickly hopped on it and peeled off.

As Markus watched Vanessa leave the alleyway, he looked up to see the two figures looking down on him. When they disappeared from his sight, he figured to disappear from sight, period. Calmly, he spoke into his left wrist.

"Find me."

Moments later, his car appeared. He walked briskly to it. He got in and hit the gas. The car's tires rolled before he exited the scene.

Back at the top of the building, Daphne De La Rosa yelled, "Damn it!"

She smacked the concrete slab in front of her. Jonathan Deadmarsh was still somewhat frozen from the whole experience. Star struck, even. He wasn't big on shooting guns, so Daphne's actions caught him by surprise. The fact he was mere feet away from a legend in crime fighting was enough to make any fanboy pass out.

When Daphne and Jon turned around, a few officers arrived to arrest the four men. The seized had illegal paraphernalia on them. The cops were looking for three out of the four, to begin with. They'd been smoked out by the two vigilantes.

While the troublemakers were being escorted down the stairwell, Jon turned to Daphne and ecstatically said, "Did you see that?! I can't believe we actually saw him, that up close and personal! And he had a sidekick with him! I can't believe this! What are the criteria for a real-life sidekick?!" He wondered aloud.

"Will you stop?!"

Daphne practically yelled at him. Her voice was raised but not to the maximum. There was a time and place for that. "Are you a psycho, or something?! These people are breaking the law, and all you want to do is see how their gadgets work?!"

"Do your job, Deadmarsh. Just…do your job," she said exhaustedly as she walked away from him.

"Daphne, wait!" He yelled.

She stopped, but it was apparent she had an attitude accompanying her. She turned and faced him.

"It doesn't intrigue you at all that you shot this man multiple times and he just jumped off a building, landed on his feet, and ran?" Jon asked. "It doesn't make you wonder, even a little bit, why it seemed so easy?"

"You know what I wonder?" Daphne asked Jon as she approached him again, fists clenched. She wanted to hit him so bad. He was just being himself. There wasn't a change in his behavior, and it irritated Daphne to no end. "I wonder why the hell I haven't had you arrested yet."

Jon's eyebrows rose. "Me, arrested?"

"Uh huh…you…arrested."

Daphne's inconsistent behavior toward him was no longer a surprise. He should've given it more thought; he would've been able to sniff Daphne's words out before she even had a chance to put them out in the atmosphere.

They now stood face to face. Jon noticed Daphne's aggressive stance, but this time, he wasn't backing down. He had no reason to.

"You couldn't have me arrested!" Jon exclaimed. "What exactly did I do? Can you even tell me what I did?!"

Daphne was silent.

"*I* don't even know what I did!" He added, defiantly looking Daphne in her eyes.

Daphne noticed the remaining officers cringe at the discomforting conversation before they left the scene. A verbal lashing from Jon was not on the short list of things Daphne was afraid of. She would let him continue. Obviously, he had some things on his mind.

"If there's anything else, I'd love to hear it," Daphne goaded.

For someone so even-keeled, Jon wasn't in the mood to deal with her attitude. He had no business talking to his superior like he was, but she couldn't just throw threats out any time she became angry.

"Look, Daphne: I may not be the best cop in the world. I may not be the toughest, or the 'so-by-the-book-it's-annoying' type. You know what, though? I do my job to the best of my ability. Even the guys up there at the precinct, the ones that call me names, they can't deny that I'm good at my job. *You* know I'm good at my job."

Daphne's expression never wavered. He'd get nothing but indifference from her features. On the inside, however, she was proud of him for standing up for himself.

"I don't know why you give me so much flak over having a superhero hard-on, as you call it," he continued. "This is who I am. I'm not the normal guy who sits and watches sports, has a beer and talks about fixing something on their car or house…I'm the guy that, when I go home, I pop open a comic book and have a candy bar. Why is that so bad to you?"

Everything at his job was separated. They couldn't be colleagues. There had to be a clear hierarchy. He didn't fit in with the mentality of the majority. For Jon, it was like high school: he couldn't be a regular student. He had to be labeled something.

"Do you want me to tell you why that's so bad? Because it's reckless," Daphne said, refusing to wait for him to answer. She had no regard for what her counterpart thought. "Can we stop there, or do you need more information?"

As Jon started to speak, Daphne brought a single finger up. She pointed at him.

"Shut up. It'll be just another excuse out of your mouth, and at this point, I can't handle another." She practically spat the words at him. "Regardless of my feelings for you, there *is* a hierarchy. There are people like me," Daphne said as she pointed to herself, "people that can do their job without letting their hobbies get in the way."

She pointed at him. He looked down at her finger when she pointed at him, then looked back up at her. His eyes told her he was on the verge of breaking. He couldn't let himself do it in front of her again.

"Then, there are people like you, dreamers…the ones that don't exactly set the world on fire."

She twirled her finger in the air. Her words were like a blur.

"Just so we're clear, I'm a doer. To me, it's just another coward in a mask. I don't care what side you say they're on…they're on the wrong side of the law, with their antics. I won't stand for it! You shouldn't, either!" She scolded, angrily pointing back at Jon. "Get your head out of your ass, before you get us killed!"

A few moments of silence.

"You know what? Maybe you're not cut out for this, Deadmarsh."

Daphne quickly walked away from Jon. She slammed the stairwell door shut behind her. She didn't know why she was so angry with him, why she reacted so harshly. His "comic book" shtick wasn't that bad.

Jon contemplated his thoughts on the rooftop. He wanted to give Daphne and the rest of his colleagues enough time to clear out. He didn't want to face them at the moment, not when he felt so hurt and disrespected…he didn't feel a part of the one thing he felt a part of.

"Stop…Stop feeling this way," he stuttered. "Just do your job and stop being so sensitive. They're just words."

As he stood on the rooftop, a pair of eyes was on him.

Meanwhile, Vanessa sped toward Markus's house. She was mad at herself for the way she handled everything. Vanessa heard the hum of Markus's car, about 50 yards behind her. As she followed the path to Markus's garage, she continuously replayed everything in her head.

My transitions are much too slow. I stayed too long in one place. I know Markus will ask me about all this. Just be ready.

The ground quietly rumbled open, providing the space for Vanessa to enter. When she did, she punched it down the corridor, which resembled a roller coaster: first up, then down. She powered down to her parking space. The bike ran for a moment before she turned it off. She dismounted the bike and watched as Markus smoothly pulled into his parking space.

Markus rested his head. This was all real. He was responsible for another human being. Her preparation – or lack, thereof – fell solely on him. He felt the sting of failed bullets on his body. They were powerful enough to penetrate, but not so powerful that they pierced his skin. It didn't stop the force of the bullets from hurting, however. He'd rather be ailing than dead.

He watched Vanessa stalk to the bathroom. She slammed it shut behind her.

In the bathroom, Vanessa peeled her mask off and laid it on the counter. She stared in the mirror. She was battered. Negativity flowed through her veins. How would she explain this to people? She traced her fingers over one side of her jaw line and winced. Bruising had formed on her features.

She slowly unzipped her suit and pulled one of her shoulders out of it. She used her other hand to help her get the other shoulder out. Her suit waited at her waistline, the rest snugly on the bottom half of her body.

She finagled a couple fingers under the strap of her sports bra, feeling for pain on her shoulder. Not too bad, she thought. She knew for sure that she'd been stomped in that area a handful of times. She viewed her skin, peering back and forth between her body and the mirror. It could have definitely been worse.

She heard a light knock at the door.

"It's open," she prompted. "It's your house, anyway," she muttered flippantly. She turned her head slightly to watch Markus walk into the bathroom, seemingly unfazed by Vanessa's dress.

It took less than a second for a woman's body to register with Markus. He didn't need to stare. Staring was not what the doctor ordered. He'd treat her appropriately, like a partner. This wasn't a date, this was survival.

"Bath: neck-deep warm water for a five-foot-ten-inch woman," Markus spoke to his bathtub. The gadgets Markus had continued to impress Vanessa, but she was too into her own feelings to acknowledge it. The water ran rapidly, with the speed of a waterfall. It wouldn't take long to fill up. "Bath: mix the formula for R-3," he commanded.

"What exactly is R-3?" Vanessa questioned.

"R-3 stands for Rest, Recovery and Rehabilitation," Markus answered.

"Not Relaxation?"

"I think the relaxation is implied." Vanessa's wry remark was matched by Markus's dry reply. She couldn't be bothered to turn her neck. It was sore. "And the water stays at the temperature asked, just so you know. I want to give you a pointer or two. I don't want to dwell on anything."

"I'm a blank canvas. Go ahead."

They both looked in the mirror at each other, Markus positioned behind her, to the left.

"Don't dwell on tonight. It's over with. If you think about all the things you should've or could've done or said, it's going to eat you alive. You made the best possible decision for that time. Deal with it and move forward."

"So you don't want to talk about tonight?"

"No. I want you to take your clothes off."

Vanessa sported a surprised look on her face until she realized that the water was off and the bath was filled. She peered into the mirror again. Markus had his eyes closed. He was such a gentleman, she thought.

"Right. Okay."

Vanessa bent over and unzipped both her boots at the same time. She ran over her curves as she peeled the rest of the suit down, past her quadriceps and hamstrings, past her knees and calves, until she was able to step out, completely. She stood in front of the mirror, wearing her black spandex sports bra/tanga combo.

She took in Markus's mask-less features. Every time she looked at him, she studied him. He was in top physical condition. He took what he did at night seriously. He showed concern over her well-being. He'd never show it – he didn't show much of anything, in her experience. She'd been around him long enough to have a hunch.

Silently, Vanessa pulled her sports bra off and tossed it to the floor. She kept her underwear on, feeling it wasn't necessary to de-brief, for lack of a better term. She then scaled the lone step that helped her submerge into the bathtub. She stood in the water for a moment before she lowered herself in. She instantly felt soothed.

"This is a godsend…my God…this is from God," she whispered.

Vanessa cocked her head back and rested it on the edge of the bathtub. True to form, the bathwater covered her, neck-deep. She looked at the ceiling momentarily and then closed her eyes, exhaling loudly while the mixture performed the task.

"Do you come down here a lot?" She asked, exhaling again. She couldn't get enough of this feeling. "You have to come down here just for Yuks, right?"

"I only use it when I need it," Markus said, opening his eyes slowly. He assumed Vanessa was completely in. Once he realized it was safe, he opened his eyes. He turned and sat on the step that led to aquatic bliss.

"I don't really view it as a mode of relaxation."

"And why would that be?" Vanessa asked.

"Because it means I didn't do something right," Markus said. Vanessa opened her eyes. They found their way to the ceiling again. "I view it more like a penalty box; I went about a plan the wrong way, if I'm in there."

Vanessa couldn't take it. She placed both her forearms on the top edges of the bathtub and pushed herself up. Markus placed his hand on her shoulder, pushing her back down. The water jumped up and hit her in the face. She tried to stand up again, and Markus did the same, pushing her back down more forcefully.

"Sit…down," Markus demanded, with a mix of softness and forcefulness in his tone.

Vanessa calmed a tad. Most of it derived from Markus's peaceful words. He didn't want any trouble. He wanted to take care of her. Being as young as she was, she had a rebellious streak in her. This could be quelled by the words of someone who genuinely thought of her best interests, even in dire times.

"I suggest that, in the future, you follow my lead," Markus said.

"Markus…"

"In the future, follow my lead," Markus repeated. Vanessa kept her eyes closed. "When you're done with your training completely, if you pay full attention and apply it, this won't happen again. This tub isn't a goal, it's a sentence."

"Yes, sir," Vanessa responded simply. She nodded her head yes at Markus's words and let herself get lost in the warm water blend. If she gave it anymore thought, she'd realize that Markus was right. Vanessa being Vanessa, she didn't want to admit that, not yet.

Admittance had its own price, on the other side of town.

Daphne slept soundly in her bed. She'd been off for a few hours, already. Dealing with Deadmarsh was exhausting, but she felt she had to. He didn't seem very self-aware. Daphne made him more aware of his surroundings, whether he asked for it, or not. She wanted to help him, and if he thought negatively about her tactics, she didn't care.

Daphne felt an itch on her nose, slowly bringing her out of her slumber. She groaned, moving her hand to scratch her nose.

"What the–"

It was restrained. She tried to use her other arm, but got the same result. Her eyes shot open as she tried to move her legs, also feeling the restraint. There he was, sitting at the edge of the bed.

He was right beside Daphne's torso, and inches away from her face.

"Cowards? I respectfully disagree. But in reality, Daphne…who asked you?"

Daphne was inarticulate. She remembered how she told Jon earlier that mask-wearers were cowards. This man had to have heard her. Was he also on the rooftop? He wasn't one of the police officers, was he? It couldn't be.

"Do you really feel safe?" The Broken Skull questioned. "In this moment, do you feel comfortable? Will you ever feel comfortable again? Let's be more tasteful, Daphne…with all things."

His words infuriated her. Her jaw clenched.

"You don't know who you're messing with." She was so angry, she felt herself getting dizzy. "I *will* track you down, and I *will* make you pay for this."

"Do you think this is some sort of…sick joke?" The Broken Skull quizzed. "Your intention is to make me pay…for what? Intruding on your sleep? Well, dear Daphne…I hope to intrude on your sleep for the rest of your days."

"What do you mean?"

"Starting at the bottom, you won't sleep for days. I'm in your house. You thought you could sleep safely, when that couldn't be farther from the case. Now, every sound you hear could mean the end. One human core need is to feel safe, to have shelter. Digest that, with time."

Daphne grunted. She attempted to pull her arms free. She became more frustrated with each second. Her arms and legs were drained, but she wouldn't stop. That's not how she was raised. Just because a maniac was in her presence, it didn't mean she wouldn't fight.

"I want to be candid with you," the Broken Skull told Daphne. "I want to kill you so badly, but my family talked me out of it. What stops me from keeping you bound while this house burns? Then it occurred to me: I don't know why I would kill you…when I could just…have fun. Now, to be clear…in the end, I *will* kill you."

The Broken Skull was pleased with his work. Everything would come together with time. To that, he had all the time in the world. He started to leave Daphne's bedroom.

"Is that it, you freaking psychopath?! That's all you have for me?!" Daphne yelled at the top of her lungs. The Broken Skull popped his head back in, if only for a second.

"Yes. I'm here to inform you that you have the attention of my family and me. We'll be watching."

She tried to spit on him, but he was too far away. The Broken Skull left, ignoring the curses and insults that followed.

She'll eventually get out. If she doesn't, she'll die of starvation. Someone will check on her, won't they? If after a day, she's not about town, I'll surely visit her again.

Jon shut his car door, parked right outside De La Rosa's residence. It was late. Even though he got some things off his chest – so did she – he felt the need to apologize. He would tell her he'd improve. He was a comic book nerd at heart, but it was time to grow up. He had to separate hobby and career.

"Just tell her you're sorry," Jon coached himself as he found himself at De La Rosa's door. He took a couple deep breaths and exhaled. He closed his hand and brought it back, set to rap on the hard wood.

The Broken Skull opened the door. Jon panicked; his eyes widened as he froze in front of the masked man, not able to speak or blink. His breathing became shallow. If the Broken Skull wanted to act, Jon's short breaths wouldn't stop him. Inwardly, he hoped it would.

"The B-Broken Skull," Jon stammered.

"You have a decision to make, detective," the Broken Skull offered, disregarding Jon's acknowledgement. "You may attempt to apprehend me, but I promise you, you would die trying. That, or…you can save your sweet Daphne."

Jon couldn't think straight. This was a lot to take in. His mind wasn't on apprehending the Broken Skull. The probability of him apprehending the Broken Skull was much lower than his chances of finding and helping Daphne. He rushed in the house.

The minute Jon ran in the house, the Broken Skull walked the other way.

"Just as I suspected," the Broken Skull muttered to himself. "I can't wait to visit you, as well."

"Daphne?!" Jon called through the house.

Daphne heard his voice. Truthfully, she didn't think she'd hear from him for a while, given the spat they had a few hours prior. Nonetheless, she was glad to hear that familiar voice; in theory, it meant the Broken Skull was gone.

"I'm here! In my room!" Daphne called.

Jon jogged down the hallway to Daphne's bedroom. As soon as he saw her, he assessed the situation. He lightly tore at the restraints, keeping in mind that her wrists and ankles were bound. It was best not to violently pull at them. Instead, he worked at them until Daphne was freed.

Instantly, Daphne shot up from the bed, wearing her tied-tight sweatpants and snug t-shirt. She didn't care how she looked. The most important part was that she was alive. Standing face to face with her rescuer, she looked into his eyes.

"Daphne, I-I just…you know…I know it's late, I just wanted to see–"

Daphne lunged at him, hugging him tighter than she'd ever hugged anyone in her life. She didn't want to let go. Jon hugged her back just as tight. Her forehead rested on his collarbone, her nose pressed against the top part of his chest. She felt safe enough to break down in his presence, so she did.

"I just wanted to see if you were okay," he whispered. His chest got warm from Daphne's deep exhalations. Her arms remained wrapped around Jon's body. He held her.

"And to say I'm sorry."

"You shouldn't be the one apologizing," Daphne said. Her voice was muffled against Jon's chest. "I should apologize to you."

Deadmarsh wasn't the ideal partner for De La Rosa, as far as relationships were concerned. She tended to gravitate towards jerks, long on appearance and short on personality. Even so, she couldn't have an impulse moment, because of this. She didn't want to alter her professional relationship with Jon.

While he apologized to her on more than one occasion, Daphne couldn't remember the last time a guy she dated was in the wrong and apologized. It was always, "Why did you make me do that?" and conversations that ended with, "This is your fault!" It was refreshing.

She pulled her head away from his chest, her eyes on his. She looked distressed.

"This is real, all of it. This guy is real. He said he wanted to have fun, that he would kill me, in the end. We have to stop this. We have to stop him."

He shook his head yes. She hugged him again, tighter than last time. He hugged her back and looked to the ceiling.

"Do you mind just…talking to me for a little bit? I don't think I'm going to go to sleep anytime soon," Daphne asked.

"No-no! It's not a problem!" Jon replied. "I'm not even tired. You know, all the adrenaline, and the 'life-flashing-before-my-eyes' thing…no, it's going to be a while," he laughed. Daphne quietly chuckled. "I'm sure two traumatized people will find *something* to talk about."

Silently, she thanked God for him.

Chapter 17

Marissa felt cold and alone. It felt like Markus had been gone forever. She looked at the digital alarm clock on the nightstand. It was after 4 a.m. She looked around. Markus definitely wasn't there.

This damn comforter!

Marissa used one hand to push the comforter down. Not satisfied, she incorporated her other hand. She pushed her bottom lip out and blew air upward before she used one of her hands to push the stray strands away from her face.

If she wasn't careful, Marissa could sleep a whole day away. Markus's comforter felt like being surrounded by pillows and clouds. She imagined she couldn't get more relaxed than she was, currently.

"I have to get up," she told herself sternly. She pulled her legs out from underneath the comforter and used her hands to push the rest away. Scratching the back of her head, Marissa stumbled to the bedroom door, finding enough energy to make her exit.

As she made it to the top of the stairs to descend, Marissa realized how cold it was in Markus's house. It showed through her shirt, as well. Why was it so cold? Was that the reason Markus had such a big, cozy comforter? She made a mental note to ask him about it later. For now, she had no idea where he was.

"Good morning, sleepyhead."

She instantly knew it was Markus. When Marissa made it to the bottom of the stair, she observed a small light on in the kitchen. It was found to be the refrigerator light, once she turned the corner. Markus had it propped open with his leg, grabbing things from it and transporting them to the kitchen island.

"Ladies and gentlemen, the only person that calls *someone else* a sleepyhead at 4 a.m.," Marissa joked. She examined some of the containers that Markus brought out of his refrigerator. She bent over and kissed his forearm sweetly, continuing her stumble through the kitchen. "Coffee?"

"Over there."

Markus pointed in the vicinity of the coffeemaker. He knew that was the first thing she'd want. She wasn't huge on cappuccinos or lattes, but coffee was her saving grace. A cup at the beginning of the day got her moving. Most everything she put in her body after that sustained her energy. A few guilty pleasures never hurt.

"So, Mr. Doubleday…what has you up so early?"

"Just another day," Markus replied. "I'm up. My mind is always working."

I think I'm going to conveniently leave out that I was just closing the basement door when I heard her, or that Vanessa's still downstairs, sleeping.

Markus smiled while he opened the containers, filled with various egg and veggie combo sandwiches. Before he placed two of them inside the oven, he looked up at Marissa.

"Do you want one?"

"Heck no! Just give me my coffee, wind me up and watch me go!" She laughed.

While he bent over and placed the sandwiches in the oven, she took in his back muscles. He was so lean that when he moved, she saw every muscle working. *Jesus*, she thought.

Markus turned and faced Marissa. "So…"

"So…" Marissa repeated.

"I think we might need to have a talk."

"I agree."

"So, we're dating, correct? I mean, there doesn't need to be this long conversation about it, right? We don't have to go and talk to the paparazzi or Jackie Reed about it, but…there's monogamy, I would think."

Marissa raised her eyebrows, mid-sip. If the coffee hadn't aroused her senses, the talk of her and Markus being an item would. She took her lips off the cup.

"Well, yeah, I thought. I-I…well…"

Markus pointed back and forth between himself and Marissa. "This is…you know…"

Marissa shook her head yes. "Right-right! C'mon, Markus…of course, we–…we?" She smiled weakly and shrugged her shoulders.

"You know I'm in love with you," Markus said confidently.

The ringing alarm of the oven caused Marissa's eyebrows to rise again.

"Someone must've just gotten a good idea."

"Markus, I'm in love with you as well," Marissa confessed, "but you have some of the worst jokes I've ever heard."

"Gotta have a weakness," he smiled. He popped open the oven and grabbed his sandwiches. He placed them on the kitchen island and propped himself up on his hands, with one leg crossed over the other. He looked at her.

"Well…two."

Marissa was putty on the inside. She could've died. The compliment was such a small gesture, but a heartfelt gesture could take someone's breath away, much like it had Marissa's. She exhaled and lightly blew on her coffee. It was still a bit hot. She took another sip.

"While your comedy may fall by the wayside, your timing could not be better," Marissa smiled warmly at her beau. "You know what to say, when to say it. Where did you get that timing from?"

Sneaking up on people, he said, in his head. "I don't know. I guess I just have a gift. Just lucky, if you ask me."

"I'll say so. So, have you heard of this Broken Skull guy?" Marissa asked. "Scary, right?"

Markus thought about the Broken Skull all the time, but that was no one's business. It wouldn't make sense to them, anyway. Vanessa didn't really talk about it. She stood a more realistic chance of running into him. Markus thanked his lucky stars it hadn't happened. The unknown was always more dangerous.

This Broken Skull guy was extremely unknown.

"It's very scary," Markus admitted. While he wasn't afraid of the Broken Skull, he was – more or less – afraid of what the Broken Skull was capable of. He was still out there, somewhere. One day, they'd run into each other. When they did, he'd be ready.

"You have a guy that's going out and wreaking havoc," Markus added. "This guy doesn't seem to care about much, except that. When you have someone that has nothing to lose, it makes a very dangerous person."

Marissa didn't want to get into the "why" of anything. She wanted him to be away from anyone or anything he could hurt. Bad people like that were people that didn't deserve a chance. She wondered to herself why the cops appeared so indifferent about the subject.

Maybe that's why her father continued to do the things he did. In her mind, her father was the lesser of two evils. In her mind, the Broken Skull was something of a terrorist, someone bent on breaking the city or state, possibly the whole country.

"So, if he shows up, and he's like, 'I'm going to take Marissa, and there's nothing you can do about it,' would you be all, 'no you're not?'" She asked Markus.

"Absolutely, without a doubt," Markus said. "I don't know how much help I would be, but I would do something." He grabbed the containers and put them back in the refrigerator. Marissa seized the opportunity presented before her: she clamped a piece of Markus's backside with her thumb and forefinger.

The hard clamp straightened Markus's back out. While his head was buried in the refrigerator, he smiled and put the last of the food away. When he finished, he pulled his head out the frig and faced Marissa. He wagged his index finger at her.

"Uh-uh. We're closed," Markus warned, winking at her. "The next one's going to cost you."

It hit her.

Markus wagged his finger at her the same way the guy that night did, the night she was in the alleyway with him. Was she mistaken? Was her memory failing her? She couldn't believe it. Markus couldn't be that guy…could he?

No way. I'm sure it was a coincidence. He's too pretty for that kind of stuff, just like I said. Or did he say that?

Her father taught her not to accuse someone of something, unless she was absolutely sure. If she was wrong, it could affect her relationship with Markus. She would hold onto that thought, for now. Maybe it was the sleep talking? Of course not, she'd had more than enough coffee to be awake, she thought.

"You know…I…have a full plate today. I'm glad I woke up, actually," Marissa abruptly – and awkwardly – notified. "It's a shoe-in that you have a full plate, too." She finished up her coffee. Marissa accepted Markus's offer to take her cup, which he placed in the dishwasher.

"You're a terrible liar," Markus offered, "but I understand."

"Okay, you caught me. My head's just cloudy. I have lots of things to think about, so I'm just going to…" She pointed back upstairs.

Markus shook his head no. "No, it's not a problem," Markus assured. At that time, it hit him: he wagged his finger the same way as when he was in the alleyway with Marissa. If she asked him, he couldn't lie. Now, he *really* wanted her to go.

Marissa nodded and turned her back to Markus, headed to the stairs.

"I'll miss you. When you're not here, it's different."

Marissa stopped, but didn't turn around. "I'm going to miss you, too…and I understand the feeling," she said warmly, as usual. The more she thought about it, the more her head became more clouded. She made her way up the stairs. As soon as he heard his bedroom door shut, his mind raced.

That mistake could cost me. I can't believe I just did that. She knows. God, she knows. Maybe I wanted her to know?

Markus crossed his arms across his chest and looked to the ceiling. For someone who'd rarely made mistakes in his life, one could argue that he'd made two in the span of less than 24 hours.

He must have been in the kitchen overanalyzing for too long. He heard footsteps coming downstairs. "Snap out of it," he said to himself. He shook his head free of overbearing thoughts as he left the kitchen. He caught Marissa's last steps down the stairs before she landed at the main level. She had her bag with her.

Markus said, "I take it you're not staying another night?"

"Well, no," Marissa answered. "We're just busy, Markus. You have so many things going on, and I have my things…it would just…we'd *really* have to move things around, and I don't want to be a pain."

"You're not a pain. I enjoy having you around. Shoot me a text or something. I just don't want us to go through our day without some sort of communication."

Markus's words cut Marissa. They hadn't spoken about it, but eventually, she would have more questions about where they stood. Markus had to know that. He might have questions to ask, and she would be happy to answer them. For now, she was on her way out.

"Also, I just wanted to add…I hope you're not mad at the whole…" he trailed off, wagging his finger again, but slightly altering the wag. "I remember you telling me about that guy doing that to you, and I can understand if you're upset about me kind of…making light of what happened to you."

His words made her feel at ease. She raised her eyebrows and nodded her head yes at him.

"I was scared, and I don't think it should be brought up in that manner. I don't think it's a trigger, but it made me feel a certain way."

"I may not have been a match for those guys but I would've done what I could," Markus said. "I don't know if I could have outrun them, but I can run really far, pretty fast," he said, trying his best to quell Marissa's concerns.

She laughed. Even though she would classify Markus under the "corny" category, sometimes, he was funny. When she finished her chuckle, she said, "I want to ask you one question, and I want you to tell me the truth."

"Anything you like," Markus said.

Inside him, his heart picked up speed. His palms perspired. He had to be ready for the probability that Marissa could ask him about his identity. He would answer her truthfully, and then, live with her reaction. He was ready.

On Marissa's side, her palms also perspired. Her heart beat rapidly. *Please don't lie to me*, she thought.

Her phone buzzed. She placed her index finger up. "Excuse me," Marissa said.

"Hello?...What? That doesn't sound right." She picked up her overnight bag and slung it over her shoulder. She pecked Markus quickly.

"I love you," she whispered.

"I love you, too," Markus whispered back.

Marissa smiled and walked to the front door. Once she closed the door behind her, she walked to her car.

"Titus?" Marissa asked through the receiver. "Okay, that was close. Can you please tell me that Markus isn't the 'wag-the-finger-at-people' guy?"

She pulled the bag off her shoulder and tossed it in the passenger's seat of her car. She slid in and looked around to make sure she was in a secure spot.

"Right! He can't be! That's what I said!" Marissa lied. She had suspicions that Markus was the guy, even if he had a perfectly good explanation for why he wagged his finger like he did. A small part of her believed he was capable of fighting crime. She wondered what his motive would be, if he had one.

It didn't make sense. Why risk his life, when he had nothing to gain from it, but everything to lose?

Back in the house, as Markus watched Marissa drive away, he heard a door open and close behind him. It was Vanessa. She looked healthy and rested. Markus examined her body: she wore boy shorts and a tight t-shirt. Most of her bare body showed, making it very easy to track her healing progress. She healed quite nicely, from what he could see.

"Feeling better?" Markus asked.

Vanessa grinned big. "I feel like your net worth, like I could sleep in that chamber for the rest of the day." She stood on her tiptoes and stretched her long arms out. She let out a small growl when she rolled her arms back. They settled by her side.

Vanessa noticed Markus looking her body over. She figured he was looking out for her, not checking her out. She extended both her arms, examining them both. The bruises were gone, like the night before never happened.

She wanted to believe that the night before was a dream. It wasn't. She peered at her legs. No bruising, and substantially less soreness. She felt no worse than having participated in a light workout.

"So, what happens now?" Vanessa wondered.

"You go to work in a couple hours," Markus told Vanessa. "I go to work in a couple hours. It's like any other day, but tonight, we're going to take a little detour…that is, if you're in."

Vanessa looked at Markus as if insulted. "I can't believe you would even wonder that, after everything that happened last night."

"I'm asking *because* of what happened last night," Markus said. "The training is fun until the first time you get hit in the face. I'm glad you're resilient, but that's tested over time, not just after one night."

"Exactly," Vanessa said. "So, what were you saying?"

"I was saying that we're taking a detour on our way out tonight," Markus repeated.

"Right," Vanessa said. "I'll be ready."

Speaking of ready, Daphne's eyes opened up, quickly and widely. She scrambled up from a sleeping position and sat up on the couch. She breathed heavy. She placed her hand on the left side of her chest.

Jon quickly placed his hands up in surrender. "It's okay! It's okay! Everything's okay." She looked at him. Her forehead was damp from sweat. He said, "I'm here, nothing happened. Are you okay? Bad dream?"

While he tried to calm her down, Daphne couldn't help but express concern for the young detective.

"You could say that," Daphne said. "I want to know if you're okay. You look so tired. Your eyes are red…did you sleep?" She asked.

Jon said, "I think so, maybe for about an hour, or something? After that, it was a wash," he snickered. "I stayed up. You moved around a lot. I sat here on this comfy couch and just thought about things, played on my phone."

Daphne stood up and headed to the kitchen. "Like what? I'm listening, but I feel like we might be in need of coffee."

While Daphne busied herself making coffee in the kitchen, Jon relaxed a bit. He was relieved he made it through the night. He was also happy he was able to provide some kind of peace of mind for Daphne. He was tired, but in good spirits. Lack of sleep was the least of his worries.

Through a yawn, Jon said, "Just thought about life, how delicate it is. Lots of things can happen, you know? This life isn't guaranteed." He closed his eyes for several seconds, and then opened them again. "So, you know, I just wanna…tell you…tell you that–"

"Tell me what?" Daphne called from the kitchen.

The smell of coffee filled the smallish house. When Daphne returned to the living room however, she realized why it didn't affect Jon: he was out cold. She smiled, and tried her best not to put the spotlight on her emotions. She was happy to have him around, even if he was an awkward, comic book nerd.

That didn't matter. He was there when she needed him most.

Chapter 18

Nightfall came.

Vanessa pulled her car into the Doubleday driveway. He had a cool pathway to his house: a mildly steep, two-lane road, with an incline lasting well over a mile. It made sense that the house sat solo. The opening and closing of his garage would create pandemonium for neighbors.

She walked to the front door and placed her hand on the sensor. Her hand outlined in green.

"Confirmed: Vanessa Vaughn."

She opened the door. Markus was waiting.

"Of course you're on time. I don't know why I thought about doubting you."

"If I had to guess, it would be because you like yanking my chain?" Vanessa questioned, smiling at her boss.

Markus shrugged and placed his hand on the sensor that led to the basement.

"Confirmed: Markus Doubleday."

The door unlocked. He opened the door and ushered Vanessa through. She stepped on the platform. Once he was sure the door was shut and locked, he mounted the escalator as well. After a few seconds, the two's feet landed on the floor of the basement.

The lights flickered on.

Vanessa said, "Peace First." A panel from the wall rotated to the right, showcasing her suit.

Markus said, "We're a go." The wall panel next to Vanessa's suit rotated to the right, also showcasing his suit. When both the suits lowered, the two snatched them off their holders and fit themselves into their garb.

While the pair dressed, Markus thought about all the things that could go wrong while they were out. Yes, it was only Vanessa's second experience with the night life, but with numerous repetitions and situations, she was bound to adapt and improve.

Once the two were dressed – save for Markus's mask – Markus looked at Vanessa.

"Is there something you need?" She questioned.

He said, "I trust you out there. I know it didn't seem that way last night, but I'm going to trust you, so we can co-exist effectively."

"Right, I understand. So, you were speaking of a detour?"

"Yes, I was. We're going to have to stop here."

He directed Vanessa's eyes to the computer screen. She trained her eyes in that vicinity, wondering what Markus was talking about.

"Computer: can you pull up the last address we talked about, please?"

The computer threw up several holograms of small houses and streets. It was an area of the city, but shown on a smaller scale. A large red arrow hovered over their destination.

"Got it?" Markus questioned.

"Yes. But Markus, who is that?" Vanessa asked.

"That's Daphne De La Rosa's house, the one that shot at us last night."

Vanessa raised her eyebrows. "And the plot thickens. That sounds quite right. I'm in the mood for a bit of intrigue."

"Just a few questions for her and we're out, Vanessa. I'd say my expectations for tonight are pretty clear, don't you?"

Vanessa smiled. "You have my solemn promise that there will be no violence at De La Rosa's. Plus, I have a sneaking suspicion she couldn't take me, anyway."

Markus liked her confidence. She definitely needed it, for this job. He walked to his car. Vanessa was a step behind.

He said, "In case you didn't know, you have similar capabilities with the computer on your bike. You just have to say the right words."

She asked, "Well, what are they?"

He smirked.

"I guess you'll have to find them."

He started his car up and pulled out of his parking spot. Vanessa started up her bike. They both pulled off quickly, hearing the familiar low rumble of the ground when the garage's mouth opened.

Just as Markus and Vanessa were leaving their domicile, so were a few others.

"Are we leaving yet?" Patrick asked impatiently. When mayhem was on the mind, waiting was the last preferred activity.

"Sweet Patty Cake, there's always time for these activities," Emma said lovingly, inches away from her twin. She looked up at him slightly. "You have to understand, the more you wait, the worse you can make it for them." She smiled and patted his jaw line.

The Broken Skull walked into the room the twins were talking in.

"It will have to wait. I anticipate no violence tonight, light, at the most. It all depends on our subjects' reactions to our behavior."

Patrick and Emma wanted a piece of the action. They'd grown tired of sitting on the sideline, even though recently, they'd gotten a pretty good chunk from Detective Deadmarsh's face.

"Light violence," Patrick huffed. "Well, light violence is better than no violence."

"Agreed," the Broken Skull said.

"Agreed times two," Emma chimed in. "Turn the temperature down, Patrick."

"The temperature *is* down," Patrick said with a shrug. "The action will come when it comes, I suppose."

"That's the positive thinking so many crave," the Broken Skull said. "Remember, all of this is a process. When Ms. De La Rosa caves into the pressures we place directly on her shoulders, you'll see something you've never seen in your life."

"And what would that be?" Emma asked.

"She could very well make her appearance on the dark side, perhaps an extended stay," the Broken Skull replied. "There are many people out there that are labeled crazy. She's the right kind of crazy, my dearest friends. Consider it recruiting."

Patrick nodded yes at the Broken Skull's assertion. He and Emma were in full agreement with the Broken Skull's tactics. They were one cohesive, unstoppable force. Their presence would be felt soon.

"Shall we go?" The Broken Skull proposed.

"We shall," Emma agreed.

The ratty-looking one-bedroom house they left out of could classify as two things: out in the middle of nowhere, and a "home base," of sorts. It was surrounded by nothing but trees. It served as a place to regroup and execute, not a place to rest their heads.

The three filed into the van that carried the Broken Skull, with Emma assuming driving responsibility. Patrick manned the passenger's seat. The Broken Skull sat in the back, most comfortable in the darkness.

While they traveled, the Broken Skull thought about his next moves. He stayed several steps ahead of the people he dealt with, and 15 minutes was enough time to think about how he wanted to tie everything together. He wouldn't do something off the top of his head. He had to measure everything.

No mistakes.

That night, Jon found himself back at Daphne's house. Most of his energy came from sleeping until early afternoon. Some of his energy stemmed from spending time with her. The night prior, they conversed until she slept. Jon took a personal day, while Daphne went to work. Nobody was going to come into a precinct full of cops and mess with her.

Daphne's drive to and from work was disconcerting, but otherwise, smooth. She'd called ahead to make sure Jon was at her house. She didn't know how long she and Jon could keep meeting like this, but she would until she figured out her next step.

Daphne exited the car, and scanned for anything out of the ordinary. Nothing found. She walked to the front door faster than she was used to and unlocked it quickly.

When she pushed it open, she called for him. "Deadmarsh?" Her heart was already beating rapidly. His absence was another reason for the imminent panic attack. She needed him to respond. "Deadmarsh?!" She cried out.

"Yes, ma'am?"

Daphne turned her head and looked down the hallway. Jon came out of the bathroom, hands wet. "I'm here, my hands are clean, and I'm ready to play Monopoly, or whatever devious plan you have for tonight."

"Sure, I'll just…you know, go freshen up."

Daphne passed Jon on the way to her bedroom. She kicked herself for freaking out. She shut the door behind her and flipped the light on. She performed a quick scan of the room. Nothing. She placed her hand on the knob of the closet door. The other hand closed into a fist and cocked back. She turned the knob and pulled the door open quickly.

Nothing.

"Okay," Daphne said breathlessly. "Get it together, Daph. Everything's okay. There's nothing here." Her breathing slowly began to regulate again.

Back in the living room, Jon waited for Daphne while she freshened up. When she left that morning, he took the time to freshen up her house. He wanted Daphne to be able to relax when she got home. Maybe the mission was accomplished? He couldn't say, for sure.

"Hey."

An unfamiliar voice. Jon whipped around. The voice wasn't alone. He recognized the two. One brought their index finger up to their mouth. Jon took the hint that he needed to stay quiet. He nodded yes.

"Can you handle this?" Ivory Fox whispered. "Would you be a lamb and stay really quiet for us? Your silence is of the utmost importance."

The young detective heeded the warning. He immediately felt star struck again. He nodded yes again.

She placed one set of fingertips at the top of her breast. "I'm called Ivory Fox."

Jon nodded once more. He knew. The message boards talked about her. He found himself wide-eyed, with childlike wonder. If not for his manners, his mouth would be wide open.

She said, “And you know him.”

She pointed with her thumb. Jon’s eyes slid over to Ivory Fox’s counterpart. He couldn’t believe he was standing in front of a legend.

“I know you don’t have a name you go by, but people on the internet call you the Sound. That one got the most votes,” Jon whispered. “Because of the…”

He quietly mimicked the tapping sound.

“Maybe we should wait until your friend comes back out?” Ivory Fox recommended. “I wouldn’t want her to miss this, since she tried to kill us, and all.”

“Maybe so,” Jon agreed. Just then, he heard Daphne’s bedroom door open.

“Deadmarsh? Are you out there?” She called. She walked down the hallway. “You’re being really quiet, like you’re out of things to talk about. Imagine that,” she joked. She saw him just around the corner.

“Everything’s just fine,” Jon assured. They smiled at each other.

As soon as she entered the living room, Daphne saw something out of the corner of her eye. Right behind Jon stood the two masked people she’d shot at the night before. She’d hit the man numerous times. How the hell was he standing upright?

Daphne got right into it.

“So, are you two working for the Broken Skull?” Daphne questioned aggressively. “Let me guess: he sent you two to finish the job he started last night. Well, guess what…you’re going to have to kill me this time. If you think you–”

“Is this the usual?” Ivory Fox interrupted the detective, using a hand to listlessly explain how disinterested she was in Daphne’s words. “Because I assure you, you’re going to have to kill *me*, if you keep on with this diatribe.”

Jon felt the need to apologize. “Sorry, it’s been a really stressful time for us. You see, she–”

“Don’t tell them anything!” Daphne blurted out. “We don’t know them, and you’re about to tell them my personal business?!” She grilled. Vanessa wouldn’t tolerate it.

“Listen, lady: I’m Ivory Fox. This is the Sound, apparently.” She pointed to herself and Markus again. “We help people. We also don’t appreciate being shot at, or in his case, flat-out *shot*,” she said, pointing to her partner. “So…maybe if you see us again, could you not to do that? It’d help, really.”

“I’m not interested in helping you, or people like you,” Daphne told the two. “There’s not much difference between you and people like the Broken Skull, people who think they’re above the law, and can do what they want without consequences.”

“Oh, we know the consequences,” Ivory Fox said. “We have psycho cops like you, shooting at us without provocation. We’re trying to help you, and we almost get killed doing it. I’ve never heard of such a thing. I don’t know if that’s police protocol, or…” she said smartly.

"Watch your mouth. Remember, you're in my house. I'm well within my rights to shoot you," Daphne said angrily. "Actually, I think that's a good idea."

She started to walk back to her bedroom. Jon grabbed her wrist lightly.

"Daphne…" Jon pleaded. "They wouldn't be here if they didn't have something important to tell us. I mean, if they wanted to hurt us, they would've done something by now, right?"

"You should listen to your boyfriend more often," Ivory Fox advised. That remark drew a scowl from Daphne.

"He's not my boyfriend," Daphne said matter-of-factly.

"I don't think that's important," Jon said. "I think they can help you, Daphne. Just tell them what happened."

"That's the thing: I don't need their help," Daphne said.

She didn't care that they stood in front of her. She would talk about them like they weren't there. She noticed the Sound lean into Ivory Fox's ear, mumbling something to her. It didn't sound like anything came out, but Ivory Fox's nodding confirmed that it did.

"Turn the lights down," Ivory Fox directed.

"I don't take orders from you," Daphne said.

Ivory Fox threw her hands up and sighed. "Christ. Well, where are they? I can do it myself." She didn't want to be courteous to this woman anymore. Out of respect for Markus, she'd continue to do so.

Without resistance, Jon followed Ivory Fox's orders. Daphne may not have been thinking clearly, but he understood. The Sound and Ivory Fox wanted to keep their whereabouts under wraps. He'd seen it a million times, in comic books.

The Sound gruffly said, "Tell us what happened."

Jon had never heard him speak. He'd never forget this night, as long as he lived. Daphne wasn't as impressed.

"Just tell them, Daphne," Jon prompted.

Daphne looked back and forth between Jon and the masked ones. Jon shrugged, as if he was telling her that it was okay. Reluctantly, she said, "The Broken Skull, he called himself. It felt like a dream when I first woke up. I was sleeping so hard. He tied me to my bed. I couldn't get out. He told me he wanted to kill me but he'd rather have some fun, instead."

"Sorry to interrupt, but…did he touch you?" Ivory Fox asked.

"No…I don't think he meant 'fun' like that," Daphne answered begrudgingly. "He said he would be back. I think it was more an intimidation tactic, than anything."

"Looks like it worked," the Sound said.

He could tell in her movements and actions. It was more than just a hunch. Daphne wouldn't acknowledge what he said, but she knew he was right. It intimidated her.

"What do you need us to do?" Jon asked. He wanted to know if the Sound and Ivory Fox had a plan, but he also wanted guidance.

"Stay safe out there," the Sound replied. "Understand the difference, detective. The only thing we have in common with the Broken Skull is that we wear masks. It stops there."

"I won't apologize for being skeptical," Daphne notified the two champions.

"We're not asking you to," Ivory Fox responded, her voice raised, somewhat. "All we're asking is that, if you see us out at night, don't try to kill us. We're making your life easier."

"You're breaking the law," Daphne said. "I'm going to give you time to evacuate my home, but I don't ever want to see you here again…either of you. Regardless of what happened to me last night, it's none of your concern. It's a police matter that will be taken care of. Next time, I won't be so nice. Goodbye."

"Is she serious?" Ivory Fox turned to the Sound. He didn't respond. She looked at Jon, who stood silent. Daphne had spoken. There was no place for further comment. She looked at a stone-faced Daphne.

"Well, good luck." Ivory Fox and the Sound left out the back door.

When Daphne heard the door shut, she walked over and locked it. She turned the knob and tugged on it, to make sure it was locked. She turned back to Jon. She walked towards him without eye contact.

In a low tone, she said, "I think I'm good."

"You're good?" Jonathan questioned. "I'd say so. You just met–"

"No, I mean…I'm good," Daphne said. She still hadn't made eye contact with him. Something was wrong. He didn't feel he had time to ask what was wrong. "They broke in here, and you let them, so…you can go back to your apartment. I'll be fine."

"They're trying to help you, Daphne," Jonathan said. He tired of this conversation. It was pretty set in stone. They even showed up and told her they wanted to help. What else could she possibly want? "You know what? I think you're right. I think it's better if I just…let me get my stuff."

As he gathered his things, she wanted to stop him. She wanted to tell him she was scared, that she wanted to figure everything out with him. After all, two heads were better than one. Instead, because of her prideful stubbornness, she decided to say nothing.

She watched him bag up his belongings. He stood silently by the door. He looked at her, trying to find something, anything from her. Instead of looking at him, Daphne looked through him. She wouldn't allow herself to say anything.

Jon pursed his lips and shook his head no. He couldn't believe she was so immovable about this topic. He wouldn't persist or persuade, he'd just go. That's what Daphne wanted, anyway.

"By the way…they didn't break in," Jon said. "The backdoor was unlocked."

He didn't slam the door when he walked out. He didn't need to make a statement. He'd made too many statements to her, as it was. He guessed it was better to let it go, than to beat his head against the wall.

Just go home, Jon, he told himself.

Jon's car pulled away from Daphne's house. Down the street, a van's engine came alive and pulled away.

"Interesting. The Main Attraction has a new helper, talking to Ms. De La Rosa and the Deadmarsh boy. Hmmm…I wonder what was discussed."

"It's not too late to find out," Patrick recommended. "The Deadmarsh boy hasn't gotten that far down the street and Ms. De La Rosa is still in there, all by herself."

"What about something different?" The Broken Skull suggested. "Perhaps we could bump into Black and Blue, and his friend? They could not have gone far. Remember, it's a process. Too much on De La Rosa, and she could crack early. The Deadmarsh boy is no challenge."

Emma laughed. "So, where to?"

"I think we can find them," the Broken Skull said. "Go that way."

Meanwhile, in his car, Markus patrolled the streets. While he did so, he thought about De La Rosa's behavior. It bothered him.

She was so hell-bent on stopping him and Vanessa's operation. There was no changing her mind. Even a visit from the Broken Skull didn't deter her thinking. He had no choice but to add her to his growing list of enemies.

Markus's thoughts were interrupted by a phone call. He looked at his dashboard screen. It was Marissa Buchanan. Markus pulled his mask off, with no fear of anyone being able to see in. His windows essentially had the functionality of a two-sided mirror: he could see out, but they couldn't see in.

"Perfect timing," Markus said with a huff, shaking his head. "Answer."

"Hey! What's going on?" Marissa said. "You look busy. Are you busy?"

"Not really. Just driving around. What's going on?" Markus asked.

"Well, I wanted to tell you some news, but if you're busy..."

"Mare, why are you so worried about me being busy? If you have something to say, say it."

It was scribbled all over her face. Markus had known her long enough to know when something was on her mind, good or bad. He was ready for anything.

"Okay...I'll say it." She was quiet for a moment. "I was thinking...well, I was going to do it, and I wanted to get your thoughts on it, because I care what you think, and–"

Markus was becoming impatient on the inside but on the outside, he gave off the look of someone patiently waiting. When he was out at night, he didn't take phone calls. Why did he, this time? Was Marissa becoming more important than the mission?

Marissa smiled. "I think I'm going to buy my contract out."

"I need a little more clarification," Markus responded.

"I'm glad you said that. The modeling contract I'm under right now, I'm going to buy out the remaining time. I'm going to give them the money back that's left on the contract and be done with it."

"Really?"

"Yes. I still have endorsements. I'm just done being stuck in France. I don't want to wait anymore. It's the logical thing to do, right? Love means more than money, and I love you."

Marissa liked having money, but never fawned over it. She thought Markus was worth more than money she could easily recoup elsewhere. She didn't want to be taken care of. She wanted to do more things, stateside.

"Well, yeah," Markus said. "I understand what you're saying. I say that if it makes you happy, do it. I like the idea."

Marissa smiled, ear-to-ear. "I knew you would understand. I know you're busy, like, all the time. I get it. I'm doing it for my own sanity, too. Being away from family and everything, it just…takes its toll, I guess."

Silence fell between the two. Marissa nervously played with her hair while Markus thought about the decision he was about to make. She'd told him the truth. It might be time for him to do the same. "Now, I have some information for you, as well."

"Really? What's that?" Marissa asked him.

A picture of Vanessa's face popped up on the dashboard and split the screen. Marissa's live feed on the left, Vanessa's picture on the right.

"Perfect timing," Markus said.

"What?"

"Nothing," Markus said. "Work calls. I'll try to give you a call later, if you're still up."

"Okay," Marissa said. Her disappointment showed as the screen went blank.

"Switch calls," Markus commanded. When he clicked over to Vanessa's call, she looked out of sorts.

"Vanessa, what is it?"

"There's a van following me!" She yelled. "Fast! I don't know the streets as well as you do! It's gaining, Markus! I don't know what to do!"

Markus mashed on the gas. The car picked up speed as he wove through traffic.

"Tell it to evade and to take you home," Markus said calmly. "I'll meet you there."

"Okay!" Vanessa said. Markus's screen went blank. He slid his mask back on. It was time to go back to work.

In the interim, Vanessa was in a pickle. The van gained on her, threatened to bump her. Even the smallest bump would make Vanessa spin out. The crash would be horrific. Her suit protected her, but she didn't want to test its limits.

She turned her head behind her. The headlights were 15 feet away, she thought. She weaved in and out of traffic, but the van sloppily stayed with her.

"Faster," the Broken Skull ordered.

Emma punched the gas. The van was almost tapped out, speed-wise. She clutched the steering wheel while she kept the van's turns as tight as possible.

As she felt the van closing in again, Vanessa held the handlebars tight. "Evade! And take me home!" Vanessa yelled.

Within a few seconds, the bike achieved a breakneck speed, weaving in and out of traffic with more precision than Vanessa showed. She was surprised at Markus's technology.

In the van, it wasn't going so well. Before the Broken Skull could say anything, Emma spoke to him. "I'm going as fast as I can," she pledged, her voice low. She concentrated as best she could, but the bike's speed was too much to overcome.

Vanessa turned around again. This time, the van was nearly out of sight. The bike revved onto one street after another. She turned around one more time. The van was nowhere to be found. Whether it took another street was not her concern.

Her heart never beat so fast in her life, not even during her skirmish last night. Vanessa breathed heavily. Near-death experiences weren't her strong point. The bike revved on, making another turn.

My God, she thought.

Markus sped toward his house. He wouldn't feel fully calm until he saw Vanessa. She sounded distressed. She hadn't called since the last time. Markus assumed she'd taken care of it.

"She's going to be fine," Markus told himself. He had faith in her abilities.

As he followed the path to his garage, Markus saw no sign of Vanessa. It then crossed his mind that maybe, just maybe, she didn't make it. She didn't call because something happened.

Just like that, Vanessa's bike shot past his car. He looked through his windshield. She turned around and looked at him. With a smirk, Markus hit the gas.

The garage opened up. The two vehicles hit the ramp, increasing speed as the ramp sloped down, with the door closing quickly behind them. Markus skidded into his parking spot and threw his car into park.

Vanessa powered down her bike, settling into her space. She threw the kickstand down and stepped off of it, just as Markus was stepping out of his car. He took his mask off. She took off hers.

"My God, that was exhilarating!" Vanessa exclaimed. Markus nodded. "This van chased me, and I've never had someone chase me in a vehicle before, it just…I feel like I'm hyperventilating! I might be an adrenaline junkie!" She performed a little shimmy with her shoulders.

Markus stared at her blankly. He didn't know what to say or do. He'd never known anyone that danced after having a near-death experience.

She smiled. "That's my Getaway Dance, I suppose. Nothing like a good chase to wake you up!"

Without warning, Vanessa closed her eyes, leaned in and kissed Markus. His lips were warm and wet, and Vanessa would've been more satisfied, but…he neglected to kiss back. She opened her eyes. His eyes were aimed on hers. She pulled back.

"Well, that definitely didn't go the way I envisioned it," Vanessa said. "Let me apologize to you. I don't know what came over me. It just kind of happened, I guess."

"It would be better if you didn't bring it up," Markus said.

Vanessa showed him a fragile smile, with full understanding that – if Markus's expression was any indication – what she did wasn't okay.

"Ms. Vaughn, I only want to have this conversation with you once: don't mix business with pleasure. You know how I feel about Ms. Buchanan."

"Right." Vanessa wouldn't look at Markus. She felt bad about what she'd just done. She couldn't take it back. How Vanessa felt about Markus was out there, in the open. What was she to do? She felt completely and utterly embarrassed. "So, you don't feel a certain way about me, is that it?"

Markus paused. He knew what she was pushing for.

"A certain way, yes. You are someone I'll protect, and someone I believe will protect me," he explained. "I love you, Vanessa, but I'm not *in* love with you. Do you understand what I'm saying?"

"Yes, of course I understand."

There was no emotion in her voice whatsoever. Although it was redundant, Vanessa couldn't stop thinking about how embarrassed she was. She wanted to crawl in a hole and die.

"Good. I anticipate this not being a problem in the future." Markus had to be stern, but he still felt how he felt about her. "Let's keep working to keep the streets clear, okay?"

Vanessa nodded in agreement. "Yeah…I'm just going to stay down here for a little while. I need to decompress, and all."

Markus understood. He nodded and walked toward the door that led to the main level.

"Markus…"

Markus stopped and turned his head slightly.

"I'm sorry."

Markus gathered his thoughts quickly. "One of the rules of business: apologize the least, and acquire the most. Don't put yourself in a position to apologize. Besides, you're not sorry about what you did. You're sorry about how it was received."

Markus left. Vanessa heard the door shut and immediately became angry with her exploits. *Half-wit! Why did I do that? Everything was fine until I did that!*

Markus was on his way back upstairs. He was human. He'd already thought about what it would be like to kiss Vanessa's lips, but he knew when he brought her in that there was a certain line that shouldn't be crossed.

When Markus left, Vanessa pulled her phone out. She clicked a few buttons and waited. A video popped up.

"When are we eating? It's easily been four, maybe five hours. All I want is some food in my belly, a warm shower and a good book. Kill me now."

In the video, Vanessa flipped the camera to her own face and pursed her lips. She also formed her fingers into a gun and pressed it to her temple. The camera flipped back around and showed the bed.

She remembered it like it was yesterday.

"Vanessa, we only just got home." The camera panned to her mother. "When we all get clean, we all eat. Sounds easy enough, right?" She asked as she placed her hands out. The camera panned over to her father for a moment.

"Besides…if you're going to serve your country well, the last thing on your mind should be eating."

The camera panned back and forth between her mother and father.

"I'm first," her father announced. The camera panned to him, following his steps to the bathroom before it panned back to her mother.

"It's only proper your dad go first," her mom said, stifling a laugh.

"So…" her mom asked.

"It's not too bad. It's very quiet," Vanessa's voice could be heard. "I don't know if I can handle all that quiet. It's just not right."

"He's going to be in there a while," Vanessa's mother said. She nodded her head yes.

Vanessa heard herself giggle a bit.

"Maybe we can find something to watch, in the meantime? What do you say?" Her mother asked.

"The book suits me right now," Vanessa heard herself say. The screen went blank. She played it again.

Vanessa didn't question or doubt her new life, but she was lonely. No one could know about her night life. No one could know about her feelings towards Markus. As high as she felt off adrenaline, the isolation Vanessa felt was sobering. She needed friends. She had to move on from the death of her parents, though she wasn't sure how she would.

Chapter 19

Jasper scrolled through his phone while alone at a restaurant.

With the help of Patrick and Emma, he chased a woman on a high-powered motorcycle. His van was no match for that. He would have to supplement the lack of speed of his van with ingenuity. To him, he was still better. He wasn't outsmarted, he was outrun. That was the difference.

Jasper was always well-dressed. This time around, he was clad in a custom-tailored white suit, with a lilac purple and white-striped shirt. His ensemble was accompanied by an expensive pair of two-toned sunglasses.

Then he saw her.

She was golden brown-haired. Jasper guessed she was a couple inches shorter than him. He'd have to get her to stand up, somehow. He wouldn't stare; he'd steal glances at the beautiful young lady. Jasper assumed he was twice the woman's age, yet, he was still drawn to her.

Hmmm...

Jasper stood up from his table and approached the young woman. When he happened upon her, he smoothly leaned on the bar with his forearm, rested it near her. She looked at his arm, and then looked at him.

"Attractiveness speaks volumes," Jasper told the woman, "but never as loud as one's intelligence. I'm Jasper. Jasper Kane." He held his hand out for her to take.

"I'm Vanessa Vaughn," she said, taking his hand in hers, shaking it lightly. "Good to meet your acquaintance, Jasper."

"The pleasure is all mine," Jasper replied. He liked her English accent. "I have a table over there, and I'd love some company."

"Well, I–"

"No strings," he interrupted. He placed his hands up barely, to show her he wouldn't pressure her. "Excuse me for interrupting what you were about to say. That wasn't my intention when I came over here. I'm going to sit back at my table. We can talk, we can sit in silence and eat…just company, is all I'm asking."

Vanessa thought it would be harmless to sit with someone. She'd just talked about how lonely she was, and this new acquaintance was simply offering her a seat across from him. She didn't think he was hitting on her. Maybe he was in the same lonely boat as her.

Vanessa shrugged. "Okay…why not?"

Although Jasper enjoyed the company of numerous women over time, the daytime life he'd been leading had become stale. It was easy to figure out a person's general needs. To figure out exactly what he needed…that was a different story.

Vanessa got up first. She looked over her shoulder and smiled as she passed him. He wasn't familiar with the lotion she wore, but it smelled unbelievable. Vanessa ate the attention up. Jasper was handsome, without a doubt. He pulled her chair out for her and motioned for her to sit.

"Thank you."

Jasper helped her push the chair in before he took his own seat. He sipped water. Through her black-rimmed eyeglasses, Vanessa nervously looked down at a menu. Jasper looked up a few times, but not for long. He also checked his watch once.

"If you don't mind me asking…what do you do?" Jasper asked.

"No, I don't mind. I'm Markus Doubleday's personal assistant," Vanessa answered.

Jasper eagerly pointed Vanessa's way, snapping his fingers.

"The-uh thing…the Pay 4 Play place, right?"

The young woman nodded and snapped her fingers mockingly. "Right, the Pay 4 Play place."

Jasper smiled. "He's the owner…you have the vault to all his secrets, don't you?"

Vanessa smiled back politely, but didn't answer.

"I kid, but I do have one question: I'm not even close to being a billionaire. I'm assuming you're not, either?"

Vanessa nodded her head no.

"What I'd like to know is…what's he like? What's a billionaire do?"

Vanessa thought about what Markus did, exactly.

"He's like any other boss. I'm asked to schedule things, make notes, things of that nature. Quite easy, really. Enough about me, though. What do you do?" Vanessa asked.

"Oh, I don't do much," Jasper kidded, taking another sip of water. While he pulled the glass to his lips, he looked over the glass, stealing another glance at Vanessa. To him, she was intoxicating.

"I'm a therapist. I do tons of listening, and like to ask questions. Would you agree that you can learn a lot from listening?"

"Sure. For instance, I know what you do for a living," Vanessa joked. Jasper smirked at her observation. "Is that what drives you?"

"Drives me?" Jasper repeated.

Vanessa nodded yes.

"Well, lots of things drive me. My biggest goal is to be the best therapist in the world. One of my small goals is something simple, like waking up in the morning. They're goals, nonetheless. Every day is filled with the opportunity to impact and explore this world. Why not take advantage?"

Vanessa needed to hear that. She hadn't been Ivory Fox for long, but she knew she had a chance to change the world. The opportunity to meet someone as refreshing as Jasper was few and far, in between. Markus was interesting, but Jasper brought a different point of view to the table. Listening to Jasper speak was liberating.

"That's a good point, I suppose," Vanessa admitted.

“You don’t have to suppose, Vanessa. Things simply are, or they aren’t. I don’t know that there’s an in-between.”

That got Vanessa thinking: things either are, or aren’t. His words sounded simple enough. She thought about her life, how there wasn’t much room for a gray area.

“Also a good point,” Vanessa said. “Apologies for cutting this short, but they’re signaling that my food is ready, so I have to…”

“No worries whatsoever,” Jasper responded, placing his manicured hands up to stop her from apologizing. “No worries at all. Listen, I don’t want to make it some kind of awkward scene. Here, let me give you this.”

He reached in his wallet and pulled a card out, handing it to Vanessa. She took the card from Jasper and studied the content: his name, his profession, and his cell number. It was a simple black and white card, but heavy. Judging on feel, the cards he had weren’t cheap. She assumed only certain people got this card.

Vanessa understood the subtlety in Jasper’s wealth.

“Communication is ever-changing, nowadays,” Jasper acknowledged. “I don’t want to intrude and ask for your number. I’m interested, but again, no pressure. Call if you like.”

She offered him a shy smile as she slid the card into her pants suit pocket.

“Thank you, Mr. Kane.”

“You’re welcome, Vanessa,” Jasper said. He made eye contact with her while he spoke, something easily forgotten these days. Vanessa certainly appreciated it.

"I'll see you." Vanessa left Jasper to his thoughts. As she walked away, she felt his gaze. She imagined he wasn't immune to studying physical features. Vanessa didn't feel bad; she'd been checking him out, too.

"Vanessa Vaughn," Jasper said to himself. He sipped water from his glass again and nodded to the waiter who'd just brought his food out. He unfolded his napkin and placed it in his lap.

She's beautiful.

Back at the office, Markus waited for Vanessa to return with lunch. He'd thought about his conversation with Marissa, and he wanted to speak to her about it. He didn't get back to her the night before. She'd called earlier.

"Phone: call Marissa," Markus commanded.

A vivid hologram appeared at eye length, showing Marissa's profile. He listened to the ring of the phone before the actual Marissa Buchanan popped up.

"Hey! Good afternoon!" Marissa said cheerily.

"There she is!" Markus smiled. "Good to see you."

"Good to see you, too."

"Everything good?"

"Of course. Listen, I want to talk to you about a few things."

"Okay. What's on your mind?"

Marissa took a quick deep breath and tried to relax. She didn't know what Markus was about to say, especially since he'd gotten off the phone so abruptly the night before. She waited for his call, but it never came. She wondered if that would be a pattern, especially since he knew he held her interest. She also thought she was over-thinking the situation.

"Well, I just want to make sure that you're sure," Markus said. "We originally planned to be reunited for good in a year's time and this is kind of a surprise. I'm not saying I don't want to do it. I'm just saying I want you to be sure."

Marissa's face looked frozen, to him. He narrowed his eyes and took a couple steps closer to the screen.

"Phone: has the call ended?" Markus asked the screen.

"No, it hasn't," Marissa said quickly. "I just thought we already went through this. I'm wondering why it's still a thing with you." She looked up for a moment before she returned her gaze back to Markus. "Maybe it's this? Listen, if you're not ready–"

Markus sternly said, "I'm ready. I just need to know that you are. I've made investments before, Mare. But when I do, no matter how they turn out, I've been sure of my intentions. This is uncharted territory for us; that's all I'm saying. Lost love is different than lost money."

Marissa looked at him again, and this time, she wouldn't wait so long to speak.

"I'm sure. Markus, for God's sake, you've given me access to your house! And not just any access…I'm talking, voice-activated access!" She smiled. The thought of him doing that made her heart flutter. "As far as I know, it's you and me, and possibly your assistant that has that kind of access. What's her name, again?"

"Vanessa Vaughn."

"Yes…her. I don't know where my head is. Anyway, I don't think something like a contract should keep us from being together, if we want to be."

"I agree."

"So, let's not pretend like money would be an issue," Marissa continued. "Let's not pretend like my parents hate you, and we're trying to elope," she said. "Let's be honest with each other: we've been in love for a long time, and everything is right about this."

"I agree again."

"Okay, then," Marissa said with gleeful cheer. "I'm scheduled to be on Jackie Reed tonight, as you know, so I'll be flying out there in a few hours. I just wanted to say goodbye to you."

There was a knock at the door.

"Of course, someone would be interrupting this," Markus huffed. "It's probably Vanessa. Door: open."

In walked Marissa. Markus took her in quickly: an off-the-shoulder tee and some hip-rocking skinny jeans. Markus wouldn't stare. Marissa had a huge smile on her face.

"Door: close," Markus commanded. The door closed behind her. "Phone: end call." The hologram vanished.

Though Markus seldom showed emotion, Marissa read it all over his face. His smile told her everything she needed to know.

She was more than willing to take in his looks: another simple suit with a cream-colored shirt. *He can pull off a simple look like this. Other people? Not so much,* she thought.

"So…Jackie Reed tonight," Markus said. His question was in the form of a statement.

"Jackie Reed tonight," Marissa repeated, nodding her head yes. "I remember you being on there, so I can't wait to be on there. Well…again," she corrected. She'd been on Jackie's show a few times, but never with news of this magnitude. This would be a must-see, according to Jackie's advertisements.

"No offense, but I don't want to talk anymore," Marissa confessed. She dropped her clutch on the floor and approached him slowly.

"None taken." He approached her slowly.

When they both met, they didn't kiss to get a taste of each other, like school-aged kids. School-aged kids attacked each other. They'd find out later that a passionate kiss didn't have to be approached with such ferocity.

Markus and Marissa both leaned in, their lips meeting. It was full with fervor, so much so, that Markus let out a short moan of enjoyment and fulfillment. Simply put, Marissa drove Markus crazy, in the best way possible.

"I just wanted to…" Marissa's lips left his, making their way to his neck. When her lips touched his neck, it gave him goose bumps, sent shivers down his spine. His hands firmly just above her hips, Marissa used her fingers to slowly undo one of Markus's shirt buttons.

"Sir, I just wanted to–"

Markus's eyes shot open.

Marissa turned to see who was at the door. It was Vanessa. Any question she had about Vanessa's access credentials was answered.

Vanessa approached them. They looked hot and bothered, to her. She felt a pang of jealousy when she noticed Marissa. Part of her was glad she walked in when she did. She couldn't put her finger on it, but there was something untrustworthy about Marissa.

Markus gave Vanessa the same look he'd give to anyone that bothered him while he was busy.

"I'm sorry. What I was saying was…here's the lunch you ordered, although it looks as if you've skipped straight to dessert." She smiled and handed him a bag.

She noticed a light, fresh coat of Marissa's peachy-nude lipstick on Markus's neck. It appeared the two of them were about to get better acquainted in Markus's office. *He'll have me ordering a new desk by the end of the day, I'm sure of it*, she said to herself.

"Thank you, Ms. Vaughn. That will be all." Markus took the bag of food. Vanessa nodded and glared at Marissa briefly before she left Markus's office.

Markus was officially turned off. Sometimes, something small could ruin the mood. Vanessa's entry effectively ended anything that could have happened in his office.

Marissa was beyond irritated at that. She could feel her then-boiling blood start to simmer again. *Son of a B.*

"I guess lunch is here. We can share, if you want?" Markus asked Marissa, opening up his container. Kale and apple salad was on the menu for today.

"No, I already had lunch today. Anyway, I was just stopping through. I wanted to see you before I got on the plane, that's all."

She sounded disappointed. Markus understood. A part of him was also disappointed. Marissa was stunning every day of the week, but when the mood hit someone, the mood hit someone.

Marissa pecked Markus on the lips once more, scooped up her clutch and walked away. She turned one more time. He was digging through his food bag.

"Markus?"

"Yeah." A welcome interruption. He stopped what he was doing and met her eyes.

"Do you remember what you wanted to tell me last night, before we got interrupted?"

It wasn't the right time to tell her the truth about his identity. Not when she was about to travel. Markus would tell her as soon as she got back from California, as soon as she walked through his house door. He was out of time.

"Yes, but it can wait. We can talk about it when you get back," Markus told her. He was trying not to lie to her again. He'd done it before; he didn't want to make it a pattern.

Going against her better judgment, Marissa didn't ask questions. She trusted Markus with decisions. Very rarely did she question him. He also showed the same courtesy to her.

"Okay. No problem," Marissa said, as nicely as she could. "I love you."

"I love you too," Markus said to her. She smiled at him sweetly before she left his office.

Markus smiled to himself. He looked at the clock, immediately calculating how much time – tentatively – he had left before Marissa would return from her trip, take the drive to his house and walk through the doors, with the expectation of an explanation.

He'd just bought himself a little more time.

On the other side of town, Daphne De La Rosa walked into the precinct, dressed in her normal police garb with dark sunglasses. She pushed open the door to her unit. She didn't sleep well the night before because Jon didn't stay. She'd slept on and off for three hours or so. She wasn't in the mood.

"Cap wants to see you."

Daphne silently passed the detective and his proud smirk on her way to Captain Grove's office. She ignored the whispers behind her as she approached his door. She'd just arrived at the precinct, and she couldn't wait to get the day over with.

She rapped on the office door before she walked in. "Captain, you wanted to see me?" Daphne said to him. He looked up from his paperwork, and pulled his glasses down toward the bottom of his nose.

"Yeah. Sit down."

Daphne took a seat across from Grove's desk and crossed her legs.

"So, do you have a relationship with Detective Deadmarsh?" Captain Grove asked. "You know, there's a lot of talk in these halls. I figured I'd go straight to the source."

Saliva accumulated in Daphne's mouth. She gulped it down. This talk made her nervous. She adjusted one of her shirt sleeves.

"Sir, a relationship? A relationship like…what do you mean? Can I have some context?" She asked.

"I think you know what I mean, De La Rosa. Are you two seeing each other?" Grove asked. "As in, dating. Do you go or have you ever been out on a date or dates with Detective Deadmarsh?"

Captain Grove's questions were abundantly clear. She had no wiggle room to misinterpret his words, or play dumb. She had to answer. She averted her eyes away from his gaze.

"No, we don't date," Daphne said.

"Did you ever date?" Captain Grove asked.

"Kind of," Daphne explained.

Captain Grove cocked his head forward and raised an eyebrow.

Daphne said, "We've shared a few personal moments here and there, but he didn't come home with me to meet my parents or anything. Trust me, nothing huge happened. All of that is over between us."

Captain Grove nodded. "I'll say. He put in his resignation."

It was Daphne's turn to cock her head forward. She barely did it, not enough to notice. She felt her eyes narrow and her eyebrows furrow. She turned her nose up.

Was it *that* serious between them, that he would quit his job? They may not have been the best partners, but he was undoubtedly valued in the precinct.

"I-I…do you want me to talk to him or something?" Daphne questioned.

"Yeah," Captain Grove replied. "We need him here. He may be one of the most awkward people I've ever been around, but it's not a win for us, if he quits. Getting rid of him doesn't make our precinct better."

Captain Grove posed a great point. Deadmarsh was an effective worker, even though she found herself at odds with his unorthodox approach. Was Superhero Code too much of a roadblock?

"Okay," Daphne said, "I'll talk to him."

Captain Grove pointed at her and said, "For once in your life, put your pride aside and do what's best for the precinct. That's not a request. I don't care if you have to give him a back massage every day for six months. Make sure he stays here."

"Loud and clear."

"Have a good day, Daphne."

She stood up from her chair and left Captain Grove's office.

I can keep the same principles and beliefs. Nobody said Jon and me have to agree, but I need to get back in his good graces, and fast, she thought.

She would muster up the courage to visit Jon.

The day turned to night. Markus sat in his living room with the TV on. He would still go out tonight, but he figured the TV in his car would only be a distraction.

A voice interrupted his thoughts.

"Hey! We're back!" Jackie said from behind his desk. He rhythmically slapped the wood surface a few times while the audience settled back into the show. "My first guest…oh, I don't know what to say about her that hasn't already been said. I can't hold in my gushing anymore! Ladies and gentlemen, I'm a volcano! Please welcome…Marissa Buchanan! Marissa?"

Iggy Azalea's "Fancy" played. Marissa emerged from behind a curtain with crinkled eyes and a smile that dominated her facial features. She dressed simple, a double-breasted vest with wide-leg trousers and pumps, all black.

She self-assuredly strode over to the plush chair by Jackie's desk. Marissa was – arguably – one of the most popular people on the planet. The reception from her adoring fans gave Marissa goose bumps.

Jackie waited for her to get to him, and when she arrived, they simultaneously kissed each other's cheek. After they shared a few words, she situated herself on the couch. The music stopped, but the crowd didn't. Marissa heard more "compliments" than she cared to count. Jackie exaggeratingly fanned his self, playing it up to the cat-callers in the audience.

"Hi!" Marissa said.

"Hello! It's good to see you again!" Jackie said.

"Good to be here!"

"I think they're glad to see you again, too!"

The group cheered wildly again. Marissa smiled politely and waved again. Her cheeks became flush. While she was flattered by the attention given, she never thought she'd ever quite get used to it.

Jackie waited until the crowd died down again, and then continued. "So…you're on a lot of media platforms?"

"Right," Marissa responded.

"Why is that?"

"I'm really just a normal girl. I watch movies, watch TV. I have things in this world I love and hate…I share them, just like everybody else does. The only thing that makes me different is that I'm in newspapers and magazines, and anything I do or say will be put out in the open."

"That's a great point."

"Thank you."

"How are things going? You've been busy," Jackie pointed out.

"Busy-busy," Marissa smiled. "Lots of things going on."

"Care to share?"

"Sure! I'm on the Jackie Reed Show. That's like, where people share things, right?" She asked, using her hands to convey her question.

Jackie nodded yes at Marissa's question. "I'm like a chaplain."

The crowd laughed. The Jackie Reed Show was notorious for announcements, big or small.

Using a comically ominous voice, Jackie said, "The world waits."

Marissa took a breath in and exhaled. She agreed to this; she didn't know why she was nervous. "Okay, here goes: I am going to take a break from modeling. I don't think its retirement, because…you know, never say never, but…you know, I'm done, for now."

Jackie's face contorted to show surprise. "Oh no! Say it ain't so!"

"Oh, it's so," Marissa said. "I'm going to focus on designing clothes."

"Clothes?"

"Yes, clothes for everyone, not just your run-of-the-mill, 115-pound model. We're going to have all sizes and all kinds of models. And tasteful colors, not things like Manatee Grey."

The audience members laughed again.

"I mean, I remember reading that in a catalog!" Marissa continued. She was on a roll. "Talk about a faux pas, I laughed at it! I didn't think they were serious, like, why on earth would you do that?!" She asked rhetorically. "I took note. My product is meant to appeal to *all* women. We're all beautiful, so I'm trying to eliminate the segregation, based on what people perceive as beauty."

"I get exactly what you're saying," Jackie said.

This crowd – and possibly the world – ate out of the palm of Marissa's hand. Jackie sensed it. He nodded in approval and appreciation of Marissa's words. The crowd remained silent while Marissa spoke.

"People in all walks of life have different stories," Marissa went on. "Some don't work out as hard as I do. Some work out harder. Some haven't gotten rid of their baby weight…and, you know, everyone deserves something nice. I mean, I'm not going to act like I haven't gone on a taco run late at night, or had chili cheese fries at two, three o'clock in the morning. We all do it."

"You're going to have a lot of time on your hands, what, with you retiring and everything. What are you going to do with all that free time?" He asked her, flat-out. She knew he was going to ask, but she and Jackie had to work the crowd a little. She feigned surprise at his words.

"What am I going to do?" Marissa said, repeating Jackie's question. Her lips formed into the largest smile ever recorded.

"Well, I'm going to move back to the states. I'm doing it to be closer to Markus Doubleday."

The place lost their collective composure when they heard that. Lots of hollering and clapping filled the studio. Marissa was appreciative of their support. To her, the unification with Markus would be epic. She believed they could be America's Sweethearts.

"Okay! Okay! We have to quiet down if we want this show to go!" Jackie said, using a hand to signal the crowd to settle. When they did, he spoke again. "So, Ms. Buchanan, this isn't the reason you're retiring, is it?"

She shook her head in a childlike manner. "No-no! Of course not! Listen, am I moving back to the states to be closer to Markus? Yes, but that's not all. I want to impact the world with my own vision, not just sell someone else's product."

"Right."

"Three things are important in this life, Jackie: you want to be loved, respected and accepted. By moving back over, I'm doing all three. Efficient idea, if I ever heard one."

The crowd clapped.

"Dazzlingly efficient, quite engaging and incredibly intelligent," Jackie pointed out. "I wouldn't expect anything less, honestly. As contrived as it sounds, Markus Doubleday is clearly the luckiest man in the world. It's always a pleasure to be in your company."

Marissa put some extra sweetness in her voice when she said, "Thank you. You too."

"All right, when we come back, we're going to–"

"TV: off."

Back at his home, Markus's eyebrows rose.

"On TV…that's big."

He sighed and shook his head before he headed to the basement, where Vanessa waited. She was somewhat impatient when it came to leaving out for the night, but the two had an understanding that Marissa was an important part of Markus's life.

"Okay, here we go." Markus placed his hand on the sensor.

As one door closed, another opened.

"What do you want, De La Rosa?"

Jonathan's words were dry. He left enough room for his head and half his body to be shown, leaving Daphne out in the hallway of his apartment building. He wasn't willing to let her in. Not again.

She'd played this whole thing out in her head a million times. She had hours to think about it, and yet, she felt like she needed more time. It was late. She was tired. By the looks of it, so was he. They'd both had enough, but for different reasons. Daphne ran a big risk by being out this late, but making things right was more important.

Just tell him how you feel, she thought to herself. Instead, she said, "I heard you were quitting."

"Yes, I am," Jon said.

"Why, Deadmarsh? You can't blame every little thing that's gone wrong between us on me."

"You know, you have a lot of nerve, showing up on my doorstep and instantly assuming that I blame you for the things that went wrong. Now, you're telling me how I'm supposed to feel? Incredible!"

"We're out in the hallway, Deadmarsh. If you're not going to let me in, then lower your voice, please. Are you going to let me in?"

"I've done that before, Daphne…more times than you'll ever know."

Jon's words floored Daphne. She read between the lines. In her heart, she knew he was right. Jon was pretty reserved by nature, so his revelation caught Daphne off-guard. She was too scared to tell him how she felt. What if he'd changed his mind? When you felt a certain way about someone, did you ever truly change your mind? Why wouldn't she just take a chance?

Daphne's voice sounded subdued when she said, "Do you have something you want to say?"

She was willing to listen to everything he had to say, if he decided to talk. Jon cracked the door a bit more, letting go of the knob and standing in front of Daphne.

Just tell her how you feel, Jon thought to himself. What came out was, "I can't do this, this thing between us. Maybe I'm too sensitive, but this seems like an everyday thing, with you."

"What seems like an everyday thing with me?" She asked.

"You dump on me! If something doesn't go your way, it's my fault! You can't stand the fact that you haven't caught your precious lawbreakers, so what do you do? You take it out on me!"

The emotion of the moment caught up to him. Daphne remained silent. She couldn't bring herself to say what she wanted to say. She wanted so badly to tell Jonathan how she felt about him. As frustrating as it was, she just couldn't do it.

For him, spontaneity took over.

"Do you know the worst thing about this?"

Jon didn't wait for Daphne to answer.

"I'm in love with you! And you know it! You're doing these things because you *know* you can, and that's not right! It's not!"

His proclamation left him visibly flustered. He looked down and bit his lip. He fought to hold it together. Daphne didn't budge. He'd said so much. She wouldn't give him anything, even though he was right. It embarrassed her. She wondered if she'd regret it later. For now, she'd protect herself.

His tone was lower when he said, "I've accepted you for who you are and what you want to be." He finally looked at Daphne, her eyes on him, as well. "All I'm asking is for you to treat me with the same respect I treat you. That's all. I need to hear something from you right now, anything to validate our conversation. Anything."

Daphne stayed silent.

He knew she wanted to say something. He couldn't be convinced, otherwise. He wanted to give her a chance to validate their conversation, not just him talking at her.

"Daphne…say something," Jonathan provoked. He sounded exasperated. "Say anything. I don't care what it is. You came over here for a reason, just…say something," he said, the sound of near-defeat ringing loudly in his voice. "I know you feel something for me, Daphne, just…"

She felt his glare. He cared about her, he loved her, he held her in high regard…and here she was, being predictable, saying nothing. There was too much residual damage. As quick as she was to pull the trigger on a criminal, she wasn't quick to pull the trigger of her heartstrings.

And then, as if awakened out of a trance, Daphne finally spoke. She gave Jon eye contact and said, "I just came by to wish you good luck."

Jon felt himself starting to lose composure. Before he did, he stepped back into his apartment and shut the door.

She knew her words were emotionless. She would deal with her feelings later, but for now, she would stick to what she was good at – differentiating her feelings from her actions. Instead of saying what she felt was right, she didn't.

She walked down the hallway. Away from him. Away from this.

Chapter 20

Marissa was en route to Markus's house, having finished *Jackie Reed* some hours before. She was anxious for Markus's reaction to her interview. She briefly wondered how he'd taken it. If he didn't watch the show, she was sure he got the news from somewhere.

She received a text from Markus about having a late dinner at Abacus, an expensive downtown restaurant. Even though she was tired of dressing up, she liked to look good for him. Tonight, she was in a fuchsia silhouette dress, with peach Louboutin shoes and a matching clutch.

She found solace knowing that in less than two hours, she'd be dressed down again. It was a small price to pay. Even when she traveled back from California, she wore a t-shirt and jeans. A pair of leggings weren't too much to ask.

Marissa spoke her name into the small receiver that sat a few feet from Markus's gate. Once the gate opened, she slowly pulled into the driveway and parked. She loved the look of his house at night.

She grabbed her clutch and walked to the front door with a song in her heart, Donny Osmond's version of "Puppy Love." She brought her hand to the sensor, but stopped short. She was about to see Markus for the first time since she announced her intentions on live TV.

"Okay…okay…don't throw up. Everything's going to be fine. Nothing to worry about," Marissa assured. She smiled and pressed her hand against the sensor. When she heard the door unlock, she turned the knob and walked through, closing the door behind her. She couldn't keep her eyes off the first thing she saw when she turned around.

"Ah…you're here."

Marissa took Markus in. He went mostly dark – dark blazer, dark slacks and dark shoes – with a white shirt and a peachy-colored tie. He looked good, as always. As he made his way down the stairs, Marissa smelled the *Sophisticated Gentleman* fragrance.

"You know, you just have a way about you," Marissa complimented.

When Markus made it to the bottom of the stair, he said, "Maybe it's just when you're around. You look like I'm the luckiest guy in the world."

She smiled. "Oh, you watched? Well, you *are* lucky, and don't you ever forget it. I don't want to mess up my makeup, so here…" She pecked him quickly and pulled back. Anything else and they wouldn't make their reservation. She licked the tip of her thumb and slowly ran it across the bottom of Markus's lip.

"I want you to promise me that, as soon as we get home, I get to put on some leggings. Something not so dressy." She used her fingers to accentuate her current state. "I have an overnight bag in my car, so–"

"And, not to mention, a lot of stuff here," Markus said. "You basically live here, already."

"Good point."

"Shall we go? I've built up an appetite, sitting here and waiting for you."

"We shall. And remember, don't eat too much, you don't want to get too full."

"Too full?" Markus escorted Marissa out the front door. He hit the button on his keychain to unlock the doors while he circled around his silver Aston Martin One-77. There were 77 of these cars built, and he had one. He pulled the passenger door open for Marissa.

She said, "I'll let you think about that one." She winked and patted his jaw line before she carefully lowered herself into the passenger seat.

He pushed the door closed and circled around the back of the vehicle. Right before Markus grabbed the car door handle, he caught Marissa's drift: he wouldn't be able to fool around later on if he got too full. Instead of mentioning it, Markus settled into his seat and headed to the restaurant.

"So, your trip…how did that go?" Markus asked.

"Oh, you know…"

Markus nodded his head no. Marissa giggled.

"I wasn't there for long. I flew in, did the show, and I was out of there. Well, no; I went to sleep, woke up and *then* I was out of there," she corrected.

"That's great. Hey, so…I know I've told you this before, but I fully support what you want to do, career-wise. I also want to be there to help you," he said, cutting to the chase.

"What do you mean?"

"I mean, why don't we go into business together?" Markus proposed. His car hugged the sidewalk on a turn. "I sell clothing…technically."

Marissa laughed out loud. "Yes, you sell smut-tastic evening wear. Your collection needs a lot of work."

Markus kept his eyes on the road while he said, "Absolutely. The world knows your ideas are superior. That's why I want you to be in charge of the fashion for P4P."

When Markus spoke, Marissa's ears perked up. Nothing made her ears perk up like opportunity, though. "I'd love to hear more."

"You'd be in charge of the night wear, but also your own fashion line, the one you were talking about starting while you were on Jackie Reed's show. I think working under an umbrella would be a safer risk. I also think it would be good for my business, as well."

Marissa thought it made sense, but, to work at the same company with your partner or spouse, or whatever their relationship status was? One of her future goals was to be married. That was no secret.

She nodded. "So far, so good…but I have a couple conditions."

Markus made another tight turn. "Name them."

"I need a big, spacious office…like yours. On the same floor, but away from you; I need to feel like I can stand alone, work-wise."

"That can be done by the end of the weekend. Just tell Vanessa what you need, and she'll make the arrangements. Next?"

"We're not going to mix business with pleasure. I won't budge on that. I want to set a precedent. I'm here to work, just like everyone else. I don't want your people to think I got into a nice, cushy office because we sleep together."

"You're showing your teeth, and I like it. I can't argue your rules; you made a lot of great points. Let me ask you, though: have you been thinking about all of this already?"

"Yes. As much as I travel, I've pretty much planned most of my life on planes. If you weren't going to make me an offer, I was going to make you one. Our names are out there; what's the downside to combining our marketing power?" She asked.

"Good point," Markus acknowledged. "It makes good business sense."

The car stopped by the sidewalk. The valet opened the car door for her. She gave him a courteous smile and took his hand, allowing herself to be helped out of the car. Marissa would've had trouble getting out of the car in tennis shoes, much less, Louboutins.

After he handed the valet his keys, Markus took Marissa's waiting hand and headed towards the front door of the restaurant.

"Miss Buchanan is entering the restaurant with Mr. Doubleday," he heard.

He continued his walk alongside Marissa. At Abacus, they never did that. Markus cocked his head back slightly and listened for more, but nothing else came out. His posture never wavered. Still holding Marissa's hand, he rubbed it with his thumb.

She squeezed his hand a couple times. "I love this place," Marissa admitted. Both of them nodded at the door greeter.

When they encountered the hostess, she said, "Mr. Doubleday, Ms. Buchanan…it's good to see you two. I'll show you to your seats."

Per Markus's request, the hostess led the two over to a secluded area. Markus paid for the few empty tables around them, for the sake of privacy. He was selfish sometimes, especially when it came to spending time with Marissa.

Marissa ate that kind of stuff up.

"Your server will be with you shortly."

Markus nodded and waited for Marissa to sit down first before he sat. The waiter brought himself over, a tall and slender fellow, ready to take orders.

"We just want to…sushi and sashimi, right?" Markus asked, pointing at Marissa. She nodded yes. Though they hadn't been to the restaurant in ages, he still remembered what she liked. "We want the tasting portion. Let's start there, and whatever wine you think goes well with it," he said.

The waiter nodded and scurried back to send the order, leaving the two alone again.

"We don't have glasses for this, but we should make a toast," Marissa said. "Should we toast to new beginnings? An overdue reunion? I'm looking for ideas, here."

"It all fits," Markus said. "Hey, listen: silly me, I have to go to the bathroom. I should've gone before I left the house."

"Yeah, because we're five years old," Marissa teased. "Get out of here. I'll see you when you get back."

Markus paid no mind to anyone as he walked briskly to the bathroom door and pushed it open. Once the door closed behind him, he looked and listened for movements in the unblemished bathroom. Nothing.

He pulled his phone out. His voice was quiet when he said, "Phone: call Vanessa." It called. He slowly paced while he waited. After a few rings, he heard her voice.

"Hello?"

"Where are you?"

"I'm around. Why? What's it to you?" She asked him jokingly.

"I heard someone say my name, along with Marissa's."

"That's pretty common, you know. People think you're popular, or something."

"I want to make sure it's a paparazzi thing and nothing else. Do you mind heading this way?"

Vanessa sighed. "Sure, why not?"

Several screams came from the dining room. His head popped up. He stopped pacing. He looked at the bathroom door. He heard lots of commotion coming from the dining room.

"What was that?" Vanessa asked.

"I'm looking."

He walked slowly toward the door and cracked it open, giving himself enough room for one eye to snoop out into the dining area. He saw one gunman. His back was turned away. Markus quietly closed the door before the gunman turned around.

"I think someone's holding the place up," Markus told Vanessa, his voice lower than a whisper.

"Good Lord, Markus! You need to get out!"

"Just get here. Meet me in the back of Abacus. If you don't know where it is, ask your bike." He turned his phone off and slid it in the inside pocket of his blazer.

Not another second passed before the bathroom door busted open. A startled Markus stared at the two men pointing their guns at him.

"Didn't you hear the man?" One of them asked. "Everybody out of the bathroom! What, are you deaf?"

"No-no-no! I just didn't hear him!" Markus placed his hands in the air submissively, chest-high. His defense mechanism in these situations was to revert back to how he thought people saw him: he was a guy who made money, not war.

The two escorted Markus out of the bathroom. He scanned the restaurant in seconds. Everyone looked terrified, as if they didn't think they would be held up while enjoying their night on the town. His outward appearance conveyed worry. On the inside, he was fuming.

His eyes found Marissa. It further infuriated him. He subtly mouthed to her with his lips, "Breathe. Eyes up." He cocked his head back slightly and inhaled, followed by an exhale.

Marissa followed suit.

He then mouthed, “Are you okay?”

She subtly nodded yes, and smiled.

One of the men jammed the barrel of his gun inches away from Markus’s cheek. Marissa’s eyes got big. All the breathing instruction was out the window. Her breathing improved when Markus gave her an assuring look.

“Hey, Chuckles…what are you so happy about? How about I put a bullet in your head? Maybe then, you won’t be so happy?”

“Okay. I’m sorry.” Markus’s eyes stayed on Marissa, his hands, still in the air

“Better be.” The captor laughed to his friend, celebrated his verbal victory. In situations such as these, Markus thought it was better to stay calm than get frantic.

“Did everyone know Marissa Buchanan is her father’s most prized possession?” He asked, approaching her. When he arrived by her side, he hovered. The small hairs on the back of Marissa’s neck stood up. She looked up at him. That voice was familiar, one she could pick from a crowd. *That son of a…*

Saying his name would exacerbate the situation. She might get her head blown off if she didn’t play it straight. It wasn’t worth taking a chance.

“What are you–…why?” Marissa asked him softly.

“Why?” Dwight repeated her words. “Why? Because I don’t have anything left to lose! I’m not valued in your family anymore. Since your daddy’s boy showed up, I’ve been shoved to the side.

Why don't I ask you? If my job is to protect him, and he doesn't feel like he needs to be protected…what's my job?!"

"Aren't you still getting paid?" Marissa asked innocently. "Have we not taken care of you?"

"It's the principle!" Dwight argued. "I wanted to earn my keep! My self-worth was tied up in that job!" His voice sounded desperate when he said, "Your daddy's associated with the wrong people, so I'm going to show him how important a job like mine is."

Marissa gulped. She had no idea what Dwight meant, but she knew enough to know her father wasn't known as an angel of goodwill.

"This is crazy. Let everyone go," Marissa sternly ordered. "If your thing is with me and my family, then it's with me and my family. These people have nothing to do with that. Let everyone go."

"You don't understand…"

Dwight firmly pushed his gun's barrel to Marissa's temple. Some gasped, some screamed. The other gunmen pointed their guns at the screamers, told them to shut up. It didn't take long.

Dwight pressed the barrel of his gun to her temple harder. "I don't take orders from the Buchanan's anymore. I don't work for them. So that means, you do what I say, or…I unload this clip in your head, and Abacus has a big mess to clean up. Do we understand each other?"

"Yes," Marissa begrudgingly buckled.

"No turning back." Dwight felt the trigger on his finger as he readied himself to pull it.

The lights went out. More hysteria.

"Shut up! If I hear anymore moving, I'm gonna shoot!" Dwight warned. "You make damn sure you're on your P's and Q's!"

Markus loved when one of the average person's senses were taken away. It allowed him to escape the two aggressors that flanked him. While Markus headed one way, Dwight headed another.

"What the hell happened to all the lights?!" Dwight was clearly panicked. In truth, Dwight didn't want to shoot anyone. He only wanted to make Marissa pay for something her father did. This quickly devolved into an irreconcilable mess.

It was then that he thought about jail time. His life would change. The idea to hurt Marissa wasn't one of his best. Most importantly, he thought about how powerful Michael Buchanan really was. Adding all that up, he was starting to have second thoughts.

Meanwhile, Markus successfully navigated through the restaurant's kitchen. He now found himself in a wide alleyway outside, where Vanessa waited.

"Sounds dangerous. Shall I come with?" Vanessa asked, smiling.

"I need you to do me a huge favor," Markus said.

Her smile lessened.

"I need you to grab my car from the valet, the silver Aston Martin. You have less than a minute before the generator kicks on, and the lights come back. When they do, I want you to drive right by the front door with my car."

Vanessa's bright features grew dim. "Just a drive?"

His car pulled up behind her, the one he used as the Sound. She turned around momentarily, and then turned back to Markus.

"Sometimes, being a hero isn't glamorous. If you weren't doing this, trust me, you'd be in there. Quickly, Vanessa; there isn't much time."

Vanessa agreed to his request with another nod. She wanted some action, but she understood the value of being a good soldier. She walked away while Markus made sure the coast was clear. When it was, he stepped into his car.

"Car: I need a backup suit," Markus said. The glove compartment opened and slid out, like a tray. On top, lay one of his suits. He started the process of undressing. The lights would be on soon.

"Don't the lights come on sometime?" One of Dwight's cohorts questioned.

"Yes! Just be patient! Don't shoot anyone unless they give you a reason to!" Dwight commanded. He didn't know how the lights worked. He was just improvising.

He heard a loud click. He looked around. He hoped that sound meant the lights were coming back on soon. He pressed the cold barrel of his gun to Marissa's temple harder, just to make sure she was there.

"That's a good girl."

"He's going to kill you for this," Marissa warned as lowly as she could. "Once he finds out, and he will…you'll be dead by breakfast."

Marissa's threatening words made him nervous. The gravity of his actions made it impossible to fix. Deep down, he didn't want to kill Marissa. He'd known her since she was a teenager. She'd grown into a woman, right before his eyes. His reservations grew louder and louder, with every second that passed.

"Maybe I should just kill you..."

The lights dimmed. People looked around the room, acclimating themselves to light again. A few seconds later, the lights fully turned on.

Tap…Tap-Tap-Tap-Tap-Tap…Tap-Tap

Silence. All eyes on the room were on a masked Markus. He cocked his head to the side. Nobody moved. People barely blinked, barely breathed.

"Get him!" Dwight angrily directed.

Two each threw a punch. Markus stepped back. They stopped just short of hitting each other. They looked at each other, breathed a sigh of relief.

As soon as the closest one turned, Markus hit him. He fell into his friend. Obscenities flew around while he struggled to shed the weight of his unconscious accomplice.

Markus faced Dwight.

Dwight's emotions moved from nervous to scared. His gaze swung back and forth, left to right. His eye caught a silver Aston Martin peeling out and speeding past the restaurant's doors. It got everyone else's attention, too.

"I can't believe you'd be with such a coward," an irate Dwight told Marissa.

Tap…Tap-Tap-Tap-Tap-Tap…Tap-Tap

A masked Markus used his baton to tap another table. He approached Dwight unhurriedly, tapping every table on his right side along the way. A few steps brought him a mere six feet away from Dwight. He outstretched his other hand. All he wanted was the gun. He motioned to Dwight.

"No!" Dwight exclaimed.

He motioned again.

"You don't understand! I've gone too far!" Dwight reasoned. "He's going to kill me! Do you understand that?! I've heard about you. You don't kill anybody! I don't fear you!"

Markus swung his baton downward and smashed Dwight's wrist. Dwight let out a blood-curdling scream, dropping the gun and instantly clutching his wrist. It was definitely broken.

Markus's actions were a necessary evil of the job. He never felt good about it, but in the end, he'd let him off easy.

Noisy sirens broke everyone's line of thinking. Sounds of relief mixed with some delirium filled the room. People scattered in different directions once the police arrived, no longer confined by the threat of guns.

As he saw police approaching, Markus scanned the building for a way out. Through all of the craziness, Marissa remained glued to her chair. He ignored all the panic and chaos around him. He held his hand out for Marissa to take.

She was initially uncertain, but allowed herself to be helped up. She picked up her pace when she felt her savior's urgent pull. She slipped off her Louboutins midstride. He pushed the men's bathroom door open and let her through before he closed and locked the slow-moving door.

He looked up at the ceiling. He stepped inside a stall and stood on the toilet.

"Hide," he muttered into his wrist. He pushed a few ceiling tiles over. He turned and looked at her. She raised an eyebrow. He intertwined his fingers and held them upside down.

"Up?" Marissa asked.

He nodded yes.

"Okay."

Her words hurried, she placed her delicate feet inside his locked fingers. He boosted her up fast. She let out a short yelp. Once she was safely in the ceiling, she was too afraid to move. Moments later, the masked man's head popped up. He hoisted himself into the ceiling with her, carefully sliding the ceiling tiles back to their original spots.

He placed his index finger to his mouth. Marissa nodded yes fervidly, keeping her eyes on the masked man as he looked forward.

This couldn't have gone any worse! I can't believe Markus ran out on me! Unbelievable! She thought. "At least take me!"

She pouted. Her words were louder than expected. The masked man quickly brought his index finger back to his mouth.

“I’m sorry!” Marissa whispered. She placed her hand tightly on her mouth as she heard the threats from the police at the bathroom door. They banged on it to further announce their presence.

Meanwhile, down on the main level, the police raided the restaurant. They caught two of the three gunmen. As told by patrons, the third was gone.

“Get them out of here.”

Daphne De La Rosa’s tone was serious. The officers roughly escorted the two men out. She jogged over to the women’s bathroom. Everything was clear. She then jogged over a few feet to the men’s bathroom. A couple officers standing outside the door let her know it was all clear.

“Did you check everything?” De La Rosa said to the officers. “Did you check the ceiling? Is everything *really* clear?” She grilled.

Marissa took a deep gulp, covering her mouth even tighter. She looked at her liberator. He looked unfazed by it all. Maybe he planned to jump down and take on all the cops? Marissa didn’t want to be on the front page of a tabloid. Nothing got you on the front page faster than a scuffle involving cops.

“Attention: we have an APB on the suspect, on Fifth and Shenandoah. All police in the area need to pursue immediately.”

It didn’t matter that she wanted the officers to keep digging. As soon as Daphne heard the call, she shot out of the bathroom. The ceiling was the least of her worries. The guy she was looking for wasn't hiding in the ceiling. He was still in the vicinity, and on the run.

"Let's go!" She yelled to a group of officers. She bustled to her car and pulled off. The rest of the police – save for a couple – followed suit. They would catch this guy, no matter what. He'd done too much to get off with a slap on the wrist.

Back in the bathroom, Marissa felt like they'd been inside the ceiling forever. She didn't know why they were waiting, but she was too afraid to do her own thing. She was a maverick, but she wasn't *that* much of a maverick.

"Markus?" She whispered. She got no answer.

He barely moved a single tile and peered down. The coast appeared clear. He completely moved the tile and hopped down, both his feet landing solidly on the lid. When Marissa peered down, she saw his outstretched arms.

"Okay, crazy night," Marissa said. She slid off the edge of the ceiling opening and – literally – fell into his arms. Her bare feet rested on the toilet lid. "And *that's* disgusting." He took a step down to the ground and helped Marissa to his level.

He opened the bathroom door slightly and listened for noise. The restaurant cleared out pretty quick. In this city, when the police had their sights set on someone, they would stop at nothing. He wouldn't complain. Their greed afforded him freedom.

"Find me," he uttered into his wrist. He exited the bathroom and slid toward the back door of the restaurant. There was no way he'd go through the front.

Marissa's feet shuffled a step behind him. "Where are we going?" She asked. He didn't answer. *This is getting on my nerves. Why am I following this guy if he's not going to talk to me? Also, isn't it creepy for someone to not talk? I'm losing patience, here!*

He pushed the restaurant's backdoor open. To the right, a black car's engine ran. He opened the car door, once he happened on it. Before he stepped in, he motioned for her to come along.

"I don't get in the car with strangers!" Marissa squawked. "Plus, I don't even know where we're going! I'm not going anywhere until you say something to me!"

"A safe place," he said.

"Okay, then." Marissa was happy to get her way.

I don't think he'd protect me, just to kill me, himself. What are the odds? When was the last time something like that actually happened? I need to stop thinking about that! That's so morbid!

Marissa stepped into the car. It sped off before she had the chance to put her seatbelt on. As she tugged to extend her seatbelt, she noticed they were headed a direction that looked more than familiar. The car zigzagged through traffic. It was reckless, yet professional. She nervously checked her seatbelt one more time.

"You don't talk very much, do you?" Marissa asked.

He expertly slithered in and out of lanes.

She narrowed her eyes. "It must be a lonely life. It's obvious you don't like to talk…what *do* you like to do?"

No answer.

"You might be an artsy type," Marissa continued. "I bet you like really nice things, like puppies and the Sistine Chapel. That sounds right up your alley." If he was going to keep quiet, Marissa would fill the void. Uncomfortable silence in cars made her squirm.

Is he an associate? Am I dealing with Markus's bodyguard, what's-his-name?

"I know you're not taking me to Markus's house. That guy left me high and dry. He trusted *you* with my life? You don't even know me! What happened to true love?" She rambled.

The car picked up speed when it passed up Markus's street. Marissa peered over at the speedometer; the car was at well over 100 miles per hour. She clutched the sides of the seat, looked up to the ceiling of the car and closed her eyes. She wouldn't talk while this maniac drove like this.

She heard a loud sound. She forced her eyes open and watched in awe as the ground opened up past the gates of Markus's house. The gates slowly swung open. She was officially scared now.

Her voice elevated to coincide with her panic. "What the hell's going on?!" She looked at the speedometer again. It was at 130.

Marissa screamed like a banshee as the car shot down the ramp that led to the garage. She dug her fingernails into the seats and stole a few glances behind her, just in time to see the ground close.

The car skidded perfectly into a vacant spot. He looked over at Marissa momentarily before he exited the car.

Marissa was furious. She unlocked her seatbelt and angrily elbowed herself out of the passenger's seat, slamming the car door behind her.

"Are you freaking crazy?!" Marissa abrasively asked him.

He continued to walk.

"What the hell is wrong with you, Markus's lackey?! You had a passenger in the car with you! Safety first! Didn't your parents teach you that?!"

He stopped.

Marissa went from angry to nervous again.

He turned and faced her.

Her heart beat faster than it ever had, faster than the robbery attempt, some months before.

He tightly grabbed the top of his mask and pulled at it, the connection at the neck ripping and coming undone.

"They did."

He pulled the mask off and held it in his hand. His unwavering steely blue eyes locked on hers. He smiled at her.

"Are you serious?" Marissa said in a near-whisper. Her eyes slimmed. "Markus…is that really you? I mean…you do this? That's you, the one on TV they're talking about all the time?"

Markus nodded yes.

"I guess you really *are* busy," Marissa said skeptically. "So, let me get this straight: you didn't leave me high and dry at Abacus?"

"No. Well, maybe for a moment. I had to change."

"I could've sworn I saw you leave."

“Vanessa took my car.”

Marissa felt some regret. She’d cursed Markus’s name the entire time they were in the car. She talked directly to the source, and didn’t know it. Until now.

“So, you just took everything I said to you, and you just…didn’t say a word?” Marissa asked.

“No, I didn’t.”

“Why not? Couldn’t you have just…laid the whammy on me in the car? You just decided to let me embarrass myself?”

“Yes. You were on a roll. Why would I interrupt you? Look, if I thought you’d deserted me, I’d be mad, too. It happens.”

Marissa was still skeptical. “I don’t mean to keep going back to this, but…so…okay, so you put your life on the line every time you’re out here, doing this?”

“Yes.”

“Well, why? Especially since you don’t have to? Have you been doing this a long time?”

“Since the end of college. You went off to pursue a modeling career and my parents had just died. I didn’t really have anything but money, and the company they ran. I had a mentor named Irving, do you remember him?” Markus asked.

Marissa nodded. She remembered Irving always being around, like a family friend, but more so after Markus’s parents passed. She constantly wondered why, but never asked.

“After my parents passed, Irving took care of me. He was a father figure, one of the reasons why I’m doing this. He’s in jail now. He got arrested for doing what I'm doing," Markus said. "I find myself having the same problem."

"What problem is that?" Marissa blurted out. She was intrigued.

"The cops. They get those blinders on and target people like myself and Irving, instead of targeting the *real* problem."

He ran his gloved over his face, from his forehead all the way down to his chin.

"The woman that apprehended Irving all those years ago is the same one after me and Vanessa."

"Vanessa?" Marissa interrupted. "Vanessa does this stuff too?"

"Yes."

"And here, I thought she was just a cream puff assistant," Marissa joked. "As it turns out, she's more dangerous than I ever imagined."

"She is," Markus chimed in. "We train together."

A moment of silence between the two.

"So, this is what I wanted to talk to you about, the thing I said could wait until you got back?" Markus notified. "I didn't want to call or text you about it. I wanted to tell you, face-to-face. I was going to tell you at dinner tonight, but–"

"Yeah, the gun to my head." Marissa formed her thumb and index finger into a gun and pressed it against her temple. "I can see where that would be a deterrent."

"I'm glad you're taking this so lightly. Is everything okay with you?" Markus asked. "I know it was kind of a crazy night."

"Everything is fine. They need to catch Dwight, though. Let the police handle it, but…you know, it kind of hurts for him to just…want to throw my life away, I guess."

Markus knew Dwight was a family friend that worked beside Marissa's father, but that was the extent of his knowledge. In fact, until Marissa mentioned Dwight, Markus couldn't say for sure who he dealt with, in the restaurant.

"I also just want to add that I'm happy with whatever you decide," Markus said. "I know I just threw a bunch of things at you right now, and I'm sorry for that. I didn't want your night to end up like this. I think that goes without saying."

"You're happy with what I decide?" Marissa wondered.

Markus nodded yes.

She had an idea of what he was talking about, but one thing would be made perfectly clear.

"I made my decision around six years ago…I'm with you."

Markus smiled with a brightness that eclipsed the sun. Marissa returned the smile, while the wheels in her mind worked.

Markus will be in trouble all the time. He'll make enemies. Someone might use me to get to him, and vice versa. This is, undoubtedly, the scariest thing I've ever been involved in. It doesn't matter. I love him with all my heart, and he loves me the same.

"I'm sorry I kept this from you for so long. I–"

Marissa pulled Markus in and under hooked his shoulders. He wrapped his arms around her. She buried her face in his chest. Through all the fabric, she could feel his heartbeat. His jaw rested against her temple.

"I don't know if I'll ever be completely okay with this," Marissa acknowledged, "but I trust you with this. Was that too anticlimactic?"

"No. I think it was the right amount of climax."

One of Markus's biggest problems was solved, and Marissa still wanted to be with him. Markus felt like a trillion dollars.

Marissa laughed. "You also owe me another pair of Louboutins."

"I don't think you're joking, but you got it."

Markus smirked as the two pulled away from each other. One of Marissa's pristine hands found its way to one of Markus's gloved hands. She squeezed it, feeling Markus's grip through the leather.

"I know you have to go," Marissa said.

"I do," Markus said.

Her smile was fragile. "I'll see you when you get home."

"I love you."

"I love you, too."

Markus pulled his mask back on and showed Marissa one thumb, to let her know everything would be fine. Once back in his car, he pulled out of the parking space and sped up the ramp.

Moments later, the garage closed, and she was alone. Marissa viewed Markus's Sound suits encased in a stand. This was real. She walked to the door that led to the main level of the house and placed her hand on the sensor. It lit green. She shut the door behind her and stepped on the motorized stair.

I can't believe he does this. I can't tell anyone, not even Titus. He's definitely not like other guys. "Hey, Marissa, what are you doing tonight?" "Oh, I'm just going to worry about my boyfriend while he keeps the streets safe. You?"

She made it through the main level door and shut it behind her. The door locked on its own, about as secure a door as Marissa had ever seen. For good reason, she thought.

She went upstairs and pushed open his bedroom door. With every step she took toward the bed, she shed an article of clothing. The night was ruined, thanks to Dwight. She wanted to feel like a queen tonight. Instead, she hung out in a ceiling. Her stomach grumbled, a reminder she didn't get a chance to eat. She looked in the mirror. Was this a way to live life? Would love be enough?

"I need to sleep on this."

She sat in her bra and underwear. In her current state, this would do. She forgot her bag in her car. She also filed that under "Tomorrow." She slid into the large bed and pulled the covers up to her neck. She rested in the fetal position while her fingers clutched the front end of the comforter.

Yeah…tomorrow.

Chapter 21

Vanessa sped down the near-empty road on her bike.

She wanted to catch up with the prick that held up Abacus before the cops did. In her spare time – between work and training – she'd studied the streets. Her goal was to know them like the back of her hand, just like Markus had prescribed.

Vanessa noticed the car the suspect was last seen in parked on the side of the road. She slowed her bike to a stop and rested it nearby. She took a few seconds to examine the inside of the car. No sign of him. She thought this guy could be anywhere.

A masked Vanessa looked left, then right. Nothing.

The broad alleyway was poorly lit. Lots of trash and garbage cans on both sides, a couple of dumpsters. Fire escapes, when she looked up. She slowly strolled, looking for any and everything while she took in her surroundings.

Her senses exploded.

She dodged.

A man smashed a glass bottle against the wall. It was meant for her, around head-high. That kind of force would put her down, she figured. She was glad he missed. As he held the neck of the half-broken bottle, he faced her.

"You're not the other guy," he said.

"Consider me a sub," Vanessa said, cheerfulness in her voice.

"Subordinate?"

"Substitute. You're the one that held up all those nice people at the restaurant, are you not?"

He nodded yes and circled. She followed suit.

As she moved about, she noticed his left wrist. It was swollen, like a bubble sat under his skin. She wasn't a doctor. She wouldn't try to analyze it. His arm dangled by his side. He grimaced as he moved. Vanessa thought it was unusable.

She said, "I shouldn't be giving you advice, but it's easier to put the weapon down and turn yourself in. I haven't the slightest, as to whether you'll accept it or not, but there are choices."

He said, "I'd rather not."

He lunged at Vanessa and swung the broken bottle, with a renewed attempt to injure. He diagonally slashed at her. Missed. He chased her with multiple swipes. She craftily dodged every effort. He tried to stab her in the ribs. She smacked his wrist as hard as she could. It made him drop the bottle.

God, he's strong.

"I should take you seriously," Dwight said.

Before Vanessa replied with a witty comeback, Dwight swung a closed fist at her. Speed was her biggest asset. She wouldn't trade blows with him. That strategy didn't stand a chance. Instead, she dodged and hit Dwight. Right, left, another right, and another left.

He replied to her chin and jaw shots with a hard right hook.

It caught Vanessa. She flew into the nearest wall. Her body smashed against the bricks. She'd never been hit like that before in her life. Her eyes began to water. She felt blood run out of her nostrils. She saw it drip onto the cement beneath her. She inhaled most of the blood, feeling it shoot down her throat. It was disgusting.

Dwight kicked Vanessa in the ribs. She gritted her teeth. Some stray blood that dripped from her nose caught her lips and dribbled into her mouth. She blew the air out of her lungs, tried to catch her breath.

He stood over her, grinned at her displeasure. When he tried to kick her again, she caught his foot and hugged it tight. She pulled her legs close. She couldn't withstand another kick. He struck her so hard in the back of the head, it cleared her sinuses. He reached down and tried to pull her up, wrenching the muscles in the back of her neck with his squeeze. She winced hard, but wouldn't let go of his leg.

Dwight raised his foot up high, ready to stomp her head into oblivion.

No time. Vanessa used the quiet moment in time to quickly roll to her back. She picked up a handful of loose trash and threw it in Dwight's face. His foot came down. She turned her body sideways. He struggled to clear his face of debris. She reared her leg back and kicked him in the groin, as hard as she could.

His knees buckled and his teeth clenched. He grimaced and fell to the pavement, using his hands to brace his fall. His guttural scream served as a reminder of his wrist injury. He rolled over to his side and held his wrist close to his body.

"You ponce!" Vanessa screeched. She spat the accumulated blood out of her mouth and wiped her lips with her gloved hand.

She circled him once. Then, with everything she had, she kicked him twice. Both kicks landed on his forearm. He howled in immense pain and rolled to his back, his legs bent upward. She knocked his legs down flat and straddled him. He couldn't cover up properly.

Vanessa unleashed a rage-filled flurry of rotating punches and forearms to Dwight's face. Blood ran. Her hands hurt, but not enough to stop. She would kill him tonight. She screamed in frustration as she pummeled her opponent. She pulled him up by the front of his shirt and hit him. His head dropped back to the concrete. She breathed hard, in and out. She stood up and took a few steps away from her attacker.

She stopped. It wasn't enough, to her.

Vanessa stalked back to her enemy and grabbed his uninjured arm. She ignored the screams while suffocating his limb with her grip. She smoothly transitioned to a sitting position, and locked his arm out between her legs.

He would think twice, the next time he thought about raising his hand to a woman – or anyone.

Dwight desperately fought the hold, like his life depended on it. Vanessa brought one of her legs to the sky, right above his head. Fear consumed his eyes. Her leg came down across his face like a hammer, rapidly and repeatedly.

Her goal: literally knock the fight out of him.

He found himself dazed from her leg attacks. She felt his body. She wasted no time when she locked his arm up tighter, this time, raising her hips. Vanessa felt him panic underneath her, kicking air and writhing violently, trying to escape. She raised her hips higher and wrenched his arm.

Snap.

He bellowed out every obscenity and vulgarity she'd ever heard. She wanted his arm for a trophy. That would please her.

Then, it hit her.

Vanessa's rage subsided long enough to come to her senses. She rolled off of him and back to her feet, proud of her work as she watched him toss back and forth, holding his arm near his body.

"Just peachy." With her glove, Vanessa wiped the remaining blood from her nose. Her actions weren't anything she'd ever done before, but she never had to. She wiped her nose one more time.

In the near distance, she heard sirens.

She said to him, "Stay here and accept your fate. I have a feeling if you don't, it could be much worse for you." She turned and walked away from him, and then brought her wrist to her mouth.

"Find me."

Vanessa ambled out of the alleyway, turning the corner just as she heard the familiar cop dialogue. They directed her defeated opponent to freeze, stay on the ground, and get his hands behind his back. Vanessa thought he'd have a bit of trouble with the last command.

Good work, not killing that bloke. I'm going to have to harness my anger and toe the line as best I can, she thought.

Vanessa stepped over her bike and bounced a couple times. She started her bike up and pulled off into the night.

A masked Markus looked down on her from the rooftop. He smiled. Though he fought the urge to be overbearing and step in, in the end, she made the right decision. She didn't even need his help. He'd taught her well, so far. He was proud of her evolution.

In the alleyway, Dwight lay on his stomach, his arms handcuffed behind his back. He was bruised, bloodied and battered. The worst part was dealing with his broken bones. He was apprehensive to move. He didn't want another dose of shooting pain, just because he was physically uncomfortable. He nominally cocked his head up.

Daphne De La Rosa knelt down next to him.

"You think it's pretty boss, endangering people's lives?" The detective asked.

Dwight exercised his right to remain silent, when it came to cops.

"You want to hear something pretty boss?" She asked rhetorically. "It's taking everything in my being not to put you in the back of my car, take you far, far away, where nobody can hear you scream…and make you scream."

She stood up just as a few officers approached. She moved out of the way while two of them gingerly picked Dwight up. They noticed he was hurt. Daphne didn't care. He could die, and it wouldn't matter to her. Threatening innocent people made him the worst kind of scum.

Seemingly, she could handle when someone endangered themselves. When they endangered others…it was such a selfish act.

It was over. Dwight Durant would accept his fate. He would survive in jail as long as he could. His mind drifted over to thoughts about how long it would take before Michael sent someone to kill him.

After Michael found out about Dwight's little stunt involving Marissa, it wouldn't take long. Dwight thought there was a realistic chance he wouldn't make it back to the police station. Time was scarce. His mind cleared. In hindsight, he should've handled it differently.

As Dwight made an effort to lower himself into the police cruiser, one of the officers pushed his head down, rushing his movements. He tried to keep his back off his injured arms, but no luck. He opted to lie on his stomach instead. The police cruiser pulled off into the night.

This was his life now.

Hours later, Markus's car and Vanessa's bike sat parked, next to each other. Markus stepped out of the car, while Vanessa lifted her leg over her bike and kicked the kickstand out. Dried blood chipped off when she wiped her nose. Some of it stuck to her glove. Markus pulled his mask off, as did Vanessa.

"Are you okay?" Markus asked.

Vanessa lightheartedly smiled. "I knew you'd ask me that…yes, just peachy." She sniffled and wiped her nose again.

"I'm going to be honest: I was on the roof top, where you had your run-in with Dwight."

Vanessa's eyes grew wide. "Really?"

"Yeah. I'm proud of the way you handled it. No casualties, unless you count an arm."

She smirked at his words. "Right. Little steps."

"I want you to be honest with me: do you think you're ready for this? I mean…the whole thing. There are only a few days off, if any. You've been exposed to it long enough to know whether this is for you or not."

She held her mask by her side, kept her eyes on him.

"Sometimes, I don't think it's for me. This guy tonight, he was twice my size, Markus. There's a twinge of self-doubt, when that happens. I feel a bit scared when I'm surrounded by three, four, five people, and they want to harm me."

Markus nodded in agreement. "I can relate. I've been scared out of my mind before."

"But…I believe in what we're doing," Vanessa continued. "I don't care if the cops are after us, or if we make enemies, left and right. If there was ever a tough enough broad to do this, you're looking at her," she laughed. "I'm with you."

"Thank you," Markus said. "You have my full support, until the end."

"Until the end," Vanessa repeated.

Markus guessed that Vanessa might need some time to decompress from the dangerous situation she was just in. They both went their separate ways: Vanessa headed to the bathroom for a recharge and Markus headed to his room, to rest. As Markus left through the basement door, Vanessa shut the bathroom door.

She looked in the mirror. She was tired and sore. She missed her parents. She still felt alone, even though she tried to branch out more. She'd made a new friend in Jasper, but she thought a few more wouldn't hurt. Her eyes welled.

Not an hour before, the emotion of that invisible line between heroism and madness was nearly crossed. It affected her. She'd been that close once before, when she pointed that gun at her parents' murderers. She'd push it down, deep into the depths of her soul, and hope that she didn't have to resort to those actions again. It was a harsh realization.

This was her life now.

Back upstairs, Markus finally made it to his bedroom. When he saw Marissa, it looked to him like she hadn't slept. Nothing was said as he began shedding his night attire, tossing his gloves in a corner, along with his mask and suit.

Marissa breathed a sigh of relief. "Okay…you're here. I couldn't sleep. Can we talk?"

Markus never broke stride. "I need a shower. You're welcome to join me in the bathroom."

She nodded yes and followed. She thought it might work better if she couldn't see his face. Maybe she wouldn't be so uneasy about talking to him.

Markus pulled his spandex shorts off and tossed them on the floor before he stepped into the shower. Clearly, he was in a rush.

Selfishly, every lustful thought commandeered her brain. She had a more important topic to discuss than Markus's naked body. She wrested her lustful thoughts away. Maybe they could come into play later, but now, it was something she didn't need to focus on.

He turned the water on and stood under it. It took seconds to warm. "What's on your mind?" He asked.

She laid the toilet seat cover down and sat on it, still in her bra and underwear. She laughed nervously.

"You know, I have a feeling my schedule's going to have to be altered. It's the funniest thing: I was so tired, but as soon as you left, I couldn't sleep. I don't know if I'll be able to, as long as I know you're out there risking your neck for so many others."

"If the tables were turned, I'd feel the same way," Markus explained with a raised voice, to accommodate the loud splash of the water on his skin. "I worried about you every night while you were in France."

Markus's considerate words made Marissa feel warm inside. His nightly deeds kept him awake, but she stayed on his mind. That was comforting, to her. He'd made her feel special numerous times in the past. This time, it just felt different, a "good" kind of different.

"After a certain time, I just couldn't date anyone anymore," Markus went on. "There was no reason to. I'd just be purposely wasting their time, and mine. You can't trust many, with the kind of information I trust you with."

"I know that, and I…I'm just glad you trust me enough to harbor your secrets," Marissa said. "I just wanted to tell you that…you know…I'm ready for this relationship. Whatever comes will come, but it won't come between us."

Markus poked his head out from behind the shower curtain and reached out with his left hand. Marissa's arm extended toward him, ready to take his hand in hers. He smiled at the gesture.

"Towel."

"Oh…o-okay," she said. *How embarrassing! I'm such a doofus!* She grabbed the black bath towel that sat atop the toilet, and waited for the shower to subside before she handed it to Markus.

Markus's torso was exposed when he stepped out of the shower. The towel she handed him was wrapped around his waist. He was dry, for the most part. He provided a very picturesque landscape for her. Maybe it wasn't on purpose, but it served one, nonetheless.

"I know it will take work," Markus recognized, "but I'm willing to. You're my one and only, Mare. It's been that way since day one."

Marissa smiled and stood up. She placed her hands on his chest. "Isn't that music to my ears?" He wrapped his damp arms around her dry body. Her lips met his.

This was their life now.

The next morning, on the other side of town, Daphne had already begun readying herself for the day. She'd all but fully processed Jonathan Deadmarsh's absence. She'd gotten back into a passable routine with her sleep. A home security system helped pacify her anxieties, somewhat. The Broken Skull was still out there. She'd find him, no matter how bloody or violent it got.

Rather than let all of these things wear her down, she decided to rise above it. She looked in the mirror with a serious face.

She said, "Deadmarsh can no longer tug on my heartstrings or cause a distraction. I'm dedicated to the law enforcement machine, hell-bent on fixing the streets. That means an end to the Sound, Ivory Fox, Broken Skull, and anyone else on the other side of my law."

This was her life now.

She flipped the radio to her favorite station and heard a familiar voice.

"We have so many people in this world that look at different things different ways, and for different reasons. One man's reasoning is not always the same as one woman's, and so on, and so forth. One thing is for sure, I'm afraid: action will always trump motivation. People will always see what you did before they have a chance to ask why."

Daphne nodded her head in agreement with Jasper's words. Action was definitely necessary.

ABOUT THE AUTHOR

Derryan Derrough enjoys talking sports, a good movie, or an awesome food recipe. You can give him a shout on Twitter: @derryanderrough or go check out his blogs at www.derryanderrough.com.

Made in the USA
Monee, IL
07 September 2021

77466445R00236